Message from Boo

By

R.G. Johansen

Shades Creek Press, LLC
Hiawassee, Georgia
Birmingham, Alabama

Message from Boo

R.G. Johansen
First Edition
First Printing, 2021
Second Printing, 2022

Book Design by R.G. Johansen
Cover Design/Final Production by Natasha Walsh,
R.G. Johansen, Chyna Tyree
Cover Image: House at Night in Winter Fog
Created by Lee Avison
Licensed through Arcangel Images, Inc., NY
Edited by Candice Lawrence

ISBN: 9781087975610
Copyright©2022 by James Randall Gober
Copyright©2022 R.G. Johansen
Shades Creek Press, LLC
Printed in the United States of America

Disclaimer

This is a work of fiction. All the characters and plot situations are totally fiction and are not based in whole or in part on any known or related person(s), situations or circumstances. This work of fiction is a total artistic creation of the author based on imagination and thought. Any similarities created are purely fiction.

"It's not what you look at that matters, it's what you see."

Henry David Thoreau

-

In loving memory of my mother and father, who taught me to stay humble, love God, cherish family, and to never forget that my freedom to live that kind of life exists because of those who sacrificed everything before me.

PROLOGUE

Do paranormal forces really exist? Detective John Williams with the Atlanta Homicide Department had always been a non-believer. His logical explanations had never given credibility to anything unnatural until he was forced to face the terrifying truth. He had been tasked with solving a series of murders that took him on a frightening journey which left him with too many questions and too few answers. The strange twists and turns in his investigations were made even more complicated by his responsibilities as a single parent to his preschool daughter, Boo. And when a passionate love interest and a know-it-all partner straight out of the New York City Police Department were added to the mix, it made matters even more complicated and unnerving.

John Williams ultimately unraveled the truth, and it was far more malevolent than he or anyone else could have imagined.

PART ONE

1

When you grow up in Central Mississippi, you are born and bred to revere the Almighty, to be rooted deeply in the Father, Son, and Holy Ghost. Weekends in the buckle of the Bible Belt included church every Sunday and prayer that all your needs would be met by a higher power. But after moving to Atlanta and taking the bartending job at the strip club, his faith had been as tenuous as a southern politician's promise to cut your taxes. He had always tended to wander, to get caught by the trap of sin, but he had always returned to the fold when he needed help. He did just that when he realized that no amount of chemo nor brilliant doctors could stop the cancer's deadly march to his lungs and brain.

At that point, his hands reached upward for a miracle. He felt as though he had no other options. But he forgot one thing. His timeline was marked in days while God's calendar was timeless. Nonetheless, he was hopeful, thinking maybe he had built up a little cache when he was a boy, when he handled those snakes at a backwoods church back home. Maybe he had proven that he was worthy of mercy and would receive prompt supernatural intervention. But when faith, hope, and prayer refused to heal his sick body, the man who had been baptized in the Holy Spirit did the unthinkable.

He knew it was a grave mistake when he struck the bargain with the one who hid in the shadows, a life-or-death miscalculation that he couldn't take back. But when you have the Big C and your time is limited with the woman of your dreams, the one you love and want to marry, you are beyond desperate; you are emotionally out of control. Good judgement is reserved for people who aren't looking over their shoulder for the Grim Reaper. As he discovered, however, the price for being cancer free was more than he was willing to pay. He would rather forfeit his life than be joined to an evil power that would ask him to forever deny his faith and live in a house of deceit, hate and wickedness. So, he refused to do its blasphemous acts and deeds of immorality. But for that, he would pay the ultimate price.

****

"Roll him over and mark his buttock before we continue with the ceremony," the deep voice commanded.

He would fight back if he could, but he had been given a witch's brew of drugs that blocked the nerves in his skeletal muscles. Beyond the daze of immobility, the wicked potion also placed him in a catatonic state that caused mutism, taking away his ability to speak or cry for help. Unfortunately, all his other senses were intact. He could hear the monotone chanting, smell the awful stench, see their contorted faces, and worst of all, feel the excruciating pain. But there was nothing he could do to stop their retribution. This was a ritual of revenge, and he would pay with his life.

"Roll him back over and hand me the knife!" The voice thundered with malevolence. The double-edged instrument reserved for this ceremony was made of molten Damascus steel. One side of the blade had a serrated edge capable of sawing through bone. And the other side was as clean and sharp as a surgeon's scalpel. It could easily fulfill its purpose of slicing through human flesh. And it did. And he felt the torture and watched in horror.

He felt cold, as though his life drained from his body. And then he looked upon what eyes should never see. Ghastly. Frightening. Fearsome.

2

Hour by hour, the disturbance intensified as a mass of black clouds swirled about in a turbulent free-for-all. The violent storm produced shrouds of rain, bolts of lightning and resounding thunder noisy enough to wake the dead. In Georgia, it was common to have thunderstorms in August, but this one was nastier than most. Old timers in the South would swear that the devil was beatin' his wife when the thunder rumbled that loudly. However, it wasn't loud enough to wake John. He never heard the rattle of the windowpanes nor saw the lightning flashes through the bedroom blinds. He was exhausted from a rough week on the job given too much overtime and too little rest.

But someone else in the house was mindful of the storm. For this gloomy night had brought with it a wicked dream, a nightmare that had awakened her from a deep sleep. The dream was bad, but nothing like the night terrors she had experienced on other occasions. Those frightening episodes left her screaming in fear, unable to leave her bed. But, tonight in the pitch-black darkness, she rose and shuffled her feet as she felt her way into her father's bedroom. Upon arriving, she positioned herself on the side of the bed and leaned over to draw near his face.

"Daddy, are you scared?" She asked. It was a rhetorical question looking for an invitation not an answer.

It was amazing the way he could sleep for hours through bowling-alley thunder, yet her gentle voice could wake him in seconds. He opened his swollen eyes to a petite effigy standing in the darkness. His daughter Boo was hugging the toy bear he had given her on her second birthday.

"Are you scared, Daddy?" she softly asked, hoping for a sympathetic reply. Clumsily, he searched for the lamp on

6

the night table until his probing fingers found the switch. He quickly triggered the light, bringing her face into focus.

"Are you going to protect me, Boo?" He asked in a raspy voice.

"Yeah, Daddy, I can protect you. Can I sleep in your bed tonight?" She asked while brushing a tear from her cheek. She appeared frightened, much like a timid lamb seeking the sanctuary of a brave shepherd.

He couldn't refuse her heartfelt request, knowing she was genuinely scared. "Okay, baby, climb onboard," John said as he slid to the other side of the bed to allow her room. John wasn't surprised when Boo left the room instead of immediately getting onto his bed. She had done this many times before.

He knew that she would quickly return, and she didn't disappoint him. Within seconds, she arrived with both arms loaded with stuffed animals. In one fast motion, she thrust her critters into the air, extended her small limbs over the side of the mattress, and climbed onto the bed in time to greet the falling toys. In an instant, there was a menagerie of two rabbits, one bear, a dog, and Boo in the middle of the pack. She affectionately embraced her animal favorites and then quickly fell asleep with the storm outside slowly subsiding.

He felt a warmth in his heart that all was right with the world as he listened to her rhythmical breathing and studied her sweet face. Watching her brought him visions of his late wife, Rebecca. He always marveled at how Boo was the spitting image of her mother. He could only surmise that God must have known that Rebecca's life would be short on Earth, and in apology, sent her gemination. John couldn't help but reminisce about the wonderful life they had enjoyed before she passed away, now almost two years ago.

7

She was a young woman of thirty years when she was unexpectedly stricken with cancer. The disease bestowed her two long years of treatment, two long years of pain, and two long years of dying. Though Boo was only two at the time, she still remembered her mother's love, the bedtime stories, and most of all, that caring touch.

After turning off the light, John lay quietly as his thoughts turned inward, thinking about the future. As a single parent, he couldn't help but wonder how he would continue to juggle the demands of his work and the needs of his family. Should he be overly protective of his little girl or teach her to be a fighter? How would he handle all the changes Boo would face in the future? Life had been relatively straightforward raising a child about to turn five years in age, but what about when she turns fifteen. Slowly, all the challenges of raising his daughter drifted from his thoughts and he dozed to sleep. Nothing could have prepared him for the day Rebecca died or the life that followed...no books to be found, no words to be spoken, life was different in so many ways.

3

An unexpected wakeup call arrived the next morning as John felt a sharp kick to his lower back. The blow was delivered by his slumbering daughter. It was a hazard he was most familiar with since she was a light sleeper and tended to toss and turn. Turning over on his other side placed him nose-to-nose with the glaring eyes of the stuffed animals Boo cherished so much. He chuckled at the notion of a grown man in bed with all of these cuddly toys, and then for a moment thought of returning to sleep. But a second wakeup call this time delivered by the annoying buzz of the alarm clock changed all of that. John had promised Boo they would go on a special trip today and a promise given was a promise kept. The day would be theirs and theirs alone.

"Wake up, Boo," he drowsily said, stretching his arms skyward. "Let's get up, eat some breakfast, and go. Come on, baby, wake up!" John knew his first attempt at rousting her from sleep would be ineffective, so he went ahead and rolled out of bed himself.

After lumbering into the bathroom, he turned on the sink's cold water and doused his face several times attempting to rescind his coma-like state of mind. It worked. The frigid water loosened his skin, allowing him to pry open his bone-dry eyelids. After toweling his face, he began an inspection of his reflection in the mirror. And while conducting his look-over, he couldn't help but make a series of crazy, contorted faces. His attempt at some early morning buffoonery brought a smile and chortle, a grown man acting so foolish.

After a quick shower and shave, John hurried down to the kitchen to prepare their morning meal. This job was usually reserved for their housekeeper Tina, but unfortunately, she was off for the weekend. She had handled the domestic chores since Rebecca's death and the description as house-keeper did not do her justice. She was much, much more. A great cook, a stickler for cleanliness, and more than anything else she had filled the maternal role left by Rebecca. Tina was a wonderful mentor for Boo and loved her as much as her own granddaughter. John knew the layer of support and encouragement she provided was priceless.

"Hey, kiddo!" John shouted up the stairwell from the kitchen. "Do you want your waffle microwaved or toasted?" Heating a frozen griddlecake was one meal he could surely handle. When he turned to yell again, he was surprised to find Boo standing in the kitchen doorway, gazing at him with those innocent eyes.

"Good morning, sweetheart." He softly spoke.

Boo's mouth turned up at both corners, exposing a mis-chievous grin that silently declared, *I've got Daddy wrapped around my little finger and I know it.* Unable to hide his pleasure, he returned her smile with one of his own that acknowl-edged, *yeah, so you do.* Happiness found in such a simple gesture as a smile. She had a way of bringing that out, that rejuvenation of his soul.

John stepped over to Boo, reached down, and lifted her upward until her back was positioned close to the kitchen ceiling. With his arms now fully outstretched, he paused to study his daughter's angelic features.

She had corn-silk blonde hair woven into the two dangling strands he had engineered the night before. It was a terrible weave. Boo's hair looked more like the real twisted tail of a piglet than pigtail braids for a little girl. Given John's lack of skill as a hairdresser, this was the best coiffure his bulky hands could muster. But Boo didn't mind, she just kept on laughing as he held her aloft and stared at her deep blue eyes. And, of course, he couldn't overlook that telltale pixie nose. Yes, she had all of Rebecca's features, even her radiant glow. She was just a smaller version of her mother. John often measured his own dimensions and substance against her dainty limbs and unspoiled spirit. And every time he did, he thanked God for sending her into his life.

"You are the prettiest little girl in the world," he said with a father's pride.

Boo responded with a series of high-pitched giggles. "Throw me up, Daddy!" She pleaded, both arms poised for flight. "Throw me up!" To John's strong arms, Boo felt as light as a feather. So, again and again, he thrust her into the air above his head. Her face was flush as she shouted with excitement. "More! Throw me more!"

"That's enough for now." He said as he placed her back on the kitchen floor. "Let's eat."

Boo was usually a finicky eater, but today she devoured her food with the speed of a half-starved puppy. John gobbled down his waffle with the same velocity. Both were excited about the surprise he had planned.

Today, he had promised Boo a trip to the zoo and nothing would delay their fun. It was precious time together since his job demanded so much. Boo was truly his escape from the foulness that often came with his calling.

4

Boo burst out the front door with John trailing closely behind. Pausing long enough to survey the house, he pondered how he would ever find time to do the needed repairs. The dwelling, an older two-story traditional of wood garnished with stone, stood on a one-half acre lot engulfed in tall oaks and Georgia Pines. The soft wood siding on the house, which was once painted a deep gray, had faded from the rays of the sun and the absence of a painter's brush. The board surface was further defaced by the vacant knot holes drilled by the chisel-like beaks of the local woodpeckers. The birds had an uncanny knack for dawn assaults on the outward bedroom wall—his bedroom wall.

John had tried almost everything to quieten their incessant pecking. He had even resorted to fastening aluminum pie plates and rubber snakes to the housing soffit in an attempt to end their reign of terror. These red-headed marauders were nobody's fool. After all, any reptile that preferred hanging upside down on a sun-bleached eve to slithering around on good terra firma couldn't be much of a threat. And the pie plates were no more effective. New tactics were needed but that would have to wait.

Water in the driveway exploded around Boo's feet as she hopped through the puddles left by the evening storm.

"Lisa Beth Williams!" He yelled. "Out of the water, please." John always used his daughter's entire birth name when formal rebuke was in order. Discipline was out of his comfort zone when it came to Boo and she knew it. She had learned early in childhood that corporal punishment was not in his repertoire, so she always pushed his patience to the limit.

One last dip.

Ker-splash!

"Get in the car," he reluctantly surrendered.

The drive seemed surprisingly short as they turned into the parking lot at the city zoo. John playfully teased Boo, telling her stories about recent animal escapes just to get a little revenge for her lack of respect for his parental authority. But mostly, he wanted to study the reaction on her suspicious face. He often played the childlike role of an older brother pestering a younger sister.

"That's not real, Daddy." She began to whimper, disturbed about the prank. "No animals got away!"

"I'm just kidding." He snickered with satisfaction.

In retaliation, she threw an open-handed left hook that missed his leg by a country mile. The tomfoolery brought a smile to her face.

Without question, Boo had her mother's spirit as well as her physical appearance. She also had her mother's love of being frightened, the trepidation of the unknown. That was the wellspring of her nickname. John took great pleasure in lurking around the house in closets, behind doors, and beside furniture; he waited for Boo and her mother to open a door or pass by his hidden location. Poised like a big cat waiting for its unsuspecting prey, he would leap from cover with paws raised, growling and grabbing for their prancing legs. It brought him a feeling of importance, a feeling that both Boo and Rebecca depended on him for protection. The message was clear. He could scare them because he would never let anything harm them. It was perfect, that loving triangle.

5

Hand in hand, John and Boo passed through the forged-iron gates of the metro zoo. Once inside, the street noise withered and the Atlanta skyline dropped away, yielding forth an uncommon landscape centered among the concrete jungle of the city. A paradise of blooming flowers and ornamental bright green plants were nestled below the tall swaying oaks. A garden of rose beds, Japanese Maples, Indica and Kurume Azaleas, dogwoods and Mahonia plants lined their path as they walked toward their first animal encounter. Eager to gain a new perspective on this feral world, Boo tugged at John's hand, pulling him towards the animals.

"Daddy, can we go see the bears first?" she asked, somewhat unsure about a rendezvous with the real thing. Her only contact with the animal kingdom had been with her pet cat and an occasional run-in with the puppies at the local pet store.

"If that's what you want to do, then it's the bears," he said. "Let's go!"

Hurriedly, the two of them walked by the savanna exhibit under the watchful eyes of two African Elephants. Side by side, their boulder sized heads rocked to and fro, swishing their trunks like two pendulums on matching grandfather clocks. John and Boo walked on, stopping only to allow a herd of rambunctious kids race by. They were like a pack of wild dogs, slowing down only to bark, howl, and growl in vain attempts to communicate with the real thing. Everyone at the zoo seemed to have some sort of affinity for these wild animals, a sort of appreciation and fear given their impressive size and lack of domestication.

Within minutes, Boo and John arrived at the bear habitat.

14

There, Boo gingerly pressed against the steel bars that prevented a careless fall into the water below. Beyond the pool, two polar bears sat on their respective rocks, sniffing the cooler air as though they sensed an end to the long, hot summer. Both animals watched as gusts of wind loosened the leaves of the shedding maples, sending the foliage fluttering just above their watchful eyes. The breeze ruffled their white fur as the bears patiently held their teddy bear like pose. Beautiful. Soft and cuddly. They reminded John of an overblown, life-like version of one of Boo's stuffed toys. In reality, they were just the opposite —an eight hundred pound killing machine, not the harmless, pudgy comics they appeared to be.

"Aren't they beautiful?" an inquisitive voice asked. The inquiry was from one of the zookeepers who had stopped to observe Boo's reaction to the bears. However, her interest was not only in considering Boo, but in John as well. She had noticed a missing wedding band from his left hand.

John noticed her too. She was tall with a trim, athletic build and a deep summer tan, very hard to overlook. She pulled back her long, tawny hair in an effort to inspect the physique of another animal named John. Up and down, she examined his frame as if she were checking out one of her primates. His six-foot, three-inch body was molded into a pair of faded jeans and a light cotton sport shirt. These loosely fitting clothes could not conceal a powerful angular frame of muscular legs, narrow hips, and broad shoulders. Like the bears, he also possessed a presence of quiet strength. Yet he also had a boyish look about him. Even with that chiseled nose and chin, he had the look of youth. Maybe it was the unkempt wavy brown hair, but more than likely it was his eyes. Sapphire blue with a mischievous glint. All in all, he was a strikingly handsome man, a man without the vain introspection typically found among those more favored by nature. It was a wonderful quality.

"Yeah, they really are impressive." John said, unmasking an enthusiastic grin. His youthful exuberance was a most unusual and attractive quality embedded in a thirty-four-year-old body that had experienced so many of life's ups and downs. "They look like they're waving us over for a game of tag," he continued.

The young woman seized the opening to impress John with her knowledge. "Oh, they look friendly enough all right, but they would go for you, like a cat after a mouse. They're very smart, unbelievably strong, and fast. About two months ago, a duck from the petting zoo escaped the building and accidentally dropped in on these two for a visit. All that was left was a pile of feathers."

Boo had listened intently to the zoological briefing on the bears. "Daddy, what happened to the duck?"

Not wanting to destroy her image of these friendly looking animals, John downplayed the story. "He probably just flew out and went straight back home."

The young zookeeper sensed that she had unsettled Boo and attempted to reverse her account of the story. "Yeah, I think he's back with his family at the Children's Zoo. Don't forget to go by there today. There're all sorts of animals like lambs, ponies, baby chicks, and even two llamas that you can pet and feed. And I'm sure the duck family would like to see you, too."

With a shrug of doubt, Boo turned away. She reached up and tugged at her father's shirt. "Daddy, can we go see the lions and tigers?"

John clenched her small hand in preparation to leave. "Sure, we can. We'll go right now."

Before John could ask directions from the zookeeper, the young woman responded. "The lions and tigers are at the

Wild Encounter. Just take this path until it dead-ends and then turn right and you'll be there." Knowing that she had blown her chance of connecting with John, she wished them both a day of fun and left to pursue her duties.

The Wild Encounter included an older building, a refuge for the cats from the summer heat. It housed a row of enclosures that allowed the inhabitants access both in and out of doors. Once inside, John and Boo glanced down the seemingly endless hall that ran the length of the structure. The fetid smell of animal scent filled their noses, causing them to wince in disdain. The odor was unavoidable. The feline occupants spent hours each day laying down the scent markers that defined their confined space as their own territories. It was as though the big cats were erecting private property signs warning their neighbors against the consequences of trespassing. The animals' only disappointment was when the zookeepers arrived to clean their tight quarters. This process of deodorizing meant that the marking would have to start all over again.

John and Boo stopped to view two Siberian tigers. With heads slung low, they stalked back and forth like two murderers prepared to commit the most unspeakable crimes. Their tails whipped about as they snarled, exposing their deadly incisors. Unlike the calm polar bears, these animals were in a perpetual state of intimidation. Everything about them implied danger, especially their size. Yet, they were also beautiful. The deep black stripes against their shiny orange coats were especially brilliant. They were magnificent creatures. John watched as Boo observed the cats and wondered if she recognized their threatening nature or merely thought of them as a larger version of her own cute pet. Never recoiling in fear, her eyes followed the tigers as though she were mesmerized by their restless motion.

After leaving the tigers, John and Boo moved on to the area that housed the king and queen of the beasts. The tan lions seemed much less neurotic than the pacing tigers. Given their nocturnal nature, the lions would sleep up to twenty hours during the day. The snoozing male, lying stretched against the side wall, raised his massive head and yawned, displaying his three-inch canines. His cellmate acted more like a sex kitten than a dangerous jungle cat. She rolled on her back, first left, then right, while an intermittent low gurgling growl called out from her throat. After rising, she strolled in a slinky, somewhat prissy fashion over to the male as though she had some burning itch she couldn't scratch. Upon reaching him, she exhaled a huff of hot breath into his ear while nuzzling her head against his thick mane. Realizing he had yet to pick up on her sexual signals, she patted his flank with her imposing paw, attempting to awaken him from his sluggish condition. Finally, the message was received. He rose, sniffed her posterior and mounted.

Boo stood watching, taking in the scene of seduction. "Daddy, what are the lions doing to each other?"

An elderly couple standing nearby had caught the amorous cats in the same coup d'oeil. Both stood with mouths agape, staring at John in anticipation of his response. Without question, he was in a quandary and needed some help and he needed it fast. And at just the right moment, he thought he had found the diversion he needed from above—no, not from heaven, but from a flutter of brown sparrows zipping about in the building's rafters. The birds caught his attention in the nick of time. Pointing upward, he exclaimed. "Look up at the ceiling, sweetheart. Look at the pretty birds."

"But, Daddy, the boy lion looks like he's hurting the girl lion," Boo retorted, looking back over her shoulder.

"No, Boo, they're just playing with each other. Come on, let's go outside and see what's going on," John said as he whisked her outside the building and into the bright sunlight.

John was befuddled by his predicament. For the first time the naked reality that he would one day face the task of explaining the birds and bees to his little angel slammed into his psyche like a stiff jab to his nose. Sex, the old equalizer, would soon enough spread its horrible seed into the innocent mind of his little girl. As she grew older, he knew her blossoming would guarantee that fact.

It would also guarantee the inevitable reproductive questions on how germination takes place. The plan had always been to invoke the wisdom of motherhood, to let Rebecca handle this facet of special education. But Rebecca was no longer available to answer that summon. It would be his responsibility, his initiation into a sacred realm of understanding…an understanding that the hands of time would not allow his little girl to sidestep puberty.

It would be difficult, but even more difficult a few years later when the unthinkable would begin. Boy meets girl and dating. He wondered if he would be one of those tedious fathers who would never accept his daughter's boyfriends. After all, those little mealy-mouthed, nasty minded reprobates would only be after one thing, breeching his daughter's undefiled honor.

Sure, he would accept them. Gagged and handcuffed to the living room sofa, he would accept them. And, of course, if one of the punks should pop the nuptial question, he would just pull out his Colt and dare them to take his baby away. Yet, he knew his thinking would change, that marriage would certainly be in her future. Thirty seemed like an appropriate age for wedlock, right after she finished medical school and her internship at the nearby hospital.

John's daydreaming trek into the hereafter was suddenly ended by the voice of his present-day daughter. Spying an ice cream vendor wheeling his portable cart, she felt the undeniable stirrings of a four-year old.

"Daddy, can I have an ice cream cone?" she asked, conjuring up her most pitiful expression.

Her plea struck a harmonic chord in his mind. This was a dilemma he could handle.

"Sure, you can sweetie!" John answered.

Boo opted for chocolate while John selected strawberry. The grandfatherly peddler was especially generous with Boo's portions as he heaped two lofty scoops into the cone. Quickly, Boo began to sculpt the sweet treat with the precision of a skilled surgeon. Her small tongue carefully swirled around the side, then over the top, not allowing a drop to miss her lips. John consumed his in larger chunks, already delving into the crunchy cone while Boo was still savoring the second scoop. Just as he finished eating the last bite, a piercing voice hailed him by name.

"Hey, John....Johnnnnnn, over here!"

Casting an eye in the direction of the voice, John recognized the zoo security guard dressed in a khaki uniform. She was one of his former classmates at the Police Academy. It had been a number of years since he had seen her, but he was certain it was Carly. He instructed Boo to finish her ice cream while sitting on the bench outside the enclosure that held several giraffes. Since Boo would be occupied and within eyesight, John decided to walk over and renew his friendship.

"It's been a long time. How have you been?" She asked in a husky voice. Her name was Carly Jordan, a somewhat attractive woman that had a tough-as-nails reputation.

"I'm doing great, Carly. How 'bout yourself?"

"Oh, I'm hanging in there. You know, it's tough tryin' to make ends meet on a cop's salary." She pinched the light brown fabric of her blouse alluding to her part-time employment.

John was familiar with a police officer's menial income and the fact that it didn't provide many extras for a family. Since he had taken on many part-time jobs himself— everything from a security guard at the stadium to a night watchman at a secluded warehouse— he knew about the low wages very well. "Yeah, you should try juggling a budget that includes a housekeeper and a four year old."

Her face was instantly soaked with deep concern as though a forgotten memory resurfaced. "I heard about your wife, John. I'm really sorry. I should have gotten in touch back then, but we all sort of went our separate ways and you never know what to say when something like that happens." Pointing at Boo on the bench, her tone once again picked up its peppery pace. "I saw your little blonde motor scooter over there. She's a little doll."

His face beamed with pride. "Yeah, she's something else. This visit to the zoo is something I promised her a while back."

"That's really great. This is a terrific place. Hell, I'm out here enough, I should know."

John noticed the fatigue on Carly's face. "Are you working here just on weekends?"

"Mostly weekends. I'm still in traffic so the schedule changes sometimes as you know. It's the same ole long hours and low pay."

"What ever happened to Larry and Bill?" John asked, attempting to change the subject.

"Larry's still in traffic with me. Bill just couldn't handle the stress, and the shitty hours so he gave it up. The last time I heard, he was sellin' used cars over in Conyers."

21

"You know, Carly, I still can't believe the four of us made it through the academy. What a crazy group. I never told you this, but I always thought you and Bill would connect with each other, and maybe, get married." John had twisted the truth in his last statement. In reality he, Bill, and Larry always wondered if Carly's sexual taste leaned toward members of her own gender. They were just too sheepish to ask.

Carly raised her heavy eyebrows and grinned as though she were about to share a secret. "You never knew did you, John?"

"Know what?" He asked, thinking she was going to tell him that she was out of the closet.

"That I always had the hots for you, not Bill."

Embarrassed by his miscalculation and her directness, he stuttered, "No...no...no, I really didn't know that."

"Hell, I tried everything to get your attention. I even got some new puppies thinking that might rev your motor."

"You got some new puppies?"

Placing her hands under each breast, she formed a cup and began an up-and-down motion, demonstrating the bounciness of her new enhanced bosom. "Yeah, I had a boob job done back then. Hell, that's all you horny dudes ever talked about. I figured a big set of pups would stir your juices. Don't tell me you don't like them."

John's face turned as red as a beet. His uneasiness was obvious. "Oh, yeah, they look great...you look great."

Carly broke into a robust laugh, pleased at exposing his natural shyness. Deciding to take her diversion a step further, she reached around her back, grabbed a buttock in each hand and squeezed as though she were testing the softness of a pillow. "Hell, I would have gotten a butt lift back then if I thought that's what it would take to get you to notice me."

Now speechless from the last barrage, he groped for a way to escape his entanglement. "Well, you know, I think you look fine the way you are."

"You sure about that?" She squeezed again.

"Stop it Carly. You're embarrassing me."

Carly was in stitches. Her involuntary laughter had almost progressed to a state of convulsion. Her short bursts of guffaw exposed her teeth as though she was impersonating a hee-hawing donkey.

"Don't worry, John boy, I'm just yanking your chain. You're a little too macho for me."

"Oh, yeah, I knew you were kidding. You were always the jokester."

John and Carly brought each other up to date on their plans and careers, and then parted. Each knew that their once special friendship had been diminished by the passing years. Today, their time at the academy was nothing more than a faint memory.

It was late in the afternoon when John and Boo ended their day stationed outside the enclosure that held a huge male rhinoceros. Perhaps it was a sign that he should have chosen a different venue for Boo's special day, for the big male appeared intent on living up to his mythical reputation as a source of procreative powers. The excited bull had aired out an impressive four-foot erection. It looked as though he was straddling a black fire hose, attaching him to the ground. John decided it was time to go home when Boo asked why the rhino had five legs. There were only so many questions a father could answer in one day.

6

It was late when John retired for the evening. Lying in bed, he gazed at the ceiling and contemplated the day's events at the zoo. Today he had stumbled on to something invaluable, a discovery that left him more baffled than enlightened. It was an acknowledgment that as time progressed, the fond recollections of his past friendships from the academy were now forgetful memories. And the realization that time drawing on would bring with it a new set of experiences with his daughter.

But for now, the circumrotation of the blades on the ceiling fan spun forth more flashes from his past, memories lost in a far corner in his mind. In a hypnotic state, he drifted back to his existence prior to choosing a more positive direction in life. An abandoned baby, three foster homes and a brief stint in a juvenile detention center is more than enough to send anyone down the wrong path. Serving in the military, especially as a member of the U. S. Special Forces changed all that.

He had even planned a career in the army. At that time, the thought of a wife and family existed only as a remote yearn held at bay by his dedication to the service of his country. Life was so clear and pure during those times. He knew he could rely on his buddies who worked and fought for the same cause. And his reason for being was found in a 535-page handbook that covered everything from setting snares, to making a thermite bomb, to raising and training a guerrilla army. And if all else failed, he could turn to the back cover of the handbook and put his trust in the Lord with the Special Forces Prayer. John whispered the unforgettable petition.

Almighty God, who art the Author of liberty,
and the champion of the oppressed, hear our prayer.
We, the men of Special Forces, acknowledge our
dependence upon Thee in the preservation of human freedom.
Go with us as we seek to defend the defenseless
and to free the enslaved.

There were no such printed handbooks to furnish him the unmixed guidance for raising a child, to provide him a unique view of life he could pass on to his adored daughter. The Special Forces Prayer was the only invocation John could summon and it was certainly inappropriate for a little girl. He pondered a prescription of church attendance to help Boo understand the purpose of her existence, to help her grasp that all life is sacred and should be honored. That solution felt right. That's what Rebecca would want him to do.

In opposite polarity, he slowly slipped into sleep, dreaming of Ft. Bragg and the training that seemed to breech the sanctity of life itself. His skills in annihilation were extensive. He could deploy a portable nuclear bomb, or if he wanted to get more personal, fire an Uzi, a Carl Gustav M45-B sub-machine gun, or a Heckler and Koch MP-5. All of these weapons of destruction provided little meaning to a child unblemished by the impurities of mankind.

His career ended at Camp Mackall inside the Bragg complex, training Green Beret recruits in the hand-to-hand skills of silent killing, in communication know-how, and in the handling of small arms conventional weapons. The overall training was a mixture of self-torture and cruelty that placed as much emphasis on malevolence as intelligence. He had to destroy any semblance of individual identity to see how each recruit would perform. This was the way the army formed the trainee into the special forces mold.

This rollercoaster ride from sadism to life-supporting team-work had finally created a mental confusion that poisoned his dedication to the service. That combined with meeting Rebecca had convinced him that life's goals were more precious than teaching young men to kill without conscience. Rebecca had always represented an essence of goodness, a willingness to transform a singular existence into a devotion of being the best wife and mother she could possibly be. Her dedication had left a profound vision of life on his restless core. It was the ineffable ties of family and love that she brought to their relationship. It made him understand life was precious and each waking minute should be enjoyed. The sound of Rebecca's laughter confirmed that passion daily. It followed their footsteps, coating them with a veneer of optimism that made the bad times more tolerable and the good times more delightful.

He had learned many things that had and would continue to serve him well. He had felt the indifferent heartache in his militia years and had experienced the divine contentment in marriage. These were all priceless lessons burned in his soul. And he was certain that a hollow heart was not for Boo. His handbook of life would be to teach and remind her that she could present to the world that same inward sense of virtue held by her mother. That there was undeniable goodness and love in mankind that would always triumph over the hatred of evil. Her life would be perfect.

7

The bedroom floor provided a convenient trap for all the dirty clothes unfamiliar with the Maytag. The room was a gauntlet of grimy sneakers, unwashed blue jeans and thrice worn shirts. It was six o'clock on a Monday morning in the deep South and John was quietly searching for his favorite shoes among the clutter. If Boo were awakened, she would demand his favor and he was already running late for work. He finally discovered the heel-worn cordovan loafers in the corner of his closet under a pile of unwashed clothes. He also found a faded shirt and a pair of wrinkled khaki trousers. After giving the shirt a quick sniff, he slipped it on along with the trousers and shoes. Now, the only missing piece to this rumpled ensemble was a sport coat. At least it was on a hanger.

"Thank God, Tina will be back today," he uttered, amazed that any one human being could create such a mess. No, he certainly wasn't the best housekeeper in the world. But given his dependence on Rebecca, he had adjusted incredibly well after her death when it came to raising a child and taking care of the household duties. He had even surprised himself on occasion, sitting up all night with Boo when she was flush with fever. But the past two years had given him a newfound respect for motherhood and its many responsibilities…mother the doctor, mother the teacher, mother the cook, mother the everything. Never would he belittle motherhood.

John stretched his tall physique to its limit as he reached for his holster and gun. It was tucked away, pushed to the back on an upper shelf in the closet. As he lifted the weapon from the shelf, his eyes caught glimpse of an old recurve bow a foster father had given him when he was a young boy. He loved that bow and had become a very skillful archer at ten years of age. Yet its effectiveness could not be matched against his firearm. The pistol, a 10mm Colt Model 1911, was an incredible piece of machinery. It took about ten pounds of finger pressure to release one of its Lawman bullets, about the same effort as lifting a gallon can of paint. A favorite of the Delta Elite, this handgun could blow a hole through an engine block. Unlike a bow and arrow, it was the epitome of aggression and death.

Bammm!

John's hair stood on end and his heart felt as though it would leap from his chest. It was Tina slamming the front door. "I'm going to kill her," he said breathlessly.

"Mister John, I'm here. Are you still here?" Tina loudly inquired.

John skipped lightly to the top of the stairs and placed his finger over his lips. "Tina, not so loud, she's still asleep," John whispered.

"I'm so sorry, Mister John." She said in a soft voice.

John mused at the sight of Tina's arms loaded with several bags stuffed with groceries. At almost sixty years of age, the diminished strength of her arms and hands strained to carry the load as she shuffled across the den floor. Her well-rounded head was all that appeared above the bags as she approached the kitchen. For a moment, John stood and stared, taking note of her facial features. Her skin was pale as though she avoided the sun at all costs. And her face framed by the sheen of her jet-black hair made her skin tone seem even more pallid. When she smiled, there was a striking dissimilarity between her yellowing teeth, dark eyes and pigmented scalp. It demanded your attention.

The cargo was about to explode from Tina's arms when John arrived just in time to prevent the disaster. Grabbing two bags, he led her into the kitchen.

"Thanks, Mister John. I'm going to cook something specially for you and Boo this dinner," she said with pride as she dropped the remaining bags on the kitchen table and began to put away the canned goods.

"Special. Cook something special," John replied placing his load on the counter. "Not specially."

Tina struggled with English, but she was very smart and had a wonderful propensity for learning. She had only been studying the language for three years and communicated quiet well. She had the same propensity for eating as evidenced by her butterball frame...at just under five feet tall, she looked like a human bowling ball.

"Sit down and I fix you breakfast," she barked, commanding John as she would her own child.

"No thanks, I'm already late. Tell Boo I'll see her tonight."

After saying goodbye, John grabbed the car keys off the kitchen counter and rushed out the front door. It was a beautiful, but unusual day. The morning air that followed the weather front was cool, almost biting. It enveloped his face and made him shudder just a little as he headed for the car. This early touch of fall was a welcome change from the last two months of sweltering heat and humidity. *Maybe a break in the electric bill*, he thought. The budget could certainly use the help since it always seemed to be in the red. No cop had ever been accused of being overpaid.

"Hey, Williams!" John's thoughts about the household budget were suddenly interrupted by a loud piercing voice. "Your cat's been crapping in my flower bed again. Are you going to do something about it or what?" The boisterous voice came from John's next-door neighbor Carl Otto. He was on his hands and knees, plucking infant weeds from his immaculate front lawn when he spied John out of the corner of his eye. Otto's lawn could pass muster as the thirteenth green at Augusta National. Its condition was in stark contrast

29

to John's lawn, the state proving ground for the development of crab grass. John knew his lack of horticultural zeal irritated the hell out of Otto. But it was just too bad. Unlike Carl who was retired, John had no free time to regularly cut his grass, let alone yank up weeds.

"Gee, Carl, I'm real sorry. I'll just take the ole roscoe here and cap a 10mm in the cat's head when I get home tonight," John sarcastically replied as he patted the bulge at his waist.

"Okay smart ass, I'll handle it myself," Otto retorted, yanking more of the troublesome dandelions from the turf.

John turned away and mumbled just loud enough for Otto to hear, "Yeah, you touch that cat and I'll personally have you declawed and neutered."

He had no time to argue. He could still see Otto shaking his fist as he slid into the car, cranked the engine and backed out of the driveway. Sure, he would get rid of the cat—as soon as hell froze over. That animal meant everything to Boo. He still remembered the look on her face when he and Rebecca gave her the kitten on her second birthday. That skinny calico female he found at the animal shelter was the best investment he had ever made. That small donation helped fill the void of companionship experienced by an only-child. Boo named her Azriel after some loony cartoon character she had seen on television. From day one, the cat tolerated any treatment dished out by her. Everything from loving hugs to ear tugs to dressing the feline in doll clothes. Sure, he would do something about it, yeah, he might buy her another one.

8

John was anxious to finish his paperwork on a recently closed murder investigation, so he arrived at the Homicide Department twenty minutes before the change in shifts. After pouring himself a cup of coffee, he momentarily sipped while surveying the surroundings.

The office was a large nondescript room on the fourth floor of Police Headquarters. The walls were painted light gray with darker gray desks lined in neat rows in the middle of the cramped enclosure. With more detectives than workstations, the shift changes were always a game of musical chairs. Exempt from this battle were the captain and lieutenant. Both were afforded fixed wall offices on either side of the detectives, with individual desks and phones. These were some of the fringe benefits of the upper echelon. Beyond that, the room lacked any personality other than a few attempts at humor—a poster on the wall that read *Fight Crime, Shoot Back*.

John had worked his way up through the ranks to detective sergeant and had finally been transferred to the day shift. This was a prized possession since it allowed him the freedom to see his daughter in the evenings and occasionally make it home before Tina's Chinese cuisine turned rigid and cold from the wait—he hated those concrete-like pork chops. He had advanced from traffic as a rookie to drug enforcement, and finally to homicide in just eight short years. Having been awarded the Medal of Merit for Bravery on two occasions aided that progress. It put him on the fast track to a detective's shield and into the field that allured him even as a boy—homicide, the most heinous and culpable of crimes. He was fascinated with murder, especially understanding the minds of those who killed.

John noticed Phil Sayers of the graveyard tour leaving his usual desk a little early, so he quickly dashed over and slid under him onto the vacant chair. After placing his coffee cup on the desk, he spun the chair in rapid circles. At the same time, he yelped with excitement as though he had just scored the winning touchdown in a closely fought football game. His excitement was abruptly interrupted by the raspy voice of Lieutenant Harold Milligan.

"John! I need to see you in my office, right now." He roared, waving his arms like a traffic cop.

John had barely risen from his chair when he was blind-sided by a fellow detective named Bob Counch. Counch quickly slid under John's buttocks and planted his own hind-quarters in their newfound home. He, like John, was looking for a workstation.

"Dammit, Counch, can't you at least wait until I get up?" John sniped.

"Six points!" Counch bellowed, pumping his arms and legs like an athlete who had just made the winning score. John was miffed, but even more aggravated when Counch imitated his earlier celebration by spinning the office chair and shrieking, "Touchdown!"

"Cut out the horse shit and get to work!" Milligan yelled, his voice strained and his face red with tension. He had been watching the proceedings through the plate glass in his office wall and was not amused with their shenanigans. "Get in here, Williams!" he commanded as he folded his arms across his chest. The lieutenant was always annoyed with his exclusion from the detective's antics, and impatiently stood at his doorway. Never accepted as one of the boys, he sought retaliation by exercising his authority over the same men who shunned him.

On his way to the lieutenant's office, John completed a pirouette and flashed an ill-willed, one-fingered salute at

Counch. "Well, at least I had the last word," John mumbled as he walked into Milligan's office.

"Williams, I want you to meet someone," Milligan said while pointing toward the stranger who had risen from his chair. "This is Victor Lechman, your new partner."

John had been given no forewarning that he was being assigned a new partner. As he extended his hand to Lechman, he began assessing the stranger's appearance with suspicious eyes. In his early forties, Lechman was a husky, bearish looking man. His paw-like hands and sturdy five-foot, eight-inch anatomy could certainly generate more power than that exhibited in the noodle-like grip of his handshake.

His bald head in contrast with his furry hands and heavy facial beard amused John. He appeared to have brown hair coming from all directions—nose, ears, eyebrows—the only Homo sapiens with body hair protruding from the top of his turtleneck shirt. His Neanderthal nose, forehead and chin were fine complements to all of that unkempt fur.

He was different, very different from John's former partner, Bob Nelson. Nelson was a smallish man of slight build with rustic features. Known as Pop to the department, Nelson had recently retired after forty plus years of service. John had been assigned as his partner when he transferred to homicide and had learned much from his tutelage. But even more, Pop had provided the rock-solid emotional foundation he needed after Rebecca's death. In John's eyes, he could not be supplanted by anyone.

"How are you?" John said withdrawing his hand from Lechman's loose grip.

"I'm all right," Lechman retorted sharply. "So, Williams, when are you and me gonna get started and clean all the perverts out of this town?" Lechman quipped as he excitedly waived his arms.

"New York, right?" John asked, pointing his finger discern-
ingly at Lechman. He had recognized the accent and gyrating motions as being from an area hundreds of miles north
of the Mason Dixon.

"Victor has joined us from the homicide division of the
Brooklyn Police Department," Lieutenant Milligan piped in,
sensing the introduction had gotten off on the wrong foot.
"He was with that department for twenty-one years, solved
some of their toughest cases. I know the two of you will get
along just fine, won't you, Williams?"

John was impressed with Lechman's credentials but was
not dazzled with his lack of Southern charm. He was about
to move the conversation up to a more misanthropic level
when the office door burst open. Captain Reid, the chief of
detectives, frantically waved a small piece of paper held in
his right hand.

"We just got a report of a homicide over in Buckhead," he
declared, looking at Milligan. "Harold, who's available and
on the clock?"

In one quick move, the lieutenant seized the note from the
captain's hand and held it out for John. "Williams, you and
Victor here are investigating this case. Get your asses in gear
and keep me posted," he said, daring John to rebuff his authority.

With a loathing look, John snatched the note. Milligan enjoyed flexing his muscle, especially in front of the captain,
but he was even more pleased with the quandary he had created. What a combination, this diehard Southerner and
know-it-all Northerner. They couldn't be more opposite.
Milligan never liked John, and this was a vengeful way to
show his contempt. John was vexed and angered by the situation. He wanted to reach over and slap that Cheshire cat
grin off the lieutenant's face. But this was not the time and
place. Besides, a stupid move like that would be

insubordination and the end of his career. It would mean that Milligan had won. He wasn't about to let that happen.

"Let's go earn our pay," John said, leading Lechman out of the office.

9

At 8:30, the morning traffic was still heavy as John and Victor turned off Peachtree Road on to Wieuca. The men were traveling north at a rapid speed toward the murder scene. Since leaving the station, the cruiser wasn't the only thing moving at full tilt. Lechman had been a non-stop source of chatter, enlightening John on how they did it in The Big Apple and on how everything was better up North. The cops. The food. The entertainment. Everything.

John's recollection of New York was quite different from the one painted by the fast-talking Lechman. In drug enforcement at the time, he was sent to Manhattan to serve extradition papers on a sleaze ball pusher who was wanted on seven felony counts in Atlanta. Two days of breathing exhaust fumes trapped between imposing buildings, coupled with big city noise and a mass of humanity, had given him the impression that this place was certainly not Mecca. Yet, the one episode that was etched most deeply in his memory involved a little old prune faced matron he encountered on his first day in the city. He had just checked in the hotel and was about to take the elevator to his room on the tenth floor when they crossed paths.

"Yoose not from New York, are you?" she queried, astonished at him holding the elevator door open, allowing her to enter first.

"No ma'am, I'm not," he said politely while shaking his head from side to side.

After the elevator rose to her floor and stopped, she stepped out and glanced back with a knowing grin, "If yoose was from New York, yoose wouldn't be doing that."

John rationalized that the pollution and noise had destroyed the brain cells of every citizen who lived in that acrimonious city, including Lechman's. Why else would anyone subject themselves to all of the human harshness when they could experience the gentility of the South by simply packing up and leaving this hostile place? No, John would never be good enough for New York and, no, he would never convince Victor that Atlanta was anything but second fiddle to NYC. He was just glad when they arrived at the crime scene. He was sick of listening to Victor ramble.

The house was located a few blocks off Wieuca Road. Victor and John recognized it immediately given all the commotion taking place out front. Parked on the street were three black and white police cruisers, an ambulance, two cars used by the lab technicians, a Fulton County paramedic unit, plus several reporters and two camera crews. Two uniformed officers were handling the street traffic while two other uniforms stood inside the yellow crime scene tape that encircled the front lawn. Residents in the area were standing around, gossiping while attempting to get a visual on what was going on. This was not your typical day in your middle-class neighborhood. Today looked more like a midway at the county fair.

After Victor parked the cruiser, he and John got out and quickly made their way through the crowd. As they walked toward the ribboned barrier, both men wondered what deed had brought them to this normally quiet neighborhood. After dipping under the yellow tape, they heard the voice of one of the uniforms, Officer Stan O'Neal. "Hey guys, you're not going to believe this one," he said, pinching his nose between his thumb and forefinger.

"Yeah, well, you know Stan, if you've seen one, you've seen them all," John attempted to sound confident, yet there was a trace of trepidation in his voice. Looking at gruesome murder scenes never seemed to bother him, but he had a queasy feeling about what waited inside the house.

37

Both men stepped inside the front door into a large living room. They were greeted immediately by a foul pungency that brought their breakfasts to their throats.

"What the hell's that smell?" Victor gagged.

Simultaneously, John and Victor reached into their back pockets, withdrew their handkerchiefs and covered their noses and mouths. The thin fabric effectively filtered some of the effluvium, yet most of the odor made its way through their make-shift gas masks and slammed into their noses.

"I don't know but it sure as hell stinks." John responded in a muffled voice as he visually measured the den. As he turned to his left, he caught sight of Dave Lewis. Since Lewis was the uniformed officer in charge of the scene, John motioned him over to get a rundown on the information he had gathered.

"Damn, Dave, how can you stand to smell this crap?" John asked while glaring at Dave's uncovered face.

Dave seemed delighted that he wasn't the only one experiencing the foul odor. "Believe it or not guys, you get use to the smell after a while."

"What have you got on this one?" John asked.

Looking down at his notes, Dave winced with confusion, "We don't have much so far. We just got here about twenty minutes ago, so we haven't had a chance to contact all the neighbors. But we do have an I.D. on the body. His name is Richard Pierce. He's resting comfortably in the bedroom down the hall." Lewis smiled.

Victor removed the handkerchief from his face and wiped the dripping mucous from his nostrils. "I've never encountered this kind of odor from a decomposed stiff before. Damn guy must have been dead for days."

Dave shook his head in disagreement. "No, according to the lab boys, the victim's been dead only six to eight hours. They can't figure out where this stink is coming from. Sure

38

ain't the body." Then, Lewis turned and pointed toward the front door. "John, if you're in charge of this investigation, it's officially your baby. I need a breath of fresh air."

John wiped the moisture from his face as he watched Dave leave. Then, he motioned for Victor to follow him down the hallway. Victor obliged and both men cautiously moved toward the corner bedroom where the bulk of the activity was taking place. Inside the room, two lab technicians and two paramedics had surrounded a queen size bed and were making wisecracks about the cause of death.

"Looks like he pissed off someone, maybe his wife or girl-friend," a paramedic sneered as he pointed at the body lying face up on the undisturbed bedding. John and Victor moved closer for a better look at the cadaver. Both were curious about the paramedic's waggish remark.

"Williams, look at this." Victor had bent over the corpse, astonished at the look on the dead man's open eyes. "You would think he shook hands with the devil."

One of the paramedics grabbed his crotch, pulled his gen-italia up-and-down and chuckled. "You'd look like hell too, if you just had your dick whacked off."

John, uneasy with the circumstances and not amused with the humor, pointed his finger at the paramedics and sternly demanded, "That's enough! You two get out!" He then turned to the lab technicians. "You know your job, get with it! For starters, I want photographs of the body and room from all angles. Measure this place, swab anything suspi-cious, and dust for prints."

John and Victor were about to examine the body when a shadowy figure appeared over their shoulders. At first, John thought one of the paramedics had returned but, when he glanced upward, he caught a glimpse of Charles Connors, the county medical examiner. He was hard to miss. The black, large-rimmed glasses stood out against his pale complexion like a billboard on a lonely highway. His body was extremely thin, looking almost emaciated. Connors had a horrible knack of exacerbating his narrow frame by wearing clothes two sizes too large as evidenced by his loosely fitted dark suit.

"Charlie, we were about to inspect the body. I'm glad you're here." John greeted Connors and then turned his gaze toward Victor. "Victor, meet Charlie Connors, M.D. to the dead. We call him the stiff surgeon." John grinned.

Victor and John chuckled, although Connors never cracked a smile. He just maintained the same pious look as though levity was not permitted in his line of work. After all, he was a forensic pathologist, an expert in the analysis of the causes of death and death wasn't a very funny business—especially murder. John held a great deal of respect for his professional abilities, yet he just couldn't help but tease Connors, hoping for a sign of diversion. None came.

The men exchanged greetings and then joined in the search for evidence. The lifeless body was that of a white male, aged somewhere between forty-five and fifty years. He was stripped of any clothing. With mouth agape, it looked as though he had sung his death song, knowing his existence in this world would soon be over. His face was calcimine and inclement with a twisted expression of bewilderment and shock.

Victor was right about the eyes. The circular pupils were dilated with a frosty opaque allure as though his demise had been one of intense anguish or passionate euphoria. Beyond those strange features, the chest and limbs were divested of hair, creating a horizontal flatness that reflected the light from the flashes of the lab tech's camera. Other than the odd look of the eyes, the most singular oddity was the severance of the man's penis.

For over an hour, the men had meticulously canvassed the corpse's hair, skin, teeth, nails, torso and legs. That's when Connors drew back from the body and began quizzically looking at the floor around the bed. "Has anyone found the missing penis?" He asked.

"No!" Victor, John, and the lab technicians responded in unison. It was as though none of them wanted to find the misplaced organ.

"All right then, help me turn him over," Connors said, gesturing a rolling motion with his hands.

With a collective heave, the crew flipped the body over, exposing the breech of the victim.

"Hey, check this out." Victor instructed the others to view the posterior.

A scarlet vertical line began at the top of Pierce's right buttock and continued to the top of the thigh. A horizontal line crossed the vertical line toward the bottom, giving it the appearance of an upside down cross. The last mark was a half-circle on top of the horizontal line at the point it passed across the vertical.

John, with a puzzled look on his face, turned to Connors, "What do you make of that?"

Connors was obviously bothered by the symbol. Sweat beaded on his forehead. "That upside down cross is the mark of the devil."

Before Connors could continue, Victor interrupted with a look of confidence, pointing to the unusual sign. "This cross with the half circle indicates that this guy was a Satanic Traitor. He may have pissed off a satanic coven or one of its members. It's used in death threats or rituals of revenge."

John was surprised that Victor knew so much about the mark. He was also a little jealous. He was still stinging from Victor's earlier dissertation about how much more advanced crime detection was up North and the last thing he wanted was a demonstration from this puffed-up Yankee. "How do you know that's what this is?" John asked.

Victor straightened his back like a knowing schoolboy called on by his first-grade teacher. "A few years back in Brooklyn, I put a psychopath in the joint. This little red headed bastard was bumping off winos, and then he would drain and drink their blood. The newspapers had a field day with the 'Vampire Runs Rampant in New York' story. As it turned out, he was a Satanist, a real Anton La Vey over the edge sorta freak. I learned the meanings of all this mumbo jumbo crap back then."

Connors wiped his right forefinger across the vertical line on the mid-buttock, smudging his finger with a sample of the red grease used to make the sign. Lifting the specimen to his nose, his nostrils flared as he inhaled, searching for any clue that might help in the investigation. "Red lipstick," he said as he exhaled. He withdrew a handkerchief from his trouser pocket and cleaned his stained finger. Again, he filled and emptied his lungs and scratched his sweaty forehead. "Something's not right," he said.

John noticed his frustration, "What's bothering you, Charlie?"

Connors pointed to the corpse and bed. "There's only a small amount of blood on the bedding. Why isn't there more blood from the wound—unless his heart stopped before the amputation? And, where the hell did this odor come from?"

"Could be some kind of heart failure," John replied. "There aren't any marks on the body. As far as the odor, I don't know."

None of the officers really had a clue, so they continued their examination in hopes of finding at least some answers to their questions. For two more hours, they slowly picked over every square inch of the body until Connors stepped back from the bed. It signaled an end to the on-site analysis, and end to the fruitless search.

"Let's get him downtown so we can do an autopsy. At least that way we'll get some answers." Connors said.

Connors packed up his gear and left the room first. On his way out, he passed Officer Stan O'Neal who was on his way in to speak with John. O'Neal, in charge of handling security on the grounds, had identified a potential witness. "We've got a neighbor outside who says she knows the deceased. She also says she was home last night when the murder occurred. Her name is Katherine Rogers."

"Have you located any other witnesses?" John asked, hoping for a little bit of good news.

"No, just her. She is waiting for you outside."

"Go tell her I'll be right out." John replied and then turned to Victor, "Get the lab boys to conduct a thorough search of the room and the rest of the house. Double check to make sure they haven't overlooked anything."

Victor was still mesmerized by the corpse and didn't look up or acknowledge John's remarks. Within inches, he hovered over Pierce's face in a cataleptic-like state of his own. It was as though he was attempting to communicate with the dead, to make some sort of telekinetic link.

John's voice reached a higher pitch, "Lechman, did you hear what I said?"

Victor blinked his eyelids as though he had been awakened from a trance. "Yeah, I heard you. I'll take care of it."

John left the bedroom, also feeling haunted by the bizarre look on Pierce's face. In all of his investigations, he had never seen anything like it. It was so freakish; it dampened his soul. But once outside, the mid-morning sun seemed to rekindle his spirit as he began his search for Officer O'Neal. After a quick visual of the grounds, he spied him standing next to one of the police cruisers with the solo witness. As he approached, he tried to create a reassuring expression by smiling and offering his hand in gentility. "Ms. Rogers, I'm Detective Sergeant Williams. I'm in charge of this investigation. Would you mind answering a few questions? It would be a big help."

Gently, she accepted his hand and answered in a subdued voice. "No, I don't mind. I'm a little shook up, but I'll help if I can." Her grim face and teary eyes signaled her disquietude.

John knew that his questions would subject her to more torture, but he had to ask. He would try to make it brief. "Did you know Richard Pierce, the man that lived here?" John pointed at the house.

Before she could reply, an unexpected squawk burst from the radio microphone attached to the shoulder of O'Neal's uniform. The scratchy noise and the garbled voices startled Ms. Rogers, making her even more uneasy. Aware of her anxiety, John asked the officer to give them a few minutes alone.

After turning back to Ms. Rogers, John asked the question again. "Did you know Mr. Pierce?"

"I first met Richard five years ago. That's when I moved here from Chicago." She pointed at a gray brick traditional house adjacent to the Pierce home. "I live next door."

"How well did you know him?"

"Not very well until about five or six months ago. He pretty much kept to himself until then." Katherine brushed the tears from her eyes and began wringing her hands. "One evening about six months ago Richard knocked on my front door, asked to borrow some sugar. He seemed very upset, like he was concerned about something. I knew he was single, and I was lonesome—I'm a widow—so I asked him to stay for coffee. He agreed and we had a pleasant conversation. It seemed like we were both very lonely and we just sort

44

of hit it off that night. About a week later, we discovered that we were both having birthdays—the terrible fiftieth." Rogers smiled. "We found out we were born about a week apart, so we celebrated together. After that, we started seeing each other on a regular basis. We got to be really good friends."

John stopped writing on the small note pad, looked up and asked, "Were you together last night?"

"No, he usually works late every night."

"Where you at home last night?"

"Yes, I was home alone all evening." She answered.

"Did you see anyone enter or leave his house, or hear any unusual sounds?" John asked as he resumed writing.

"No, nothing."

CLAAANGGG!!

A rackety noise pricked their ears, forcing their heads in the direction of the front door. The sound was from a mobile stretcher that had dropped from the concrete porch, down the brick steps to the sidewalk below. The misguided fall caused the metal wheels to clatter like the symbol on a drum.

For John and Ms. Rogers, the sound should have been nothing more than a mild irritant. But a negligent attendant had left the gurney rails in the down position while transporting the black body bag with Pierce tucked inside. The jolt from the plunge dislodged the body, sending it aloft like a miniature Zeppelin. When it landed, the deceased was resting diagonally across the cot, rigor mortis somewhat preventing its collapse.

Meanwhile the lead attendant had fallen, tumbling across the grass while his pal frantically scrambled, trying to catch, balance, and stop the runaway stretcher. Barnum and Bailey could not have choreographed a more burlesque scene. John bit hard on his lower lip, hoping the pain would abrogate the laughter he felt rising in his torso. Ms. Rogers didn't share the sentiment. She covered her face with her hands, and again burst into tears. Seeing her friend thrown into the air like a misdirected pancake hit her hard. .

Her emotional outcry made John more curious. "Ms. Rogers, were you and Mr. Pierce more than just friendly neighbors?"

"We were in love. We were going to be married next March!" Unable to contain her feelings, the sobbing rose to a howl. Any additional questions would have to wait.

John motioned for O'Neal to escort Ms. Rogers back to her house. He had her phone number and would follow-up later when she had regained her composure. In the meantime, he decided to check with his new partner. He perused the sea of faces standing inside the yellow tape. He spied Victor striding toward him, rocking side to side, as though his bulky body was incapable of forward motion. As Victor drew closer, he pointed at a man standing outside the cordon.

"That guy lives two doors down. He hangs out at the club where Pierce worked. He said Pierce was diagnosed with a brain tumor about a year ago. Said it was terminal. Then lo and behold, five months later he's cured." Victor hesitated, keeping the rest of the story to himself. It was as though he wanted John to search for the answer to Pierce's miraculous recovery.

John, curious and annoyed with Victor's tactics responded, "Soooo, what happened?"

Victor's face beamed like a twelve year-old who had just found the last item on his scavenger list. "Pierce had too much to drink one night and told this guy that after he was released from the hospital, he was depressed about his limited time here on earth. So, he somehow contacted a man who practiced black magic. Anyway, the shaman had Pierce pray psalms of vengeance, which he had to copy, lay under his pillow, and sleep on each night. The next phase of his treatment included placing six knives under his pillow and

46

sticking six more knives in the wall over his bed. Can you believe that shit?" Victor wiggled his hands in the air as though he were beckoning the spirits, "Some real spooky stuff, huh?"

"So, what happened next?" John asked, his curiosity now at a fever pitch.

"Well, nothing. I mean Pierce went back to his doctors and they said it was a miracle. The tumor was gone. Oh, yeah, this guy also said Pierce became really disturbed after that. Said Pierce joined the church and started reading the Bible. He turned into a religious fanatic."

"Don't tell me you've got the poop on the bar where this guy worked, too?" John asked, expecting a positive response given Victor's apodictic thoroughness.

"Yep, I've got all the details."

John was pleased with the information Victor had gathered, yet he was still unwilling to compliment him on a job well done. "Let's go back in the house and wrap it up."

As the detectives walked toward the front door, John gazed at the traditional ranch style home and contemplated the odd venue. This neighborhood conjured up images of children on bicycles, older couples strolling arm-in-arm, and joggers trotting down the tree-lined streets.

He was still struck by the homey, rather ordinary places where violence and sudden death occurred, and this place was no different. Even after eight years in law enforcement, he was still surprised that wickedness could be found in such a tranquil place. But once inside the house, the indistinguishable odor burned his senses, making it clear that no community is immune from the homicidal acts of a maniac.

John and Victor searched for the next four hours with their only discovery being an oddly shaped amulet, hung from a worn leather hawser. Frustrated by their lack of success, they moved outside where they canvassed the neighborhood door-to-door, trying to locate witnesses whom probably didn't exist. The long shot didn't pay off, so they went back inside the house and broke camp, instructing the uniforms to seal the crime scene and leave.

Outside, the newshounds were still laden with camera equipment. The crews were bunched up like a pack of electronic hyenas, sniffing the air for blood. John knew that conversing with anyone outside the police department would only mean trouble. For even though these so-called journalists used recorders during an interview, they rarely got the story right. Perhaps sensationalism took precedence over accuracy. Whatever the reason, John didn't care. He and Victor exited the house and ignored the barrage of questions by silently boring through the pack. Quickly, they boarded their russet Chevy, and left without acknowledging the reporters' existence.

As John drove the cruiser south on Peachtree, he, once again, never had the chance to jump into the conversation. Victor had resumed where he left off, talking non-stop about New York, covering much of the same material he bragged about earlier. John mentally blocked the monologue until a noisy rumble from Victor's paunch caught his attention. The men had been so engrossed in their work, they had forgotten to eat lunch. John peeked over at Victor while he maneuvered the sedan through traffic.

"You hungry?" John asked.

"Yeah, I'm starved. It just hit me like a ton of bricks."

"I'll take you to Atlanta's finest eatin' house. It's just down the road on North Avenue."

"Weese gonna have some chicken lips and grits?" Victor asked sarcastically.

Victor's off-hand remark was stereotypical for transplanted New Yorkers. That was John's thought anyway. He was certain that all those damn Yankees had a *Gone with the*

Wind vision of the South. A vision that included servants in white gloves, serving up fried chicken and cat-head biscuits to all those fat Southern gentlemen and well-bred ladies. The dinner, of course, would be followed by a round of mint juleps on the front porch swing.

Yes, John was angry, and he wanted to strike back at Victor for his mendacious cliché, but he exercised the utmost restraint. In lieu of releasing a verbal lashing at this uncivil Northerner, he elected to outwit him. This would be Bull Run revisited.

"Tell me Victor, how long have you been in Atlanta?"

"Five weeks."

"Before you moved here, how many times did you visit Atlanta or any other city in the South for that matter?"

"On our way to Miami, back a few years, me and the wife drove through Atlanta. We ate dinner in a little hick town just north of the Florida line. It was one of those barbeque joints that are so popular down here."

John grinned as though he had the opening he wanted. "So, your only exposure to the South is five weeks in Atlanta and a barbeque joint in South Georgia, right?

Victor didn't answer. He was too busy searching the vista for any building that might smack of this famous restaurant. The hierarchy of needs was definitely at work here, placing his hunger about four levels above the geographic repartee with John. Thank goodness, they had arrived.

Victor eyed the lot as John searched for a place to park. "Damn, look at all the cars." Victor seemed disappointed as his eyes searched for a spot in front of the restaurant.

"Don't worry, the Varsity has six hundred parking spaces. We'll find a spot."

John drove into a parking space in the back, placed the gear shift in park, and cut the engine. He was still disgusted that Victor never answered his question. "Let's go."

49

Now mid-afternoon, the heaviest crowd had come and gone, leaving the Varsity somewhat free of the usual masses that gathered around noon to devour their favorite iconic hot dog or burger. Victor bolted from the car and led the way to the restaurant's front door. Once inside, the aromas of fried meat, onion rings and hot grease assaulted his nostrils. The smells were irresistible. Victor looked left to right in pursuit of the food, while John searched his jacket pocket for his mobile phone.

"Victor, I'm going to make a call home, I'll catch you in a few minutes."

Victor, focused on the servitor of fast food standing at the counter, never affirmed or disaffirmed John's remark. Drawn like a grizzly to a honey tree, he made a beeline for the counter while licking his chops. Meanwhile, John stepped away from the noisy counter and called home to check on Boo. Talking to her always seemed to lift his spirit and he certainly needed a lift today. Three years of observing senseless homicides kept him in need of steadfast reminders that good things do exist in life.

"Hello," Tina answered his call.

"Tina, this is John. Just checking in. Is everything going okay?"

"Yes, everything is good here," she answered.

"Would you get Boo? I'd like to talk to her for just a minute."

"I'll get her," Tina answered.

His daily calls were routine, and Tina wasted no time locating Boo.

"Daddeeee!" Boo's voice was shrill with excitement.

"Whatcha doin', baby?" John's face was instantly transformed from police-hard to daddy-soft.

"Playin' school with Azriel...and...and...watchin' TV with Tina. You comin' home now, Daddy?"

"No, sweetheart, but I'll be home before you go to bed."

"Wait, Tina wants to tell you something."

"Okay. I'll see you later. Love ya."

"Love ya, Daddy."

Tina's anxious voice was revealing. Although everything was in order at the Williams' dwelling, it wasn't at Tina's house. "Mister John, it's my granddaughter. She's not feeling good. I need to go home to see about her."

Tina rarely asked to leave early or arrive late, so John knew that her young granddaughter had to be very ill.

"That's alright, Tina. Go next door and ask Jennifer to babysit Boo until I get home. Make sure she has my phone number and tell her I won't be late. Give me a call if she can't make it."

"I will. Thanks so much, Mister John."

John returned the phone to his pocket and hurried to the counter. Since Victor had a head-start on lunch, he needed to order a hotdog of his own and then catch up with his new partner. Within a minute he was served, so he began the search for Victor. He found him plunked down at a table in one of the restaurant's side rooms.

John seated himself in a chair on the opposite side of the table. He figured Victor would be hard pressed to deprecate this old Atlanta landmark, especially given the amount of food he had on his plastic tray. John starred in disbelief at four chili dogs, two fries, one order of onion rings, and a jumbo chocolate shake. This man surely had a set of copper arteries and a cast iron stomach.

Victor never looked up to acknowledge John's presence. He just kept shoveling in the food, not waiting to devour the previous bites before cramming another chunk of frankfurter in his mouth. His cheeks pooched in all directions, giving him the appearance of a gigantic chipmunk that was stock-piling chili dogs for the winter.

"So, how do you like the food, Victor"? John asked.

"Good, real good." His voice was muffled from the mouthful. He dispatched his third hot dog in two bites and his fourth in three. After ingesting the last morsel, he picked up the chocolate shake, swished the straw around the bottom of the cup and sucked with the absorption of a Hoover vacuum. Upon siphoning the last drop, he placed the empty cup on the tray and announced his gratification with a low phonic belch. He followed the burp with a silly grin—silly because his upper lip was rimmed by a grayish brown mustache left by the chocolate malt.

John watched the proceedings, unable to believe the display put on by this incredible eating machine. But he was even more affected by seeing this side of Victor. It seemed strange how something as simple as his eating habits exposed a human side, a frail side that imparted a message to John that Victor was indeed vulnerable, that he possessed human frailties just like anyone else. John knew that they had to trust each other, to depend on each other for their survival regardless of their backgrounds. In their line of work, it was just that simple.

After John finished eating, he turned to Victor. "You ready to go? We need to get back to the office so we can start following up on our leads."

With a somewhat confused look on his face, Victor leaned hard to his left and looked over his shoulder. He was attempting to gain a view of the serving counter. "I think I'll get one more to go," he simpered. I'll eat a light dinner."

And so, John and Victor left with Victor's extra dog in tow. Minutes later, as John was driving south past the stately Peachtree Center complex, Victor consumed the last morsel of his last hot dog. One final belch reconfirmed his pleasure.

"I've got to tell you, those are some of the best hot dogs I've ever eaten—and I've had some of the best, you know, they don't get any better than what we've got in New York." That was as close to a compliment as Victor could muster. It was close enough for John.

"Yeah, it's a good place to eat if you're not watching your diet," John replied as he glanced down at Victor's midsection.

Victor patted his stomach and burst into laughter. "Hell, pal, the only diet we have to worry about is the one served up by a Saturday Night Special, you know, the lead kind."

John laughed along with him, now feeling more at ease with his new partner. He knew that Victor wasn't wrong about the risks in their profession. Any police officer who says he's not afraid is a fool. Sure, their work was basically ninety-nine percent investigations followed by the bureaucratic rigmarole of report writing, but you could count on that boring routine being interrupted by unexpected moments of sheer terror.

Such was the reason why so many officers keeled over from heart attacks—all that high test adrenaline sporadically shocking their systems. John tried not to dwell on a stray bullet from a strung-out dope dealer or a knife stab from a mentally ill wacko. You never know who is standing behind the door when death comes calling.

These iniquitous thoughts never crossed his mind until the genesis of his daughter. Until then, he never accepted his own mortality. Yes, it was that blessed event that affected him so profoundly. Rebecca, pregnant with Boo, wolfing down her favorite treat for the baby—ice cream chased with more ice-cream. John had prepared her a second cone of sherbet when her water broke, splattering on the tile floor in the kitchen. There she was, standing with ice cream cone in hand, refusing to believe that motherhood had arrived. After all, the little one wasn't due for three more weeks. Meanwhile, John stood frozen, viewing the puddle beneath her dress, thinking she had gone insane. Why else would she pee on the floor? It wasn't until she screamed that he realized she was in labor.

They rushed to the hospital just in time. Thirty minutes later, a petite nurse emerged from the delivery room and handed the beautiful newborn to her anxious father. While cradling Boo in his arms, a rejuvenating sense of goodness filled John's being, a feeling that brought forth tears of joy. He wasn't a religious doubter, but he wasn't a religious fanatic either. Yet, at that moment in time, he was certain of one thing. He was sure that this tiny baby was a message from Heaven, a message that God really does exist. For whom else could create something so innocent and beautiful as a child?

Fearing that she would think him weak, he never told Rebecca about those special feelings. He wished he had. He wished he could turn back time so he could tell her. But he couldn't, so he often told Boo the story, hoping her mother could somehow hear his words.

After arriving back at the station, John and Victor went through the motions of explaining the crime scene to their superiors. Nearly everyone in the department had already heard about the case and wanted to know the details. Repeating the story to all those interested parties, along with doing the preliminary paperwork, ate up the early evening hours. When John and Victor finally left for home, they both agreed to resume their work in the morning.

10

John arrived at the house at eight o'clock in the evening after a stressful day on the job. He opened the front door and stepped inside, doing a once-over with his eyes and ears. The lighting was dim, almost obscure, and earsplitting music fused the house. It caught him off guard. His initial impulse was to locate Tina.

After all, this wasn't the first time she had hatched a musical celebration in the Williams' house. Tina enjoyed country music a lot. John was always amused that a little Asian grandmother would be in to all the drinkin', lovin' and fightin' songs. But she was. And she especially loved the beat and swagger of Bocephus.

But these sounds were very different from southern rock. The phonetics sounded more like hip hop music, street speech from an American teenager, Jennifer, the babysitter. After turning on the light, John located the guilty culprit. Lying on the sofa, Jennifer was attempting to comprehend her chemistry homework while being zapped by the noise from a music station on the television. John surmised that the study habits of today's generation were a hell of a lot different than those practiced when he was a young boy. He could just picture himself, ten years in the future, counseling Boo on a difficult homework assignment, while his eardrums and brain cells were being destroyed by rock 'n roll rondeau.

The sudden glare from the bright light startled Jennifer, causing her to recoil from the sofa to her feet. "Oh, Mr. Williams, you scared me. I didn't hear you come in." She grabbed the TV remote control and quickly turned down the volume.

John, about to chide her for creating the racket, lost his concentration when his eyes caught her shapely seventeen-year-old figure. There she stood, facing him with an apologetic smile on that pretty, young face. Her mid-drift blouse allowed him a quick glance at a smooth plateaued tummy and cute belly button. And he willingly took it. The loosely fitted garment was held forward, away from her torso by two perky breasts. The thought of her braless condition made his face turn red with embarrassment. And, of course, he couldn't help but notice the twin peaks through the mid-drift's thin fabric.

He was even more abashed by her lower extremities as he copped a glance downward at a pair of blue denim shorts that clung to her well-proportioned hips and slender legs. Yes, his eyes pored over every inch of her, including her bare feet and long tresses of hair. And heaven forbid, he even had a sexual thought about her, a shameless want that surprised even himself.

But, fortunately, common sense prevailed, and his flight of fancy quickly ended. Perhaps the stark reality of statutory rape did the trick. His law enforcement memory evoked that thought. Jailbait. Nevertheless, it had been a long time since he had those kinds of thoughts about the opposite sex. And, it certainly had been a while since he thought of himself as an engaging sexual partner. The feeling ruffled his passion, attempting to awaken it from a two-year slumber. This just wasn't the right situation to stir that kind of fervor.

Trying not to get caught gawking at her features, he looked away and asked, "Jennifer, how in the world can you study with all the noise?"

With a sugary, almost innocent intonation, she responded, "Oh, I can't study in a quiet room, and besides, Boo loves to pretend she's one of those dancers on the music videos. You should have seen her strutting her stuff down here a little while ago."

Turning his head, he looked up the stairs, "Is she asleep?"

"Right now, she's in her room playing school with the cat."

John reached into his pocket and withdrew several folded bills while Jennifer waived her hand, attempting to refuse any payment for her babysitting services. "You don't have to pay me for this evening. It was really no trouble. As a matter of fact, I'll be glad to do other things for you if you need me to."

Not about to touch that invitation, he paid her, thanked her, and quickly escorted her out the door before his impure thoughts returned to his head. He watched until she entered her house, and then returned inside. Without hesitating, he made his way up the stairs and headed toward the right corner bedroom. Boo had always felt a sense of security in that small retreat, so John was not surprised to find her there. After quietly opening the door, he stood outside in the hallway and watched as she lectured her inanimate students. She had written a word on her marker board and was reciting it to an assortment of stuffed animals that she had arranged in a semi-circle on the floor. Not to be overlooked, she did have one student with a heartbeat. Azriel was sitting in the middle of the make-believe classroom.

Gato

"*Gato*, means cat. Say, '*gato*'," she instructed each recruit to repeat her words. Boo erased *gato* from the board and replaced it with a new word.

Pero

"*Pero*, means dog. Say, '*pero*'," she repeated the lesson pointing to her toy white dog.

John watched silently as Boo continued her instructions, declaring and defining each new word and then moving on to the next. Tina had been trying to teach her Spanish during the day and it was sheer merriment listening to them both pronouncing Spanish words with an Asian intonation or Southern drawl. John suspected it was Tina's way of getting even with him for correcting her English grammar. He tapped on the door.

"Well, Miss Teacher, do you have any new Spanish words for me?"

"Daddy!" she exclaimed; her eyes wide with excitement. She jumped into his arms, and they exchanged a kiss and hug.

"What have you been up to, sweetheart?"

"I've been playin' school, and...and me and Jennifer played like we were dancers on TV, and...and we talked to her boyfriend on the phone," she replied succinctly and with total honesty.

He was impressed with how her language had blossomed in the past year and how she always spoke with complete candor, directly to the point.

"She told me not to tell you that her boyfriend kept calling on the phone."

John placed Boo back down and smiled with a knowing assurance that she trusted him above all others. "Well, I'm glad you told me. Have you eaten dinner already?"

"Yeah, Tina fixed me something to eat and she said to tell you that she left you something in the refrigerator," Boo answered.

"Thanks for telling me, baby. Slip on your jammies while I fix your bed. It's time to go to sleep."

Normally, Boo would argue about retiring for the evening, but tonight she obediently slipped on her bright pink pajamas while John rearranged her stuffed animals on the bed and pulled back the spread. After grabbing her favorite bear, Boo climbed onboard and under the covers. John bent over, preparing to tuck her in when she unexpectedly hit him with a big surprise. With lamblike innocence, she looked to her father and with the sweetest voice, begged for his protection.

"Can I sleep with you tonight, Daddy?"

"Boo, you need to sleep in your bed. I have to get up early in the morning and would wake you up if you slept with me. You're not afraid are you, baby?"

With total sincerity, she answered, "Mommy has been coming to see me at night. She said that there were bad people trying to hurt us." She squirmed and then squeezed her bear.

"Oh, sweetheart, you just dreamed that she was here," John replied as he soothingly stroked her hair and brushed her cheek. Sensing she needed further comfort, he softly asked, "Do you want me to read you a bedtime story? Will that make you feel better?"

The anxiety on her face was instantly replaced by an expression of joy and anticipation. "Yeah, would you read me the crocodile story?"

"Yeah, sure I will," he responded and then turned to look for the book on her dresser.

Quickly, she sat up and pointed under her bed. "It's down there, Daddy. Mommy left it there after she read to me last night."

Not wanting to encourage the imagined visits, he ignored her words, bent down, and retrieved the book. He sat on the edge of the bed, but before he began reading, he paused for a moment to remember his sweet Rebecca. She had been so zealous when it came to Boo's education. She believed that a child's edification should begin at an early age and had demonstrated her commitment by teaching Boo rudimentary spelling and reading early in life. *The Crocodile in the Tree* was one of many books she had purchased for Boo's childhood development. John was certain Rebecca would want him to continue her teachings. So, he began the story until Boo's eyelids grew heavy and she finally fell asleep. After tucking the blanket around her, he affectionately kissed her forehead and quietly left the room.

John was still contemplating Boo's remarks about her mother when he arrived in the kitchen some twenty minutes later. He found a plate of spicy chicken that Tina had left him for dinner and he mistakenly, over-heated it in the microwave. He was preoccupied with Boo's bizarre story. The mere thought that her fantasies were anything but a dream provoked the hairs at the nape of his neck. *Just dreams. Perfectly normal for her to miss her mother. They'll pass in time.*

John only ate a few bites of his burnt chicken; he had lost much of his appetite anyway. After dropping the charred leftovers in the trash can, he retired to bed, pondering the unusual events of the day.

11

Rrrrrrrrrrrrrrrrrrr!

The Stryker saw produced a high-pitch inflexible noise as it pierced the brain cavity of the lifeless body resting on the examination table. The morbid sound greeted John and Victor as they arrived early at the morgue. The detectives made an appearance in the autopsy room just in time to catch the postmortem proceedings on Richard Pierce. The chamber seemed cold and impersonal, far removed from the warmth of living creatures. It smelled of a mixture of spirituous alcohol and partially decomposed corpses. An eerie way to begin one's day, to witness the dissection of a human body.

John stood for a moment feeling off balance and nauseous. He clamped his teeth and sucked in several long deliberate breaths, hoping to send his morning meal back down from his gullet. The gorge of acidic food moved up and down in a wavelike manner producing the same queasy feeling he had experienced on a rocking charter boat down on the Gulf of Mexico. Finally, he regained his sea legs enough to focus on Charlie Connors and the unknown man twisting the skullcap off Mr. Pierce's corpse. Connors, who was eating a jelly stuffed doughnut, looked up in time to recognize the officers when they walked in. He nudged the short, chubby assistant who was performing the autopsy, hoping to stop his fellow chirurgeon from any further dismemberment.

"John, how ya doin'?" Connors seemed felicitous when solving the enigma of death. Anatomical jigsaws really turned him on.

"I'm fine, Charlie, how 'bout yourself?" John asked as he watched Connors bite through his pastry, squirting purple jelly in all directions.

"Real good," he replied. "John, this is Paul Weatherman, my brother-in-law. He's a pathologist with the medical examiner's office in Birmingham. He and my sister Shirley are in town for a few days, so I asked him to come in this morning to take a look at our boy here." Connors chuckled, exposing his lavender stained teeth. "You know, us stiff doctors gots to stick together."

"Nice to meet you, Paul." John was about to introduce Victor when he lost sight of his fellow officer. He spied him delving into the box of doughnuts on a metal cart near the autopsy table. He frantically dug for his favorite cream filled pastry.

"The big guy heisting your goodies over there is Victor Lechman." John pointed in Victor's direction.

Victor never looked up from the doughnuts He simply murmured salutations toward the stranger and continued his search.

Connors picked up the lull in the conversation by chirping in, "Before you came in, Paul and I were arguing on how long your hair continues to grow after your heart stops. I say two hours; he says three. What do you think, John?"

"I don't have a clue. I didn't know hair continued to grow after you were dead!"

Now, John knew why Charlie was aglow. A man in his profession rarely had the opportunity to match wits with one of his own kind. This pathological tête-à-tête had stimulated Charlie's keen mind and stirred his competitive juices. He wanted to solve the mystery and best his kin in this game of homicidal smarts. Meanwhile, Weatherman was back at work, wasting absolutely no time in his search for answers. He continued examining the brain, hoping to import what Pierce's eyes must have seen, what his nose must have smelled, and what his ears must have heard on the fateful night of his demise. He glanced up at Connors and spoke,

"Cerebrospinal fluid looks good, dura and pita mater good, cerebrum okay. No brain tumor. No trauma here either."

"Have you found anything yet, Charlie?" John asked. "Anything that might explain the cause of death?"

Connors' beaming face suddenly changed back to its usual serious guise. "We still have more work to do," he said, his voice expressing his annoyance.

John sensed Connors somehow expected to solve Pierce's demise based on physical evidence inside his brain cap. John was certain that he was disappointed in the negative findings.

"Sorry I asked," John retorted. "I mean, I'm only conducting a murder investigation here."

"I'm the one that should be sorry. I'm just frustrated. I need a break." Connors explained.

Victor had been so busy sampling the pastries, he had missed much of the exchange between John and Charlie. "So, what's the story on this one?" He asked in a muffled voice.

Connors pointed at the various body parts they removed in the examination. "Look at these eyes. They're silver. I mean this guy was blind, but not until right before he died. His optic nerves, commissure, and tract are absolutely charred. It's like someone took a sauntering iron and pushed it through the vitreous humor without touching it, and then scorched the hell out of the nerves and spheroid bone. Even in my wildest imagination, I can't explain how this could happen."

Weatherman stopped dictating into the over-hanging microphone and stepped from behind the examination table. He switched off the recording device and looked up at the detectives, revealing a jowly face that seemed discolored by a living form of postmortem lividity.

He took one short breath and began his explanation, "There are no congenital heart defects, no arteriosclerosis, no rheumatic heart disease, no myocardial infarction, no nothin'! All his fluids were clear. Mr. Pierce here, should have been running a marathon, playing tennis maybe, anything but lying on his deathbed."

Connors stood beside his overweight brother-in-law and continued the run down. "The lungs were congested but there was no evidence of natural disease, nor was there any sign of disease elsewhere in the body. With regard to his gastrointestinal tract, the stomach was about half-full, indicating some post ingestion prior to his death."

"You guys care to estimate the time of death?" Victor inquired.

"Paul thinks it was about four in the morning. I'd say somewhere between four and five," Connors answered.

"Wouldn't there be more digestion than a half-full stomach if he died at that time?" Victor asked, proceeding with the questions.

Connors edged forward and placed his hand over his stomach. "Yeah, unless he ate a really late dinner or...."

"Or what?" John asked.

"Well, the digestive process can be drastically altered if a person is knocked unconscious after a meal or if he is frightened. We initially suspected that he had been knocked out or possibly had a stroke. But there was no evidence to support those suspicions," Connors continued.

"So, that leaves fright," John looked around for confirmation.

Connors and Weatherman didn't speak right away. They just gazed at each other as though they were afraid to say what was really on their minds. Connors reluctantly spoke first. "Gentlemen, this is strictly an off the record, nonprofessional opinion. You understand?"

"Yeah, yeah. We understand," John said. "What is it?"

"Well, if we didn't know better, we'd say that this guy saw something that literally scared him to death," Connors answered.

Victor burst into rambunctious laughter. "That's just great. Scared to death, huh! So, tell me how you account for the missing dick? I suppose it got scared too and just fell right off. And what about the stink that was in the house?"

Connors refused to look at the burly New Yorker, and instead began to stack the surgical instruments in the steel tray. "The penis was removed by a serrated, sharp instrument. The smell we can't explain. The tissue showed evidence of retaining the odor from the house. I'm sending samples to the toxicologist for analysis. You'll just have to wait for the report. That's all we know." He slammed the last scalpel in the tray with a little extra emphasis.

John recognized Connors was annoyed with Victor, and the perplexing paradox of Pierce's death didn't help. He gestured to Victor, indicating that it was time for them to leave. "Thanks for your help, Charlie." He turned to glance at Weatherman, "Nice to meet you, Paul. We really appreciate your input on this case."

When the detectives arrived back at the homicide office, Captain Reid met them at the entrance door. Reid was soft-spoken, often described as having the charm of a Southern gentleman. He was also well respected by everyone in the department. His snow-white hair foretold his years of experience solving homicides. "John, I've got some bad news and some worse news. The lab boys came up empty on any prints at the Pierce homicide scene."

"So, what's the other bad news?"

"We need a volunteer to instruct the self-defense course at the YWCA on Friday night. It's the one that the department sponsors."

"Geez, don't tell me you volunteered me," John said in protest.

"No, I didn't, but Milligan did," Reid answered.

"That bastard!" John retorted.

"John, watch your mouth." Reid pointed his index finger in John's direction.

"I thought Mouse Curtis taught those classes," John said.

"He does, but he's on vacation this week, so Milligan drafted you."

"He never asked me about it, Captain."

"I know, John. Just do this for me. I'll handle Milligan. And by the way, we've got another possible homicide reported in College Park. You and Victor add this one to your case load." Captain Reid handed John the address and then turned away, walking toward Lieutenant Milligan's office.

Victor and John weren't disappointed in the lab technician's failure to uncover any fingerprints. There was about a one-in-a-thousand chance of finding a latent print that didn't belong to the victim, his relatives or friends, or the officers who answer the original call. All that dusting with black powder and the intense inch-by-inch examination was simply what the public expected the department to do. Even if they found a discernible print, it would usually be of little value unless the detective had a good idea of the print's owner. An unidentified print had to be compared with fingerprints of people who were suspected of a crime and if the person hadn't been arrested on a federal charge, his or her prints wouldn't be in the FBI central file anyway. Physical evidence could certainly convict a criminal, but it rarely solved the crime.

The detectives followed up on their last assignment by spending the remainder of the day at the home of an elderly couple, a dead elderly couple. These soulmates were found in each other's arms in a final embrace of death. Holding

66

their suicide note, a crucifix, and a picture of Christ and the Apostles at the Last Supper, they had ended their time on Earth by taking an overdose of sleeping pills.

It was a peaceful ending to the suffering they endured in their waning years, peace at last. John was certain that their clutching of the cross and picture was a powerful signal indicating the couple was asking for forgiveness for their own self-destruction, hoping for permission to enter heaven's gate. The inquisition was short, an open and shut investigation. Cops referred to it as a platter case. To John, it was just another impersonal account of death, another terrible confirmation that people die for nothing. Every day, he had come face-to-face with the worst impulses of men and women. He had witnessed it all, from serial killers' horrible brutality to the infirm and weary's suicides. The job seemed to run against every good grain a person could have in his body. Yet, he just couldn't stay away.

12

Lieutenant Milligan confronted Detective Sam Trout as he entered the homicide room on this unusual Wednesday morning. Milligan was verbally assaulting Trout for arriving twenty minutes after the change in shifts. Lieutenant Bad Ass Milligan, as he was known by the detectives, was making certain that everyone in the office could witness his performance—the king in reign over his wee empire. Milligan, about five-five in height, possessed a terrible Napoleon complex, no doubt a result of his minute stature.

He went out of his way to make life miserable for the troops, and in reciprocal fashion, they felt compelled to return the favor to the aggravating little bastard. Phil Sayers, Trout's partner, had observed the dressing down his pal was getting for his late arrival and decided retribution was in order. Knowing Milligan would usher Trout into his office for the final censure, Sayers picked up his phone and called Eddie Tombrello at the front desk. Tombrello, a veteran sergeant on the force, disliked Milligan more than a speeding driver abhors a traffic cop. He was more than willing to be a party to the practical joke that Sayers had in mind.

"Eddie, this is Sayers. How 'bout connecting me to the mayor and then to Bad Ass? Conference all three of us on the same line," Phil requested while motioning the other detectives to eyeball the lieutenant in his office. This was not the first time Sayers and the others had conducted a bit of espionage. Their jobs were sobering enough without having to put up with Milligan's swaggering bravado. In order to maintain their sanity, the officers had to revert to something youthful, something silly, and sometimes, something down right nuts.

Within a minute, Tombrello was making the connections. First, he contacted Sayers, conferencing him in the three-way call and letting him know the trap was being set. Next, he contacted Milligan, and finally, the mayor. "Lieutenant Milligan, this is the desk sergeant. I have a call for you."

The detectives snickered like a pack of high school kids as they scrambled around, attempting to gain a better visual through the glass pane in Milligan's office. The low-level laughter grew in intensity as they watched the lieutenant bring the phone to his ear.

"This is Lieutenant Harold Milligan."

Sayers, then attempted to impersonate Milligan's voice, "Excuse me Mr. Mayor, but you are the dumbest, bald-headed prick I've ever known. How can you expect us to do our job when you keep cutting our budget!"

"Milligan!" The mayor screamed. "You are in deep shit!"

"Mayor, that wasn't me." Milligan attempted to explain, but the mayor wasn't willing to listen.

"I'll show you what a real prick I can be when I talk to your superior!" The mayor slammed down the receiver.

John, Victor, and the others tried in vain to suppress their laughter as Milligan vaulted from his chair, stomped out of his office, and to the front desk. Tombrello expected him. He knew Milligan would accuse him of playing a role in the prank and he knew, of course, that he would deny it. The detectives could hear Milligan yelling at Tombrello all the way down the hall. Meanwhile, Trout danced around the homicide room, delivering high-fives to his compadres.

The laughing finally ended when Milligan settled down and returned to his office. With the subterfuge over, John and Victor put pen to paper. This report writing process consumed the morning and afternoon hours. A team of detectives could easily amass thousands of scraps of information, any one of which could prove to be the vital link or clue necessary in solving the crime. The investigative operations plan was essential in order to record, minute-by-minute, feedback of the investigation. Both men also prepared Investigative Action Forms for field information control. The intricate system required everything be in writing. The reports would serve them if, and when, a criminal was brought to trial.

The detectives had planned an early evening visit to the bar where Richard Pierce had previously worked. Canvassing for witnesses, or hoofing as it was commonly called, chewed up a lot of shoe leather. Contrary to popular belief, detectives are not Sherlock Holmes clones, deducing tiny elements of evidence into some esoteric sequence just in time to arrest an incredibly shrewd murderer. Neither are they hoodwinked idiots screwing up all their cases just so some TV private eye can solve them. Instead, they combine a dedicated tenacity of running down leads and asking a hell of a lot of questions—all of this in the face of endless red tape.

It was eight in the evening when the detectives completed their reports. They quickly walked to the parked cruiser in the police garage. As they drew closer to the car, Victor picked up his pace in order to arrive before John. "Okay if I drive?" Victor asked as he grabbed the driver side door handle.

"Sure, why not. You'll fit right in with all the other maniacs out there."

John held his breath as Victor weaved in and out of traffic. He attempted to avoid watching the swerving cars by focusing on the tall buildings reared against the evening sky. Atlanta was beautiful downtown, especially at night. The twinkling lights made the city seem magical. It really had a special charm, especially to those familiar with the unique communion of the metropolitan area with the surrounding rolling fields and red clay hills. But the city was also misunderstood.

Too many people, unfamiliar with its progress still believed that the city was deeply rooted in its past. Passing the historic Ebenezer Baptist Church brought forth a comment from Victor not uncommon to people unacquainted with present day Atlanta. "So, is the Ku Klux Klan still a problem down here in Georgia?"

Victor was oblivious to the fact that the Invisible Empire's white hooded stooges had not been visible in this part of the country for a long time. "Well, Victor, the KKK isn't a problem here anymore. As a matter of fact, most people from Atlanta link the name Martin Luther King, Jr. to this area, more than the KKK. Did you know that King was born and buried here, and he preached at the church we just passed?"

Victor avoided a response by swearing at the red Nissan that had just cut in front of his path. However, John was not about to lose the opportunity to school Victor on the city's claims of distinction. The venerable Bobby Jones, golf's Grand Slammer and baseball's Home Run Slammer, Hank Aaron, were two of the more notables John touted as Atlanta's own. Coca Cola, TBS, and Delta topped the corporate ladder of fame with Margaret Mitchell's big book, *Gone with the Wind*, of literary notoriety. He continued to list the attractions from Stone Mountain to Cyclorama, from Six Flags over Georgia to the Georgia Dome. He even cataloged some of the offerings of the Atlanta Historical Society—Rebecca had taught him that.

John felt a tingling vindication as he finished the mental tour. Funny thing was, Victor seemed sincerely interested in the lesson. Yes, Atlanta had a lot to offer including miles and miles of eye-busting expressways. And along with those expressways came miles and miles of cars driven by thousands and thousands of would-be Bill Elliott's. The only problem was that their steering skills came up a tad short of those

71

possessed by hard chargin' Bill when he was driving on the NASCAR circuit.

Victor succinctly illustrated that by slamming on the brakes to avoid the blue Dodge that recklessly swerved in front of their police car. In retaliation, he stomped on the gas pedal and cut through traffic as though he was driving the last lap of the Atlanta 500. After catching the speeding Dodge, he cocked the steering wheel to the left, gunned the gas and executed a power slide in front of the menacing roadster, almost sheering its front end. It was as though these drivers were the enemy and Victor felt a need to mix it up with them—dog-eatin' dog, Junior Johnson Style.

"Can you believe these damn drivers? Where the hell did these idiots learn to drive down here?" Victor complained.

John repositioned himself and retorted, "Down here! Look, pal, 'these idiots' were trained in your backyard—the New York, New Jersey, and Massachusetts schools for the vehicular insane. Hell, half the people in this town are from somewhere else anyway." John was about to continue the exhortation when he caught glimpse of their final destination. He motioned for Victor to slow down as he took several deep breaths, attempting to get his heart rate back to normal. "Here's our place, Fireball. Pull it over while we still have the fenders intact."

After parking the sedan, the men paced toward the entrance to The Foxes' Den. The establishment was a local cocktail lounge off Piedmont that mixed libation with nude dancing. Some called it a strip joint, some called it a gentlemen's club. It all depended on your savoir faire—country redneck or downtown executive. Regardless of the label, the detectives hoped questioning the owner and employees would yield some fruitful information on what happened to Pierce.

John couldn't help but get in an extra prod or two about Victor's wild driving as they flashed their detective's shields and stepped past the burly bouncer at the front door. Once inside, the area billowed open, exposing an assemblage of young, unclad women tripping the light fantastic atop what appeared to be a sea of platforms. For the uninitiated, it was truly an unbelievable scene. Each cockboat-like table was manned by a crew of gawking seadogs attempting to keep their torpedoes intact while stuffing their hard-earned money into the garters wrapped around the honeydew legs of these dancing donnas. John and Victor stared in disbelief at the surrealistic view of all the free- flowing hair, bouncing breasts, and cupcake bottoms. They thought it had to be some illusory creation of their depraved minds. But this was no illusion.

The exposed dancers varied in height as well as anatomical dimensions. Some were redheads, some blondes, and some brunettes. There were Asian Americans, African Americans, Native Americans, and there were even some European Americans. An inconceivable mixture of the female population...a giant smorgasbord for the lascivious. The officers bellied up to the bar, identified themselves, and asked to see the manager or owner of the establishment. The young woman behind the counter agreed to help, but John noticed her shaking hand as she dialed a number on the phone. Her voice even quivered when she asked the men to wait momentarily while she contacted the manager. After completing the call, she pointed at an indistinct figure approaching them from the shadows.

"Sugar Bear will show you to the office," the girl behind the counter said all atwitter.

As the murky image crystalized, John leaned toward Victor and reassessed the bar maid's description of the upright bestial. "Looks more like a freakin' grizzly bear to me."

73

His assessment was on point, for if bears are viewed as flesh-eating animals with shaggy fur, heavy bodies and wide heads, then this person fit the bill. The goliath plodded forward and with deliberate intent, stopped directly in front of the detectives. Without uttering a word, he scanned them from top to bottom with a malevolent stare. It was as though he was inspecting his next meal. John knew some large and powerful cops, but none could match the eminence and expanse of this carnivore. His body was thick and unwieldy. His beady eyes were brown and vacant, seemingly disconnected with anything human. That horrible face was covered with a scraggly, snuff-colored beard that met his unkempt hair in a menacing union that seemed to alert the detectives to danger. He had huge, hardened arms that protruded from his sides like the limbs on a grotesque tree that had grown from radioactive soil. And scariest of all was his contorted mouth. When his thin lips parted to speak, he exposed a darkened set of crisscrossed incisors and bicuspids, well developed for tearing and grinding his main diet, constable fricassee.

"So, you pigs want to see Marty, huh?" he said in a slurred voice. His lower jaw impatiently jutted in and out, revealing his disfigured malocclusion. At that moment, he looked more like a bulldog than a bear.

Before John could respond, Victor stepped in his path. "Yeah, if Marty runs this place, then we want to see him." John could see the hair on the back of Victor's neck rise with electricity. The two behemoths fronting each other seemed destined for a confrontation—black bear versus grizzly bear. Sensing the tension, John stepped to the left of Victor, hoping to draw Sugar Bear's attention away from his partner.

"Would you mind taking us to Marty?" John asked, using the most courteous voice he could muster.

Still leering at Victor, Sugar Bear responded, "Follow me!"

Sugar Bear turned and slowly began the trudge through the bar to Marty's office. Victor and John obediently followed in the shadow of this moving mountain while, again, taking in the night club's more shapely attractions. Along the way, they passed a multitude of tables, leaving in their wake the seductive dancers that were still in hypnotic motion with each beat of the music. Trying not to be obvious, as though he had not paid for the entertainment, John peeped left and right pouring over the totally nude figures. He was captivated at how effective the girls were at getting the patrons to give up their hard-earned money. A coy smile or sexy jiggle was all it took. It was a potent message—look all you want but leave your cash and don't even think about touching the cookies. The erotic tour finally ended when they arrived at a door at the left rear of the club. Sugar Bear knocked with his right paw and announced their arrival.

"Cops are here to see you, boss," he growled.

"Come on in," Lococo answered.

Inside the room, the officers found the lord and owner of the club. He sat in a chair behind a large flat top desk, and was counting the early evening take, stacking the bills in neat piles of ones, fives, tens, and twenties. Upon seeing the officers, he stood up and offered his hand in a conciliatory manner.

"I'm Marty Lococo, the owner. I hope Sugar Bear wasn't rude to you gentlemen. He's one of my best bouncers but he has a little bit of a temper. You know the customers sometimes get drunk and carried away with all that hot prancing flesh out there. So, Sugar has to show them the door. You know, get a little physical." Lococo snickered.

"No, he wasn't rude, just a little tense. Maybe he's been working too hard." John had a slight smirk on his face from his cynical words. "I'm Detective Sergeant John Williams and this is my partner Detective Lechman."

"Well, he just doesn't appreciate our men in blue like the rest of us." Lococo looked directly at John, winked and squeezed his hand in a friendly gesture. There was a hint of sweetness in Lococo's voice and in his mannerisms. Gracefully, he emerged from behind the desk, sauntered over to the wet bar and mixed himself a drink. There was a sort of off-beat prettiness about him, a nonchalant and unhurried calmness that seemed to settle down John and Victor. The reprieve allowed them to forget about Sugar Bear and to focus on the investigation.

"You gents care for a highball?" Lococo asked, spinning his smallish figure in a half circle while holding up his drink for inspection.

"No thanks. We just need to ask you some questions about one of your former employees," John withdrew the pad containing his notes from his pocket and began the query. "How well did you know Richa—?"

Lococo interrupted before he could complete the question. "Richie worked here for two years. He was one of our best bartenders. All the girls loved him. Hell, everybody loved him. We were all devastated when we heard about his death."

"What did you hear about his death?" John asked.

"Just that he committed suicide. He was very sick, terminally ill as a matter of fact. We figured he didn't want to go through all that chemo and suffering." Lococo took a slow sip of the drink.

"Who told you that he committed suicide?" John asked.

Lococo answered, "Oh, I don't know. Someone here at the bar, I guess."

"Did Pierce have any enemies that you know of?" Victor chirped in.

"God, no! Like I said, everybody loved Richie. Everybody!" Lococo took another sip and returned to his chair.

However, he never offered the same courtesy to John or Victor. He let them stand in front of his desk like two insubordinate employees being called on the carpet. "Why do you ask that?"

"Pierce was murdered, that's why," Victor answered.

"Murdered?" Lococo acted stunned.

"Yes, murdered!" John answered this time.

"Who would want to do that?" Lococo rhetorically asked.

"How about somebody here at the club? Did he have any run-ins with any employees?" Victor asked. "Any customers?"

"No! I've already told you that!" Lococo snapped.

Victor had obviously struck a nerve. Lococo refused to make any further eye-contact with Victor or John. Instead, he turned his attention back to the unstacked bills on his desk. The detectives were determined to finish the interrogation even if Lococo was annoyed with their inquiry. So, the cross-examination continued for about twenty more minutes with John asking most of the remaining questions.

Marty provided little, if any, additional information. Victor, however, had picked up on one additional tidbit. He had noticed an odd piece of jewelry draped around Lococo's neck. It was a thin silver chain that held a cross-like charm with a half-moon above it. It was emblematic of a black mass. Lococo explained away the satanic token as a gift from some unremembered admirer. Of course, the officers didn't believe him, but they were frustrated and out of time, so they stepped outside the office in preparation to canvass the other employees. Surely, there was one living soul in the place that knew something about their case.

Victor motioned John to move away from the office door. "Can you believe this lying squirrel?" he asked, his face full of contempt. "What a bunch of bullshit." Now mocking Lococo's high-pitched voice, "Oh, we all just loved Richie. We

77

are so upset that he died." Victor's face was as red as a hot pepper. "That little piece of shit knows a hell of a lot more than he told us. And did you see his eyes? He was on something more than alcohol."

John knew that Lococo wasn't on the level with them.

"Yeah, I know, Victor, but I don't think he has the balls to commit murder."

Victor's anger continued, "Hell, I don't think he has the balls for that either, but I know he's hiding something."

The two detectives slowly simmered, and they made wise cracks as they walked back through the maze of nakedness to the main bar. They were about to question the jumpy young bartender again when John noticed the familiar outline of Sugar Bear Mountain, pacing quickly in their direction. John nudged Victor, alerting him to the impending threat. Both men watched as the club's clientele parted like a multi-colored sea, allowing the big man to pass unimpeded by their tiny presence. When he arrived, he stopped directly in front of John and began swaying like a snake attempting to hypnotize its prey. His eyes possessed a demonic stare. It was as though he was un-joined with anything rational.

"I think it's time for you two pig shits to leave," Sugar spat, the drool excreting from the corner of his mouth.

Given the earlier friction between Victor and Sugar Bear, John had expected the madman to confront his partner, not him. This unexpected move caught him momentarily off balance.

"Look pal, you just go on about your business so we can do our job. If we have any questions for you, we'll let you know before we leave," John responded in a serene, unruffled voice. Both officers were well trained to deal calmly and coolly with a disrespectful public, especially when confronted with insulting language and aggressive behavior. However,

Sugar Bear had not received any reciprocal training when it came to dealing with police officers.

"I'm not your pal, you low-life motherfucker! You can either walk out now or I'll kick your ass all the way out the door!" His face was boiling with indignation. It turned a bizarre crimson in color.

By now, a small crowd had formed, encircling the confined space occupied by John, Victor and the Bear. The men were shoulder-to-shoulder with the customers jostling for a better view. Their heads bobbed up and down like marionettes being yanked about by a clownish puppeteer. Once more, John suppressed his temper, trying to detach himself from the verbal assaults so he could act in a professional manner.

"Sir, you have two choices. Number one, get out of my way so I can do my job, or number two, we're going to place you under arrest."

Both options were totally unacceptable to the Bear as he edged even closer to John. "I hate pigs. A stinkin' pig killed my brother, Bobby. A sorry bastard just like you. I'm gonna' get even for Bobby by whippin' your ass so bad your mama won't even recognize you. That's the least I can do for your killin' Bobby."

By now, Sugar was so close it felt like he and John were about to have a fist fight in a phone booth. So close, John could smell the bear's foul breath. With his back penned against the bar, John knew there was no reasoning with this psychopath. Something bad was about to happen and like any cop in this predicament, he was hopeful that his partner was there to back him up.

Having not heard even an utterance from Victor, John was tempted to look around to check on his whereabouts. He knew, however, that any lack of attention in Sugar Bear's direction would be an unwise move. Trusting Victor to watch his six, he refocused his thoughts on his next move.

Unfortunately, he never had the chance to consider a move or anything else. Sugar Bear had rocked to his back foot, preparing to throw a knockout blow to John's head. His shift in weight signaled the arrival of the knuckled paw and the plunging body that followed close behind. John saw it coming so he pivoted to his left and skillfully parried the accelerating right arm with his left forearm. The subtle maneuver directed the assailant's momentum past John, sending him belly first into the bar. Stepping backward to clear some distance, John directed a wicked kick to the outer side of Sugar's lower right leg. The well-placed blow struck the peroneal muscle and nerve that are attached to the fibula, dropping the Bear to one knee.

"You son of a bitch," the giant howled as he grabbed his injured calf.

John paused, deciding to let Sugar reconsider his earlier position. He knew the psychological reaction to pain was more likely to control Sugar's behavior than a hail of blows that might make him fear for his survival. John removed the handcuffs from his belt and eased forward, preparing to place the Bear in shackles. Unfortunately, the Bear was still kicking. He had pulled his massive girth up from the floor and grabbed a half-full beer bottle that was resting on the bar. He then quickly twirled, sending a spinning back-fist loaded with a Bud Lite over John's ducking head. This latest attempt at decapitation sent a new surge of adrenaline, and worse yet, anger through John's body. Diplomacy was no longer an option, since his instinct for survival had kicked in.

The bear, open and off balance, presented a wealth of targets for the detective's expert hands and feet. In a millisecond his brain inventoried the vulnerable areas in search of an option—nose, eyes, throat, ears, mastoid, temple, sternum, abdomen. And in a nanosecond, he made the decision to send the rigid heel of his right hand into Sugar Bear's sweaty snout. The violent blow crushed Sugar's bridge backward into the tender ethmoidal nerve and produced a sickening snap, a pop, like that expelled from a small caliber handgun. Blood exploded from the wounded bear's nostrils, sending it indiscriminately on the nearby rubberneckers.

A following smite from John's knee found the bear's vulnerable groin, delivering the final coup de grace. A faint, guttural moan slipped through the bear's jagged teeth, a sound symptomatic of the piercing malaise now shooting through his body. The furry giant collapsed on the sticky floor, still wet from the numerous spilled drinks and gamey blood. John was convinced the fight was over, but before he could expel a sigh of relief, an unexpected shove blindsided him, propelling him into a female bystander. After quickly rising to his feet, he discovered the source of the impetus. He squinted, refusing to believe the warfare that was taking place in front of his eyes.

Victor had latched onto a second bouncer who was a replication of Sugar Bear in vastness and in bad attitude. This one simply lacked the fur that was present on the original version. Victor's steely hands were clamped on the man's thick neck in a bulldog grip of death. In an attempt to escape, the employee peppered Victor's face with a series of close-fisted blows. Unaffected by the punches, Victor squeezed even harder, drawing the marbling blood vessels to the face of the bouncer who was growing weaker by the second. Victor seemed possessed, like an angry pit bull clinging to its tormentor. There was no bark, no scowl of face or twitch of eye, nor was there a menacing snarl. He had simply submerged his fangs and was chewing the life out of this young steer. When the bouncer dropped to one knee, John wondered if he would have to sever Victor's head. After all, once a pit bull starts gnawing, that's the only way to pry him loose. John patted Victor's back, hoping to wake him from the combative trance.

"Victor…Victor! Let him go. It's over, pal." John pulled at Victor's arms, trying to free his hands. It was a useless attempt. John was about to panic. He realized that the bouncer was fading fast, and he needed an answer. So, he positioned his face directly in front of Victor's mug, looked directly into his vacant eyes and begged him to return to reality.

"Victor, it's me, John. You've got to let him go. You're killing him. Come on, pal, turn him loose."

Victor released some of the pressure, but his hands were still clamped around the bouncer's neck.

"Victor, please! You're gonna' kill him. Let go!" John pleaded.

John's words finally sank in. Victor slowly freed the asphyxiated man, allowing him to crumple to the floor. Victor then took a couple of steps back and brushed the sweat from his brow. When he finally spoke, John knew he had somewhat recovered from his rage. "This guy was about to part your hair with a beer mug when you and Sugar Bear were discussing your ancestry. I had to stop him. I got a little carried away but I'm okay now. I'll cuff him and your friend over there if you'll call for backup and EMS." Victor said, pointing to Sugar Bear.

John agreed, but before leaving, he carefully watched Victor to make certain he had fully recovered. He knew there would be a delayed reaction to the fracas, and he was right. Victor was now breathing in heavy gulps as the shock hit his nervous system. Yet, he still went about the business of cuffing the assailants. John was convinced that he was all right, so he walked over to the bar to use the phone while mentally rehashing the violent episode. He knew the potential sanctions awaiting an officer accused of using excessive force. He also knew of their right to protect themselves if their lives were at risk. Given the intent of the bouncers, he felt confident that their actions were righteous.

After John completed the call, his point of view switched to a small group of patrons gathered in the middle of the bar. He was surprised to see a young woman lying on the floor in the middle of the crowd. He hurried through the bystanders and kneeled down to assess her condition. She appeared unconscious.

"Did anyone see what happened?" John looked up to the crowd for an answer.

One of the dancers who had watched the fight was first to speak. "You knocked her down when those other two guys ran into your back. She went down like a ton of bricks hit her."

John returned his gaze to the floored woman who seemed to be regaining her senses. She had opened her eyes and pushed with her elbows, attempting to lift herself from the floor.

"Whoa, wait a minute. Don't get up! You may be hurt." John tried to push her back down.

"No, no. I'm okay. I was just knocked off my feet," she answered.

"Are you sure? Paramedics are on the way and they can check you out."

"No, really. I'm fine. Just let me sit here for a minute. I'm still a little dizzy." She smiled and looked directly into John's eyes.

She wasn't the only one having a dizzy spell. The jasmine scent of her perfume and her striking features made John a little woozy himself. He couldn't help but stare at her sable eyes and flowing black hair. And there was no way he could overlook those lips. Replete and ripened red, they were utterly seductive against her milky smooth skin.

"You really should wait until they get here," he pleaded.

"I'm okay now. Just help me up off of this filthy floor."

John obliged by easily lifting her from the deck. It provided him a second opportunity to sample her perfume. Embarrassed by his lustful thoughts, he looked away hoping she couldn't detect the avarice in his eyes.

"Are you certain you're okay?" He asked again.

"Yes, I'm fine," she responded.

For what seemed like ten minutes, she continued to sweep the grime from her dress while John stood frozen, saying nothing as the curtain of silence grew thicker by the second. His cat-like reflexes had slowed to a snail's pace for he was truly groping for a way to continue the conversation. He was taken aback by her beauty, yet he was totally unaccustomed to wooing the opposite sex. His mind continued drawing a blank, failing to fill his mouth with words of wit and charm. Desperate not to let her slip away, he spied Victor approaching from his left flank and devised an alternate strategy. In quick succession, he curled his fingers in and out, motioning for Victor to draw closer.

"Victor...Victor, come here. I want you to meet someone." Victor stopped beside John and straightened his back in preparation for the introduction. "Victor, I'd like you to meet—," realizing that he had yet to get her name, John's complexion approached a shade of plum.

She offered her hand for Victor's reception. "I'm Lorelei Lamb. My friends call me Lori."

Victor's hand folded around her dainty palm as he grinned from ear to ear. "Nice to meet you, Lori. I'm Detective Victor Lechman. Are you a friend of John's?"

Amused by his question, Lori playfully laughed. "Well, I guess you could say that. We just bumped into each other tonight, and I mean bumped into each other," she responded while staring at John.

John's face now turned an odd mixture of predicament rouge and waggish claret. He looked as though he had a temporary case of wind burn. His only out was to laugh at himself, and so he did. He then extended his hand, offering Lori a warm introduction. "Lori, my name is John Williams. It's a pleasure to meet you. I sure hope you're not hurt from the fall."

"Oh, no, I'm fine. I shouldn't have been standing so close anyway. I was curious about the crowd, you know, sticking my nose where it didn't belong. I can't believe how the two of you handled those big gorillas. I could have used some of that self-defense stuff on my last date. He just wouldn't take no for an answer."

Victor's eyes darted over his left shoulder, locating the cuffed bouncers. "Speaking of gorillas, I'd better go check on the boys. Lori, it was nice to meet you."

"Same here, Victor."

Another uncomfortable silence fell between Lori and John. After securing the leather purse on her shoulder, Lori turned her head and surveyed the crowd as though she were searching for a missing companion. Finally, she broke the silence. "Well, I've got to go. I was supposed to meet a girlfriend here and it looks like she didn't show up. I'm not sure why she picked a place like this anyway. I've never been to a strip club in my life. John, it was very nice to meet you." Lori's dark eyes were fixed on John's baby blues as she hesitated, allowing him another opportunity to make the next move.

His clumsiness in the subtle art of flirtation compelled him to blurt the first thought that entered his mind. "Look, Lori, I'm teaching a self-defense class at the Decatur YWCA tomorrow night. The session starts at seven o'clock. Why don't you come by and I'll give you a few pointers on handling those pesky dates?"

"I don't know, John. Maybe I will," she replied, turned, and walked away. By the expression on her face, she seemed disappointed that he wasn't more aggressive in his pursuit.

John watched as she slowly disappeared in the shadows. As he walked back to the bar, he reprimanded himself in a subdued voice that only he could hear. "John, you're a real dumb ass. What a detective. Hell, you didn't even get her phone number. And what a stupid move asking her to a YWCA class on Friday night. She's probably had a half dozen better offers than that while she was in this place."

He had made a mistake and he knew it, yet he sensed that he still had time to remedy his blunder. He quickly turned around and prepared to sprint after her. However, before he could take the first step, a tug at his shoulder impeded his progress. It was the young bartender he and Victor had spoken with earlier. There was a visible change in her emotions. A switch from nervous jitters to trembling fear. She peered from left to right as tears flowed from her puffy eyes, leaving a trail of diluted black mascara. It was as though she had been injected with an overdose of adrenaline. She spoke in stuttering phrases as she stuffed a folded piece of paper into John's front pocket.

"There's a name and number on...on the paper. It's a guy who may know what...what happened to Richard. You're not going to get any straight answers from anyone around here. I think this guy can help you."

As she turned to walk away, John grabbed her arm. "Wait a minute. Who is this guy you're talking about?"

Before she could respond, a combative Marty Lococo yanked John's hand from her arm. "Turn her loose!" He yelled so loud his voice transcended the music echoing off the mirrored walls. "You get back to work, you little slut. And as for you, Detective Williams, I'll have your badge before you make it back to the station. Your superiors will be hearing from my attorney! You had no right to hurt my boys the way you did!"

John's fingers and palm coiled around Lococo's thin bicep, squeezing the muscle as a python would compress a feeble mouse. "Listen to me you piece of shit. I don't give a damn who you report this to. If I find out that you're even remotely involved in Pierce's murder, I'll arrest your scrawny ass, throw you in jail, and throw away the key. I'm sure some of the good ole boys would love to have you as a cellmate."

John released his grip, allowing Lococo to rub his twisted tendon and reconsider his threat. Lococo seemed unaffected as he licked the sweat from his upper lip and grinned an eerie grin. Suddenly, his face turned wickedly red as he stared directly into John's eyes and issued one last warning. "You have no idea what you're dealing with here, detective. Don't push it."

That horrible look on Lococo's face startled John. It was as though he had reshaped his facial features. Being the consummate pragmatist, John dismissed it as nothing more than the diffused light from the kaleidoscope suspended from the ceiling. Still, it was quite weird. He watched as Lococo walked away, displaying the wet perspiration in the seam of his skin-tight trousers. "What a twit," John said in disgust.

With the confrontations over, John and Victor continued their search for anyone who knew anything about Pierce. Having no luck uncovering any witnesses, they gave up and departed The Foxes' Den around midnight. It had been one hell of a night.

13

John hated squirrels. The scampering sounds from the attic was one of the reasons why. Many a morning at the Williams' house began with the bushy-tailed rodents prematurely awakening him from a peaceful sleep. John listened as they ran and jumped from the inner timbers supporting the bedroom ceiling. Around and around, they raced in a seemingly endless game of tag until, as if on cue, he rose and they darted outside. Their annoying play reminded him that the well-gnawed hole in the cedar siding had yet to be repaired.

John blinked from the bright sunlight streaming through the bedroom window, and then managed to find his way into the bathroom. As he made the short journey, he contemplated a most gruesome demise for the bothersome critters. He had not sampled a spicy squirrel stew since his boyhood days, and he was certain that the .22 caliber handgun he had hidden in the closet would do the trick. The thought of revenge was nice, but as he stood urinating over the toilet, he quickly shifted mental gears to last night's encounter with the lovely Miss Lorelei Lamb.

As he flushed the john, a queasy feeling pulsed through his body as though any chance of seeing Lori again had likewise been flushed away because of his timid behavior. He had yet to think of himself as being competent in the pursuit of the opposite sex and this lack of confidence unearthed doubts he had never experienced before. His hopes rested on the possibility that she would show up at the self-defense class tomorrow night. The odds were against him, but it was all he had. If she did, it would provide him one last reprieve to make a move.

Showered and dressed, John moved slowly, almost sauntering down the stairs and into the kitchen. Azriel greeted him at the doorway, begging for her favorite chicken and tuna dinner. She paced back and forth on the tile floor and purred while rubbing her furry sides against his ankles. As usual, the action left a handful of shedding white fur on his black cotton trousers. She quickened her back and forth movement and began emitting high frequency meows as he opened the can and spooned the smelly mixture onto her dish. At that moment, he noticed his pants were covered with missing pelt from Azriel's flanks. He dislodged some of the fur with his hand. "Damn, Azriel, you make me look like I've been in a cat fight," he scowled.

John poured himself a cup of coffee, then stood at the kitchen counter and ate his meal while watching the cat gobble down her last bite. Afterwards, Azriel just sat on the floor and stared disdainfully at him until she wandered into the den and threw up a hairball on the carpeted floor. John could clearly hear her gagging from the kitchen. *That damn cat!* It was almost time to leave for work and that's the last thing he needed. Maybe Carl Otto was right after all. Any animal that threw up all over the house, stared a hole in him for no apparent reason and, constantly, made his life miserable by marking his trousers may be better off dead. Were it not for Boo, he might at least consider giving the cat up for adoption.

John quickly finished the last bite of his own meal and stacked the dishes into the sink. He then paused when he noticed something out of the ordinary on the kitchen table. It was one of Rebecca's most prized keepsakes, a time-worn Bible that had been passed down through three generations. The sacred book was a special link between daughter, mother, and grandmother. Tina or Boo must have removed it from its place of safekeeping he thought as he reached down to pick it up. As he lifted it from the table, he noticed that one of the open pages had been creased at the corner.

There were underlined passages on the same page, and he gently held the Bible while reading the verses from Ephesians 6:10-16:

> *10 Finally, my brethren, be strong in the Lord,*
> *and in the power of his might.*
> *11 Put on the whole armour of God, that ye may*
> *be able to stand against the wiles of the devil.*
> *12 For we wrestle not against flesh and blood,*
> *but against principalities, against powers, against*
> *the rulers of the darkness of the world, against spiritual*
> *wickedness in high places.*
> *13 Wherefore take unto you the whole armour of God,*
> *that ye may be able to withstand in the evil day, and*
> *having done all, to stand.*
> *14 Stand therefore, having your loins girt about with truth,*
> *and having on the breastplate of righteousness;*
> *15 And your feet shod with the preparation of the gospel*
> *of peace;*
> *16 Above all, taking the shield of faith, wherewith ye shall*
> *be able to quench all the fiery darts of the wicked.*

A feeling of sick excitement surged through John's body. It created an instant burn in his stomach as though a match had been struck and then doused with water. The nauseous feeling was followed by his heart pounding his chest. His initial thought that the Bible and the scriptures were meant to warn him of some impending danger quickly gave way to an elementary-my-dear-Watson explanation. As his heartbeat returned to normal, he chuckled at the notion that this time-seasoned veteran of law enforcement would jump so quickly to such an absurd accounting of the obvious facts. A warning, how ridiculous!

"Good Lord! John, how can you be such a dumb ass?" Looking upward, he continued the monodrama. "Sorry, Lord, no offense intended." Concluding the digression, he closed the Bible and placed it out of reach on top of the refrigerator. He then walked upstairs to check on Boo.

Boo was still in deep slumber when John cracked open her bedroom door. The sound of her gentle breathing was a soothing measure of reassurance that the only hobgoblins he had to fear were those conjured up in an overactive imagination. As he closed the door, he heard Tina arrive. Her timing was impeccable, always appearing when he needed to depart for work. He skipped downstairs to meet her in the den.

"Good morning, Mister John. How are you this day?" Tina asked, as she passed him on her way to the kitchen.

John followed her for the sole purpose of seeking a second opinion on the mysterious Bible. "I'm fine, Tina. How about you?"

"Very good, thank you," she answered.

"Tina, I found Rebecca's Bible on the kitchen table this morning. Do you happen to know how it got there?"

Tina winced, displaying a furrowed brow. "No, Mister John. I no have the Bible," she answered as though she knew the answer to the riddle but was afraid to reveal the secret.

John smiled and attempted to ease her fears. "Well, I didn't think you did. Boo probably found it and played with it not knowing it was important." As he turned to leave, he remembered his Friday night commitment to teach the self-defense class. "Oh, Tina, can Boo stay with you tomorrow night? I have to work late and won't be home until eleven or so."

"Yes, it's no trouble. We love to keep her."

"Oh, and Tina, would you mind cleaning up the hair ball in the den?"

"No, Mister John. I saw it when I came in. I'll take care of it."

John thanked Tina and left the house. As he drove to the station, he remained in a pensive mood given the odd circumstances of the morning, but especially of the last four days. He made a mental note to question Boo in the evening when he arrived home from work. His inquisitive persona wouldn't let the enigma of the Bible rest until everyone had been cross-examined.

14

The news of the encounter between John, Victor and the bouncers at The Foxes' Den had spread like wildfire throughout the department. As the two detectives entered the homicide room, they were greeted by the officers who were beginning the day shift and those ending the night tour. The brotherhood gathered in the middle of the room displayed a mixture of attire that ranged from banker style three-piece suits to vagabond style faded shirts and jeans. The department had a liberal policy when it came to appropriate dress, so their accouterments were a direct reflection of their personal appetite for clothes as well as a visual image of their inclination toward a conservative or liberal sense of humor. Phil Sayers, the department comic, was appropriately garbed in a pair of madras green trousers and a baggy Hawaiian shirt that was imbricated with lime green orchids. Sayers emerged from the crowd, yielding the colors of a circus clown, ready to entertain the troops. Desperately fighting to hold back his laughter, he approached John and Victor, preparing to deliver a one-liner as he snickered between breaths.

"Well, well, look whose here, Atlanta's own Robocops. What say, guys, we cruise on down to that strip joint off Piedmont? Me and the boys understand that they have an opening for two bouncers. We heard that the pay is not so hot, but they have a helluva fringe benefit package—you know, all the ass you can eye-ball and wild bears you can shoot in an eight-hour shift," Sayers rolled his eyes and crowed with laughter.

The response from the assemblage of officers was quick and loud. The noise of their laughter brought embarrassment to John's and Victor's faces as well as the unsettled attention of Lieutenant Milligan. In fact, Milligan appeared in the doorway to his office wearing a veneer of rage from his head to his toes. His visage alone was enough to quickly disperse the group of chuckling officers as well as gain the notice of John and Victor. Milligan spied the two detectives as they attempted to intermingle with the diffusing cops. Their hopes to walk away unnoticed were cut short by the lieutenant's angry voice.

"Williams...Lechman...get your asses in here on the double!" Milligan's thumb, extending from his closed fist, was pointing back toward his office.

John sensed Milligan was ready to explode into a censorious tirade. He couldn't help but observe his rigid posture and clenched teeth as he and Victor walked past him through the doorway. Milligan slammed the door and began spewing a vicious fusion of spittle and castigation.

"I had a call from a Mr. Lococo this morning. He tells me that he intends to press police brutality charges against this department. He said that two homicide detectives entered the office at his club last night, slapped him around, and then without provocation, proceeded to beat the crap out of two of his employees! What the hell do the two of you know about this?"

John began explaining the evening's events with detailed accuracy. His calmness seemed to infuriate Milligan even more. Before John could finish his report, Milligan moved closer to the standing officers and began a second barrage of words and spit that sprinkled their faces with another round of censure. Milligan was clearly hoping for a heated reaction from John which might support a claim of insubordination.

"Shut up!" Milligan's voice erupted across the room as his ragged brows bounced up and down in a flutter of exacerbation. "I want a complete report on what happened last night on my desk, before the day's out. And, Lechman, I'm real disappointed in you. I've come to expect this sort of behavior from Williams, but I thought you would know better."

Before Victor could respond, the office door swung open and Captain Reid leaned in interrupting the excoriation.

"John...Victor...I want to see the two of you right now," Reid said in an authoritative manner. Looking directly at Milligan, the captain ended any further rebuke. "Harold, I could hear you ranting all the way down the hall. I heard what happened last night and I know John's and Victor's actions were justified. From now on, they are reporting directly to me on this case. Do you understand?"

Milligan's eyes revealed his frustration and displeasure at his failed attempt at reprisal as well as his loss of authority. His response was laden with sarcasm. "Yes sir, I sure do."

John and Victor left Milligan's office and followed the captain to the entrance of the homicide room. When they arrived at the doorway, the captain turned and faced the detectives. He made eye contact with them both, signaling a silent message of *don't let me down for backing you up.* He then began to speak, "We just received a report of a homicide up in Dallas. The nude body of an adult male was found this morning in a barn located on the property of a local farmer. The man had been hung from the barn rafters, and his penis had been severed. His name was Dr. Frank Rimmon."

John's memory was instantly triggered by the name of Dr. Rimmon. He removed the folded piece of paper in his shirt pocket given to him by the disturbed bartender at The Foxes' Den. He unfolded the note and held it in front of Victor and the captain so they could read it.

"Dr. Frisbie Rimmon," they all said in unison as though it had been rehearsed.

"This is the lead I got from one of the employees at the nightclub. Looks like someone didn't want us talking to this guy. That is, if Dr. Frank and Dr. Frisbie are one in the same," John said.

The captain motioned the two men out the door. "Contact Chief Goodwin at the Dallas Police Department. I'll call him and let him know you're on the way."

15

John and Victor hurried toward the car. John removed the car keys from his pocket and proceeded to drop them twice as he attempted to unlock the door. His impatience, fused with the anticipation of viewing this new crime scene, made ordinary movements more difficult. Nonetheless, his persistence paid off. On his third attempt he released the door lock, and within minutes, they were traveling on Highway 278 toward the rural town of Dallas.

Neither man spoke on the way. John nervously thumbed the steering wheel as Victor stared blankly out the car window into space. Both sensed that this case was about to become a great deal more complicated than a one-time, one-murder homicide investigation. The similar pattern of death between Pierce and Rimmon implied that this work was possibly done by the same perpetrator. Both detectives had investigated serial killings and knew that these cases were the most frustrating. Not the least of their problems was the distinct possibility that the culprit may be in the area for only a short time—time enough to run up a tangle of victims and then move on to a new location to kill again. The fact that Satanism may be involved with the serial angle simply complicated matters even more. It also pointed to non-rational motives, that the killer or killers may feel they are compelled by forces beyond their control. The thought that they may be dealing with this type of psychopath or sociopath created a queasy, almost toxic feeling in the detectives' guts.

Dallas, a small town, located about thirty-five miles northwest of Atlanta claimed all of those who lived in the area. The town, the seat of Paulding County, was rich in history and tradition. The residents still embraced the bygone customs and values of years gone by. Even the architectural lines of the buildings held fast to those yesterday times. For this old fashioned town, change had come slow.

The detectives scanned the old buildings that lined the narrow main street that carved its way through the center of town. The buildings seem to lack any single feature that distinguished them from the others, save the two that boasted the aging gas pumps. Yet, Victor was able to distinguish the police building from its adjacent look alike brothers.

"On the left, John, the building is on the left," Victor remarked while aiming an index finger at the station.

John also saw the sign marking the police station and quickly turned the steering wheel, pulling the car into a parking space adjacent to the building. In one quick move, Victor released his seat belt and rolled out the passenger door before John could completely stop the car and return the gear shifter to park. Yet, John had little trouble catching up.

Within seconds, he was following closely behind as the two men entered the front of the station through a creaking wooden door that appeared bleached from the midday sun. Inside, the room was large and functional, decorated sparingly with a foursquare bulletin board on the east wall. Two vintage telephones were located on the desks situated in the back of the room. In the front, a strategic counter prevented their entry into the office. The entire area smelled of the musty oil that preserved the extinct wood floor beneath their feet. It was a smell that symbolized that the station and town still represented a retrospective mark in time. As the two men scanned the unoccupied office, the entrance door behind them noisily opened, creating a passageway for a large, lumbering mound of humanity.

"Are y'all the detectives from Atlan'ter?" the voice asked.

John and Victor wheeled to find a uniformed man walking through the doorway. He appeared brief in height yet broad in girth, about two biscuits shy of three hundred pounds. His side to side rolling gait created a multiform visage against the up-and-down motion of his oversized belly. He stopped within two feet of the detectives and gave them both a misgiving look.

"I seed yorn Fulton County tag on yorn car outside. Captain Reid tole me y'ald be comin'. I'm Hootie Goodwin. I'm the chief in these parts." Goodwin extended his hand.

"Nice to meet you Chief Goodwin. My name is John Williams, and this is my partner, Victor Lechman." John responded with a courteous smile as the ceremonial handshakes were completed.

"Hell, jest call me Hootie. That's whut everybudy in these parts calls me," the chief grinned, exposing a jagged set of teeth painted with tobacco juice and decay. "Hain't no need fur furmalities," Goodwin said, as he motioned the men past the front counter to the back desk in the office. The detectives obediently followed. When they arrived, he slid two chairs across the floor, and offered the seats to the waiting men. "Plant yorn back sides here boys, and sit a spell," Goodwin said in a slow, muffled voice. The wad of tobacco pooched in the chief's left cheek, mixed with his deliberate delivery of the English language, produced a string of syrupy verse that had Victor stirring in disbelief.

"Look, chief, we don't have time to sit down and shoot the breeze. We're here to see if there's a link between Frank Rimmon's death and a murder we are investigating in Atlanta," Victor blurted in a rakish fashion.

Chief Goodwin's brown eyes once again dawdled up and down Victor's thick body, making a second assessment of this out-of-town slicker. With precise accuracy, a glob of saliva jetted from Goodwin's lips. Flying in a long brown arc, the cheroot landed in a green metal wastebasket positioned within inches of Victor's left leg. The snuff-colored projectile was a message to Victor that ole Hootie didn't appreciate his restive attitude.

"You hain't from Gawjuh, are you son?" Goodwin asked, while his left eye twitched uncontrollably. It was as though Victor had tossed a handful of Yankee salt in the chief's portly face.

In a quick attempt to prevent Victor from responding, John took a half step between the two would-be adversaries and interceded before the conversation could continue. He grabbed the outer chair and instructed Victor to take the seat, while he positioned his chair next to the chief.

"Look, chief, we really appreciate you letting us get involved in your case. Victor didn't mean to be disrespectful. It's just that he's a little uptight about the possible connection between Rimmon's death and our murder investigation in Atlanta. Hell, Hootie, we're both a little tense about this investigation," John apologetically said. He was hoping for an amiable response from the chief.

Fortunately, the twitching stopped in the chief's eye and a dose of Southern grace reappeared on his face. Leaning forward he launched a second glob of brown tobacco juice neatly into the foul-smelling waste basket. "Hell, boys, furgit about h'it. After lookin' at Rimmon's body this mornin', I got me a case of them thar heebie-jeebies myself. Skert the hail out of me. Damnedest thing I ever seed." The chief winced as he licked a trickle of perique from the corner of his mouth.

The chief's anxiety about the corpse heightened the detectives' senses as every muscle in their bodies drew into a hard knot.

"Where's the body now?" John asked.

"It's still in the barn out on the farm," Goodwin replied. "We hain't moved it since we know'd y'ald be comin'."

"Who owns this farm?"

"It's Frank's daddy's place. It's not fur from here, jest north 'round New Hope."

"Did he live on the farm with his family?" John inquired, as he withdrew a black notepad from his pocket.

"No, he lived in Atlan'ter. I figer he wus jest comin' up here to visit. His mama an'nim said they wern't spectin him. Course, that's whut he do. You know, show up un'spected."

Victor just couldn't grasp the chief's jargon, so he decided it was time to, again, enter the parley. "Who is this Mama-nim person that wasn't expecting Rimmon?" Victor asked Hootie.

Acting as an interpreter of Southern colloquialisms, John turned to Victor in a plea for his silence. "The chief is talking about Rimmon's mother and them—you know, Rimmon's relatives." In a hushed tone of voice, John continued, "Victor, please, just keep your mouth shut and let me do the talking." Turning back to the chief, "Hootie, can you take us out to the farm?"

"My d'spatcher, Wilma, and my deputy is out today so I kan't go back. But… I kin give y'all d'rections on how to find thu place. When I was out thar I tole Frank's daddy, Virgil, that y'ald be comin'."

"Well, we'd appreciate any assistance you could give us. But, before we leave, you mind if I ask you a few questions about Rimmon." John asked.

"Hell no, you can ask away." Hootie answered. "Jest long as New York over thar shets up!"

John agreed to Goodwin's conditions and for the next hour, he and the chief discussed the similarities of their respective investigations. Victor reluctantly obliged as well. Although he sat in silence, he did twist and turn like a man who had his trousers filled with hot coals. Not being able to ask questions was driving him crazy. But John hit all the key interrogatories so his help in the matter was really not needed. As their conversation came to a close, the chief confirmed that Frank and Frisbie were one in the same, although he had no explanation why Rimmon had been tagged with the alias, only that he thought he had acquired the nickname from friends in Atlanta. Finally, the chief completed a sketchy map with directions to the farm. Handing the diagram to John, the chief escorted the men out the station door to the sidewalk in front of the building. Before leaving, the detectives' offered to provide technical and investigative support on the case. The chief had neither the manpower nor forensic support to properly pursue a complicated murder investigation. He gratefully accepted the offer.

16

The Chevy cast a veil of dust as it slowly traveled on the dirt road. This was a far cry from the high-speed, mortared streets of Atlanta. The remote roadway continued on, winding peacefully through a stand of unbroken pines. Finally, the gentle curves gave way to a straight byway that passed a deep ravine that was green with a network of kudzu. The violet blooms from the creeping plants filled the air with the fragrance of late summer in the country. The vines extended out and up, smothering the ground and trees in a choking reminder that the sweet smell of the flowers oftentimes conceals the malevolent intent of the creeping vine.

Their journey to the Rimmon farm finally ended eight miles into the wilderness. They had arrived at a gabled old cabin nestled against a wooded hillside. Both men stopped and turned to survey the property after they stepped up on the boarded porch. The bottom land in front of the house extended for several hundred yards, halted only by an upland hill dotted with pines, oaks and maples. The property was a testament to the pioneering ingenuity that built the log-sided farmhouse, and the fertile soil bespoke of the hard labor that sowed the sun-drenched crops.

It also told a story of rural hardship and dispossession. The cabin's oak bark roofing shingles and squat stone chimney were of the same natural materials used by settlers in the region decades ago. Much as these pioneers used a crossbred mule for tilling, so did Virgil Rimmon. Their style and quality of life quietly declared their independence, that everything on the farm was put there by their hearts and hands, mixed with their love and caring for the land. It was simply enough. After the detectives finished their examination of the property, they turned and walked across the rickety planks to the cabin's front door. An eerie high-pitched squeal followed each of their steps. It was a baneful warning.

Victor used his hands to shade the low rising sun from his eyes as he gazed through the screen on the half-hinged door. John gingerly knocked with his right hand while shading his own face with his left. That's when he noticed the ceiling on the front porch was painted an odd shade of blue. The unusual paint on the ramshackle structure triggered a memory deep in his mind. Rebecca's grandparents were from the Lowcountry in South Carolina and she once told him that they painted their porch ceiling blue to keep the spirits from entering the house. John simply dismissed the weird superstition as coincidental and began another series of raps on the door frame. Finally, the elderly Mr. Rimmon emerged from a back room in the cabin. Speaking no words, he stepped through the doorway past the detectives while motioning them to follow. At the side end of the porch, he methodically placed three of his crudely made chairs in a small circle and asked the detectives to sit down.

As John seated himself, he couldn't help but stare at Mr. Rimmon. His heavy skin was tan and weathered. The acute wrinkles on his forehead, cheeks, and neck followed the conformation of his face, much as the deep furrows he had farmed conformed to the neck of his land. He was old in time, yet young in spirit. This man with hickory hands and silver-white hair was pushing eighty years, yet he was a man that still possessed great physical strength. And when John gazed into Rimmon's sharp blue eyes, he sensed that his spirit held that same vigor. But today, his gritty resolve was clouded with confusion. His one and only son had been killed and he didn't understand why.

"I'm Virgil Rimmon, Frank's daddy," he said in a subdued voice. "Y'ald be the police from Atlanter?"

"Yes sir, Mr. Rimmon. I'm Detective John Williams and this is Detective Victor Lechman," John responded while shaking the farmer's calloused hand.

"Hootie tole me y'ald be 'round today, so I's been 'spectin you," Mr. Rimmon said with a troubled expression. "If y'all need to ask questions 'bout Frank, I'll tell y'all what I know. My wife h'aint takin' his dyin' too good, so I'd be grateful if y'all leave her be."

John and Victor gratefully accepted the offer and began the inquiry. Virgil was more than cooperative. The only problem was his speech. By degrees, he answered their questions in that twangy backwoods drawl placing his accents on whichever part of the word struck his fancy. At first, John was having a hard time understanding him. But after about twenty minutes, he had broken the imperfect code and was starting to appreciate the rhythmic dialect. He even began introducing a few doublewords in his own sentences, and without thinking, began to blend his nouns and verbs as though they were of liquid.

"Chief Goodwin tole us that Frank was a doctor-man practicin' in Atlanta. Did Frank ever say anything to you about a patient, or anyone else for that matter that might wish to harm him?" John asked.

"No, Frank was a rubbin' doctor so I don't know why any of his patients would want'a hurt him. 'Sides that, he'd only come 'round 'bout once a year. Never talked to me 'bout his payshunts. Jest stay'd long enough to visit his maw a'spell and then he'd leave," Mr. Rimmon answered.

Victor finally heard two words he understood, "What do you mean by a rubbin' doctor?"

"He'd be a bone cracker. A kirepracter. As fur as I know'd, he'd didn't make no enemies doin' that. The boy never done nothin to deserve to die like that," Mr. Rimmon's voice trembled. The tears in his eyes spoke loudly, a father should never have to outlive his son. His attention was fixed on the barn as his hands wiped the drops from his cheeks.

John could feel an immense need in Rimmon's voice. It was as though the weight of the world bore squarely on his shoulders. "Is there anything you can tell us that might help us find the person who killed your son?"

Suddenly, the teardrops were supplanted by a vision of anger as Rimmon's face reddened with hate. "I know'd who kilt my boy!"

"Who killed your son?" John asked as he slid to the edge of his chair, awaiting the answer.

"Last night he come down from the mountain over thar," Mr. Rimmon said as he pointed to the wooded hills. "I know'd he was comin' cause the dogs were a'howlin', and the cows low'd and low'd cause they wus skerd. I looked out the window and seed all my chickens run up to the porch and that's when I seed him comin'. Ridin' a coal-black rig bein' pulled by a coal-black horse, he come from over yonder. H'it were dark...real dark, but I know'd it was him. When he stopped his rig by the barn I could tell."

Mr. Rimmon paused to catch his breath. His account of the evening had stirred his heart to an off course, galloping pace. His brief moment of rest allowed John enough time to view the barn from the porch in an attempt to understand what the farmer had seen.

"Mr. Rimmon, your barn is some two to three hundred yards from this house and I don't think there was a moon out last night. How could you recognize anyone, let alone see anything from this distance?" John asked.

"I know'd sir, cause I'm a preacher-man on Sunday. And any preacher-man know'd that only the devil can bring with him that kind'a stench. The air was foul. I smelt it. It were the smell of death and it come callin' on my boy last night. The devil come callin'."

106

Rising briskly from his chair, Victor closed his notepad with a loud slap. "Well, that will about do it. I haven't understood much of what you said, sir, but I think I got the gist of it." Victor turned back to face John. "John, what say let's zip back to Atlanta, get a warrant on Mr. Lucifer, zip back here, run up the mountain, and place the ole cuffs on the unholy one." Victor's impatience and disbelief in Mr. Rimmon's story was apparent in his face and gestures. It was also apparent that Mr. Rimmon didn't appreciate Victor's disgust with his account of the strange events.

"I don't care whut you think, mister. That thar's the truth!" Rimmon's eyes narrowed.

Sensing that Victor's vehemence would hinder the investigation prompted John to take quick action. Much like his strategy with Chief Goodwin, he asked Victor to leave him alone with Rimmon and to begin the review of the crime scene in the barn by himself. John knew that his absence would allow him to continue the questioning without being interrupted by any outbursts of emotion.

John's strategy worked, although a half-hour of additional questions provided him very little information. Mr. Rimmon's knowledge of his son's activities for the past few years was vague at best. John did learn that Frank had left his parents and the town of Dallas about ten years ago to pursue his chiropractic education and career in Atlanta. Evidently, Frank wanted out from under his father's puritanical thumb. It didn't take John long to understand why. Mr. Rimmon had begun to give him a fire-and-brimstone sermon on how mankind should live by a strict and rigorous religious doctrine.

Virgil was one of a vanishing breed of homespun country preachers on Sunday, and a hardworking farmer during the week. Intent on quoting the Scriptures, Mr. Rimmon spoke of nefarious pacts with the devil and how his son had become

God's rival because of his incessant quest for knowledge and power. The Book of Isaiah was his divine reference as he recited the consequences of making a covenant with Hell. After John realized he was making little progress, he rose from the split-bottomed chair, preparing to walk to the barn. He concluded that Rimmon's tale of his son's death was an explanation espoused of grief intermixed with a pulpit view of life, not one based on logic and reality. Excusing himself, John thanked Mr. Rimmon for his cooperation, stepped off the porch, and proceeded to catch up with his partner.

A subtle, uneasy feeling embodied John as he walked across the grassy pasture toward the barn. It was farfetched, but Rimmon's story still hit him hard. Unlike Victor, he hadn't dismissed it as the ravings of a lunatic preacher. Perhaps Mr. Rimmon opened up a Mason jar filled with moonshine and had a few snorts. Or maybe it was a simple case of an old man with dementia, distorting what he really saw. John just didn't know what to make of it. He did know, however, that as he approached the aging barn, he began to feel numbness in his hands and feet. It was as though his body was being restrained from moving forward by some unknown centrifugal force.

His vast experience of viewing grisly murder scenes refused to counter this powerful apprehension. The terrible numbness in his body instantly turned into a wave of nausea as he approached the barn's open double doors. Suddenly, he gasped for air. It was as though he was being suffocated by the foul breath of death wafting from the rafters. It was a stench so bad it caused him to shake as the odor drew closer. With all his senses now ignited, he convinced himself to take two more steps. But then the thought of turning back crept into his mind. *Victor can handle the details on the corpse.* He thought. *I need to turn around and get away from here.*

John followed his instincts, yet as he turned about, he found himself face to face with something much worse than a decomposing corpse. It was a muscular, black bull. Yes, he was almost nose to nose with two thousand pounds of mean-spirited beef. The animal had been grazing in the pasture surrounding the barn and had taken notice of this out-of-place stranger.

It's eyes, dark with danger, had been carefully appraising John's movements. The agitated bull shook its wide head, side to side, as though it was warning John to go the other way. John stood as motionless as a pillar of salt while he hastily considered his options. The choice became as clear as the cloudless sky above. Chances for survival with a decomposing stiff were infinitely better than those with a hostile ox. He made one more about-face and quickly sprinted inside the barn.

Gloomy slithers of sunlight carved their way between the gaping planks on the side of the barn. The lack of illumination created a lurid setting given the brightness of the outside world. With hands protected by latex gloves, Victor was busy turning the suspended body, ignoring the smelly breeze and absence of light when John came rushing in.

"Look out, John!" Victor yelped, as he watched his partner draw near.

John failed to see the animal carcass laying in his path. As he stumbled over the remains, he wildly grasped for any hilt of balance. His hands found only the loose, rancid skin of a disjointed cow as he fell clumsily to the ground.

"What the hell!" John exclaimed as he recoiled to his feet from the fall.

"Say hello to Elsie," Victor laughingly said.

"Here... catch," he said, tossing John a cylinder-shaped flashlight.

John caught the flashlight in both hands and, nervously, thumbed the switch to the on position. Quickly, he aimed the beam toward the ground. The artificial light did its job by helping his myopic eyes focus on the bulging heifer. It was ghastly. A metamorphic night had converted the cow's serene face into one of sunken terror. John stared in disbelief as a swarm of flies buzzed in and out of the animal's vacant eye sockets. As he fanned the light up and down the swollen carcass, he also noticed that the cow's tongue, udder, and reproductive organs were missing.

"Damn, why would anyone mutilate an animal this way?" John asked, as spasms once again found his belly.

"Let me tell you something, pal. We've got the work of a big-time Satanic cult here—a big-time cult! They cut out the animal's parts so they can use them in their rituals," Victor responded with an authority of both excitement and disgust.

"Even the cow's sex organs?" John inquired as he reeled from the nausea.

"Especially those. These Satanic cuckoos believe the sex organs contain power. They believe that the release of sexual energy is one way they can reach a higher level of consciousness. By taking the sex organs, they think they can add power to their rituals. And I'll bet you dollars to doughnuts that the cow's blood has been drained."

"Remember, Rimmon said he heard the cows bellowing last night. That's when this must have happened," John remarked, as he continued to shine the beam up and down the dead body.

"Maybe, maybe not. These fruitcakes usually use an electric prod to stun a large animal like this. Knocks them right off their feet. Then, they'll spray the face and neck with Freon so the cow's alive, but not alive. Usually no sound. The commotion the old man heard last night could have been caused by something else."

"Great, this is just great," John said.

"Come over here, John. Take a look at this. The cow's not the only one missing a sex organ." Victor's voice was painted with disgust.

Between the side stalls, in the hub of the barn, the naked body of Frank Rimmon hung upside-down, tethered by a hemp rope that was tied to a large timber that supported the roof. With both feet bound together, the six foot, two-hundred pound body drooped laxly as though without bones. John couldn't help but notice Rimmon's bluish arms as they dangled toward the wheat-strawed ground.

And Victor was right. A dangling penis was AWOL. Just like Pierce, Rimmon's severed organ was nowhere to be found. Victor pulled John's attention to another part of Rimmon's anatomy by spinning the body around and pointing to the buttocks. An inverted cross of crimson had been smeared on his right cheek. He also instructed John to take note as he pried open Rimmon's swollen eye lids, providing him a palpitating view of two dilated orbs, milky white in color. They were just like Pierce's bleached eyes. Finally, Victor pointed to the ghastly mouth that spoke without speaking. It was agape, in a grinning bow of horror. The question of whether the death of Pierce and Rimmon was related had been answered with an awful certainty. The stink, the cross, the eyes, it was all there, and not one drop of blood could be found.

The detectives were persistent. For almost two hours, the vein-like beams from their flashlights jittered up and down the corpse, and then on the ground underneath. Other than the obvious, they came away with nothing other than a case of Hootie's heebie-jeebies. Both men seemed unable to train their light on Rimmon's abhorrent features any longer. Besides that, they were growing exhausted from their search in the difficult light and stench inside the barn.

111

"Victor, let's step outside. I need a breath of fresh air," John said as he wiped the sweat from his forehead.

"Yeah! So do I. This is all like a bad dream," Victor nervously replied.

The bright sun restored their sense of balance. It made them momentarily forget that humanity could be capable of committing this kind of evil. Yet, both men were unaware that this temporary reprieve would soon be lost, unaware that they were destined for a long, horrible ride on a wicked carousel that would have them questioning everything. For now, it was best they didn't know. They had too many unanswered questions regarding Rimmon. Both agreed that the situation called for technical support—lab technicians, pathology, the works.

They also agreed that Victor would continue the investigation at the barn, while John contacted the necessary personnel. The only problem was that the Rimmons lacked even the most rudimentary conveniences, including a telephone. In addition, the detective's mobile radio could not reach the station from this remote distance and there were no cell phone towers for miles. Left with no options, John had to leave the farm. It was a preordained trip, anyway, given his desire to leave the premises. As he walked to the car, he cautiously watched for the menacing bull that had earlier impeded his path. No bull this time, although his path was still blocked. This time, it was a pint-sized matron, the mother of Frank Rimmon. She confronted him squarely in the middle of the open pasture. Threadbare in dress, decorated only with a pair of silver-rimmed spectacles, she seemed restless, troubled as if her life was completely off-center. Her voice, forebodingly quiet, seemed sapped of the strength it normally possessed.

"I'm Alma Rimmon. I seed you on the porch with my husband. Are you gonna find who kilt my Frankie?" she asked as tears stained her sullen cheeks.

"Mrs. Rimmon, we're going to do everything in our power to find out who did this," John responded but his words lacked the commitment being sought by a tormented mother.

"Promise me. Promise me y'all find who did this. An eye for an eye," she said, her voice now trembling.

John frantically searched for the perfect words to say to a grief-stricken mother. With knowledge that hundreds of murders go unsolved each year, he hesitated to make such a vow. Yet, he knew it would bring her solace. With all of life's sorrow and confusion, the promise would be the perfect words she needed to hear, the commitment she so desperately wanted. In the darkness of her son's death, it would be her the light of justice.

"Yes ma'am, we'll find who did this. I promise."

With pledge in hand, she seemed more at ease. John took the opportunity to ask her some questions regarding her son. From odd bits of information, he learned that on previous visits, her son had spoken to her about an invisible torment, of changing his ways and, most importantly, of meeting his Maker. Frank Rimmon's words to his mother were a self-fulfilled prophesy. Finally, Mrs. Rimmon confirmed her son had arrived unannounced last night, and that she nor her husband knew of his presence until they discovered his body this morning.

17

The Chevy left a cloud of dust behind as it departed the rut-
ted dirt road for a smoother, asphalt thoroughfare. The return to civilization cued John's eyes to search for a landline
phone as he continued the drive. A number of four-score
homes scattered along the route provided him ample opportunity to stop and impose on the occupants' hospitality. Most
of the dwellings were wired with the convenient utility that
he sought. And occasionally their rural property was im-
planted with something else, a convenience not found in the
city. Shelters were impregnated in the earth, furnishing the
landowners with an asylum from a once potential nuclear
war with mother-Russia. Emblematic of atomic paranoia,
these once common chasms now provided a harbor of safety
only from an occasional tornado. Scanning a house for a sign
that anyone was at home brought John's focus to a standing
road sign nearby. The black metal marker provided directions to the entrance to one of the state's historic sites. Confident that a telephone could be found on the premises he
angled the Chevy off the main road and into the park.

The historic landmark was located a few miles north of
New Hope. The bordered sign, fronting the visitor's center,
lamented a long-ago time, a deadly struggle of house against
house, of brother against brother—the Civil War Battle of
Pickett's Mill. Inside the center, John phoned Captain Reid
in Atlanta to report on their investigation. Reid listened carefully and then instructed him to wait at the center for his return call. It would take twenty or thirty minutes to arrange
the needed personnel and coordinate their meeting in Dallas. John then asked the attendant working at the visitor's
desk if she would notify him when his superior called back.
The elderly attendant happily agreed and then suggested he

stroll one of the walking trails in the park while he waited. After the bizarre morning at the Rimmon Farm, he needed the break, so he left the center and headed for the first trail outside.

At first, his decision to walk the park seemed like a smart choice. The mere smell of the piney woods had a sobering effect on his senses. Rhododendron and witch hazel were in abundance, along with a blending of sweet gums, scrub oaks and loblolly pines. As he walked downward along the trail, he was also struck by the pungent scent of ferns and the mossy smell of the plummeting damp ravines. He felt much more at ease. He had even begun noticing the signs that were strategically located along the path. Each placard described one facet of the historic engagement that took place on May 27, 1864.

He was enjoying the peaceful discursion as he stopped to read one of the informative plaques. The history lesson was a welcomed change. Besides being a fascinating part of Georgia's past, it had taken his thoughts completely away from the morbid murder of Frank Rimmon. After he finished reading the plaque, he paused to view the remains of an ancient rifle-pit.

It was then that a strange black cloud shaded the forest floor from the sun's bright rays. The curious eclipse made it impossible to read the historical marker. A sudden rush of air swept down the narrow valley. The gusty wind grew and grew until it howled like a banshee. John was certain he could hear the moans of dying men in the breeze. He shivered as the air became clammy, icy cold. It was as though this day belonged to an up-North winter, instead of a down-South summer. The trance-like loss of balance he experienced on the Rimmon farm had again seethed into his soul. But this time, the trance was more powerful, more like a state of suspended animation. He was there, yet he wasn't there.

It was the present, but it was the past. His eyes were open, yet he couldn't see reality before him—only the unreal drama taking place in the valley below.

Can this really be happening? That was all John could think as he felt himself rising upward, suspended in midair like a hovering bird. Twenty feet up, he looked to the woods below, unveiling a vision of death and destruction. The bottom of the ravine, dense with underbrush, was flanked by the steep slopes that hid the awaiting gray clad rebels. The Yankees, tired from their march, stumbled along the narrow creek in long vulnerable columns, unaware of the waiting ambush. Suddenly, the still woods erupted with the sounds of cannons and bullets flying thick through the air. The destructive wall of Minnie Balls and shrapnel found the confused Federals and, instantly, the earth became littered with the dead and the dying.

Meanwhile, John just hung there in this terrible dream, unable to move, unable to hide his eyes or cover his ears, unable to awaken, unable to do anything but watch. The violent specter continued as the demonic cries and shouts grew louder. Repeatedly, soldiers in blue charged, only to be raked by the murderous barrage of infantry and artillery fire. *God help me. Why am I here?* John wondered again and again.

John continued to question his role in this terrible nightmare until the sun faded on the horizon. It was then that the fighting finally stopped, revealing the aftermath of the horrible slaughter. As the moon slowly appeared, its silvery rays found the pallid faces of the dead and the scared faces of the wounded and dying. There were so many hurting young men. Yet John's eyes were drawn to only one.

It was a gray coated rebel, a young officer who had been wounded while charging the Yankees from the back of his white steed. A .44 caliber bullet from a Henry rifle had pierced his flesh, knocking him to the thick underbrush

116

below. As John gazed downward, the young soldier looked up, and their blue eyes mysteriously met. And at that exact moment, John was stunned beyond belief. For the young man below was him. John could now feel the agonizing pain in his own chest, yet he could find no wounds. He could feel the sadness in his heart, yet he could find no tears. *God help me*, he thought.

"Sir...sir, your phone call. Your call came in," the puzzled attendant said as she jabbed John's right shoulder. "Are you alright? You look like you've seen a ghost," she remarked, staring at his colorless face.

The glittering sunlight seared his vision as he abruptly awoke from the trance. "Yeah...yes ma'am. I'm fine. I think I was just daydreaming." He squinted, looking all about in search of the soldiers he had just seen. Of course, they were not there. It was only a dream, only a bad delusion.

"You look a little pale. Why don't you follow me back to the center and I'll get you a cool drink of water," she said.

"A cold drink sounds good," John answered while still looking around for the ghosts.

As John followed the elderly woman back up the rock-lined trail, he continued to look over his shoulder toward the creek bottom below. He still couldn't believe what happened. Once inside the air-conditioned building, the clerk pointed to the phone and motioned him to sit and take his call while she went for the water. After the horrific vision in the woods, he welcomed the chance to relax for a moment and regain his composure. He spoke with Captain Reid and received instructions to meet his associates back in Dallas at Chief Goodwin's office. The sound of the captain's voice on the phone helped him come to his senses. By the time he hung up, the attendant had returned with a paper cup filled with water. John thanked her for her kindness and then took the opportunity to do what detectives do best...ask questions.

"Since you work here, you must be the expert on this piece of history," he stated, as he took a sip.

"Well, I know a bit about what happened, although I'm no expert," she answered.

"Were there many soldiers killed in the battle?"

"I think the Yankees lost between 2,000 and 3,000 men. It was a slaughter. Some called it the Hell Hole at Pickett's Mill because of the killin'," she said. She was unable to recall the Confederate casualties. "Those hillsides are full of pits and holes that hid our boys from the Yanks. They never knew what hit 'em."

John asked several more questions about the battle, finished drinking the water, and then thanked the cordial woman for the information and her help. Then, he left for Dallas to meet the technicians. He spent the remainder of the day in a fog. This rebel never knew what hit him.

18

It was around six o'clock in the evening before John arrived back at his house. He would have arrived sooner were it not for a two-hour stop at a local pub. The visit provided him the normalcy of some light conversation chased by several rounds of nerve soothing libation. Given the earlier events in the day, it was time well spent. His psyche was still in a state of disorder. Rebecca's Bible found without explanation in the kitchen, the investigation at the Rimmon farm, and most of all, the mesmeric trance in the woods were all violations of the laws of nature and physics. At least the alcohol numbed his senses, allowing him a temporary reprieve from the insanity.

Tina met John at the front door and gave him a run-down on the day's events. She also reminded him that Boo would be with her the following night. He had forgotten about his commitment to teach the self-defense class until she jogged his boozy memory. As she walked out the door, she told him that Boo was upstairs in her bedroom. He thanked her and then turned to find his daughter. He stumbled through the house attempting to avoid a collision with the furniture. All of that alcohol on an empty stomach had left him with the balance of a one-year-old toddler. Slowly, he stammered up the stairs until he finally made it to the top. His dexterity didn't improve as he moved down the hallway. He bounced from wall to wall until he reached Boo's bedroom.

It was there that he found his daughter, playing her favorite game of school. Peeking through the doorway allowed him to observe the goings-on unnoticed. Her room was small and cozy. The soft pink walls provided a dainty backdrop for the whitish curtains that accented the windows. A chest of drawers, double bed, and chair were placed along three of the four walls. The remaining wall was lined with a toy box and a three-legged wooden stand that supported her often-used marker board.

Boo didn't notice her father enter the room. She was too busy writing a foreign word on the board. It was time, once more for her stuffed animals, crowded on the bedside, to learn more about the Spanish language.

Chica

"Say cheee-cu," she demanded while pointing her index finger at the board. If Cervantes ever heard Boo's pronunciation of his romantic language, he would assuredly roll over in his grave. This was not of the enriched Castilian dialect or of a Galician tongue—this elocution was more of a lengthy Georgia drawl.

Unable to withhold his amusement, John laughed. "Well, tell me Miss Boo, do you have room in your class for me?"

"Daddy!" she yelled with excitement. She instantly forgot about the lesson, ran to her father, and leaped into his arms. "I didn't know you were home," she said as she gazed into his eyes.

"Yeah, sweetheart, I just got here. Did you miss me?" he asked as he returned her gaze.

"Yeah, will you play with me, Daddy?" Boo asked, sensing he might be in a good-natured mood.

"Sure, I will. What game do you want to play?"

"Let's play hide-and-seek," she answered.

"Okay, I'll be it and you can hide."

"Yeaaaaa!" She screamed as she dropped from his arms and scampered for her first hiding place.

For the next hour, John gradually sobered up as he stalked through the house, searching for his daughter. Upstairs and down, back and forth, he found her concealed in the strangest places. Inside obscure closets or under an overshadowed bed, Boo retreated to hideaways most four-year-olds would find unnerving. An animate giggle she could not suppress always revealed her location when he drew near.

After the games, they ate dinner, watched television together, and then prepared for bed. John had little trouble convincing Boo to retire. She was exhausted from their high jinks, but not so tired that she didn't request a bedtime story from her agreeable father. After pouring her limber body onto the bed, he granted her wish by reading her favorite storybook. Afterwards, he tucked the covers around her small limbs and gently kissed her forehead. Boo appeared quite content, so the moment seemed ideal to ask her about the Bible. Its strange appearance on the kitchen table was still gnawing on his mind.

"Boo, this morning I found your mother's old Bible on the kitchen table. Do you happen to know how it got there?" John asked, with caution in his voice, careful not to alarm her of his concern.

"Mommy had her Bible last night when she came to see me. She must 'a put it on the table," Boo answered with complete candor.

John bristled as an alarming chill swept through his body. It felt as though his blood pressure had suddenly dropped to a balmy low in reaction to Boo's response. He fought to keep from trembling as he canvassed his mind for some plausible explanation of his daughter's remarks.

"Sweetheart, I'm not going to get mad at you if you did it. I just need to find out how it got to the kitchen."

"I didn't do it. Mommy did," she said with a faint cry. "I'm scared. Mommy said there are bad people out there."

John lifted Boo and wrapped his arms around her small frame. She returned his embrace by gently hugging him back. How could he doubt her words? Her explanation of the Bible was less bizarre than an account of his own encounters during the day. "I believe you, Boo. I believe you. And don't worry. I won't let anyone hurt you." He kissed her forehead and placed her back on the pillow.

After leaving Boo, John paced to his own room, undressed, and then entered the bathroom in preparation for a shower. The hot water from the spigot peppered his face, bringing back the pragmatic reasoning of a seasoned police officer. Bottom line, all the day's incidents could be accounted for with rational explanations. The Rimmon murder was no different than the hundreds of others he had investigated. Just another lunatic blaming his rabid actions on a force beyond his control. His uneasy sensations at the farm were probably a touch of the flu. After all, the bug had arrived early in Atlanta this year. As for the trance at Pickett's Mill, it was nothing more than an unusual flash of unconsciousness. Something akin to momentarily falling asleep at the steering wheel of a car, only to wake before leaving the roadway.

The Bible puzzle was as easy as *habla usted espanol*. Tina did it. She acted awfully flaky that morning. John surmised that she must have been guilty of something. The final mystery of Rebecca's visitations with Boo was no mystery at all. It was merely a young child having difficulty distinguishing fantasy from reality. She dreamed of her mother and simply thought she was awake at the time. Now he had all the answers. Now everything was back to normal.

John stepped out of the shower, toweled himself dry, and dressed in his pajama bottoms. To no surprise, when he walked into his bedroom, he found his daughter lying peacefully on his bed. She was surrounded by three of her favorite stuffed animals and deep in sleep with an aura of contentment on her face. John made no attempt to move her back to her own bed, instead he lay down beside her, tenderly stroked her hair, and gazed at her innocent face. Somehow, in his gut, he knew that he had none of the answers he so desperately sought, that his life would never be normal again. Sleep did not come easy.

19

Victor Lechman was not a man endowed with the inventive imagination of Thomas Edison, nor the quick wit of Mark Twain. He did, however, have a pit bull persistency combined with the patience of Job. That was how he solved crimes...sheer perseverance. He arrived at the homicide office two hours before the change in shifts; he had been piecing together the fragments of information that had been gathered the day before at the Rimmon farm. He was driven by the baffling circumstances surrounding these murders. Unlike some hot dog rookie joining the force to seek danger, Victor, much like John, pursued the unthinkable, the explanation why any human could commit such sordid acts.

John passed the detectives leaving from the night shift as he entered the office and approached Victor who was sitting at his desk. John appeared fatigued. It had been a restless night. His dreams were consumed not with the unpleasant picture of Frank Rimmon hanging from the barn rafters, but of the lingering image of himself as the wounded soldier at Pickett's Mill. That, along with Boo's squirming kicks to his lower back, made for a fidgety evening.

"Damn," Victor said, "You look like hell. You feeling any better today?"

"Yeah, a lot better than yesterday," John answered, producing an undecided grin.

"Well, it's Friday and payday. That should make you feel a little better. Plus, I've got a little present for you," Victor replied as he arched his bushy eyebrows. In his typical boyish fashion, Victor wanted John to guess the secret he was withholding.

"What have you got?" John's voice deepened with irritation at his partner's antics.

Lifting a folded piece of paper off his desk, Victor smiled, while waiving it back and forth like a flag. "What do you think it is? Come on, guess," he said with a vexing smirk.

Friday and payday aside, John was simply not in the mood to play the game. "It's a damn round-trip ticket to Hawaii you bought for me. Now, any more questions?"

Feeling a tinge of remorse, John wished he could withdraw his words unheard. His overreaction was more a symptom of stress than that of Victor's prankish diversion. Even so, his partner never acknowledged his harsh tone. That kind of reaction was not uncommon in Brooklyn, Victor's former haunt. Oftentimes, subtle courtesies would give way to urban irreverence in that city. That was John's opinion, anyway. He thought the use of the profane was simply how one communicated with another.

With smile unbroken, Victor asked once again, "Okay, last chance. What do you think it is?"

John's impatience yielded to Victor's waggish expression. An ear-to-ear grin exposed Lechman's central incisors, producing the look of an excited, overstuffed chipmunk. The look provoked a silent laugh, reversing John's earlier state of tensity. "Okay, pal, I give up. What is it?"

"It's a warrant."

"An arrest warrant?" John asked, in disbelief that his partner had solved the murders and was about to seek out and arrest the culprit.

"No. It's a warrant to search Rimmon's office. Judge Hines signed it last night around ten o'clock. I knew you'd want to be there when we searched the place. You ready to go?" Victor asked while rising from his chair.

"What about our report on Rimmon? I haven't lifted a finger filling out the paperwork."

"Not to worry, compadre. I just finished our report. It's on Captain Reid's desk right now."

John's mood instantly brightened. Putting a pen to paper was his least favorite task of being a police officer. Since the captain was a stickler on turning in progress reports, Victor's efficient handling of the matter was a welcome relief. "Yeah, I'm ready. Let's go."

As Victor rose from his chair, he paused for a split second. "Oh, I almost forgot. We need to stop by the coroner's office on our way out. I stopped by and saw Charlie Connors earlier this morning before I came in. He said he would have some preliminary results on Rimmon's autopsy by now."

"Let's go," John cheerfully replied, the strain now leaving his entire body.

Fifteen minutes later, the detectives arrived at the coroner's office. Once inside, they found Connors poised above the naked body of a juvenile male lying across a stainless-steel table in the middle of the autopsy room. The M.E. was carrying on a one-way profane conversation with the kid. Good thing Connors wasn't a funeral director. In Georgia, a mortician could lose his license for using obscene language in the company of a corpse.

Charlie badly needed the deflection. This was already his second examination of the day—a teenage boy, shot by a drug dealer for a nickel bag of cocaine. The fluorescent lighting produced an odd, reflective glare off the shiny table and tile that lined the walls and floors of the room. It also produced an albino, almost mad doctor appearance on Connors' waxen face. He was completely consumed by the autopsy. He never looked up to acknowledge the detectives' arrival. Instead, he kept on talking as he lifted a narrow black hose and proceeded to rinse an entry wound on the corpse as he probed for the slug that ended the young man's life.

"Bingo," Connors remarked into the microphone dangling above the body. "Entry wound pierced the pectoralis major muscle, severed the left costal cartilage of the left rib and angled slightly upward. The bullet perforated the pulmonary artery and then stopped just inside the inner layer of skin on the middle back." With a pair of tweezer-like forceps, he withdrew the slug from the body. "By the size and twist, it looks like a .38 caliber, about a 158-grain bullet." Connors left the probe in the wound and proceeded to snap several photos which would be used as evidence. He then removed his blood tattered smock, turned to Victor and John, said hello and gestured them to follow. "Let's go in my office. I need a break."

Inside the office, Connors motioned for the detectives to take a seat. Afterwards, he seated himself and lifted a box of doughnuts from the corner of his desk. After helping himself to one, he passed the box to John and Victor. John declined but Victor, of course, grabbed two jellies. For a few minutes, the only sounds in the room were the smacking phonics made by Victor and Charlie. John watched in disbelief as they dipped into the box again and again. Connors finally spoke when the box made its last lap.

"Thanks for the doughnuts, Victor. I appreciate it."

At that precise moment, it became crystal clear to John that Connors had befriended Victor for the mere price of a box of pastries. Why else would the ornery M.E. knock himself out to complete an early morning autopsy on Rimmon? Yes, Victor had been by the morgue earlier, he had stopped by to deliver the bribe and to kiss a little ass. John felt like a jealous child, deprived of a brother's love. Irritated at Victor and Connors' chummy relationship, John began to speak in an effort to end their camaraderie. "Hey, when you two pigs get through stuffin' your faces, let me know. After all, we do have two murders to solve."

"Okay, okay. Relax, John. Charlie will bring us up to speed," Victor said as he grabbed the last doughnut.

Connors' shoulders slumped with disappointment as he began to speak. "I've got to level with you guys. I've done more autopsies than I care to remember, but I've never seen anything like these deaths. Like Pierce, Rimmon was blind at death. I mean the same silvery eyes, same charring of the optic nerves. He was also unconscious before he died. Tissue on his neck showed signs of trauma, like maybe he was popped with an electric prod of some kind. Other than that and the missing penis, there were no other cuts or abrasions."

"What about blood stains? There had to be blood or some other evidence in the barn," John said, with a confused expression on his face.

"That's the damnedest thing. His body was completely drained. I mean not one drop of blood anywhere," Connors nervously remarked as he lit a badly needed cigarette to help soothe his frayed nerves. "I did find a hair sample under his fingernails. Lab boys said it had some of the characteristics of animal hair, the Bovidae family."

"Speak in English, Charlie. What's a Bow-vu-die," John asked with a peevish grimace.

"It's the goat family. You know, two horns, a beard," Connors answered.

"I didn't see any goats on the farm yesterday. Did you see any?" John asked, turning toward Victor.

"No, I didn't see any goats," Victor responded.

Rising from his chair, Connors crumpled the empty doughnut box between his hands and tossed the remains into the metal wastebasket beside his desk. He crushed his smoldering cigarette in the ashtray, rose from his chair, and stormed toward the office door. "I didn't say it was a goat hair. I said the lab boys said it had some characteristics of goat hair. Hell, they can't identify what it is for sure."

"Anything else, Charlie?" John asked, hoping that Connors had withheld some tidbit of information.

"Look, John, all I've got so far are two dickless stiffs and a lot of unanswered questions!"

Connors turned and left the bewildered detectives sitting in his office. Four deaths the previous day had left him with too many bodies and too little time. And John and Victor had been left with too many questions and too few answers.

20

Victor veered in and out of the heavy traffic as he and John made their way to Frank Rimmon's office. New York congestion was primarily stop-and-go, whereas, in Atlanta, the pace could be more like stock car racing on a motor speedway. As their vehicle approached a crowded intersection, Victor stomped on the gas pedal to beat the changing traffic light. John stared incredulously at his partner as his back stiffened bracing for an expected crash. In contrast, with one hand on the steering wheel, Victor appeared relaxed as though he were on a Sunday afternoon drive in the country. With pie-eyed anxiety, John watched as they narrowly missed a crossing pick-up truck.

"Watch out!" John exclaimed. "And slow down!"

Victor ignored John's explicit order and continued whipping in and out of traffic, serpentine style. In only two short weeks, Victor had undergone a metamorphic transition. He was now infected with that rare Atlanta disease reserved only for those who travel the city's thoroughfares—a toxic dystrophy that consumes rational brain cells, turning a once conservative driver into a Mr. Hyde of the roadways.

Traveling north to the Five Points business district finally ended in a traffic gridlock at a junction of intermingled streets, an intersection that only an inebriated traffic engineer could design. Given Victor's driving skills, John was relieved to arrive unscathed. He scanned left and right until he spied Rimmon's office and then he pointed Victor toward a parking space a half-block away. The chiropractic office was located just off the corner, nestled between a local bar to its left and an attorney's office to its right. A paradox of commerce—one could partake of a few cocktails, drive on this hodgepodge of accident-prone streets, seek advice from a contingency-starved television attorney, and have one's spine realigned without traversing more than fifty feet. This was truly a tidy combination of businesses for anyone interested in cashing in on the litigation lottery.

After the car was parked, John led the way. He quickly stepped out of the vehicle, walked down the sidewalk and to the office door. Victor followed close behind as the detectives stepped through the doorway. Both men were greeted by a smallish woman, barely five feet in height. She was standing next to a filing cabinet, peering through a pair of black horn-rimmed glasses while struggling to balance an armful of patient files and papers.

"You guys the cops here about Dr. Rimmon's death?" she asked, as she dropped the stack of files on a nearby desk.

"I'm Detective Williams and this is Detective Lechman. We're in charge of the investigation. Can we ask you some questions about Dr. Rimmon?" John said, displaying his detective's shield.

"My name's Connie, Connie Best. As for the questions, ask all you want. Fact is I don't know much," the young woman responded with a blank stare. "I've only been working here two weeks. Craziest job I've ever had. I knew something was screwy when I started. I mean this guy paid me for a month in advance, a month mind you. And he's only been in twice since I've been here. And when he was here, he acted like a scared puppy. Only stayed ten or fifteen minutes and then out the door."

"What did he do when he came in?" John asked.

"He'd go straight to the treatment room or his office. I'd hear him messing around with the equipment or something back there, and then boom, he'd blow by my desk and tell me not to take any appointments. Then out the door. I mean, how can you run a chiropractic business and not treat any patients?" She responded with a look of disgust.

Although John and Victor didn't expect to discover any revelations from Ms. Best, they had to ask the questions anyway. It was their job. Their instincts were right. After a thirty-minute interrogation, they didn't uncover any new information, so they gave up. They asked her not to move any files or other items in the office. Afterwards, they proceeded to search every square inch of the premises.

Fortunately, their exploration of Rimmon's office was far more productive than the interview with Ms. Best. Their search uncovered a bizarre mixture of devilish paraphernalia—three amulets of assorted colors along with one particular piece of jewelry that spoke of hedonistic charm. It was a yellow, oval amulet displaying the sign of Baphomet—a goat head inside an inverted pentagram within two circles. They also discovered a number of cowrie shells, mandrake roots and vials filled with oils. The detectives were particularly interested in two crumpled pieces of parchment paper found within the upper left-hand drawer of Rimmon's desk. The first document contained the nine Satanic Statements, the guide to those energized by the negative forces of sin. John and Victor half-whispered the verses as their eyes followed the impious words.

1. *Satan represents indulgence instead of abstinence!*
2. *Satan represents vital existence, instead of spiritual pipe dreams!*
3. *Satan represents undefiled wisdom, instead of hypocritical self-deceit!*
4. *Satan represents kindness to those who deserve it, instead of love wasted on ingrates!*
5. *Satan represents vengeance instead of turning the other cheek!*
6. *Satan represents responsibility to the responsible, instead of concern for psychic vampires!*
7. *Satan represents man as just another animal, sometimes better, sometimes worse than those that walk on all-fours, who, because of*

his "divine spiritual and intellectual development," has become the most vicious animal of all!

8. Satan represents all of the so-called sins, as they all lead to physical mental or emotional gratification!

9. Satan has been the best friend the church has ever had, as he has kept it in business all these years!

The second paper contained notes made by Rimmon. The writings were a series of fragmented sentences, disturbed thoughts and questions from a man caught up in some diabolical struggle between good and evil.

John felt a familiar chill as he read the annotations.

"The serpent isn't slimy, nor does it squirm on its' belly. It is shiny and beautiful. It walks on two legs and has the cunning of the master. The serpent will not let me turn back. I hunger for—"

The notes abruptly ended, leaving the detectives to ponder what Rimmon had meant. Although they didn't know the meaning, they were encouraged by the evidence they were finding, so they ignored the note for the time being and methodically continued their search. Their persistence paid off. Within a closet, the men found what appeared to be some type of black ceremonial robe and a gold scepter with an inverted pentagram fixed atop one end.

Last but not least, they discovered a lethal assortment of knives hidden on a top shelf in the supply closet. This was not the customary equipment of a practicing chiropractor, unless the good doctor had abandoned the art of massage for the pursuit of pleasure through superstition, charms and black magic. Their perusal of the office ended with a review of the patients' files. It was then that they uncovered the most incriminating piece of evidence. It was a file on Richard Pierce, the first murder victim.

21

It was late Friday afternoon when John and Victor finished their shift. Their remaining time on the clock had been spent combing through the patient files they had confiscated from Rimmon's office, making phone calls, and writing lengthy reports. Only one additional tidbit of information emerged from their scrutiny—a file on Marty Lococo, the owner of The Foxes Den. Lococo's file, along with the one on Pierce, presented a powerful link connecting them to Dr. Rimmon. It was a bold statement that they were all somehow tied together by an odd psychotic energy.

Victor seemed restless, constantly glancing at his watch. His mind was fixed on the upcoming weekend and not on the investigation. Even though he was consumed by his work, it was time for him to block out the memories of the misaligned day and to concentrate on the quality time he would spend with his family. John's thoughts were also off the case. He was focused on the evening, hoping that the lovely Lori Lamb would make an appearance at his self-defense class. At the end of the shift, each man wished the other a pleasant weekend and departed for their intended destinations.

The police department encouraged all officers to participate in community affairs. As in John's case, sometimes the encouragement took the form of a direct order. Although in this situation, he didn't mind. Even though he had complained about the assignment, he really enjoyed sharing his knowledge. It was the least he could do since the department had spent so much time and money training him. While at the academy, John thought the schooling would never end, from self-defense, to basic first aid, to cardiopulmonary resuscitation, to the Heimlich maneuver. He was tutored on just about everything, including the simple task of how to make a suffering individual comfortable while calling for medical assistance.

John arrived at the Decatur YWCA in time to change into his sweats and to spend a few minutes thinking about his upcoming lesson. The demanding defense techniques taught at the academy included too many esoteric tasks for the untrained students. There was no need for them to learn how to search and handcuff a suspect, or how to approach a stopped vehicle, or where to stand once you are beside the car. These seemingly routine procedures could mean the difference between life and death for a cop, yet for a housewife or a teacher, they had little value.

Police officers were also instructed in the fundamentals of judo and boxing intertwined with a mixture of other self-defense techniques. John knew that their training was important. He also knew that combative suspects rarely adhered to the Marquis of Queensberry rules and that officers involved in a real knockdown, biting, kicking, scratching brawl would often forget what they had learned.

A fight on the street never took the form of those seen on television or the movies. Street fights were usually violent explosions of feet and fists along with neurotic screams laced with panic and hostility. In these furious exchanges, however, officers usually remembered to use the one hold that has saved the life of more of their brethren than all the other exotic techniques combined. The pandemonium often ended with a policeman securing a headlock around a face covered with blood and hate. To be used only if an officer's safety or life was at risk, this straightforward wrestling move was always followed by the execution of a choke hold. A simplistic move where a baton or forearm slid down an assailant's face, securing a new position around the throat so a squeezing motion could be applied.

The pressure from the strangulation restricted the flow of oxygen laden blood from the carotid artery, causing a momentarily loss of consciousness. Used sparingly, it was a better option than the lethal force of a sidearm. No, the women weren't candidates for chokehold techniques, nor any other advanced self-defense training. John just needed to teach them a few defensive maneuvers they could remember during an assault. He would be satisfied if he accomplished that goal.

As John walked into the open gymnasium, he was met by a heavy odor. It was the stinky smell of perspiration, the aftermath of a week's worth of workouts and games. Without hesitating, he headed straight for the middle of the basketball court. It would be there, on an island of multi-colored tumbling mats, he would conduct his class. When he arrived, he couldn't help but test the pudding-like pliancy of the mats with his bare feet. He even thought about tumbling around like a five-year-old boy, but an early arrival of students changed his mind.

The women had begun pouring into the open gym. And ten minutes later, the arena was saturated with the chattering sound of forty women discussing their forthcoming lesson. In the manner of an army drill sergeant gathering the troops for roll call, John instructed the women to align themselves around three sides of the mats while his eyes scanned left and right in a fruitless search for Lori. Although he was disappointed by her absence, he had a class to conduct so he proceeded by introducing himself and laying down the ground rules for the lesson. He then asked some questions regarding what the women expected from the session. Their expectations ran the gamut from how to handle an overly aggressive date, to dealing with a rapist or mugger.

"I hope everyone understands that the purpose of this class is to teach you some very simple and practical ways to deal

136

with aggression. It is not my intent nor is it possible in two hours, to teach you some sort of rigid, ancient fighting style such as karate or jiu jitsu," John spoke with sternness in his voice. "So, let's get started with rule number one. Although this may be unfair, men are, in most cases, bigger and stronger than women."

Rule number one was greeted by a series of jeers and scoffs. Albeit true, the women felt this was truly, a quintessential chauvinistic remark. With palms down, John waived his arms, gesturing the women to calm down.

"Okay, okay, listen up," he said, exposing a mischievous grin. "Time for rule number two. In a real emergency, you must keep your wits about you and not panic."

An elderly woman, with a round, delicate face raised her grandmotherly hand and posed a question. "Are you saying that we shouldn't be afraid if we are attacked?"

"No ma'am, I'm not saying that at all. It's just that if you panic, your chances of surviving aren't good. Now, as for being afraid, that's normal. It's the best thing you have going for you. Fear produces adrenaline and adrenaline will make you stronger. It will also make you less sensitive to pain if you're injured and help you run like a deer if you're trying to get away." John continued, "Any more questions?"

There were plenty of inquiries. For the next twenty minutes, questions came one after another. The women's exuberance about the lesson had piqued John's interest, giving him a slight boost of his own adrenaline. He was now completely embroiled in their class.

"All right, let's start out by discussing the easiest and best self-defense technique you can use. Does anyone know what that is?" John asked as he surveyed his students.

An unknown voice from the back of the crowd yelped, "How about a Smith and Wesson .38?" The answer to the question gave rise to a roar of laughter from the women.

John swiftly responded, "No, it's not a gun or a knife or any other weapon. The best defense is prevention and that includes being assertive."

John's explanation was logical. Nature had betrayed the opposite sex with a cheaper allocation of strength and size. As such, any ideas that a petite, 100-pound girl trained in self-defense could nonchalantly cripple a 250-pound linebacker with a quick flick of her hand, had to be immediately dismissed. Nature had also unfairly bred a sense of passivity in women when confronted by an aggressive male. This oftentimes would manifest itself in an outward appearance of fear. A collage of movements from hunched shoulders, to a nervous, fast-paced walk will telegraph signals to any would-be mugger that they have found an easy mark.

As the detective explained, it was critical for the women to break any prior latent conditioning and to take control of their body language. Phase one of this process was to consciously breathe in slow deep breaths so as to keep oxygen flowing to the brain and muscles. Phase two was to walk erect with your head held high, to never avoid looking directly at those who may intend you harm. In the manner of a schoolyard bully shouldering aside those who stand in his way, the lesson was to move with confidence.

The final phase was that the women must reprogram themselves to get fighting mad when anyone invades their personal space. The goal was to replace a frail smile with a saber-tooth gnashing of the teeth, to change a face of submission into one of hate and rage. A combination of screams and yells was the final ingredient, thus the transformation would be complete—a scared rabbit would become a roaring lioness.

John addressed other common-sense methods of avoiding felons. He asked the women to understand that, in most instances, crimes occurred because of opportunities.

Therefore, it was important to practice safe habits. The session had been going well, but now it had reached a tedious lull. John was addressing the humdrum subject of why you should keep your car locked and why you should park in a lighted area when a feisty, young woman in the group sprang forward, exposing her boredom.

"This stuff is all well and good, but I came here to learn how to defend myself if some Bozo doesn't buy all this growling and snarling jazz," she said with a tinge of anxiety in her voice.

John promptly responded, "All right, I understand what you're saying. So, why don't we talk about some counterattacks that you can use if your bark or posture isn't convincing enough? Would anyone be willing to let me empty their purse on the mat to show the class some of the weapons you carry that you're not even aware of?"

The bored woman who prompted this part of the session offered her handbag for perusal. John gratefully accepted and dumped the purse's contents on the outer edge of the mats. He then made a careful inventory of the contents and began his lecture.

"These are weapons that can be used for stabbing," he said as he displayed a rat-tail comb, a metal nail file, and a ballpoint pen. "Any of these objects can be used as a dagger."

Sifting through the remaining items, John discovered a set of car keys and a can of hair spray. Positioning the keys in the palm of his right hand, he closed his fingers around all but one key which he allowed to protrude from his closed fist. He then raised his hand, demonstrating his newly found weapon. "Carry your keys with the sharp edge of one key sticking out of your fist. Use this key as a slashing weapon across the face or any other exposed flesh of an assailant."

John dropped the keys and picked up the can of spray. "This can be used to temporarily blind someone if you give him a good dose of this stuff in the face." After one last glance of the purse's paraphernalia produced no new weapons, John concluded that part of the session and began the last segment.

This was the meat of the course. It involved a discussion, along with demonstrations, on the use of weapons more natural than those made from plastic or compressed in an aerosol can. These armaments were sculpted by God's hammer and chisel. The graceful arms and hands, the angular legs, knees, and feet. The Almighty One never intended his artful work to be used as personal weapons, yet in his wisdom he must have known that man's cruelty to man would someday create a world where we would need to use these masterful creations to stay alive.

John had merely taken the use of these body parts to a level of lethal response. His knowledge and competence in the fighting skills of karate and jiu-jitsu were extensive. And since he had been an all-SEC wrestler in college, he had proven himself to be an effective grappler as well. Yet, the art in which he really excelled was Aikido. His prowess in this field was unmatched by almost anyone other than a few of the remaining masters still practicing in the Far-East. For some uncanny reason, learning this complex style of fighting had been easy for him.

He never knew why since Aikido involved so many intricate maneuvers, so many specialized techniques that required perfect timing and precision. All of those bending and twisting actions applied against an assailant's fingers, wrists, elbows, and shoulders also required exceptional speed and agility. Tonight's lesson would include none of those complicated moves. Instead, he would concentrate on identifying vulnerable areas on a would-be aggressor and a simple weapon that could be used to inflict the pain.

John knew of many vulnerable areas on the human body. His task was to concentrate on the vulnerable points that matched up with the strengths of his students. The typical response from a woman being attacked usually included sheer panic along with beating the assailant's chest with the underside of her closed fist. This was somewhat akin to hunting tigers with a slingshot—you may get off a few shots, but the result is an angrier feline, or in the women's case, a pissed off felon.

"Here's one of your most effective weapons," John said as he held up his hand and outstretched fingers for viewing by the class. And here's the most vulnerable area on a man's body," he remarked, pointing to his eyes.

"I thought that the weakest area would be a tad bit lower, like in the balls!" The loud comment came from the back of the crowd. It drew a round of laughter as several students stepped aside, allowing the comic to step forward and approach the center stage.

John felt a nervous, school-boy punch of excitement hit his mid-section as Lori Lamb emerged from the parted billow of ladies. The thirty-year-old woman sashayed forward, stopped at the edge of the mats and stood, facing him with her hands resting seductively on her hips. Unable to speak, he remained motionless, gawking at the sight of this vexing woman. Even the grey, loose fitting warm-up could not diminish her form. Her flowing black hair was styled into a cute ponytail. The coiffure gave full exposure to her face, a face that John knew had no equal.

The dim light at The Foxes Den had shielded her beauty, for the brilliant light from the gymnasium ceiling highlighted her face, removing all the unwanted shadows. It was not necessary for John to speak. His silence spoke volumes. Her visage was the completion of a commissioned work of art, of every man's dream and every woman's yearn for perfection.

Her natural symmetry seemed almost unnatural as a gaggle of pie-eyed women stared jealously as she walked by. It was an understandable reaction.

When John finally recovered from his state of suspension, he replied, "Well, that's a good point, but I'd still go for the eyes on the first blow. Once the assailant is blind, you can pretty much go for any area."

For the next twenty minutes, Lori stood with a row of students directly in front of John, prompting him to speak in a somewhat slurry fashion. This was something of an embarrassment for a seasoned police officer who was accustomed to dealing with stressful situations. Yet this stress was nothing like the pressure he felt when dealing with a disfigured two-bit hood. This was the overpowering kind that attacks the brain cells when a bashful cop is confronted by an unabashed brunette. Nonetheless, he attempted to gather his composure and continue the lesson by describing other vulnerable areas of the body such as the nose, throat and ears.

In an effort to distract himself from Lori, John refocused on teaching his students how to identify natural weapons. Since the women lacked any expert training, these weapons would be used more as a means to pierce or maim rather than to kill. The fingers would be used for jabbing, the teeth for biting, the head for butting, the elbow for smashing, the hand for hitting and grabbing, and the feet for kicking. John's treatise on how to stab someone's eyes with a rigid index finger or the twisting and squeezing of a man's scrotum with an open hand had many of the women reeling with repulsion. Several appeared to be on the verge of passing out or throwing up. He was careful to explain that these techniques should not be used to fend off an unwanted kiss at a party, but instead should be saved for assaults stitched with threats of brutality and venom. The unanswered question was whether many of these timid personalities could complete

142

the metamorphic trip from a loving housewife or dedicated teacher to that of a creature lashing out with convulsive fury. If they failed to finish the journey, if they made it only part of the way, then the outcome would be a halfway defense destined for tragedy.

John had allocated the last thirty minutes of the class for actual demonstrations. These physical techniques required student volunteers, so he stepped forward in preparation to ask for a participant. Before he could finish the announcement, Lori took a step up on the mats and offered her services. Her action brought a satisfying smile to John's face as he welcomed her participation.

"Okay, now that we have a volunteer, I'm going to show you how to deliver some defensive blows if an assailant grabs you from behind," John said as he positioned himself in front of Lori. "Miss, I want you to walk up behind me, reach around the outside of my arms, and lock your hands. Don't be afraid to hold me tight." His reference to Lori as "Miss" was a feeble attempt to act cool and indifferent, as though he didn't remember her from the night club.

She obediently wrapped her arms around his trunk and tightly clasped her hands. As she drew closer and closer, John could feel her warm breath as it fanned the nape of his neck. He could also feel the softness of her breasts as she pressed against his stiffening back. He was intensely aware of her shapely presence, sensing that an old burning desire was about to be ignited. Her scent was clean, almost jasmine in smell. Feeling flooded with heat, he wanted to turn around and kiss her full lips instead of demonstrating some self-defense head butt or elbow jab. However, he resisted that lustful urge and attempted to concentrate on the lesson at hand. It was a useless effort. The fever had already begun.

"Okay, pay attention. Even though my arms are pinned, I can still deliver a blow with the back of my hand," John demonstrated the move by leaning to his left and striking downward toward Lori's groin using a common judo chop. Stopping short of making contact, he continued the demonstration by acting as though he was grabbing a pair of testicles. "You could also grab and twist if there isn't enough room to swing your arm and hand."

Tapping her hands, he gestured for Lori to release her grip. He then commissioned her to exchange places, allowing him to be the aggressor and her, the victim. It was time for her to evince the ability to execute the blow. Stepping behind her, he allowed his arms to envelope her torso just beneath her breasts. With planned precision, Lori positioned her buttocks snuggly against John's groin. She then shimmied her bottom as though she were seeking the most comfortable fit. Her slow movements had become the wellspring for an aching throb inside his sweats, a swelling that brought an embarrassed red glow to his face.

In response to John's reaction, Lori widened her stance and pressed even harder. John's thoughts were now consumed with how he could conceal the impromptu bulge in his sweats without exposing his infatuation to the entire class. His predicament faded quickly, however, for Lori initiated her own unexpected self-defense maneuver. Leaning to the left, she swung her arm and hand downward toward John's crotch. Instead of executing the abbreviated judo chop that he demonstrated, she continued the motion with her open hand seizing his private parts. Although the pressure she applied was not enough to drop John to his knees, it was enough to bring a grimace to his surprised face and certainly enough to deflate his aroused condition. Air exploded from his mouth as his eyes rolled upward, signaling the pain.

John squealed involuntarily as Lori slowly released her grip. Many of the women convulsed with laughter while several simply stood with mouths agape, unable to believe what they had just witnessed. Lori had completed an about-face and was attempting to apologize for her actions.

"I'm so sorry. I don't know why I did that. I just got caught up in the demonstration." Her words were spoken with a hint of remorse, but also with a trace of mischief. John wondered if she was playing some sort of mind game, if she was teasing him by using an uncommon mix of affection and torture. "Are you all right?" She asked.

"Yeah, I'm okay," John responded weakly as the pounding slowly subsided in his genitalia. In a sluggish fashion, he asked Lori to join the others as his voice oscillated from high to low in reaction to his injury. In an attempt to avoid further abuse, he paired the women together to practice the self-defense moves he had demonstrated. A half-hour later when the class concluded, John again restated the need to exhibit assertive behavior. He also emphasized the need to practice the techniques they had learned, and above all, to practice safety to avoid becoming an unwitting victim in the first place. As the women disbursed, Lori made her way toward John.

"I am so sorry for what I did. Will you forgive me?" She asked.

"Sure, I'm okay now anyway. I was just surprised by your move." John smiled.

"I don't know if you remember me. I'm Lori Lamb. We met at The Foxes Den the other night."

With a soft chuckle he replied, "Of course, I remember you, Lori. That's some way to reintroduce yourself though. You gave me quit a scare."

"Well, I told you that's the most vulnerable area, not the eyes." Lori smiled unable to hide her pleasure at making her case.

"I don't think I would argue that point, right now," John sensed that it was an opportune time to ask her for a date since she seemed in an obliging mood. Hoping that this time his mind wouldn't betray him, he clumsily searched for the right words to say. "Lori, I was thinking that if maybe…you know…sometime if you're not doing anything…. Well, I mean maybe we could get together for dinner or something."

John's words were anything but a deft invite from a smooth-talking Southern gentleman. Instead, he seemed more like a thirteen-year-old teenager struck silly by puppy love. It was as though he was unable to voice anything but fragmented sentences.

However, Lori wasted no time. Her response was short and sweet. "When?"

Somewhat stunned, John silently prayed that a small pinch of charm would find his lips along with a little courage.

"Well, what about tomorrow night?" He said, speaking with a little more confidence.

John had not noticed that Lori had written her phone number on a small piece of paper while he was tripping over his tongue. She handed him the note and answered, "Call me tomorrow."

22

It was three a.m. when John anxiously awoke from a deep slumber. Beads of sweat had materialized on his forehead as his heart raced out of control. As he sat up in bed, his breath was short and erratic. He attempted to recall the details he had experienced in his dream. Rebecca had appeared in his sleep before but always in an aura of peace. Her face was a portrait of agony in this unwanted nightmare. She stood before him, holding her Bible in extended hands as though she beckoned him to accept its tidings. His muddled memory was unable to retrace any other events after that.

He rose from bed feeling woozy and disconnected as though he had no ties with the real world. This was a nauseous flush. It was a sick feeling much like the dismal emotions he experienced when Rebecca died—it began in the heart and slowly filled the body with a horrible emptiness. John made a quick trip to the bathroom and returned to bed hoping the sensation would depart.

John drifted off again and slept like a baby until nine o'clock that morning. He had forgotten the dream, and was again thinking about Lori. Obsessed with his upcoming date, he began the day in his bathroom where he spent considerable time conducting an inventory of his toiletries. He wanted to make certain he had all the items needed to groom himself for the evening's encounter. On the countertop next to the sink, he arranged his concoctions in meticulous order until he had convinced himself that all was well.

Afterwards he took inventory of his evening dress since he wanted to take Lori to one of Atlanta's more stylish restaurants. This process took all of five seconds to complete. His formal wear amounted to one, somewhat faded, camel-brown sport coat and one nine-year-old navy-blue suit that was missing several of the jacket buttons. These were not the clothes of a well-paid man-about-town. They were, however, the trappings of an underpaid cop who had to learn to think five-and-dime when it came to his wardrobe. The sport coat would have to do. He spent the remaining morning and afternoon catching up on some much-needed yardwork followed by a quick trip to the barber.

The phone rung just minutes before John walked out the door. It was Lori. She said that she had been shopping with a friend and asked if he would mind meeting her at the restaurant. He thought the request was a little strange but agreed to do so. After arriving at the restaurant, he parked the Chevy and glanced at the rear-view mirror for a quick assessment of his appearance. Satisfied that every hair was in place, he exited the car, walked across the parking lot, and entered the building. He caught a glimpse of Lori chatting with a tall, overly aloof maître d' at the welcome podium. She saw John at the same time and waived him over.

She introduced him to her new friend. The maître d' never bothered to offer John his hand. Instead, he stared disdainfully at his jaded sport coat and tie as though he had no business in this swanky establishment. But his indifference didn't bother John because there was someone else who seemed genuinely excited to see him. Yes, Lori's big smile and the affectionate kiss she planted on his cheek was a clear declaration of her interest.

John was certainly glad to see her too. That sexy body in a tight black dress, that faint smell of perfume and that gorgeous face had him feeling like an out-of-control alley cat. Had the maître d' not instructed them to follow, he probably would have pounced on her right then and there. He even thought about grabbing her as they walked through the dining room. But he controlled his animal instincts and made it to a secluded corner table without breaking any city ordinances. After they were seated, the maître d' exhibited his usual air of starched formality as he left them two leather-bound menus and then slipped away to continue his predictable deportment.

The restaurant's decor was a dark combination of maroon-like walls accented by black, overly refined Edwardian fixtures and furniture. It presented the appearance of a lavish brothel rather than a French café. The candles positioned on the unspoiled, white tablecloths did little to enhance the obscurity. They did provide, however, the setting for a romantic dinner. And Lord knows, John wanted it to be romantic. He was just having a hard time coming up with any fanciful comments to get the evening kicked off to that quixotic start.

Fortunately, the awkward moment didn't last very long. A waiter quickly glided to their table and offered them their choice of libation. With an air of comfort, Lori ordered a glass of a particular wine while John opted for the working man's martini, a long neck Bud. His nervousness continued as he fumbled with the menu and realized the entrees were described using very little English and an abundance of French. Unlike the haunts he usually frequented, this was a classy place. This restaurant sported Chateaubriand and duck mousse, not deep-fried catfish and black-eyed peas. Devouring anything he couldn't pronounce made him queasy. He glanced above the top of his menu and noticed Lori staring his way.

"John, you've got to let me order for us. I majored in French at school and rarely get the chance to speak the language."

"You'll get no argument from me. I have enough trouble with the English language, let alone French."

John was feeling more at ease with his surroundings and was about to continue their conversation when the wine steward arrived with their drinks followed by the waiter who

149

was ready to take their order. Lori requested an appetizer of cauliflower simmered in wine, broth, and onions. For their entrees, she selected veal prepared with mushrooms and shallots flavored with demi-glace, cream, and white wine. Her smooth elocution of the French language was striking. It fashioned a tinge of shallowness in John as he intently listened and sipped on his ordinary beer. *Why would anyone with her beauty and sophistication be interested in an unpolished, homespun Georgia boy like me?* That was all he could think about.

His doubts quickly vanished though as Lori directed a barrage of inquiries his way as if she was a prosecutor cross examining a witness. She wanted to know everything about him—the past, the present, even his thoughts about the future. She absorbed his every word. This was a new experience for John since he was usually the one conducting the investigation. Lori gazed deeply into his eyes as though they held the key to his soul, his innermost thoughts.

When the steward arrived with a second beer and a refill of wine, John's confidence grew even more. He continued talking about the future including his plans for Boo and his career with the police department. It was the portrait of an everyday drama, the allocation of precious time between a doting father and a career-minded cop. The talk of his past consisted of his fascination with solving mysteries from his childhood to his high school and college days, and his tour of duty in the military.

The conversation flourished until his account of the past arrived at Rebecca's illness and her eventual death. At that point, John's words gave way to silence, and a stillness grew between them. It was like the forest at dusk, a time when God's creatures turn mute until dawn and the new light. Lori's good looks and personality aside, these were dear memories for John, keepsakes best left undisturbed.

Lori recognized his uneasiness and quickly changed the subject. "Look, here comes our food. I hope you like what I ordered," she said.

With graceful precision, the waiter bordered the elegant china with shiny flatware. He then presented the appetizer with a side of sweetbread. Before leaving, he carefully arranged the vase of fresh flowers and repositioned the candle. Fifteen minutes later, he returned with the main course.

The meal was superb. Cauliflower was a food for which John held no fondness, yet this whitish vegetable was laced with a flavor that made his mouth yearn for more. As for the veal, each morsel was the origin of a succulent explosion that tickled his palate. A sorbet for dessert was the finish to this gastronomic success. The evening was going marvelously. John could feel a flame of affection building in his heart until the waiter arrived with the check—a peek at the tab quickly doused the fire. John nervously pulled his wallet from his trousers and fumbled through the small bills. He was definitely short on cash, so he handed the waiter an often-used Visa hoping his limit would bear the evening's fare. It would be a shame to end the dinner with an embarrassing declined credit card.

His once calm behavior had been instantly replaced by fidgety movements and uneasy speech. However, luck was with him. The waiter returned, requesting John's signature on the credit slip. Not knowing the appropriate tip for a place so fancy, John filled in the blank with what he could afford, signed the slip, left a copy for the waiter who was standing close by, and quickly escorted Lori toward the exit. He wanted to leave quickly before the waiter had a look at the gratuity and, in French, told Lori what a cheapskate she was dating.

Lori exchanged one last burst of French locution with the maître d' who was hanging around the dining room entrance. Both grinned and giggled as their words and phrases rose and fell like a phonetic roller coaster. John stood by like a puttering bank guard looking over his shoulder for the pissed-off server. Feeling a little paranoid, he couldn't help but wonder if he was the source of their amusement, if Lori and the host were talking about his lack of savoir faire or maybe the fact that he was as poor as a church mouse. When the conversation ended, Lori grabbed his right arm and nestled her head against his shoulder. On their walk to the car, she softly kissed his cheek and declared her joie de vivre with him and the dinner. This cop was on cloud nine.

John and Lori arrived at the car just in time. The low hung sky had begun to sprinkle and the distant sound of thunder signaled that a downpour wasn't far behind. They scurried to get inside. Again, John felt somewhat awkward, so he spent a few moments adjusting the delay switch for the windshield wipers. Meanwhile, Lori, impervious to the weather, seemed fascinated by all the police paraphernalia in the unmarked squad car. Like an impish eight year old, she twisted the dials and switches on the radio with one hand and detached and clamped the blue emergency light with the other. John's eyes flicked back and forth between scouting traffic and watching Lori's lissome features. Since the streets were void of the usual weekday traffic, he spent most of his time staring at her.

Her low-cut, short black dress did little to shroud her figure. Her heaving breasts and sexy legs had him back in that tomcat frame of mind. And for John that was truly rare. He had never felt this kind of sensation before, not even with Rebecca. But Lori had ignited a two-year reserve of high octane testosterone. It had him searching for some cunning strategy on how to get her into bed. His desire was not one of endearment, but one of pure lust.

"Do you want to stop somewhere and have a drink?" John asked, hoping to get a read on what she was thinking.

Diverting her attention from the radio, Lori leaned back onto the vinyl seat and cast a knowing smile. "I've had enough to drink. Let's go someplace where we can relax."

At first John couldn't decide how to respond. The caroming action of his revitalized sex hormones ultimately made the decision for him. This was no time for shyness. "We can go to my place," he said, with an understanding that it might've been a sink-or-swim proposition.

"What about your daughter. Won't we wake her up if we go there?"

"No, Boo is spending the weekend with my housekeeper. We'd have the place to ourselves."

"All right then, your place it is."

Sliding across the car seat, Lori positioned herself next to John and snuggled against his side. She sensed that all sorts of emotions were churning through him, that she had awakened a fervent energy. She was right. John gave an extra punch to the accelerator pedal, and fifteen minutes later, he made a right turn onto his down sloping driveway. He and Lori quickly dashed from each side of the car and ran across the driveway to the front of the house. The drizzling rain suddenly erupted into an intense downpour, accompanied by lightning and thunder. As they say in the South, it was a frog wash.

John secured the door and turned to find Lori gazing at him from the shadows. There was no pretense or disguise about whether she shared his passionate feelings. In a fluid move, she stepped closer allowing him to view her dark eyes and rain moistened lips. He welcomed her embrace with open arms. He also welcomed the kiss that followed. It was long and slow, very passionate. When they finally broke, he drew back in an attempt to regain his composure.

As he gasped for a breath, his heart somersaulted as though he had just finished running a marathon. He wasted little time recovering as, once more, his arms found her waist and his tongue hungrily explored her lips and mouth. Signaling her arousal, she sensually moved her abdomen against his groin and upper thigh. He could feel the heat from her lower body as she continued to writhe, now brushing her breasts against his chest. As they broke from their last kiss, Lori began to softly whimper, making wordless, beguiling sounds of desire. Her shimmering black hair, damp from the rain, brushed against his cheek as he left a trail of unbroken kisses down and across her neck. He slid his hands down to her buttocks, stroking and touching, while she swayed and purred in delight. It was her erotic appeal, her raw beauty, that drew him to her.

For several more minutes, they continued the sensual fore-play until John was certain he could wait no longer. Frantically, he searched her dress for a zipper as he attempted to guide her toward the stairway to the upstairs bedroom. But their need was too great to make the journey. In a wild moment, John hiked up her dress as she unbuckled and dropped his trousers. Clinging together, they collapsed to the carpeted den floor and continued the fervid pace as shadows from the flashes of lightning danced about the walls and ceiling. She arched her back while he strained, pushing hard with his muscular legs.

"Oh," John moaned.

"What is it?" She asked.

"I'm having a hard time getting it in."

"Push harder," she insisted.

Without hesitating, he followed her instructions, pushing harder and harder until, in a flash, he was powerless to continue. It ended as fast as it started. Not a real cool move, but he was helpless to prevent it. His two-year abstinence from sex, wed with the pleasing struggle, had produced a mercurial climax. Unfortunately, Lori was not on pace with his quick as lightning speed.

Slowly, his breathing returned to normal as his elbows began to ache from the strain of supporting the bulk of his weight. Flush with embarrassment, he felt like an out-of-control teenager experiencing sex for the very first time in the back seat of a car. He was afraid to look at her, afraid that she would be disgusted with his lack of sexual stamina. He needed a plausible explanation for his untimely finish, and he needed it fast. "Lori, I don't know what to say. It's been a long time since I've been with anyone."

"Don't worry about it. I understand," Lori said, patting his back in a gesture of forgiveness. "It would have been easier if I weren't a virgin. You need to let me up though. I've got to visit the bathroom."

John had noticed Lori's chastely condition given the struggle. Yet he was still surprised that anyone with her maturity and good looks would still be a virgin, especially in today's indiscriminate society. Feeling as though he had stolen something precious and pure, he chose not to pursue the delicate subject as they rose from the floor and gathered their loose garments. He felt guilty enough already. However, Lori did get a little revenge for his lack of consideration. His partially clothed condition prompted her to snicker as she followed him up the stairs. Unclad from the waist down, he was still wearing his sport coat, shirt and tie.

"What's so funny?" He blushed, thinking she had found amusement in his premature ending.

"You just look like you're about to go to a formal dinner without your pants," she burst into laughter.

"Yeah, I bet I do look funny," he said with a sheepish grin.

Lori grabbed his hand and pulled him up the stairwell and into his bedroom. Within minutes, she appeared from the master bathroom and began to slowly walk toward the bed. Lying there in wait, John watched her form slowly bloom as she drew closer and closer. This was the first opportunity he had to study her naked features and he didn't waste the chance. Seductively, she walked to the bedside and stood before him, allowing his eyes to drift over her body. The light in the room was dim, but there was enough illumination to reveal her nipples still firm from their earlier embrace. Visible as well were her narrow waist and hips. And, of course, he couldn't help but notice those long legs. Her striking beauty had, again, rekindled his desire. His arousal had not gone unnoticed.

Climbing on top, she straddled him. Then she whispered, "Let's try it again."

PART TWO

23

When John arrived at police headquarters, Victor greeted him immediately. The detectives had spent the last three days following fruitless leads, so Victor decided outside help might be useful. He asked John to follow him into the interrogation room where, once inside, he sprang his little surprise.

"John, I want you to meet Dr. Susan Brown. She teaches at the university."

John viewed the outsider with a suspicious eye. He had always considered himself a capable detective and he suspected her presence might mean he was doing a poor job on the investigation. However, he refused to let his distrust prevent him from being social. He exchanged the usual courtesies and shook her sturdy hand. He was surprised by her strong grip given her petite size and grandmotherly features. Her hair, short and gray, bordered an unadorned, yet warm face. There was a glimmer of knowledge in her clear, green eyes. It divulged not only her educational achievements, which included a Ph.D. and Th.D., but of her lifetime of experience as well. But John was still not convinced he needed her help.

"So, Victor, what's the deal?" John asked as he turned in Victor's direction.

"Dr. Brown is an expert on cults, devil worship, you know, the kind of crazy stuff we've been running into on the Pierce and Rimmon cases. I asked her to review our files. I think she may be able to shed some light on the murders."

John turned back to Dr. Brown. "Is that right, doctor? Are you going to solve these murders?"

Recognizing John's skepticism, she smiled and finger tapped the conference table that centered the room. "Mind if we sit down?" She asked.

"No, of course not," Victor responded.

"No, Detective Williams, I'm not here to solve your cases. As a matter of fact, I'm not sure if I can provide you any help in these investigations whatsoever. But, after reviewing your reports and from what Victor has told me, I do know that you're dealing with a satanic coven. If you only approach these incidents from a scientific perspective, you'll probably never catch the people responsible for these deaths."

"Oh, does that mean we are supposed to ignore forensic science? All we need to do is break out a Ouija Board and crystal ball and our case will be solved?" John's voice was bitter. In truth, however, he wasn't upset about Dr. Brown being there. He had used experts like her many times in the past on other cases. He was red-hot mad because Victor had not consulted him before asking the doctor to assist them on these homicides.

Dr. Brown faced him, crinkled her eyes, and insightfully smiled. She realized the meeting was headed for trouble. In an attempt to allow heads to cool, she reached into her back-pack and withdrew a pack of cigarettes. "It's such a nasty habit. I hope you don't mind if I smoke."

Before the detectives could respond, she had lit a king-size smoke and deeply inhaled several puffs. "What you're confronted with is the worst impulses of man. We are talking about people who run in packs, like dogs. People who look for meaning and fulfillment in worshipping evil and practicing black magic. They look just like you and me, yet they wouldn't think twice about sacrificing a child in order to seal a pact with the devil. These people are very secretive and very clever. The more you know about how they think, the better your chance of catching them. That's what I'm saying, Detective Williams."

Feelings aside, John knew that enlisting her help was the right thing to do. He also understood that she was right about the killer—or killers—appearing normal. It was this mask of normalcy that camouflaged their criminal activities and made it even more difficult to uncover their double life. "Since you've read our reports, you're familiar with the crime scenes and how we found the victims. Can you tell us anything about what kind of cult would do this sort of thing?" John asked.

"I don't think it's an orthodox or traditional sect," she said.

"Why do you say that?" John responded.

"Well, those sects tend to be more open. They worship Satan in an active sense. That is, they tend to be highly organized, operating in full view of the public. They usually stay away from rites that involve sacrifices, leaning more toward spiritual ceremonies. This doesn't mesh with the people you're looking for."

"Well then, what does?" Victor asked, as he excitedly drummed his fingers on the tabletop.

"Something more like Santeria."

"Santeria?" Victor quickly replied.

"Santeria is an occult art that has its roots in Africa. It began in the Yoruba tribe in southwestern Nigeria. Their belief system revolved around worshipping a lot of different deities. Each god had its own identity and special powers. It evolved over the years and eventually made its way to this country."

"Why do you think this is the group we're looking for?" John asked, as he watched the doctor extinguish her first cigarette and light another.

"Well, I'm not saying it is a Santeria sect. I'm just saying that it could be. Santeria believers do sacrifice animals. They also have elaborate ceremonies and, depending on the deity, offer whatever they think will please their god the most."

"Have humans ever been sacrificed in their rituals?" John asked.

"There are documented cases where that has happened, but I don't think your victims were offered as a sacrifice."

"Why not?" John asked.

"Well, the markings on the victims' buttocks for one thing. The inverted cross with the half circle is used in death threats or in rituals of revenge. Your victims must have somehow betrayed their coven. Their deaths were simply retribution for their betrayal."

"We suspected that, Dr. Brown," Victor said excitedly, knowing he had made that connection at the first murder scene. "What we don't understand is the cause of death and why their penises were severed."

"Yeah, and what about the stench at the house and in the barn?" John retorted as he leaned across the table. "That odor was nothing like anything I've ever smelled."

"Okay, okay. Slow down," Dr. Brown said, motioning to the detectives to calm down. "I'm no pathologist so I can't help with the cause of death. But as for the severed organs, there's a logical explanation."

Both John and Victor squirmed in their chairs as though they were about to have their masculinity sliced from their bodies.

"In satanic religion, there is a belief that the release of energy, specifically sexual energy, is one way to reach a higher level of consciousness. In other words, invincible power can be gained from the sex organs. Satanists, of course, want anything that can add power to their rituals, so removing the victims' penises is a way for them to have some of that power for themselves."

"Are you saying the cult members keep the sex organs for their own use?" John asked.

Brown exhaled a plume of smoke and then answered, "Well, they could but most likely the organs are given as a sacrifice to the deity they worship."

"Do you mean that these wackos worship some sort of sex god?" John asked with an incredulous stare.

"That's exactly what I mean, detective. Probably the Santeria god, Oshun. Since this god controls sexual energy, the organs were probably given as an offering to it."

"Well, what about animal mutilations? Would these people consider the sex organs of a cow to be an appropriate offering?" Victor asked.

"Sure, a cow would be acceptable, although Oshun would be appeased more by a goat—more specifically, a female goat."

Victor and John made the circumstantial connection between Dr. Brown's comments and the evidence found at the Rimmon farm. Both surmised that the animal hair found under Rimmon's fingernails was linked to the presence of a goat in the barn. Like inseparable twin brothers sharing the same psyche, both men were ready to play their next hunch.

"Can you tell us about any other characteristics that might be unique to this cult?" John asked.

"Yeah, like any symbols that might distinguish them from other sects," Victor joined in.

"Well, they favor yellow necklaces and charms, and they are especially fond of gold. They also like to use cowrie shells to cast and break spells."

"Would a gold amulet inscribed with a goat head be something you would associate with these people?" John asked.

"Oh, definitely. That's something a shaman would normally wear and use for enchantments," the doctor responded and then took another drag on her cigarette.

"Are you talking about a witch doctor that casts spells?" Victor asked.

"Sure. For instance, the witch doctor could cast spells to heal or inflict sickness, or he may want to stir up a little love between two individuals, or maybe a lot of hate. Better yet, if he has a direct pack with the devil, he supposedly has the power to cast a black spell that would cause the death of another person."

"Do you know of any cases where someone has died because of a spell?" John asked.

The doctor grinned and chuckled. "That's an odd question from someone who only believes in scientific explanations but, the fact is, I don't. The only so-called documented cases are the death spells cast by witch doctors among the aboriginals in Papua, New Guinea."

For the next hour, John and Victor continued to question Dr. Brown. Both men surmised that Pierce had sought help from Rimmon for his terminal illness. They suspected that Rimmon had cast some mystical spell in an attempt to excise the tumor from Pierce's body. After that, the evidence indicated that both had, for whatever reason, betrayed the coven and as a result were murdered. Dr. Brown could provide no logical explanation for the cause of death nor the foul odor at the scenes. She did, however, provide them a theory on Pierce and Rimmon that supported the detectives' suspicions.

Dr. Brown spoke as she continued to light one cigarette after another. Her account was straightforward much like her smoking. She explained that to understand the connection between demonism and black magic, one had to understand the Bible and Christianity. With the ease of a seasoned evangelist, she quoted scripture after scripture while relating its meaning to demonology and the events in the murders.

"Pierce and Rimmon," she said, "had attempted a clean deliverance from the cult by renouncing Satan and commanding he and his evil spirits be ousted in the name of Jesus Christ. Afterwards, both had tried to maintain a relationship with God by praying and studying the Word."

John had been calmly listening to Dr. Brown's explanation and taking notes until she began to paraphrase Ephesians 6:10-20...*the believer must use the whole armor of God against the powers of evil.* At that instant, a chill of monumental force hit him, gripping every nerve in his body. The ball-point pen he was holding, fell from his shaky hand and bounced across the table. He remembered reading those same words when he found Rebecca's Bible in the kitchen. His training to rely on logical explanations begged him to dismiss this as another mere coincidence, yet his subconscious beseeched him to seek a more mystical reason. He took several deep breaths, picked up his pen, and chose to accept the voice of reason.

Although John believed that Dr. Brown's quotation was coincidental, he still wanted to ask her why she chose that particular scripture, and more importantly, what it meant. However, he didn't get the chance. Dr. Brown ended the session abruptly. Realizing she was late for a class, she quickly doused her final cigarette, rose from her chair and ended the meeting. Victor asked if a second meeting could be arranged, and Dr. Brown politely agreed.

24

Boo met John at the door and leaped into his outstretched arms. Her pint-sized limbs encircled his neck and waist. Leaning back, she grinned, while her glimmering eyes lingered on his features. He knew she was studying his disposition. *Did Daddy have a good day or a bad day at work?* It was her barometer, her measure of her father's willingness to play games before she retired to bed. He was completely exhausted from the mental and physical rigors of the murder investigations, but his fatigue was overshadowed by the guilt of ignoring his daughter for the past several days. Besides, he had a second date with Lori on Friday which meant he would have to shuttle Boo off to Tina's again.

"Hey, sweetheart. What have you been doing today?" John asked, as he mustered a big smile.

"I've been playin' with Azriel...and....and....Tina and me played school." Boo responded, sensing that her father might be in a playful mood.

"Well, it sounds like you've had a busy day. I bet you're tired from—"

Boo surmised that John was about to cut the evening short, so she quickly interrupted. "But, Daddy, Tina won't play hide n' seek with me. Can we play hide n' seek?" Her mouth curled downward, preparing for dejection. She had learned that the mere threat of tears was usually enough to sway her father around to her way of thinking. This was part of the intellectual expansion of a four-year-old daughter...daddy control.

"Sure, I'll play hide and seek, but not until I eat dinner."

Unable to disguise her pleasure, Boo delivered a high-frequency squeal that would curl the ears on a Doberman.

165

"Hurry up and eat!" Boo exclaimed, baring her baby teeth in a broad grin.

John chuckled softly as he carried her into the kitchen. He was always amused at her delight at being startled. For Boo, the game of hide-and-seek was just that, a game of trepidation. It included him not only concealing his presence, but also him lying in ambush and leaping from a closet or pouncing from behind a couch. The game was a simple way to nurture her vivid imagination while at the same time providing reassurance that she would never be harmed.

John found Tina in the kitchen, standing next to the table. With a large wooden ladle, she was shoveling his evening meal onto a plate. Her repasts were always a culinary adventure. She would oftentimes mix spices and herbs unique to her homeland with American fare. Tina thought American recipes were too bland; they lacked the special punch provided by ingredients such as red crushed peppers and a spicy dose of cumin. John prepared himself to try her latest concoction. It was a fricassee unlike any he had previously eaten. The first bite assaulted his senses, instantly producing a pair of teary eyes and a runny nose.

"Good grief, Tina, this stuff is hot," John blurted as he wiped the beads of sweat and mucus from his upper lip.

Tina quickly spooned a small helping of the spicy meat from the skillet and sampled its flavor.

"It's a new meal I try for you, Mister John. I'm sorry you don't like," Tina said, in a disheartened voice.

John saw Tina's dark eyes well with tears. Her value to the Williams family was far more important than him having to endure a saucy, three alarm supper.

"No, no, Tina, I mean it's hot, you know good hot. It tastes really good."

Tina's frown was promptly recast as a smile as she approached the table with skillet in hand. "I'm glad you like it,

Mister John," she said, as she spooned an extra helping on his plate.

Tina stood close by, watching John until he had consumed the very last bite. John wondered if this was her way of getting even. The thought that she might be vindictive, however, was dismissed as the heat from the peppers finally left his mouth. He knew that this caring woman didn't have a vengeful bone in her body. Eating a spicy meal was a small price to pay for the loyalty and care she provided, a very small price. Besides, her motive for waiting became clear as she waved a cheese covered ladle in Boo's direction.

"Boo, would you go up to your room and play for jest a little bit. I need to speak to your father," Tina said, her voice thick with tension.

Boo reluctantly rose from the chair. She had been patiently waiting on her father and was miffed at having to postpone the game.

"Daddy, I don't want to go to my room. I want to play now," Boo retorted.

"Go on up, sweetheart, I'll be up in a few minutes," John said.

"No, I want to play hide n' seek now," she said with an air of defiance.

A little bribery was now in order. "Listen, sweetheart, if you'll go on up now, I'll let you hide first, and I'll read you a story when you go to bed." The bribe worked. Without hesitation, Boo gathered Azriel from the floor and scampered up the stairs.

John turned back toward Tina and observed a softening around her eyes as she sat down at the table beside him. Her light, round face had a very concerned appearance as though she were the bearer of bad tidings. At first, he thought she was going to tender her resignation, a notion that made him shudder with anxiety. She was, simply, irreplaceable, as far as he was concerned.

"Mister John, there's something I need to tell you," she said, wrenching her hands.

"Don't tell me you're quitting. Boo loves you and I really didn't mean anything when I said the food was hot, really. I enjoyed every bite of—"

Tina interrupted John by shaking her head and reaching across the table, patting his hands in a gesture of reassurance.

"Oh no, it's nothing like that. It's about Boo. She has been telling me stories about her mother, that's why I worry."

"About Rebecca? What kind of stories?"

"She say that her momma comes to visit her every night when she is in bed."

"Oh, jeepers, Tina, she told me that same story last week. Heck, it's just her imagination, that's all, just her imagination." John answered, attempting to dismiss her fears.

"No, I don't think so. She tell me all about her momma. What clothes she wearing. What she look like. What she say. It scares me, Mister John."

John squeezed Tina's hand in an attempt to allay her fears. "Tina, she has seen a lot of pictures of her mother. She can describe her looks or clothes from those pictures. Believe me, it's nothing to worry about. Just a child's vivid imagination."

"But she say her momma tell her that we are in trouble, in danger. That bad people will try to hurt us. Why would she make up something like that?"

"I'll talk with her about all of this. But you don't worry. She's just having a little trouble distinguishing the difference between fantasy and reality. She either made this up or she's just having some bad dreams," John replied with authority.

Grudgingly, Tina accepted his explanation. However, just to be sure, John continued to preach his account of why Boo had brewed up such a farfetched story while Tina washed the last of the dirty dishes. His insistence on restating his interpretation of the events seemed to be more for his benefit than hers. Finally, he felt a little more at ease as he escorted her out the front door and watched her big Buick back out of the driveway. Before leaving, she agreed to keep Boo on Friday night, so the plans he had made with Lori were secure, although his mind was on anything but his upcoming date.

Like an unwanted inhabitant, the thought that Boo may have actually seen her mother refused to vacate his mind. His sanity kept demanding a sapient explanation which meant it was only a dream, much like the dreams he experienced right after Rebecca's death. For months he had often viewed her in his sleep. Standing before him, she exhibited the same troubled facial expression each night. She always wore the same royal blue dress, and she always held out her hands.

It was as though she was clinging to his world, and she had refused to forsake their love by accepting the hand of death. Boo was merely undergoing a delayed version of his own life-like visions. At the time of her mother's death, she didn't have the intellectual development to grasp what had happened. Soon to be five years in age, she had begun to understand and react to the reality that she didn't have a mother, so a make-believe mom would have to do.

John crossed the den and walked up the stairs. As he reached the doorway to Boo's bedroom he was startled by a hair-raising scream. Boo had been hiding in the hallway closet, patiently waiting on her father to walk by. Leaping from her hiding place, she grabbed his trousers and released an earsplitting scream of excitement. "Gotcha!"

Swallowing hard, he forced his heart out of his throat and lifted her off the floor. "You little imp," John cried out with laughter. "You scared me to death."

"Put me down, Daddy," she yelped, still burning with desire to play the game. "Go downstairs and count to a hundred. Then come find me. Go downstairs," she demanded, squirming to free herself from his hold.

He returned to the kitchen and waited. His thoughts were still consumed by the supposition that Boo may have seen her mother. It was a ghostly concept for a storybook, but in real-life, it simply didn't wash. Again, he allowed explanations to pass through his mind, and in an orderly fashion he rejected all but the most logical ones...just a dream or her imagination. Finally, he concluded that it was simply a child's invention. He reasoned that this was her defense when she felt lonely. He also remembered Rebecca referring to children, who contrived imaginary companions as gifted and creative. And in his mind, Boo certainly fell in that category. Case closed.

Returning upstairs, he began the search for his hidden daughter. He explored his bedroom in the darkness, but was unable to locate her hiding place. Moving through the deep shadows, he entered Boo's bedroom, knowing that it was her favorite retreat. Looking from left to right, his eyes finally rested on the closet door. Keenly aware of her tendency to select closets as hideaways, he slowly opened the door anticipating her bolting from the obscurity.

"Okay, Boo, I've found you. You can come out now." John said, as he peered into the darkness. From within, there was no movement, nor was there a whisper of a sound. Yet he sensed her presence. Clumsily, he felt for the light switch thinking the illumination would expose her hiding in the corner. His search for the switch, however, was adverted by his attention to the sounds from above. It was the scratching and clawing of the troublesome squirrels in the attic. He intently listened while the pesky critters began to bark as though they were delivering a warning signal of impending danger.

Suddenly, he heard three loud sounds from the attic which could not have been caused by the squirrels. A thump. A clop. A thump. The noise was followed by an increase in the cadence of the squirrels' barking.

John became more concerned. But in a flash, his concentration was broken as he felt a pair of small hands grab his lower legs.

"Gotcha!" Boo screamed as she jumped up and down in delight.

"Jeez!" John shrieked as a shot of electric current charged through his forehead. "You scared the daylights out of me." For a few seconds he felt unable to think clearly, as though his faculties had been zapped by lightning. He strained to listen for any more bizarre sounds as Boo tugged at his trousers.

"I was hidin' under the bed, Daddy. You thought I was in the closet, but I was under the bed."

"Yeah, you really fooled me, sweetheart. I would have never found you under there," John replied as he heard another loud thump and a clop from above.

"Listen, baby, I need to go up in the attic and check to see what the squirrels are into. I want you to put on your pajamas and get ready for bed. I'll be back in a few minutes."

"I don't want to go to bed. I want to play some more," Boo retorted as she displayed her most pitiful expression.

John had not bothered to look down as he continued to audit the sounds from above. Intent on investigating the attic, he again resorted to bribery.

"Look, baby, if you'll get ready for bed, I'll read you two bedtime stories. Okay?"

Boo stood motionless, contemplating the new offer. To forfeit a game of hide n' seek for two bedtime stories was a decision of monumental importance for a budding little girl. The stillness was finally broken as she delivered her verdict.

"Okay, Daddy, I'll go to bed," she answered, knowing the odds of playing another game of hide n' seek were slim or none anyway.

Twenty minutes later, Boo heard her father's footsteps descending the attic's collapsible ladder. His exploration above had been fruitless, even the squirrels had left. John found Boo in bed trying hard to resist the drowsiness that tugged at her eyes. Recognizing her lackadaisical mood, he only read one brief story, and then stroked her hair with a singular tenderness that can only come from a father's loving hand. Words of endearment had always been difficult for him to voice, even with Rebecca, so his feelings of love were often expressed by a caring touch or a delicate kiss. Boo, just like Rebecca, knew of his love and welcomed his unspoken caresses. He watched as she fell to sleep, then he listened to her rhythmic breathing. After he kissed her forehead, he turned off the light and left the room.

Hours later, John fell asleep still listening for sounds from the attic. He was annoyed at not discovering the source. The fact that he had not questioned Boo about the stories she had told Tina had left him off balance as well. But the main cause of his insomnia was the intuition of a veteran cop—an eerie feeling that he was being watched.

25

It was an unproductive morning at the office. Forensic science had come a long way since the day of Jack the Ripper, yet John and Victor had uncovered no new leads in the investigation. Even the quick-witted Charlie Connors, with the assistance of the crime lab had come up empty. There were no fingerprints, no bloodstains, no weapons, no fibers, nothing other than the unusual animal hair. There was simply nothing to tag, test, match, or identify. The crime scene and the condition of the victims were more an omen of the psychosis of the assassin rather than a source of physical evidence.

All that was left was conjecture. Was the murderer a serial killer, a cult member seeking revenge, or merely a sexually deranged individual with a well-defined motive for killing? Victor and John decided to retrace their steps. That afternoon they returned to the Rimmon farm, and again scoured the barn and surrounding grounds. Finding no new evidence, the men decided to call it a day. Both agreed that a follow-up meeting with Dr. Brown on Monday would be their best option.

Few words were spoken as Victor maneuvered in and out of the Friday afternoon traffic. The mystery behind the murders seemed to leave them speechless. Besides, John's thoughts were off duty as he daydreamed about Lori and their approaching date. His enchantment with her beauty and charm was a disquieting feeling. He could only reason that his infatuation was one of captivation, a curious desire that had been locked away in a far corner of his mind.

This hunger was suppressed during his years of marriage, possibly due to the strong need to be a good provider and father. But deep inside, John knew that it had nothing to do with being a husband or father. It had everything to do with Lori. She was so different from Rebecca. Her hair was dark, in stark contrast to Rebecca's flaxen tresses. The dissimilarities continued with Lori's perfect figure and flawless features. Rebecca was more often described as pretty with a cute body than beautiful with a brickhouse build. For John, Rebecca provided the constancy of a loving wife while Lori was the flight of fantasy he could only make up in his imagination. For now, his fanciful creation was real.

26

John felt uneasy as he walked past the tall, white columns. His sense of being out-of-place continued as he and Lori entered the stately home of Reed and Polly Garrett. Attending a party given by Atlanta's upper crust was not his idea of a fun evening, yet Lori had insisted that they make an appearance. As they walked through the huge-marbled foyer, he was taken aback by the lavishness of this Tara-like abode. The mansion was filled with French furniture, spiral stairs and crystal chandeliers.

John's initial thought of making himself invisible by melding into the crowd quickly dissipated as he realized it was a select gathering of intimate friends. Somehow, he would have to find a way to fit in and bandy words with this elite group of blue bloods. He could hear the murmur of conversations as Reed guided them down a long hallway that emptied into a large, elegant room. The voices hushed as the threesome walked through the doorway into the chamber.

However, the stillness was quickly broken as Reed delivered the formal presentation of John and Lori to the small group. His words were well chosen and proper, as though he were introducing a king and queen instead of two everyday mortals. This stuffy announcement made John even more uncomfortable than before. After the initial courtesies were finished, Lori ushered John to each of the individual guests for a more personal introduction. To John, the members of this social clique seemed flawless in their appearance and demeanor. The women were adorned with glimmering jewelry and beautiful dresses that displayed the polish, breeding, and money that came with their state of affairs. The men were refined, bearing the personalities of smooth politicians, always ready with a witty quip to spice up the conversation.

After about an hour into the evening, John had all but forgotten his apprehension and was beginning to relax among the guests. But when Reed returned with a second round of drinks and an arsenal of questions, his anxiety returned.

"So, John, Lori told me that the two of you met during a brawl at one of Atlanta's finer drinking establishments. That had to be quite an encounter," Reed remarked with an inquisitive stare, as though he were laying the groundwork for a follow-up question.

"Well, I must admit, it was out of the ordinary," John responded, turning to smile at Lori.

"Were you at the club on police business?" Garrett asked, "You are a police officer, aren't you?"

"Actually, I'm a homicide detective. And yes, I was on duty when I was at the club."

Without hesitation, Reed quickly continued the cross examination. "Was someone at the club a suspect in the Pierce homicide? I read about the murder in the news."

"I really can't talk about the case. It's still under investigation," John replied with the usual police protocol, yet he was intrigued by Garrett's keen interest in him, and his curiosity regarding the Pierce case. "Did you know Richard Pierce?" John asked, looking squarely into Garrett's eyes.

In an instant, the smooth refinement was replaced by a nervous, uncouth jitter as Reed answered the question. "Oh, no, I didn't know the man. Like I said, I just read about the murder in the newspaper and thought you might be handling the case. Are you in charge of the investigation?"

"Well, as a matter of fact, I am," John answered.

"How about the Rimmon murder? I read about that one in this morning's paper. Are you in charge of that investigation too?" Reed asked.

Before John answered, he paused and watched Reed nervously lick his lips. Garrett's left eye also began to twitch, broadcasting yet another signal that he was anxious about the conversation. "Tell me, Reed, why are you so interested in these murders? Do you know something about these cases?"

Fortunately for Reed, Polly Garrett arrived before he could answer. "Reed, leave John alone. I'm sure he has better things to do than discuss your fascination with the morbid murders that happen around this city. Anyway, Harvey Longstreet has agreed to entertain us with some of his magic."

Without hesitating, Polly grabbed John and Lori by their arms and accompanied them into an adjacent sitting room. The other guests were seated in a semi-circle around Harvey who was standing behind a wing chair in the middle of the room. As John stood with Lori behind the row of guests, he was unable to clear his mind of his suspicion of Reed. A good cop always plays his hunches, and intuition told him that Reed's interest in the murders was more than a mere fascination with death. Besides, he had uncovered stranger connections than this one over his years of police work. His deliberations continued until the voice of Longstreet snapped him from his presumptive thoughts.

"Okay, I need a volunteer. Who wants to be first?" Longstreet asked as he glanced from right to left, seeking to cull out an easy mark.

John was unaware that Longstreet was a practicing psychologist who used hypnotism as a means to treat many of his misaligned patients. Any cocktail party at the Garrett house usually included a session where Longstreet would place an unsuspecting person into a trance hoping to entertain the other guests. Everyone watched as an elderly woman volunteered to be the first subject. Longstreet was calm and unhurried as he instructed her to relax and clear her mind in preparation for the spell.

To John, Longstreet had the profile of a typical shrink. The doctor was short in stature at five feet, five inches in height. At fifty pounds overweight, he obviously was a non-believer in the body being a temple. His face was covered by a graying beard that hid a swollen complexion, red from too much rich food and booze. He should have practiced what he preached, for a few sessions of self-hypnosis could have helped him curb his overeating and excessive drinking.

Longstreet had some unusual characteristics, but his most noticeable trait was his soft rhythmic voice. His words flowed in smooth succession from his lips producing the serene vibration of a dulcet song. In a matter of minutes, he had coaxed the woman into a hypnotic state. This was no vaudeville act where some side-show Svengali transforms a stand-in stooge into a clucking chicken. Instead, Longstreet merely suggested that the woman was unable to lift her arm due to its enormous weight, and lo and behold, it worked. No matter how hard she struggled, she could barely lift her arm an inch above her lap. John snickered at the antics until Longstreet questioned the matron about the pain she had been experiencing.

In an instant, he recognized the signature of the deadly disease. It was the same plague that robbed Rebecca of her own beauty and youthfulness. All of the omens were there. The wig and the sunken checks spoke volumes. The blight of leukemia and the devastation of chemotherapy had stolen her radiant hair and elegant face. It had given this forty-year-old woman the appearance of a grandmother. John's silent laughter ended.

All the painful memories had returned; his throat ached from the emotion. He even felt the onset of a measure of sadness until he caught a bird's eye view of the peculiar necklace the woman was wearing. The chain of gold held a trinket he had observed once before. It was identical to the amulet he and Victor had found at Rimmon's office. It brandished the same goat's head positioned inside an inverted pentagram. John was so deep in thought about the coincidence, he hadn't noticed that Lori had volunteered him to be the good doctor's next victim. He quickly awoke, however, when he heard Longstreet call his name.

"John, you look like you've seen a ghost. Come on over and have a seat. Relax." Longstreet curled his fingers in-and-out, gesturing John to comply with his request.

John attempted to resist, but Lori urged him to move forward by pushing him toward the chair.

"Oh, no, not me. Get someone else." John insisted.

"Come on, John. It won't hurt, I promise. If I do anything to hurt or embarrass you, you can pull your police revolver and shoot me," Longstreet quipped as he rolled his eyes in a make-believe gesture of fear.

John was bedeviled as to why everyone knew his occupation. He could also smell a rat and this affair had all the makings of a set-up. A little voice inside his head begged him to walk away, yet his thirst to learn more about these individuals implored him to go along with the escapade. Reluctantly, he moved to the chair and took a seat.

"Okay, Harvey, I'll be your guinea pig. But I think you're wasting your time trying to hypnotize me. I don't believe in all this hocus-pocus stuff," John said.

"Of course, you don't. You're a police officer. If you can't tag or fingerprint it, then to you, it simply doesn't exist. But let me explain something to you about hypnotism."

Longstreet launched into his brief dissertation explaining that the hypnotic state was a condition similar to sleep, yet more of a dream-like state. He expounded that hypnosis was simply a condition where a person partially withdraws from reality by allowing themselves to be receptive to suggestions. The hypnotist merely asked his subject to allow a suggestion to go to the subconscious without the conscious mind first applying logic and reasoning. Longstreet went on to explain that a subject would not do anything that he or she didn't want to do, and that a subject would never do anything against their moral principles.

John had dismissed most of Longstreet's lecture until the doctor concluded his discourse by saying that the more imaginative and intelligent a person, the easier they are to hypnotize. This reverse psychology placed John in a position of appearing ignorant and shallow if he failed to free his mind and accept Longstreet's suggestions.

"Okay, John, just sit back, relax, and try to free your mind of any conscious thoughts. I want you to concentrate on the coin and listen to my voice."

Longstreet held the whirling coin within inches of John's eyes and, again, asked him to remain calm.

"I'm going to count to twenty. As I'm counting, your eye lids will become heavy and they will slowly close. By the time I reach twenty, you'll be completely relaxed."

As John studied the spinning disk and listened to Longstreet's soft voice, he unexpectedly found himself falling into a peaceful languor. Initially it was a feeling akin to falling asleep at the wheel of a car while listening to soft music on the radio. But then, slowly, he began to drift backward through time on an amazing journey that had unhinged him from the present. The first image he beheld was a vision of Rebecca on the day Boo was born. Then his dreams revealed two of his foster parents bathed in a heavenly light. After he caught a brief moment of two individuals who were complete strangers, all the faces began spinning by in rapid succession like a movie on fast forward.

There was a measure of surprise in Longstreet's voice; he did not expect John to be such a receptive subject. Within a moment, however, he had regained his tongue and began to ask an array of subliminal questions.

"John, this is Harvey. Can you hear me?

"Yes, I can," John answered.

"Are you okay?"

"Yes, I'm fine."

"Can I do anything to make you more comfortable? Would you like a drink?" Longstreet asked, noticing that John's eyelids were fluttering in violent spasms.

Suddenly, John's body began to shudder, then it stopped, and then it began again. A few seconds later when the trembling ended, his face became waxen as though the nip of a wintry breeze had frozen his features. Longstreet assured the guests that nothing was wrong and then squared himself in front of John's face to take a closer look. Before he could complete the examination, John's back stiffened as his voice exploded with the answer to Longstreet's question.

"DA MICHI SIS CEREVISIAM DILUTAM!"

Longstreet was sent reeling backward from the blast of John's delivery. He was even more startled by the pitch of John's voice. It was an octave lower than his normal tone. Longstreet turned to reassure the guests that this reaction was not out of the ordinary, but he was lying. He knew John was having a rare hetero-hypnotic experience.

"Why is he shaking?" Lori asked with a look of concern.

Before Longstreet could respond, Polly Garrett fired a second question. "And why is he talking that way? It sounds like Italian."

"Actually, it's Latin. He just asked for a light beer in Latin," Longstreet said with a knowing smile. "John may be having some type of recall. I've had several patients under hypnosis that shook like that when they remembered a present-life experience, and I've even had one woman who had recall of a former-life."

"I think you should bring him out of this right now," Polly retorted.

"Believe me, there's no cause for alarm. The moment I think he's in any trouble, I'll snap him out of it. In the meantime, let's see where this takes us."

Longstreet was able to cajole John into an even deeper sleep which brought about another seizure. This time his trembling became more violent and lasted longer than the first episode. When the attack finally ended, Longstreet attempted to calm John down.

"John, listen to me. You're completely relaxed. You're feeling very peaceful and still. You feel like you're weightless, like you're floating through time."

Longstreet was talking to the wind, for John could hear none of his words. He was already on a journey, drifting back in time. He was experiencing the same sensations he felt when he stopped at Pickett's Mill. This time, however, he had traversed to a period long before the Civil War—the epoch was 1000 B.C. John was there, he could see the glimmering blue sky and hear the wind whistling in his ears, yet he could not find his physical being. He was a voyeur in another time, but he was a voyeur that recognized the time, the land and the people. He could see it clearly.

The Philistine army held a position on a slope along the western side of the Valley of Elah, while the Israelites were strategically located on the eastern side of that same valley. Both camps watched as a giant clad in armor made of wood and strapping leather, swaggered down to the valley. John carefully listened as the champion of the Philistines issued his formidable challenge. With defiance, the giant invited the Israelites to choose their champion to fight with him until death. The prize for the winner and his people was to assume a master's role, while the defeated troops would serve as slaves to the reigning army. The Israelites stood motionless.

To accept the challenge would mean sure death, yet John could feel himself move forward.

The sea of men parted, allowing him to walk past them, down the green valley toward the giant. As he approached, he noticed a servant bearing a huge, dense shield standing beside the great warrior. With indignation, the ten-foot titan brushed aside the smallish servant. The giant had seen John approaching and was angry that the Israelites would send such a puny combatant armed only with a staff and a sling. He would not need the protection of an armored shield to dispatch such an unworthy opponent. One mighty blow of his broad sword would quickly end the confrontation.

John felt himself stop short of the reach of the giant's sword. At this safe distance, he was able to survey all of the gaudy brass and iron in an effort to find a vulnerable target. The giant's unprotected face provided the clear mark. The giant spewed insults as he raised his weapon in preparation to move within striking distance of John. But before he could take one step, John placed a smooth, round stone into his sling, and with the precise skill of an expert marksman, released the rock toward the giant's bearded face. With the accuracy of a bullet, the stone whizzed through the air until it struck the giant's exposed forehead. A sickening sound pierced the air. Seconds later, the Philistine fell to the ground. John seized the giant's heavy sword and raised the weapon to sever the head while declaring his allegiance to the One that gave him his courage.

"I AM 'EBED YHWH. I AM THE LORD'S SERV-ANT." John roared with excitement raising his arm to strike a blow. But before he could smite the fallen giant, a scream woke him from the trance.

"John! Wake up!" Longstreet shouted as he shook him.

John's eyelids slowly opened revealing a glaze of disunion. His right arm continued to move up and down as though he was beheading the titan.

"John! Dammit, snap out of it," Longstreet panicked as he attempted to restrain John's chopping right arm.

"I am 'ebed yhwh." John repeated his declaration of loyalty, but this time it was spoken softly, in his own voice. "I am 'ebed yhwh."

The glassiness slowly left John's eyes as he collapsed back on the chair. He was as out of breath and as exhausted as a tired boxer after a twelve-round bout. The circle of guests that surrounded him expelled a simultaneous sigh of relief as they watched him regain his senses. Within seconds, he had returned to his former state of consciousness. But now, his feelings were a mixture of confusion, anxiety, and embarrassment. Not wanting to engage in a question-and-answer session with the guests, he sprang from the chair and quickly found Lori.

He brushed aside Longstreet and the others as he pulled Lori toward the front door. Longstreet followed, begging him to return. He ignored the doctor's pleas as he burst out the door, pulling Lori down the walkway to his car. Lori pleaded for him to at least say goodbye to the Garretts. He refused. A return to the house would mean an explanation as to what he had experienced. He could not explain something he did not understand. Besides, given his suspicion of Reed Garrett and the other guests, he wasn't sure he wanted them to know about the incredible vision he had just seen.

27

John stared through the office window as Monday's rush hour traffic crept along at the usual snail's pace. He was at the university waiting for Victor and Susan Brown. His thoughts were centered on the past few days; his psyche was still in an upheaval. It had been a restless weekend for a number of reasons. Lori had yet to forgive him for his unexpected departure from the Garrett's party. They had even argued over what she described as his childish behavior. His treatment of her friends angered her, but she was not so miffed that it cooled the enthusiasm of their love making. No, in that land of passion they kept surprising each other by reaching a new and more intense zenith each time they became as one. But their sexual encounters provided only a brief respite from his preoccupation with his visions and the murders.

Victor and Dr. Brown abruptly interrupted John's unsettled musings. With arms loaded with books, Dr. Brown struggled to dig the office key from her backpack. John grabbed some of the textbooks and passed the extras to Victor and she unlocked the office door. The workplace was homey, but with a touch of clutter. It was a reflection of Dr. Brown's informal, easy-going style.

"I've got a class at nine, so let's get started," Dr. Brown said, as she opened a spiral bound notebook "Any new evidence in your cases since we last met?"

Victor shook his head. "No. We went back to the Rimmon farm after the last time we got together but didn't come up with any new leads."

Dr. Brown took a deep drag on her cigarette and blew a cloud of smoke upward in the air. She then flicked the ashes into the tray and immediately closed the cover on her notebook. "Well, then I really don't think I can tell you anything else."

The murders aside, John did not want to miss the opportunity to ask Dr. Brown about the odd things that had happened to him since the investigation began, but he feared Victor would think him insane. He'd need to finesse the maneuver.

"Dr. Brown, you quoted a Bible scripture when we saw you last. It had something to do with using the armor of God against evil. Do you remember the scripture?" John asked.

"Yes. I believe you are referring to several verses I quoted from Ephesians."

"Do you think these verses have some special meaning to do with these murders?" John asked.

Dr. Brown dabbed her cigarette stub in the tray, extinguishing the flame. She then looked squarely into John's eyes. "Tell me, John, do you believe in God?"

Before John could answer, Victor joined in with a matter-of-fact response, "Of course, we do."

Brown never turned away from John, "I'm asking John the question, not you Victor."

"Yes. I believe there is a supreme being," John pronounced with an air of certainty.

"Do you believe there is a devil?" Brown asked while lighting another cigarette.

"I'm not too sure about that," John replied.

"Well, John, given your profession, you of all people should know that there is good and there is evil. And if you truly believe there is a God, no matter what form, then why do you find it so hard to believe that there is a devil?"

"I do believe that there are a lot of bad people out there. I just have a hard time accepting the existence of some so-called Prince of Darkness," John answered.

"Well, your attitude is exactly what the devil wants—to be thought of as a figment of our imagination. It's the perfect disguise. It allows him to oppose everything God stands for in a way that doesn't bring attention to his role."

"But what about the Bible verses? What does all of this have to do with these murders?"

"No being is cleverer at manipulating people than Satan. And I think that's exactly what's happening in these murders. The members of this coven are being controlled by evil. In order to solve these murders, you must understand the role of the devil and God's role. You shouldn't be afraid to look to God for answers. That's what I was referring to when I quoted the verses; you have to look beyond the physical evidence."

Unable to refrain from joining the conversation, Victor immediately chimed in, "You mean to tell me that we should be looking for a dude with horns and a pointed tail?"

Dr. Brown chuckled as she exhaled a column of smoke. "Well, there you have it. Victor, didn't you hear me say that Satan is very wily, that if we think of him as a comic character with horns and a tail, he can do little harm other than an infrequent nightmare? His shroud is much more cunning than that. According to the Bible, the whole world lies in the power of Satan. That means he hides behind everything—government, education, religion, music, our ability to reason—everything."

"So, what are we supposed to do? If we can't see, hear, or touch this evil—if it's not physical—how do we find it?" Victor asked.

"I didn't say that it couldn't be in some physical form. In the Garden of Eden, the devil was in the form of a serpent, but not in the form of a snake, as we would normally think. In original Hebrew, serpent meant something shining and beautiful, similar in meaning to Lucifer. At that time, the

187

serpent walked on legs and he was referred to as the beast of the field. So then, as now, Satan and his angels may be able to take on many forms, as well as possess existing forms such as man."

"Hell, I didn't know that Satan had any angels. I thought angels only came from Heaven," Victor said in disbelief.

"Well, in this case, hell is the operative word," Brown replied. "The Bible tells us that Satan was once a very powerful angel. He was known as Lucifer, which meant the light bringer. But he got caught up in his own power and beauty and became twisted and impure. He was jealous of God's power, so, he led one third of the angels in a rebellion against God."

"So, what happened then?" Victor asked.

"Well, like I said, hell is the operative word. The revolt was repelled. Lucifer became Satan. His band of angels became demons, and they were all cast from Heaven to you know where."

"So, you're saying that the devil could be on Earth, disguised as a person, and that these murders may have been committed by Satan?" Victor asked.

"Quite possibly by Satan, but more likely by one of Satan's demons such as Oshun or by someone who is being manipulated by Oshun," Dr. Brown replied. "For some reason, Satan must feel that he can effectively corrupt certain individuals by using Oshun. All of your evidence points in this direction."

"I'm still having a hard time imagining me and John slapping the handcuffs on the devil," Victor cracked a cynical smile.

Dr. Brown appeared annoyed by Victor's response. "Well, I wouldn't feel too macho if I were you, Victor. God promised that the seed of woman would ultimately conquer Satan, not the seed of man. So, you may want to keep your handgun holstered for now."

"I didn't mean any disrespect. I was just kidding," he apologized.

"Look, if you aren't going to take this seriously, I'm not going to discuss it anymore. Just keep this in mind. When God asked Satan from where he came, Satan replied, 'From going to and fro on the earth, and from walking up and down on it.' So, he's here all right; he's here with his demons watching you and me and everybody else. And he's waiting on his chance to spread his energy," Brown said. Her voice was edgy, and her eyes darted about as though she could feel the presence of some forbidden power in the room. She quickly rose from her chair signaling the end of the meeting. It was almost time for her first class. John stood up at the same time and leaned over the desk.

"Can I speak with you alone, just for a few minutes?" John then turned back toward Victor, giving him a knowing stare in an effort to coax him out of the office. Dr. Brown glanced at her watch and reluctantly agreed.

After Victor departed, John gave her a brief summary of the flashbacks he had experienced at Pickett's Mill and at the Garretts'. He even detailed the mysterious appearance of Rebecca's Bible and the bizarre fact that the pages were turned to the scripture Dr. Brown had quoted at their first meeting. He told her everything, including Boo's insistence that Rebecca had visited her at night. When he finished his story, he could see that Dr. Brown was deeply moved. However, the softness in her face quickly gave way to a look of hard concern.

"Remember when I said that Satan had convinced one-third of God's angels to rebel?" Dr. Brown asked.

"Yes, I do."

"Well then, needless to say, two-thirds of the angels remained with God. And I believe that depending on your faith, when you die you either ascend to Heaven to join God's angels or you are cast to Hell to become one of Satan's. And, as I said before, I believe that all of us are being watched by both the heavenly angels of God and the fallen angels of Satan. Now, to some that may sound fantastical, but I think that is what's happening to you, but on a much more personal level."

"I'm not sure I understand."

"John, I believe you and Boo may be in danger and Rebecca is trying to warn you." Dr. Brown watched as doubt gathered on John's face.

"I'm having trouble accepting that line of reasoning, Dr. Brown. I'm trying to be open minded about this, but it's hard."

"I can see that, and it's exactly why Rebecca is visiting your daughter. It's Boo's innocence. She is willing to accept her mother as being real, and Rebecca knows this. Rebecca also knows you are too pragmatic to believe this, so she is trying to communicate with you through Boo."

Dr. Brown's voice brought a sense of reason to John's situation, yet her explanation of the events was still difficult for him to accept. Before she left, she scribbled a name and phone number on a piece of paper and handed it to John. It was a psychologist that Dr. Brown hoped would help him fathom his predicament. Dr. Brown squeezed John's hand reassuringly, told him she would pray for him and Boo, and then she left him standing outside her office.

28

The notion that police work is inherently dangerous to one's spirit was never more evident than on this early Tuesday morning. If a murder scene was a signature of the person who did it, then this individual was the epitome of evil. The Pierce and Rimmon murder investigations had been frustrating for John and Victor, yet, this new turn of events made it maddening.

Clothed only in his briefs, Sugar Bear's strapping body appeared mangled and bloated. He lied face down on the kitchen floor in a huge pool of drying blood. He hadn't gone down easy. The trail of blood in the apartment weaved from room to room, finding itself on the floor, walls and furniture. Both detectives tiptoed around the red ooze in an effort not to disturb the evidence.

Victor surveyed the personnel in the room and immediately took charge. "Who found the body?" he asked a uniformed officer standing to the right of the cadaver.

The officer cupped his hand over his nostrils to filter the room's oppressive scent. "The next-door neighbor. She smelled the odor and reported it to the station," the uniform replied in a muffled voice.

"Is Charlie Connors here yet?" John asked as he gazed around the room with a blank stare.

"Yeah, he's in the bedroom," the young officer answered.

John seemed unable to focus on anything but the corpse. Make no mistake, there was no love lost between the detectives and Sugar Bear, yet John still felt a tinge of sorrow mixed with bewilderment. He wondered if the Bear had repented and now belonged to God's band of angels or if he had shunned salvation and was enlisted in Satan's corps. It was something he might never know.

"Get him in here now," John commanded, now back to business. "And somebody round up the neighbor. We need to question her and the other residents in the building."

The uniform left the room and returned with the weary medical examiner. Connors looked dog-tired. Given the heavy hours he had worked over the past two weeks, it was understandable. Yet his physical exhaustion had not diminished his energy to understand what had taken place in the apartment. He still craved the answers to the mystery.

"Damnedest thing I've ever seen," Connors said as his eyes shifted left and right, viewing the blood splattered kitchen cabinets.

"You got any lab boys here?" John asked.

Connors nodded. "Yeah, I've got two technicians in the bedroom collecting blood samples. It's going to take a while to sort through this mess."

"How about fingerprints?" Victor asked.

"They finished dusting about twenty minutes ago," Connors replied.

"Any latents?" Victor continued.

"Lots of 'em. Problem is they probably all belong to our dead friend here," Connors answered, bending down for a closer inspection of the corpse. "Although, I did find something I think the two of you would be interested in."

"Let me guess. You found the murder weapon," John said, knowing the odds of finding the real weapon at the scene were a million to one.

"Not hardly. But take a close look at his back." Connors motioned.

"Yeah, it's big, hairy, and punched full of holes," John continued his nervous sarcasm.

"Look closer," Connors replied.

192

"I see it," Victor said with an air of excitement.

"There's some loose hair around the wounds, and it doesn't belong to our dead compadre here."

"That's right. It looks like the same type hair we found under Rimmon's fingernails," Connors said.

"You mean the goat hair?" Victor continued.

"We never determined if it was goat hair for sure. Just that it had characteristics of hair from the Bovidae family, of which goats just happen to belong," Connors answered.

John was unstrung. The fact that Victor noticed the hair first simply added to his vexation. "Well, we won't know that for sure until it's tested in the lab!" John snapped. "Besides, I don't remember seeing any goats inside or outside this building. So, let's just concentrate on identifying the real suspect, not some farm animal."

"Damn, John. You pissed off about something? You've been awfully edgy since we got here," Victor noticed.

"No, I'm not pissed off. I just want to get on with this investigation."

John could sense a strangeness about the apartment even though everyone else was treating the murder as your basic run-of-the mill homicide—everyone except Connors. With painstaking care, he brushed the portable vacuum up and down Sugar Bear's decaying back, attempting to collect any trace materials that may have been left. At the same time, he took mental notes of the unusual wounds. The large red patches of trauma around the lacerations were uncharacteristic of your typical stab wounds. It was as though the jagged instrument that inflected the damage was coated with a deadly poison. Connors switched off the vacuum and filled the detectives in on what he thought happened to Sugar Bear.

"In all my years of viewing stiffs, I've never seen anything like this," Connors said as he placed the vacuum back in the black case.

"So, what about these wounds?" Victor asked.

Connors pointed to the oozing U-shaped lacerations on Sugar Bear's shoulders. "Look at these wounds and how they are connected. Then tell me what's odd about them."

Both John and Victor leaned forward to study the discolored tissue.

"If I didn't know better, I'd say they looked like bite wounds," John said in a much more studied voice.

"I'd agree, except the puncture holes are not your typical set of molars. They are too narrow and deep. It looks more like they were caused by the sharp edge of a steel trap, not by human or animal teeth," Connors replied, pulling apart the torn flesh to demonstrate his point.

"Damn, that's nasty," John drew back in disgust.

"Let's take a look at his front side. Can we roll him over now?" Victor asked Connors.

"Yeah, I'm finished with his back," Connors answered.

It took the heave of all three men to roll Sugar Bear over on his backside. If they had an inkling of what had been hidden, they may have foregone the effort. For none of the men were prepared for what they were about to see. Instead, they found a new look into evil, a visage of horror that stunned even these seasoned veterans. They seemed to gasp in unison as they caught their first glimpse of Sugar Bear's disfigured face and battered torso. The nose that John had broken at The Foxes' Den was now nearly severed. It hung only by a thin thread of skin. His waxy eyes bugged from their sockets with a wild look of fear. And below, a mutilated tongue protruded between his yellow, jagged teeth. The fleshy organ had been bitten in two. His neck, chest, arms, and hands exhibited a morbid mixture of contusions and gashes while his heavy beard was caked with curing blood. He looked like some enormous alien, an extraterrestrial that accidentally ran into a buzz saw.

John swallowed hard, attempting to hold down his morning meal. "Damn, someone really did a number on him."

"Yeah, but not without one helluva fight," Connors said. "Look at the bruises and cuts on his hands, arms, and chest. These injuries hint of an upright struggle. This guy was in a battle for his life and he knew it. Hell, just look around this apartment. By the blood trail, it looks like the fight began in the bedroom, moved to the den, and ended in the kitchen. It had to be vicious, and my guess is he was fighting someone he knew."

"Why do you say that Charlie?" Victor asked.

"Number one, no signs of forced entry. I'd say he was awakened in the middle of the night by someone at the door," Connors continued with the sketchy details.

"How did you come to that conclusion?" Victor responded.

"Well, the bed was unmade and all of his clothes were put away. Indicates he answered the door in his underwear, maybe had a brief conversation and then probably moved to the bedroom. There's not as much blood there versus the hallway, and there's even more blood in the den and kitchen. And oh, by the way, the blinds are drawn on the bedroom window, so someone on the street may have been able to see inside the apartment," Connors said as he probed at the open wounds.

Still feeling queasy, John rose to his feet, averting his attention from the corpse and Connors. It offered little relief, as the apartment reeked of decomposition, coagulated blood, and the putrid, unidentified stench. It was a wakeup call that on this bright morning, a darkness had fallen on earth. John could just feel it. He just didn't know what to do about his disquietude. His thoughts quickly returned to the investigation as Victor's voice brought him back to the reality of the murder.

"John? John, are you listening?" Victor asked, as he pointed to Bear's swollen neck.

"Yeah, I'm listening."

"Look at all these bruises on his neck. Charlie and I think the perp must of had a death grip on our pal's throat. Had to be incredibly strong to hold this big guy by the neck while he ripped him to pieces. I mean really possessed," Victor said while shaking his head in disbelief.

"Oh, so now are you saying that the killer was under some sort of demonic possession?" John scoffed.

"It's possible. We had a guy back home that killed his wife. Said he was possessed by the devil. The little runt only weighed about one hundred twenty pounds, yet it took six cops to handcuff him, and he broke the cuffs five minutes later. Snapped them like sewing thread," Victor said.

"Well, that's just great. Our two prime suspects are a goat and a midget with superhuman strength. Now let's see. How about this theory—Sugar Bear was possessed by the devil and he stabbed and choked himself to death? How does that sound?" John displayed a curled lip.

"You know, John. Come to think of it, remember that weirdo in Decatur who claimed he was possessed by a legion of demons? The guy was about to axe his neighbor when the police arrived. He was shot six times in the chest and still stood and laughed at the cops until he took one on the head. Remember that one?" Connors asked John.

Reluctantly, John partially agreed. "Yeah, I remember it. But everyone thought the guy was a fraud. He was hyped up on drugs when he was shot."

"I did the autopsy back then and I can tell you that he had no drugs or alcohol in his system, and two of the bullets that hit him in the chest, pierced his heart. The guy was dead on his feet, yet he still kept coming," Connors shook his head from side to side.

This was a time of amazing progress, a scientific age when man could understand and explain even the most arcane evidence at a crime scene. Man could also scientifically understand phenomena such as the genesis of our universe and the evolution of the human race. As a matter of fact, man could just about explain anything with some measure of scientific means. And it was clear to Victor and Connors that John was stuck on the side of science, that he simply would not accept any doctrine not espoused by a highbrow academician. Unnatural explanations founded in the field of superstition and folklore were not an option for him to consider. If there are no demons, then all the depraved acts of human beings could be traced to causes other than supernatural evil. Again, his rational side had taken over in an effort to explain his troubled feelings.

"Could have been a massive adrenaline rush. That's been known to give people superhuman strength. We've all heard stories about a person having the strength to lift a car in an emergency situation," John said.

Victor and Connors ignored his theory and continued with their search for evidence. John also gave up on his theory and joined in by questioning neighbors and directing the work of the photographer. Several hours later, photos had been taken, statements recorded, and all but one piece of evidence had been catalogued and bagged. Still their labors produced no solid leads—a lot of crazy theories, but nothing of substance. The three men watched as two lab technicians and three uniformed officers struggled to lift the final piece of evidence onto the stretcher. It was Sugar Bear's corpse. For him, there would be no more days of menace, no more exploding temper or violent outbursts. Now his massive body was powerless. The detectives were emotionally drained. Two solid weeks of investigations had left them without a suspect.

29

There is a special union between a mother and daughter. It is a bond that begins at conception and continues throughout eternity. There is no force in the highest reaches or lowest depths that can diminish the tie or destroy the love. Such was the bridge between Rebecca and Boo. In complete candor, Boo had repeated the same intriguing story of her mother appearing at her bedside, gently stroking her hair while expressing her never-ending love. Before departing, she would tenderly kiss Boo's forehead and beg her to deliver a warning to her father that a dangerous peril was nearby, and that he should keep a watchful eye. Boo's latest disclosure came the evening after the detectives had investigated the murder scene at Sugar Bear's apartment. The combination of the grisly crime and her account of the visits had left John in a state of sleeplessness.

John was miserably tired when he rose the next morning. But his insomnia had allowed him to do a lot of thinking. He had decided to make an appointment with the psychologist recommended by Dr. Brown. Perhaps Dr. Michael Goodall would have some answers. John showered, dressed, and stopped by Boo's room before he left for work. He found her sleeping soundly, clutching her favorite stuffed bear. He stared at her innocent face and then softly kissed her cheek. At that precise moment he somehow knew that his daughter truly believed that her mother's visits were real. Be it by dream or imagination, it really didn't matter. She was his beloved daughter and she, above all others, trusted him. How could he now deny her words?

He missed Rebecca so much and wished Boo could bring her mother back in flesh instead of in spirit. He could still vividly remember Rebecca's last day in the hospital. She had endured such horrible suffering, yet on that final day she seemed at peace. That was what John remembered most, the look of joy on her face as she lay in bed, pressing Boo to her bosom, whispering softly in her ear.

Both mother and daughter had found solace in each other's arms, remaining motionless for hours, drifting in and out of sleep. Both had been pulled into a dream where Rebecca was teaching her daughter about the beauty in life and of God's love for all His children. As John gazed at Boo's tender face, he could see Rebecca's bright aura. And at that very moment, he knew, their souls were inseparable.

30

In the hallway outside the homicide department, a large gathering of reporters waited impatiently for any warm body that entered or exited the office. Like sharks smelling blood, they immediately circled John in a frenzy to determine if he carried the scent of the murders. He took pleasure in silently pushing aside the newshounds; on more than one occasion, his words had been twisted in order to emphasize sensationalism over fact. Besides, he was convinced that the media's prime time presentation of cases like this one had the exponential effect of stirring up every neurotic copycat within airwave transmission of Atlanta. His time was stretched enough without adding these kooks to his caseload. As he was about to enter the squad room, a female reporter from one of the local television stations screamed his name followed by an ill-timed accusation.

"Detective Williams! Detective Williams! Sources say that you had something to do with the death of Sugar Bear, that there was bad blood between the two of you. Do you have any comment to make about his death?"

John paused at the door as a rush of blood filled his face. He wanted to respond but he knew it was a no-win situation. Anything he said would be ground up and spat out in a headline that would make him the prime suspect. He remained silent, biting his lower lip and stepping through the open doorway. He was sure that he had avoided all the trouble until he entered the homicide department.

Lieutenant Milligan bolted from his office when he saw John enter the open room. John made a quick turn and slid between two other officers in an effort to avoid him, but it was a useless maneuver. Milligan caught up with him as he reached his desk.

"Williams! Don't try to avoid me. I've got some questions for you."

"Why in the world would I want to avoid you, Lieutenant? You know I just love our little conversations," John replied with his best straight face.

Milligan's face was ugly with displeasure, "Don't be a smart ass, Williams. I won't hesitate to bring you up before a review board if you disobey my orders!"

"You know I would never do that, Lieutenant. Besides, I don't believe you've given me any orders." John could see Milligan hated his lack of reverence.

"What about the reporters outside? You know it's against department policy to answer questions about any ongoing investigation," Milligan countered.

"Well sir, for your information I haven't spoken to any reporters."

"You'd better not. And I'm not happy with the progress you're making on these cases. You got any suspects?"

Milligan had finally found a raw nerve. No one was more frustrated than John with the headway he and Victor had made on their investigations. "No, not yet, but we're workin' on it," John bristled.

"Have you asked for a profile from Quantico?" Milligan asked.

The FBI's behavioral science unit in Quantico, Virginia ran information on murder suspects against their database. The analysis was done in order to profile the killer. John knew that the lieutenant was aware that the profile had been ordered. It was standard operating procedure to do so on cases of this nature.

"Yes, Lieutenant. You know it's been done."

"Well, I want a report on the progress you made yesterday, and I want it before the end of the day! You got a problem with that, Sergeant?"

"No, sir," John said, doing his level best to control his temper.

Milligan twirled, hitched his pants, and stormed back to his office. John yanked open his desk drawers searching for the stack of blank forms. He would need a quick start on the report if he was to meet Milligan's deadline. He shifted to Victor's desk as he continued to open and slam the sliding compartments. His search suddenly ended when he viewed the contents in Victor's bottom left drawer.

He had stumbled across something that caught him totally by surprise. Inside were two small bottles of Freon and a leather holster that held a taser-gun. John remembered Victor's explanation that occultists used electric prods to stun animals before spraying Freon on their throats. This tactic kept the sacrificial lamb quiet while an embalming tool was used to drain their blood. Even though John had found a stun-gun designed for use against humans, he knew it would be effective against a large animal as well. It wasn't standard issue for homicide detectives, and he certainly wasn't familiar with any law enforcement technique that required the use of Freon.

A disturbing thought entered his head. Could his partner somehow be involved in the murders? He grappled for a reasonable explanation. He never finished his headwork; Charlie Connors startled him from his ten seconds of contemplation.

" Hey, John! I've got an update for you. Let's meet in the interrogation room." Connors waved his left arm, motioning John to follow.

John nodded, closed the bottom desk drawer, and dismissed his apprehension. He followed an unnerved Connors down the narrow opening between the desks and into an indistinct room that held a small table and two metal chairs. John immediately noticed a restless, almost dirty look on

Connors' face when he entered the room. It appeared as though the many years of performing autopsies, the fallout of coping with the sordid aftermath of so many murders, had found a home on his facial features. His vacant eyes revealed the emptiness he was feeling while his sagging skin warned that he was close to physical exhaustion.

"Rigor mortis and blood coagulation indicates that the time of death was between two and three o'clock in the morning," he said in a nervous, almost neurotic fashion.

"You mean Sugar Bear?" John asked.

"I worked through the night, finished the autopsy about an hour ago." Connors withdrew a handkerchief and blotted his sweaty brow. "Won't know the cause of death for sure until I get the toxicology report from the lab."

"Got any guesses?"

"Shock from the loss of blood would be my first guess, but..." Connors paused.

"But what? You suspect some other cause?"

"Like I said, I won't know for sure until the chemical analysis is done, but the tissue inside the puncture wounds was inflamed. It had the reddish, black appearance of a burn. His vital organs, especially his lungs, had a similar appearance."

"What do you think caused that?" John asked.

"I'm not sure, but it looked like trauma from poison. A substance like phosphoric acid could do that type damage, sulfuric acid is a possibility as well," Connors responded.

"You know something, now that I think about it, that stink at the apartment, the same smell that surrounded Pierce and Rimmon, had the scent of sulfur," John replied.

"I agree, but I still don't know what caused the odor."

"What else you got?" John asked.

"Well, from the angle of the wounds, I'd say the assailant could be between five foot six and five foot ten. Since the blows came from both directions, I can't determine if he is right or left-handed. May even be ambidextrous. Could even be more than one assailant. Just don't know. Bruises on the neck didn't help in that matter, either. But there is one thing I can tell you," Connors stopped to gather his thoughts as an incredulous glaze formed on his eyes.

"What's that?"

"Victor was right about the strength. Had to be incredible. The victim's larynx was crushed, and I mean flat. That's why none of the neighbors heard any screams," Connors continued.

"Why is that?" John asked, leaning forward in his chair.

"The larynx is the cartilage box that contains the vocal cords. Assailant crushed the vocal cords to keep the victim quiet, and for good measure, severed his tongue. I think that was done early in the struggle so the assailant could take his time. He wanted to inflict a lot of pain, he wanted to torture the victim, but he didn't want to raise a ruckus."

"Damn, it sounds like this was some sort of execution," John winced.

"This killing may have been a helluva lot messier than the Pierce or Rimmon murders but make no mistake, they all smell of executions, no pun intended," Connors quipped, allowing some wry humor to break the tension.

"The murders may be similar, but there is one big difference between Sugar Bear's death and the other two homicides," John countered.

"And that is?" Connors asked.

"Sugar Bear still had his dick! If some kind of sexual pervert was involved in all of these murders, why was his penis still intact?"

"I have a theory about that. I've been doing some reading on Satanic cults, and I think I have an explanation. I found semen in Sugar Bear's shorts."

"You found what?" John laughed.

"I found spermatozoa in his underwear."

"So, what the hell does that prove other than he may have had a wet dream before he was killed?"

"Last night the chemist analyzed a sample that I gave him. And it was dead spermatozoa."

"Wouldn't you expect sperm to die outside of a body after a short period of time?" John asked.

"No, John, you don't understand. It means that Sugar Bear was sterile."

"Good grief! So that's why you think he still had his Johnson? Because he was shooting blanks? I don't know, Charlie, that's a stretch," John said.

"Just think about it. These cult members covet sexual potency, and that potency surely includes being fertile. No, he may not have been a eunuch, but he sure as hell didn't get any cards on Father's Day, either!"

"I see where you're going with this. The fact that they didn't sever his penis means that they knew him. They knew he was sterile." John looked at Connors for confirmation.

"That's what I think," Connors said.

"Oh my god!" John's mind whirled with visions of the three dead victims. He was beginning to see wisdom in Connors' theory, but he still lacked some of the answers.

"But why was Sugar Bear so brutalized when the others weren't?"

"I don't know unless they wanted to make an example of him, to frighten anyone who may think about opposing the cult. I do know that the hair fibers we found in Sugar Bear's wounds were the same type we gathered at the Rimmon farm."

"So that means the same person was at both places," John stated.

"No, not at all. The hair fibers aren't human. We still don't know what they are for sure, so we sent a sample to the FBI lab for DNA testing. We should know something in about a week."

"What about the wounds? Any ideas on what kind of weapon was used?" John asked.

"Two types of injuries, two different weapons. A blunt instrument, something club-like caused the contusions. Lots of hemorrhaging under the skin. As to what caused the entry wounds, I haven't a clue. I've done hundreds of autopsies and I've never seen lacerations like that. All I can tell you is that the instrument was jagged and very, very sharp. How the poison got into his body, I don't know. I do know that the fight was savage, and I think the struggle lasted for at least two hours."

"How did you come to that conclusion?" John asked.

"Remember we found a dozen or so small pools of blood throughout the apartment, and one large pool in the kitchen with the body."

"Yeah, I remember."

"Remember how bruised his hands and knuckles looked?" Connors asked.

"Yeah."

"Indicates that Sugar Bear fought with the assailant—or assailants—was knocked down in each location, bled, got up, and fought again in a new spot. He finally dropped for good in the kitchen."

"This is just all too crazy. The guy had a smashed voice box and a severed tongue, and he fought like hell for two hours before he died. I don't know."

"Look John, all I can tell you is that's my take on what happened."

"I still don't understand why no one heard anything. That apartment looked like a war zone. Someone must have—"

Like a bolt from the blue, Victor burst through the doorway. "Maybe somebody did." Victor said with excitement. He had overheard John's last comment.

"What do you mean?" John quickly asked.

"A uniform arrested a young kid about a block away from Sugar Bear's apartment. The kid was arrested the same morning Sugar Bear was killed. Uniform said the kid kept babbling about a fight, about a guy getting killed in an apartment. Said he could see in the apartment window from the street," Victor declared.

"Where is the kid now?"

Victor appeared ready to crow. "He's downstairs in the tank."

John sprang to his feet. "Let's go."

31

The city jail is not a place for the faint of heart. It's a foul, noisy, and oftentimes violent enclosure for those awaiting their day in court. It is not designed to punish or rehabilitate, nor is it meant to provide recreation or an education. It is simply a holding pen. As John and Victor entered the lockup area, the stench of vomit and urine provided the first slap to their faces. Both men ignored the musk and continued walking past the cells toward the holding tank at the end of the corridor. Along the way, they were greeted by a second slap consisting of a hail of insults and a volley of spit. The angry inmates had recognized them as one of the screws that put them in this despicable place and they happily took the opportunity to show their disfavor. However, neither detective heard the disparaging jeers nor felt the rain of spittle. They were too focused on the young man at the end of the cell block.

The uniformed jailer unlocked the gray steel door allowing the detectives entry into the hold. Both men gazed right and left as their eyes finally rested on a silhouette coiled in the corner of the cell. It was a tearful vision. A combination of fear and despair marked this man's features. Not yet twenty in years, he cast the figure of a man twice his age. A complete erosion of his body and soul had occurred in less than six years. His weary eyes were replete with rivers of crimson veins while his wrinkled skin had all the coloration of a starving vampire. His long, unkempt hair was dirty brown, slicked to his scalp by a residue of grimy oil. Thin and sickly, his gaunt body was that of skin and bones. It was indeed a sad sight, the result of living on the street, scrounging for food in smelly dumpsters, stealing to support an odious habit, an addiction to crack cocaine.

He had seen the detectives enter the cell, and in response, slowly rose to his feet. His oversized green flannel shirt and baggy jeans were more suitable for Og the giant rather than his anemic frame. They were tattered and gamy, overripe from too much wear and not enough cleaning. The strong smell of body odor followed him as he moved toward John with an old man's shuffle.

"You want to know about the fight?" The boy asked, staring blankly at John.

"Yeah. I'm John Williams and this is my partner, Victor Lechman."

"Nice to meet you. I'm Roger Baneda," he said as he extended his frail hand to John.

What can you tell us about the fight, Roger? John asked.

"Not a whole lot, man. I was a little out of it that night."

"What do you mean?" Victor asked.

"I'd been usin'. I was buggin' real bad. I'd smoked a rock right before I saw it," Roger answered as he wiped sweat from his brow with his dirty sleeve.

Roger's admission sucked the energy from the detectives. Both men felt as though the unbearable weight of the unsolved crimes had again dropped squarely on their shoulders. They knew that the kid's recollection of the evening would be tainted by the cocaine. It would be suspect at best.

"Look, Roger, why don't you just tell us what you saw?" John invited the boy to continue.

"I saw this little guy fighting with this big guy."

"Where were you when you saw this?" John asked.

"I was on the street lookin' in the window," Roger answered.

"Can you describe what the men looked like?" Victor asked as he withdrew his note pad from his pocket.

"I couldn't see their faces. I was too far away, and it was too dark inside the apartment. But I could tell that the big

210

man was throwin' a lot of punches. They didn't seem to faze the little guy though."

"Why do you say that?" Victor asked.

"The little guy didn't flinch. He just had the big guy around the neck, and it looked like he wouldn't let go. They were only in front of the window for a few seconds. Then they moved away," Roger said.

"Did you see anyone else in the apartment?" John inquired.

"No, just the two," Roger said as he bit his quivering lower lip.

"Are you all right?" John asked.

"No, I need to get out of here. Can you get me out?"

"No," Victor retorted.

"Are you sure you didn't see anything else?" Victor asked "Anyone on the street, around the apartment building, anything?"

"No, nothing."

"Well, so much for this lead," Victor barked with sarcasm as he slapped his note pad closed, turned, and walked out of the cell.

John remained for a few minutes, watching the trembling boy return to a fetal position in the corner. He attempted to ask some more questions about the night of the murder, but the boy ignored him by babbling about an invisible cell mate that wouldn't leave him alone. The boy reminded John of his days as a cop on the beat. Daily confrontations with sick junkies were routine back then. Unfortunately, the flow of drugs to America's youth had gotten worse since those days, and as such, this boy's story wasn't much different from many of the others.

Born to loving parents in a middle-class neighborhood, his first contact with drugs came at age twelve—an after-school experiment with cigarettes and alcohol. He then added infrequent marijuana use with his so-called friends until they moved up in the world of drug abuse with daily reefer smoking and booze. At age fifteen, Roger's destructive pattern continued with a hell broth of cocaine, speed and heroin. By seventeen, his drug-abusing career culminated with crack cocaine. Before his arrest, he used at least one drug daily, depending on his ability to deliver or sell narcotics or his willingness to steal to support his habit.

Yes, John had seen it all, the homeless kids on park benches, in alleyways or abandoned buildings. He had even seen them sleeping on graves in dark cemeteries. He wondered why a child would opt for this sort of withering life. Yet he knew it was the drugs. The explosions of hate aimed at those who love you the most, the anxiety, the apathetic attitude toward school, the disbelief of a higher power, it was the drugs, always the drugs.

He listened as the gibbering stopped and the boy began to cry. Although the drugs had emaciated his physical being, his real suffering was one of mental despair. His youthful spirit, his innocent soul had been stolen. His prison was not this hideous jail. It was, rather, the torture of living in loneliness, of having no hope, of knowing that until you return to your loved ones and ask for help, your pain will never go away. He sobbed louder. It was a cry to go home

32

"Come in, John, have a seat. Susan told me a lot about you."

John entered Dr. Michael Goodall's office expecting to find dark shelves filled with Freudian books, an analysis couch, and a manic-depressive atmosphere. Instead, he encountered a bright, airy room with upright furniture and a warm, healing ambiance. Goodall was a clinical psychologist; his field was one of studying human behavior and senses rather than investigating and treating mental illness. The friendly room was a dictum of his relaxed style. It was the tonic that helped put his clients at-ease, allowing them to openly express their feelings and thoughts. It was doing its job for John's initial impression was positive.

"Well, I hope you don't think I'm a nut, Dr. Goodall," John said as he seated himself on the chair in front of Goodall's desk.

"Oh my gosh, no! I just hope I can help you make some sense of what you have been going through," Goodall said as he withdrew a writing pad from the desk drawer.

A dose of apprehension abruptly darkened John's otherwise sunny disposition as he surveyed the scholarly diplomas hanging from the wall. The hourly rate for someone with his credentials and monetary needs didn't fit well with a cop's menial salary.

"I appreciate that Dr. Goodall. I'm just not sure if I can afford much of your time."

"First of all, please call me Michael. Second, don't concern yourself with my fee. You can pay me whatever you can afford. I'm more interested in talking about what's been happening to you," Michael reassured.

John breathed a sigh of relief knowing he wouldn't have to live a hand-to-mouth existence in order to pay the doctor's bill. He spent the next thirty minutes recapping the recent unusual events. Michael patiently listened, interrupting only to ask an occasional question. John felt as though Michael understood something about all the twists and turns, and that he had a special sense about what had been happening.

"Tell me, John. Have you experienced any unusual dreams?" Michael asked in a soft voice.

"I'm not sure what you mean. I've had my share of wacky dreams just like everybody else," John answered.

"No, what I mean is, have you had any dreams similar to the flashbacks you experienced?"

"No. Nothing like that. Why do you ask?"

"Well, I have a couple of theories about what you experienced when you drifted back in time."

"Like what?"

"First of all, there are a lot of ways to channel into the past. Research has documented that the human brain can subconsciously receive information from sources beyond our physical world. It has been done through hypnosis, like what you went through, and sometimes, it happens in dreams. And some people even claim that they know about the past because they lived during that time— they are reborn again and again."

"Oh, man, are you talking about reincarnation?" John's face gathered with doubt.

"Don't look so shocked, John. It could explain your ability to speak Latin when you were under hypnosis. For example, have you ever heard of Bridey Murphy?"

"Bridey who?" John asked.

"Bridey Murphy." Goodall spoke a little louder.

"No, I haven't."

"Well, let me tell you about Bridey. She was a woman who had never been to Ireland yet, under hypnosis, she spoke of a place in Cork called the Meadows. And she spoke with an

Irish brogue. She claimed to have lived there in the eighteenth century. She was able to accurately describe the area, and I mean in great detail."

"I don't know. This all sounds a little far-fetched to me." John looked doubtful.

"Look, I'm not saying that I believe in reincarnation either. Heck, modern science completely discredits the concept. All I'm saying is that I have an open mind about the possibility it could happen."

"All right, I'll try to be open minded as well. Hell, after what's happened to me, I've got to think anything is possible. Can you tell me more?" John asked.

Michael exposed a pearly smile. He was delighted John was willing to at least consider rebirth as a possible explanation for his hallucinations. He knew that it was a giant step for a pragmatic cop to embrace any theory not found in a science book.

"The belief in reincarnation has been around for centuries. Even Plato accepted the premise. Over time, it was believed that a soul was strengthened or weakened by the lessons learned in each of its lives. It was a way of explaining how people had special gifts—like explaining child geniuses such as Mozart or Chopin. Do you have any special talents, John?" Goodall asked.

"Oh, yeah, I can play chopsticks on the piano. And with both hands!" John burst into laughter.

Michael chuckled and then responded, "No, you know what I mean. Anything come natural to you?"

"Now that I think about it, martial arts have always been easy for me. It's as though all the moves are instinctive. It's always been that way, even before my training in the army."

"My gosh, that's quite a coincidence." Michael replied as he furiously scribbled on his notepad.

"What, what's a coincidence?" John asked.

"You were in the military, right? You were a soldier?"

"Yes."

"Your flashbacks. When you saw yourself in the flashbacks, you were a soldier?"

"That's right."

"Don't you think that's a strange coincidence?"

"I guess so, but maybe that's why I saw myself that way. Because I was in the army," John shrugged his shoulders...

"I don't know, John," Michael disagreed as he stopped writing. "It could be, but why are the martial arts so natural for you? Could be that if you have lived past lives, you've been trained before?"

"I don't know. I'm trying to keep an open mind, but I can't. Besides, my strict Southern Baptist upbringing tells me that once you die, your spirit either goes to heaven or hell—no second chances."

"Okay then, let's talk about my second theory."

"All right, what's that?" John asked.

"Extrasensory perception," Michael continued.

"Good grief, I know I don't have ESP," John rolled his eyes in disbelief.

"Wait a minute before you dismiss this. First, let me explain," Michael leaned forward. "Although many religious leaders would argue that the Bible discounts the possibility of reincarnation, these same theologians would agree that spirits have been around long before man."

"How does ESP fit into this?" John asked.

"Well, if there are no immortal souls through reincarnation, but there are spirits, then once your mind becomes receptive to suggestions, these spirits may be trying to communicate with you."

"I'm not sure that I understand."

"Okay, let me put it another way. The Bible validates that spirits, good and evil, have been around for eons, right?"

"Okay, I'll buy that." John slid to the edge of his chair.

"All right then, if spirits have been around for eons, then they can remember what has taken place in the past," Michael stated. "So, once you open your mind to suggestions, such as when you are under hypnosis, then these spirits may be able to describe historical events through you."

"I understand what you are saying, but I still don't understand why I'm involved."

"I don't know the answers to that, John. I wish I knew, but I don't."

"What about the things Boo has been telling me about Rebecca visiting her at night?" John leaned closer to Michael's desk.

"She may be dreaming about Rebecca. Remember when I said earlier that spirits can contact you when you are receptive?" Michael answered.

"Yeah, but how does that fit in to all of this, Michael?"

"Well, your subconscious is very receptive to suggestions when you are asleep."

"So, you think it's all just a dream?" John wasn't sure how to take Michael's words.

"Maybe yes, maybe no. It could just be a dream or Rebecca may really be trying to communicate with Boo," Michael answered.

"In her dreams?" John asked.

"Yes, in her dreams."

"You know something, Michael?" John laughed. "For-a-well-educated-down-to-earth-psychologist, you've got some pretty far-out ideas."

Michael laughed melodically, "Well, you're not the first person who has called me a crackpot."

"I was just kidding," John apologized.

"I know you weren't serious. But all kidding aside, I do believe that either of my theories is possible. I've documented other cases similar to yours."

"Well, I guess that there's no way to test your theory, so we may never know."

"There is a way to test my ESP theory if you're willing to try."

"Oh, no. No more hypnosis." John shook his head.

"No, I'm not talking about hypnosis. It's called psychometry. Have you ever heard of it?" Michael asked.

"Are you talking about psychics?"

"Yes, psychics can psycho-metricize when touching specific objects."

"Yeah, I remember a homicide I was working several years ago. We had a suspect in custody but couldn't find the body of a young boy. We had a psychic come in from Macon to help us find him. She asked for some of the boy's clothing, his favorite toy, or anything special to him."

"Yes, your psychic knew she would receive her strongest signals when touching these objects."

"So, what do you have in mind for me?"

"I think Rebecca's Bible might be able to provide you some answers if you're willing to try an experiment. "I'd like for you to sleep with the Bible. I think you may have another vision if you do."

John was dumbfounded, "I'm not sure that I want to have another vision."

"You do want some answers to what's happening to you, don't you?"

"Yes." John emphatically answered.

"Then why not try this?"

"I don't know, sleeping with a Bible?"

"At the very least, place it close to you, like on a nightstand next to your bed. It's important; it could provide you with the clue you're looking for."

Grudgingly, John agreed. "Okay, I'll try."

"Oh, by the way, one more suggestion."

"What's that?"

"Drink a glass of orange juice about an hour or so before you go to bed."

"What's the juice for?"

"The sugar in the juice will enhance your dream state. It helps stimulate the neurological tissues in the brain, but not so much that you can't sleep."

"Would it help to spike the juice with vodka?" John asked in jest.

"No, no alcohol. And don't eat any grains for dinner. Both tend to dull your ability to dream."

Although John wasn't completely convinced Dr. Goodall's prescription would solve his mystery, he had no other option. And at this point, he was willing to try almost anything. Michael ended their session with one last explanation of his theory. The doctor was convinced that dreams brought individuals understanding because they reveal what is in the subconscious mind. He was certain that the subliminal threshold was the spiritual insight into the core of a person's being. So, by analyzing dreams we unlock the door to our psyche, to our inner being. John simply wondered if the door was meant to be opened.

33

Police officers who bear witness to man's most sordid acts need an occasional escape from the deadly storm. This safe harbor was oftentimes provided by a waggish portion of antithetical, juvenile behavior. It was an effective way to purge the unwanted cynicism from their bodies. Although their teasing and silliness occurred most every day, Fridays always seemed to bring their antics to a new, higher level of playfulness. On this sixth day, Lieutenant Milligan, a.k.a. Bad Ass, was once again the brunt of their jokes.

Phil Sayers and Mouse Curtis had concocted today's prank. It was a clever scheme aimed at exploiting the Lieutenant's reputation for being the consummate moocher. Although Milligan was quick to help himself to any doughnuts or pastries brought in by the other detectives, he was dirt-cheap and slow to contribute his fair share when his turn came to ante-up. Maybe he thought his sponging was a privilege of office. The other detectives certainly didn't think so.

Sayers and Curtis had delivered a fresh batch of bagels along with a mixture of cream cheese and chives, or so it looked like chives. It was actually finely chopped lawn grass. When blended with the aromatic cheese, it was almost undetectable. The wily cops knew that unless you had descended from a cow, your digestive tract was unable to process the sedge. The result would be the same as that experienced by an ordinary dog or cat when they decided to graze in the back yard.

The rubbernecking began as the lieutenant spread a generous portion of the grassy pate on two of the baked rolls. All eyes followed as he munched on the first bagel while slowly walking back to his office. Sayers, the king of knaves, fought back the laughter as his eyes welled from the revelry of pulling off the gag. Like a clowning schoolboy, he danced around the squad room while sticking a finger in his gaping mouth. He, like the other detectives, snickered under their breath, pretending to conduct business as usual when in fact, they anxiously waited for Milligan to burst from his office.

It took all of twenty minutes for the fermentation to be complete. Milligan dismissed the first subacid ache as a touch of his usual sour stomach. He quickly gobbled down an antacid and continued working, thinking the pill would solve the problem. The second attack of pungency, however, refused to react to the same treatment. This vinegary assault was escorted by the uncontrollable urge to spew forth the fodder. Without hesitation, Milligan rose, hurried from his office, and staggered across the floor. Cupping one hand over his mouth while rubbing his cramping stomach with the other, he tried to hold the bagels in check. He had barely reached the hallway when the laughter erupted. It filled the squad room with a cleansing spirit, a revelry that the detectives had actually pulled one over that miserable son of a bitch. The rejoicing continued with congratulatory handshakes and back pats while Phil and Mouse bragged about their success and hid the incriminating evidence. It was a riot, a high-spirited riot—that was until the lieutenant returned.

The hullabaloo instantly ended with the reappearance of an angry, visibly shaken Milligan. Still queasy, he rocked back and forth like a drunken sailor. His twisted, pale green face confirmed his discomfort while a mouth full of obscenities bespoke of his anger.

"Which one of you assholes did this? Milligan yelled.

A sea of faces gazed at Milligan with all the innocent wonder they could muster. How could this man suspect such a saintly group of choir boys?

"Dammit, I want to know who's behind this!" Milligan's eyes narrowed on Phil Sayers. "I know you had something to do with this."

"Why, Lieutenant, is there something wrong? You seem awfully upset." Sayers responded in his most saintly voice.

"You bet I'm upset. Somebody put some kind of shit in the cream cheese, Milligan screamed, his Irish green face now returning to fuming red.

"You must be mistaken, Lieutenant. We've all been eating the bagels and cheese this morning and nobody here has gotten sick." Sayers replied with a contorted face, straining to hold back the laughter. He looked around the room as the other choir boys shook their heads in agreement.

"I want that cream cheese now!" Milligan barked. "Curtis, go get it."

"Gee, Lieutenant, it's all gone. I ate the last bite about five minutes ago," Mouse answered.

"You bunch of assholes!" Milligan knew he had been gigged, and he also knew that his attempts to debunk the sham were useless. He stormed to his office while the detectives had another round of high-fives.

The wisecracking finally ended when the detectives caught sight of Marty Lococo entering the squad room with his infamous attorney, Felix Lovelady. Lovelady was well known throughout the Atlanta Police Department, especially by the officers who investigated the multitude of traffic accidents that occurred around the city. He was famous for arriving on the scene just seconds after the mishap. In short, he was an ambulance-chasing weasel in a pinstripe suit, ready to play the legal lottery in hope of extorting a pound of flesh from any would-be defendant with one nickel in his pocket. "Ethics" was a word not found in his vocabulary. Even the brethren in the trial bar had distanced themselves from this Machiavellian con man. Both Lococo and Lovelady, however,

222

were welcomed into Milligan's office. Ten minutes later, John was sternly summoned to join the sidebar.

John entered, took the remaining chair and made a visual assessment of Lovelady. The pot-bellied barrister and his undernourished client were diametrical opposites. Unlike Lococo, Lovelady was grossly overweight sporting a hippo build with a puffy moon-face. His stubby nose and shifty, ferret-like eyes were two of his more attractive features. A gnarly, coal-black hairpiece raked back into a ducktail coiffure was one of his least. The wig had all the earmarks of a rain-soaked skunk, roadside swollen from an untimely run-in with a Mack truck. But perhaps more repulsive than his looks were the nauseating sounds he made while sucking his over-bitten, yellow teeth. To John, this oversized cue ball with a bad toupee spelled trouble.

"Williams, I think you know Mr. Lococo." The lieutenant then pointed at Lovelady. "And this is Felix Lovelady, his attorney," Milligan said.

"Yeah, I know who they are," John replied, not bothering to offer his hand in greeting.

"Mr. Lovelady here, says he is preparing to file a police brutality lawsuit against the department—and more specifically against you." Milligan looked at John with a piercing stare.

"Brutality! That's a bunch of bullshit!" John retorted.

"My client was verbally assaulted and battered by Detective Williams at his night club." Lovelady said as he probed his teeth with a flicking tongue.

"This is crazy. If I battered Twinkle Toes over there, he'd be in a hospital, not here making these ridiculous charges!" John's anger was quickly escalating.

Lococo sprang from his chair pointing an accusing finger at John. "I told you I'd have your badge. You should've never hurt me or my boys!"

"I don't have time to listen to this crap. I've got four recently open cases on my desk, Lieutenant. I've heard enough. I'm out of here." John rose from the chair.

Milligan leaped to his feet, joining John and Lococo. "Williams, sit down and stay until I give you permission to leave!"

"This is garbage, and you know it, Lieutenant!" John said, refusing to return to his chair.

John was right. Milligan did know it. Even though the two men had an adversarial relationship, they were in agreement about the frivolous charges. Besides, the lieutenant disliked attorneys even more than John. Since his nasty divorce, he had held fast to a Shakespearean maxim of what to do with officers of the court. "All right.! Everybody be calm and have a seat. I've got a few questions I want to ask," Milligan said. "Now, Mr. Lococo, are you alleging you were battered by Detective Williams at your club?"

"Yeah, that's right, my client was physically abused by your officer," Lovelady quickly interjected.

"I'm not talking to you, Fat Boy," Milligan snapped. "I'm speaking to Mr. Lococo."

Milligan's sarcasm did not fall on deaf ears, a huge smile appeared on John's face. He was pleasantly surprised to find the brass on his side.

"Now, what happened at your club?" Milligan continued.

"Detective Williams grabbed and twisted my arm," Lococo answered with a fabricated whimper.

"His actions caused severe physical injuries, emotional distress, and mental anguish to my client," Lovelady interrupted. "And please don't call me Fat Boy."

"I thought I told you to shut up, Fatso," Milligan fired back. "If you interrupt me one more time, I'll do more than call you names. I'll have your fat ass kicked all the way down Peachtree Street." Milligan turned back and stared at Mr. Lococo. "Now, I don't see a cast on either of your arms, no sling, no bandages, no anything. So, how badly can you be hurt?"

"It's not that he hurt me, it's his attitude about—"

"Be quiet, you shouldn't say anything else about your injuries," Lovelady interceded once again.

"All right, that's it!" Milligan rose, walked to the office door and opened it for their departure. "If you want to file a lawsuit, file it. Otherwise, get your asses out of my office—and oh, by the way, Lococo, from what I've read in the reports, you're still a suspect in our investigation. So, don't leave town."

"We'll see you both in court!" Lovelady said, attempting to get in one last jab.

"Yeah, yeah. I'm really afraid, counselor," Milligan replied, motioning the two out the door.

John watched as Lovelady and Lococo sashayed out of the office. He was beginning to feel sympathetic toward his boss, apologetic about the cruel pranks they had pulled. He even thought that, maybe, he should be treated as one of the guys. His compassion was short-lived, as Milligan quickly directed his poison back at John.

"Did you hurt that little twit?" Milligan spat.

"No!" John replied.

"You sure about that?"

"Yes, I'm sure. I don't know what brought this on. I just called him a few names, that's all."

"If you did anything to him, and I find out about it, I'll have your badge. You understand?" Milligan barked.

"Yeah," John scoffed, turned his irreverent back on the lieutenant and left the office.

John had returned to his desk when a disturbing thought entered his mind. Why was Victor excluded from the inquisition? After all, he had mangled one of Lococo's prized bulls. John made a quick visual search of the busy room.

Unable to find his partner among the turmoil, he grudgingly decided to explore the inner sanctum of his partner's desk. He paused momentarily, feeling pinched between his curiosity and the silent moral voice that was chastising him for considering such an act. Curiosity prevailed. He opened the bottom drawer and rummaged among the contents.

The fact that the taser gun and Freon were missing caught him completely off guard. He also discovered another unwelcomed surprise. The sight of the demonic charm caused his heart to skip and his hair to bristle. It was cast in the same mold as the amulet he and Victor had found in Rimmon's office, a goat's head inside an inverted pentagram within two circles. The troubling thoughts made him dizzy. Why would Victor have such a charm? And, what happened to the Freon and taser gun? John's head was overloaded. He was so deep in reflection he hadn't noticed his partner approaching from the rear.

"Looking for something?" Victor snapped with a steely Brooklyn accent.

An embarrassing rush of adrenaline instantly flooded John's body. "Yeah, I just need a pen. Mine ran out of ink." John nervously said as he quickly closed the desk drawer. It was the best excuse he could conjure up on such short notice.

Victor's knitted brow and half-closed eyelids telegraphed his displeasure with the ransacking of his property. "Pens are in the top drawer. Just ask next time and I'll get it for you."

John slithered back to this desk feeling ashamed. He arrived in time to catch the airborne pen Victor tossed. As he prepared to deliver a second explanation for his actions, his telephone rang. It was Lori calling to confirm their evening date. There was something about her sweet voice that made him forget all of his worries and woes. It sent him spinning in thoughts about her beauty and style, her radiance and charm but most of all, her perfect symmetry.

For the remainder of the day, John pored over the lab reports from the murders. He also examined all the crime scene photos and interview reports. His review yielded no new information or fresh leads. If a workable clue was to be found, he had missed it.

34

John was in an exuberant mood as he drove south on I-75. Boo was spending the night at Tina's which meant his entire evening was open for Lori. She had asked him to pick her up at the Garrett's house. He wasn't thrilled about returning to that place, but he was so upbeat about seeing her, he really didn't care. Tonight, nothing could extinguish his energetic fire. He tapped the steering wheel to the earthly tones of the country music twanging from the radio and did his best to sing the lyrics. His out-of-tune voice bellowed like a lovesick hound baying at the moon. Merle Haggard, he wasn't. But it didn't matter; he loved the song. It was a working man's ballad, an old fashion, everyday discourse about a little bit of cheatin' and fightin', and a heavy helpin' of drinkin' and lovin'.

As the song ended, John felt a passionate urge to pop the cap on a Budweiser, light a Marlboro, and have a tattoo of Willie Nelson inlayed on his left bicep. The unusual impulse quickly parted as he dialed in another station offering a harmonic mix of progressive jazz and R&B. The tapping began again, followed by an urge to pop the cork on a bottle of Korbel, light an expensive Havana, and have a tattoo of Alicia Keys stippled on his right bicep. Urges aside, he loved it all, from country to classical, to blues to pop, all except the mind-bending sounds of heavy metal. His musical ear had never learned to appreciate the obstreperous sound of punk rock. Boo would have to teach him the finer points when she reached her teenage years.

He watched a panoramic view of downtown appear through the windshield. The city was an engineering wonder, a delight to the eye. It was defined by a rare blend of glistening, new skyscrapers and stoic, low-rise brick buildings. The city wasn't perfect. It had its fair share of crime and traffic and all the other sins that are wed to a large urban area. But its unique blend of the old and the new more than offset its shortcomings. It offered up diversion for all whether it be a boot kickin' country saloon or a laid-back blues café, linguini with clam sauce or chicken fried steak with milk gravy, from nouveau riche art galleries to bourgeois pawn shops. Yes, you could find your pleasure in Atlanta.

John drove on, losing the view of the city as he exited interstate onto West Paces Ferry Road. He headed east for about a mile and then searched for the residence. He remembered the Garretts' curving driveway was bordered by a green canopy of southern magnolias that rose above the tended lawn. He also recalled that the trees, tall and thick, partially veiled the antebellum home from the street. So, he slowed the Chevy as he strained to see the distinct white columns which marked the Garretts' front porch. As he was about to pass the house, he jammed the brakes, sliding the car in the entrance between two of the more established magnolias.

"Whew, that was close!" He switched off the radio, rolled down the window, and enjoyed the minty smell of the evergreens as he drove up the driveway. After he parked the car, he stepped outside, took several deep breaths and smiled. The flora tickled his nose and within minutes, his eyes would relish her beautiful face. Life was good.

Excitedly, John headed up the long passage to the house. It was walkway overarched by a roof of trelliswork intertwined with dangling vines. It had the wicked appearance of a lurid den laden with menacing green snakes. It was spooky. As he looked about, he quickened his pace to the speed of a traveler about to miss his plane. The sunny attitude that made him so chipper, suddenly turned into dark uneasiness.

He was frightened, but it wasn't fear. More correctly, it was apprehension, a premonition, a warning that something bad was about to happen. The goosebumps on his cold flesh confirmed it. John's prophetic feeling became realty as the dreaded flashbacks returned. But this time, the vision came in fragments, stabbing his consciousness in quick, measured blows. It was as though his antenna to the past had a case of bad reception, only able to hold the picture for a few seconds at a time.

"Come on," he said, fighting off the horrible feeling, "Keep going. Just get out of here. Don't let it happen."

The icy wind intensified. Like an invisible hand, it swirled, pushing his tall body around in a circle. That's when he heard it. The voice.

"John," it said in an indistinct whisper.

Over and over, the blinding, white flashes pierced his senses, burning his watery eyes. He was unable to discern the ghostly figures in the flashes, but without a doubt he heard the voice again.

"John," the sound was now behind him.

"John," now it was in front.

"Who is it? Who's there?" John yelled, not really wanting a response.

The answer did not come. Instead, the flashes continued with one vision lasting long enough for him to gain a perspective. It was a full-blown picture—a picture of horrible chaos. The spectral figures were divided into two forces struggling against each other in an unearthly battle. A wicked black minion fiercely attacked a host of white celestial beings on what appeared to be a heavenly field. Hand-to-hand, they fought in the most contentious confrontation John had ever seen. The visage was shocking, intense and haunting. John was momentarily stunned, off balance and unable to fathom what he had just seen. His earlier visions were alarming, but this snapshot was cataclysmic.

"Please stop!" He begged with outstretched hands, feeling only the snake-like vines.

His fervid request was answered. The ethereal trance suddenly ended as the calm evening air blissfully returned. As he tried to restore his natural vision, he felt the firm grip of a hand seize his right shoulder. The unexpected touch chilled his blood and sent his heart spiraling.

"WHAT THE...!" John lurched forward as his head twisted around, seeking the origin of the contact.

"John, what's wrong?" The soft voice asked.

His blurry eyes finally cleared, allowing him to focus on the image. It was Lori. There was a look of disbelief etched on her face.

"Are you okay?" She asked, still alarmed.

"Yeah, I just got a little dizzy. I'm fine," John said, wiping the sweat from his brow.

"I heard someone yelling when I was in the house, and I came outside and found you here. Who were you yelling at?"

"Nobody, it's nothing."

"Well, you were talking to somebody. What's going on?" Lori pried.

John fashioned his best reassuring smile, reached down, and grabbed her hand. "Come on. Let's go. We'll talk about it when we get away from here."

John wasted very little time as he drove on the downtown streets. Lori begged him to slow down, but her words had little effect. He blew past two stop signs and pushed the Chevy at speeds way over the limit. Fortunately, they made it to Lenny's unscathed. John had picked this pub because of its reputation for having lively music and good food. Yet, his interest was now in restoring balance, not devouring a hearty meal.

Still, a little libation seemed like a good idea. It was the perfect antidote for his mental anguish. And drink he did. One quick beer. Then another. The third beer finally had a soothing effect on his frayed nerves, allowing him to regain his composure. Meanwhile, Lori just sat and stared. Content to wait and watch, she knew he would talk when he was ready. Slowly, his troubled eyes mellowed, and the worry lines disappeared from his forehead. Lori affectionately lifted his hand and kissed his open palm.

"Do you feel like talking now?" She asked.

"Yeah, I do. I hope you won't think I'm crazy, though."

"Don't worry. I'm sure I'll understand."

He stopped denying the strange events. He would no longer pretend that they were his imagination, hallucinations, dreams, or even nightmares. After all, Brown and Goodall had diagnosed him sane and explained the past incidents in a more bizarre manner than his own. His sanity was intact. Coming to terms meant he would describe what had happened in a calm, matter-of-fact way that avoided all the labels of paranoia or lunacy. For an hour his words flowed from his lips like a tidal flood after a storm. It felt good, comforting to express his thoughts, to cleanse his soul.

Lori was an excellent listener. She never interrupted the monologue, just an occasional nod or an understanding smile. When he finished the account of what had been happening, he leaned forward in the chair, nervously rolled the beer bottle between his palms, and waited for her response.

"It's incredible...what you've been going through. And these doctors that you've seen, do you think they know what they are talking about?" She asked.

His exuberant mood returned. He feared Lori's reaction would be one of shock, a mistrust of him for being strange or, worse yet, she would think him a lunatic. Instead, she reached across the table and squeezed his hands. Her under-standing gesture made his heart sing with joy.

"I don't know. I'm hoping that this is just temporary, that it will go away." John smiled.

"And if it doesn't, what will you do?"

"Well, I guess it's back to the shrinks." He laughed "And if that doesn't work, I move on to tarot cards or a Ouija board." The bon mot continued.

"Don't forget about voodoo." Lori burst into laughter, joining the celebration.

For several minutes, their eyes were wide and voices loud. They took turns lampooning the situation, cutting silly re-marks and one-liners. They were in stitches, but these were healing stitches. Slowly, the revelry simmered, permitting their eyes to soften and their voices ebb. John gave his beer one last anxious spin and looked up to find Lori staring at him with her dark, enchanting eyes. It was the first time in the evening he had allowed himself to hold fast to her beauty. His approval rested in his own eyes, and in the eyes of every other red-blooded male in the place. The rounded manner of Lori's body in the tight red mini had not gone unnoticed. The ripples began the instant she walked through the pub's front door. All that agitation, all of those manly hormones zinging down to their unmentionables; John was no excep-tion.

"What are you thinking?" She asked, watching John cop a glance at her breasts.

"Oh, nothing."

"Nothing?" She said in disbelief.

"I was just thinking about the time we met," John replied, keeping his lustful thoughts hidden.

"Do you believe in love at first sight?" She asked.

"Why do you ask?" Lori's question caught him completely off guard.

"Don't answer a question with another question, John."

On the spot, that's where she put him, and with a loaded question. "I believe it can happen." He responded, taking a quick slug of brew for extra nerve.

"Good answer." Lori leaned forward and affectionately kissed his lips.

The question never came up again. It never had the chance. A blast of upbeat music had suddenly filled the room, making it difficult to have a conversation. The band's melodic vibrations found Lori's ear, lifting her in rhythm from the chair. Instantly, her mood tripped from being a wistful advisor to eroticism in motion. No longer interested in table talk, she pulled at his arm in an attempt to get his unwilling body to the dance floor. He resisted at first, but then gave in to her insistence.

She knew that he needed the diversion. He knew it too. It was just that this type of recreation wasn't recommended for someone with two left feet. Well, maybe he didn't have two left feet, but he was rusty. The high school prom was the last time he had cut a rug. But he quickly discovered that his ability to swing with the beat was of little consequence. Lori did enough gyrating for them both. He merely remained in one spot, feigning a few awkward steps while she circled with the effortless grace of an agile feline. It was exciting, her lissome body in harmony with the lively music. John just stared, shuffled a little, and stared. So did all the other tomcats in the joint. Meanwhile, Lori continued working her paws and swishing her tail. That was until the music slowed, allowing her an embracing dance with an embarrassed cop.

"I can't believe I'm out here trying to dance. I'm afraid I'm not in your league," John pulled back to gain a view of her face.

"Shush, don't talk. Just hold me tight," She purred, not looking up to meet his gaze. She just pulled him closer, rubbing her body on his.

Her warm embrace combined with the booze helped his awkward feet move with the smoothness of Fred Astaire, transforming his unwieldy soft-shoe into the winged footwork of Mercury. He felt lightheaded, smelling her sweet perfume, feeling her silken hair again his face...and her body...it was Heaven. They were as one, swaying in unison as though they were wrapped in a cocoon. Inside, their senses were on fire, ignited by the flow of the music and the heat of their touch. They danced until their desire could no longer wait.

John tracked down their server and hastily paid the check. Unwilling to wait for their meal, he and Lori hurriedly left for his house. Food was the last thing on their mind. Their type of fervor had, certainly, never been contemplated by Maslow when he developed his hierarchy of needs. Of course, Maslow had probably never seen anyone who looked like Lori.

As he drove, Lori snuggled against his side, whispering, allowing her fingernails to flutter along his thigh. He wanted to roll down the window and scream. Instead, he punched the gas pedal even harder, pushing the Chevy to a zenith meant only for cars varnished with bright numbers and bold ads. In record time the finish line appeared. They had arrived at the Williams' abode.

Without hesitating, they found the bedroom and then, the bed. The adoration was beseeching, almost prayerful, the way they moved aimlessly over one another. As though blown by a guiding wind, he followed her curves and dips, while an unswerving current carried her along his bends and swells. Both loved the foreplay, the kissing, the touching, the exploring. To John, it was nirvana. Her nipples tasted of berries, her lips of sweet wine, her inviting body of honey and cream. Lori returned the affection with a vibrance that made him shudder. When they finally met, both rocked in rhythm, spinning in time, coming again and again. He was surprised at his prowess, his need to have sex right after having sex. Usually that was the only time a man didn't want it. But the real surprise came when she whispered in his ear.

"John, I think I love you."

35

Outside the bedroom window, the persistent woodpeckers stabbed away at the stained wood siding. John pulled the blanket over his head in a futile attempt to doze. The noisy pecking continued until it finally forced him from bed. He had hoped to sleep-in since Lori was insistent that they stay up until the wee hours of the morning. The active evening had left him tired, a little sore, but very satisfied. Surprised that she had not awakened him instead of the woodpeckers, he reached across the bed to find her missing. Apparently, she had whisked away earlier, leaving him a note that she had plans for the morning, that she would take a cab instead of waking him from his peaceful sleep.

After slipping out of the covers, he rubbed his eyes and re-read the note. He felt a little unsettled about her leaving without at least saying goodbye, but it was too late to complain, so he shuffled over to the bedroom window and took out his frustration on the birds. He drew the blinds, rapped the pane, and screamed at the top of his voice. The noise was effective. The birds darted from the eaves. As John stared out the window, his attention was diverted to the south where the sky appeared heavy and dark. A billowing mass of black clouds were forming a horizontal wall, a sky-work of malevolence that was crawling upward toward Heaven. It was a foreboding sign that a blackness was about to enter his life. All of his puny attempts to dismiss his flashbacks, of explaining away Boo's visits from her mother, of accusing Tina of moving Rebecca's Bible about the house were wasted. He would soon discover that all of the so-called coincidences were about as coincidental as the sun rising in the east and setting in the west. He didn't know it, but his nightmare was about to begin.

John might have anticipated the pain, but the signs were too heretical for an analytical cop. His only expectation was to meet Lori for another night of ecstasy, not of some unknown future misery. After her expression of love, his emotional reckoning was at hand. He had avoided voicing his feelings until now, but tonight she would surely resurrect the subject and expect an answer. Problem was he didn't have one. Was he a lover or libertine? Was his intent pure as snow or did he harbor lustful deceit? If it were lust, could it grow into love? If it were love, could he be sure the lust would continue?

Would he be sincere and tell her he was unsure, that he really needed a little more time or would he lie like a snake and tell her that she hung the moon, and a constellation or two for good measure? He decided on the typical male response: *I care about you a lot, more so than anyone else I've ever known. And I really, really would like for us to spend more time together. You know, so we can get to know each other even better.*

"Yep, that's it," John said, rehearsing his elusive lines while watching his reflection in the bathroom mirror. In practice, he flashed his honest blue eyes and summoned up his most earnest look. Amused by his appearance, he broke into laughter. "Man! You look like a snake oil salesman at a county fair. Needs more practice."

He stopped rehearsing the facial expressions long enough to shower, shave and brush his teeth. In the meantime, he continued to work on his lines until Azriel broke his concentration. The cat was at the back door, howling for permission to enter the house. He heard her all the way from the bathroom. He dressed and then ambled downstairs to check on the cat. He opened the door and he gazed upward for another look at the disturbance while Azriel dashed inside like a breeze. After closing the door, he moved to the cupboard and found a can of her favorite fare. He also found a surprise that sent an eerie shiver up his spine.

It was Rebecca's Bible, resting on the Formica countertop next to the refrigerator. The horrible discontinuity had returned along with all the questions. He had visited the kitchen last night and the Bible wasn't there. He couldn't blame it on Tina or Boo. Only he and Lori were in the house and he felt certain she had not found its hiding place. Besides, it was absurd to suspect her of even looking for the Bible. Uneasily, he looked around and listened as though he might hear the obscure voice or footsteps of the guilty party. The only sound was Azriel purring louder. John was disturbed, so disturbed that after feeding the cat, he prowled the house like a second-story man seeking a Picasso. He knew it was a useless effort, but he did it anyway. It was futile.

He spent the remainder of the morning catching up on laundry while his afternoon was filled with a little work on the lawn. When he finished cutting the grass, he heard the shrill ring of the phone. It echoed off the kitchen walls, producing the sound of a policemen's whistle. It was bad news. Lori had called to cancel their date for the evening. Something about caring for a sick Peggy Garrett. Disappointment swept through him like the stiff wind blowing outside. It left his male ego bruised, damaged by what he viewed as rejection when, in fact, it was nothing more than a friend helping another friend.

It sent a blinding surge of insecurity into his veins, driving him to concoct all sorts of fiction about what she was really doing. His distortions were far-reaching, everything from suspicion of another lover, to a precipitous attempt at ending their relationship. He allowed his imagination to stew until early in the evening. It was then that he permitted himself to be foolish, to act as a jealous teenager, driving back and forth in front of the Garrett mansion. He was embarrassed, but he did it anyway. He saw nothing that confirmed his paranoid suspicions. Tonight, there would be no need to confirm his love. His evasive lines and disingenuous stares would not be necessary.

36

The earthbound mind often dismisses reasoning joined to powers of the spirit. It is always difficult to accept forces we cannot not see, feel, or smell. In the past, John had been no exception. To embrace guidance from the air was not a belief he had held, but he was slowly becoming a believer. Tonight, would be another test of his faith. The mysterious reappearance of Rebecca's Bible had convinced him to follow Dr. Goodall's advice. He had placed the Good Book on the nightstand next to his bed before slipping under the covers.

John sensed that the haze was about to clear, that the twilight would bring the answers he so desperately sought. He stared at the shadowy ceiling; his face wore the contemplative look of a man about to venture into some forbidden zone not meant for mortal creatures. Although he was puzzled, he was not afraid. He did feel somewhat foolish though, until he remembered the words from his foster parent Mama Ruth. *Johnny, you can always find solace in the Good Book*, she would say. *You can always find the answers in the Scriptures.* It was a popular tenet among all good Bible-Belters and although his Mama Ruth wasn't known as a thumper, she was certainly a woman of strong faith. Throughout the time he lived with her, she had baptized him in the sacred Word. All of it. From Genesis to Revelation, she would read the verses, and then explain the meaning behind the scriptures. And even though his convictions had strayed at times, he was Southern born and bred to revere the Almighty and he would always come back to those righteous words. She had taught him that important lesson before she died. A lesson he would never forget. That comfort would allow him to partake in Goodall's experiment—that comfort, and his burning curiosity for the truth.

Tonight, John's usual pattern of taking twenty to thirty minutes to fall to sleep was broken. He was under within ten. Within minutes, he had progressed to stage-three, the stage known as the theta phase. It was this peaceful slumber that opened the door for his trip back in time. The wakeful memories of Mama Ruth had planted a subconscious thought in his mind. It had prompted a dreamy return to his boyhood days at home with her. He found himself there, lying in bed, watching as the covers were tucked around his boyish limbs while listening to her musical voice. His eyes were drawn to the golden aura that surrounded her tender face. It was beautiful. So peaceful.

"Would you like me to read to you, Johnny?" She asked.

"Sure, Mama Ruth. I'd like that very much," John answered, unable to stop staring at her visage.

Ruth opened the book and began softly reading the text.

"Finally, my brethren, be strong in the Lord, and in the power of his might. Put on the whole armour of God, that ye may be able to stand against the wiles of the devil. For we wrestle not against flesh and blood, but against principalities, against powers, against the rulers of the darkness of the world, against spiritual wickedness in high places. Wherefore take unto you the whole armour of God, that ye may be able to withstand in the evil day, and have done all, to stand. Stand therefore, having your loins girt about with truth, and having on the breastplate of righteousness. And your feet shod with the preparation of the gospel of peace. Above all, taking the shield of faith, wherewith ye shall be able to quench all the fiery darts of the wicked."

Slowly, she closed the worn covers of the Bible and looked at John for his reaction.

"Did you like the story?" She asked.

"Where did you get that Bible, Mama Ruth?"

"It's Rebecca's. She gave it to me. Did you understand the story, Johnny? Do you know what's going to happen?" She asked while caressing the book.

"No, I don't understand. Why did you read those verses?"

"Victor said he would hurt me if I did, but I did it anyway. It's important that you understand." Ruth looked over her shoulder as her face grew with apprehension.

John could see that her tranquil aura had changed to trembling fear. She was afraid of something waiting in the shadows. He strained to get a visual picture of the obscure figure in the corner of the room, but his eyes measured nothing.

"Why would Victor hurt you for reading the Bible?" John tried to wipe the tears from her cheek as she answered between quivering breaths, but his hand felt nothing.

"Because...Because he's the—"

"SILENCE!" The sinister voice rumbled like thunder. "I told you what I'd do if you disobeyed me!"

Out of the shadows stepped what appeared to be Victor Lechman, or part of him anyway. The creature's hoofs clopped with a noisome, malevolent pitch as streams of vapor spurted from his open nostrils like hot gas from a volcano.

"Please don't hurt my boy. You can hurt me if you're mad about what I did, but please don't hurt Johnny," she begged.

"Shut up, you bitch! I'll do what I please!" Victor's voice roared as he moved forward.

Now within reach, he paused, allowing John to size up his strength and power. John stared with his mouth agape. He could only imagine that the beast had been evoked from some terrible colony of demons summoned to keep defiant mortals in line for disobeying their blasphemous commands. Victor looked horrible. Standing upright, he bore the resemblance of a disrupted creature that was part human and part animal. Above the shoulders, he held his own natural face, distorted only by the outpouring of steam from his snout and the imposing horns that curved inward like evil hooks. But below, his normalcy was grossly interrupted by the black, bestial body of an enormous bull. He was menacing, thick with massive ox-like muscles that surrounded a swag belly. Sweat glistened from his lathered hide as he swayed back and forth, swinging his cloven forelegs.

"So, you want some answers, Johnny boy? Victor hissed. "Is that why you're here?"

"Yeah, I want some answers." John snapped at the creature with all the courage he could muster.

"Are you afraid," Victor smirked.

"I'm not afraid of you," John whispered.

Victor erupted into a profane laughter as he stepped even closer. "Your mama can't help you now." Victor's eyes turned blood red with a glare as Ruth disappeared from the scene. "You see, your mama left you by yourself. She doesn't even care about you."

"That's not true! She would never leave me. You made her leave. Now bring her back," John cried.

"Time to go, boy. I'll take you with me and tell you what you want to know."

John yanked the bed covers over his head as Victor reached downward with his deformed limbs. John broke from the terrible dream and sat up like a jack-in-the-box. His fearful screams had propelled him from sleep in an explosive awakening. If this dream was a message from beyond, its dark tidings were a mystery to him. Gradually, his heart rate slowed, allowing him to relax and ponder his nightmare. He was certain Dr. Goodall would take great stock in his dream, especially with Victor appearing as a Minotaur. The doctor would surely conclude that the strange creature was a symbol of some hidden fear buried deep in John's soul.

And Goodall would probably surmise that John's guise as an adolescent may well suggest that he was acting immature, and the appearance of Mama Ruth was a signal for him to be more tolerant and understanding. Then again, he may conclude that the bizarre vision was symbolic of nothing other than an over worked imagination. John decided to leave the interpretation to the experts. He pushed the blankets off his sweat soaked torso and made a quick trip to the bathroom to empty his swollen bladder. Returning relieved, he reclined back in bed.

After an hour, he slowly drifted back to sleep, hopeful that he had seen the last of Victor's hideous apparition. He had seen enough demons, ghosts, and goblins to last a lifetime. A dream of a chimera evening with a sexy blonde bombshell would be a welcome substitute, but he had an eerie feeling that the night would hold anything but bouncing bosoms and slender legs.

Soon, he would learn that his premonition was true. Returning again to third-stage sleep, he found himself back at his foster home. This time, he was a mature thirty-year-old. The action began as John passed through the dark doorway to the den. It was there that he found him, resting in his favorite chair, watching the evening news. He watched his foster dad's ashen eyes shift from the television to him, staring with a look of quiet anguish. John felt a mix of love and sadness.

He was a teenager when his Papa Dan unexpectedly died in a mining accident and John had always regretted not having the opportunity to say good bye. Papa Dan was the man he loved and respected most, the man who had taught him to follow his heart, to listen to his soul. The cast of his foster dad was as he had remembered him, face covered with ember soot and work clothes in tatters. The vision pulled at his heart as he stared at his Papa Dan's transfixed eyes.

Dan's visage reminded him that his papa was reared as a dirt-poor east Kentucky boy who learned that the measure of a man was more than the position he held or the gold in his pocket. For ten years, John listened and watched. And for ten years, he absorbed the undefined wisdom of a workaday coal miner with a third-grade education, a time-hardened man who knew more about life than all the highbrow intellects on earth. While Mama Ruth taught John to be faithful by citing the Scriptures, his Papa Dan schooled him on courage and honor by living the same words she so passionately quoted.

"Papa Dan, is that you?" John asked.

"Yeah, Johnny, it's me. I've missed you, son. I've missed you a lot," he said in a soft voice.

"I've missed you too. Where have you been?"

"I've been away, away for a long time," Papa Dan answered.

"But you're not going away again, are you? You're going to stay." John felt a wave of sadness and attempted to move to the man he cherished. He desperately wanted to welcome him back with a loving hug, yet he was unable to budge. His feet were held fast to the floor and his impassioned prayer could not be answered. The barrier between them could not be broken.

"No, son. I ain't comin' back. I can't. But you've gotta listen to me."

Again, John attempted to move forward, but his effort was useless. The invisible barrier was too powerful, "What is it?"

Rising from the recliner, Dan turned to face him. His pale blue eyes were piercing; the white orbs were bordered by his blackened face. "Johnny, I've seen your daughter. She's so beautiful." He smiled.

"Yeah, she really is," John said with pride of his own.

"She's in danger, Johnny. You've got to protect her." His smile disappeared and worry returned.

"I don't understand. Why is she in danger? Is somebody trying to harm her?" John asked.

"I can't tell you, son. But you've gotta wake up and make sure she's all right."

"Boo's just fine, Papa Dan. I want to stay with you. I want to make sure you and Mama Ruth are okay."

"Listen to me, Johnny. Me and your mama are fine. We're at peace now. But you can't stay, it's not your time. You've gotta wake up now."

The dream was so real and his need to commune with this man was so strong, but Papa Dan always spoke the truth.

"Okay, I'll check on her, and then I'll come back."

As John turned to leave the room, the Minotaur appeared from the darkness. The beast swung its forehoof, striking John above the right temple. He never saw it coming. As odd as it seemed, he was out cold, unconscious in his own supernatural dream. Whether or not his foster dad's warning was a message of some waking danger facing his daughter was of no consequence, he simply could not wake from this unearthly slumber.

It could have been five minutes or five hours. John didn't know. But he had recovered from the blow and was lucid again, back to dreaming. It was then that he heard the faint cry of her voice in the mist. It was Boo, calling his name.

"Daddy," her voice sounded like a far-off chime.

"Boo, is that you?" John spoke to the wind as he pulled himself to a sitting position.

"Daddy," the voice grew dimmer.

247

The bleary fog cleared from his eyes in time to turn dream into nightmare. Rebecca and Boo, his two perfect loves, were in a bright aura. Both were standing before him, clutching each other's hand, staring intently at his face. He watched in bewilderment as the wind rushed about, blowing their hair, and billowing their dresses. His heart shivered as he watched them slowly fade into the radiant light. In despair, he rose to his feet and attempted to run to their side. But, again, the barrier could not be broken.

37

RINGGGGGGG!

John awoke from the nightmare to the shrill ring of the telephone on the nightstand. The vivid details of the dream sent a shock wave through his nervous system strong enough to spike his wavy hair straight. He was frightened, cold with sweat, so afraid that the imagery of his dream was more than a creation of his subconscious mind. Frantically, he slapped at the phone until, finally, his clumsy hand found the receiver.

"Hello?" He said, still breathless.

"Mister John, it's Tina."

"Yeah, Tina. What is it? Is everything okay?"

"Someting's wrong with Boo. She's very sick." Tina's voice trembled.

John scrambled from the bed with lightning speed. "I'm leaving right now. I'll be at your house in ten minutes to pick her up."

"No, Mister John. We're not at my house."

"Where are you?" He could hear the sound of sobbing on her end of the call. It sent a chill up his spine. "Tina, where are you?" He pleaded.

There was an unsettling pause of silence, then he heard the murmur of voices, and then a stranger spoke.

"Hello, Mr. Williams. This is Ann Morgan. I'm a nurse at North Lake Hospital. Your daughter is with the doctor. You need to come here right away."

"What's wrong with my daughter?" His voice now filled with manic anxiety.

"You can speak to the doctors about that when you get here. Just come up to the fourth floor."

John never bothered to say good bye, instead he dropped the phone and bolted for the closet. There he found a pair of jeans, a tee shirt, and sneakers. His mind, now awash with disorderly thoughts, made even the simplest task of dressing an awkward affair. The tee shirt on backwards, the jeans difficult to zip, and the left shoe on the right foot. Finally, he got it right. Then came his unskillful attempt at starting the car. He dropped the keys twice on the Chevy's floorboard before he finally inserted the ignition key into the starter. It was all part of the hurry, all part of the confusion.

The speeding Chevy never bothered to stop for the red signs or red lights. To John, they simply didn't exist. He just kept driving, talking to himself in a strange, monotone voice, and driving faster. Fortunately, there was little traffic on the Sunday morning streets. So, he moved on, his voice growing silent as he switched to nervously biting his fingernails. The flow of adrenaline finally slowed when he caught glimpse of the medical center. As he approached, he slowed and looked for the main entrance. North Lake was no different than most other hospitals—its unclear signs and one-way streets made for difficult maneuvering. The layout had to be the work of some maniacal engineer hell-bent on adding to the emotional strain of those visiting the premises. For John, the scheme had served its purpose.

Once inside, he found the directions no better than those outside. His eyes darted about until he located a sign directing him to the elevator that would take him to the fourth floor. It was then that the grip of fear made his racing heart stand still. The placard revealed that the ICU was on that same floor. Cops are trained to remain calm in all sorts of intense situations, but all of that training takes flight when their loved ones were at risk. He knew something was terribly wrong; the feeling had descended to his heart.

Fear turned to panic as the silver doors opened and Tina and Nurse Morgan were waiting on the other side. It wasn't the tears from Tina that delivered the horrible news, but the grief swollen eyes of Ann Morgan. Medical professionals, like cops, are also schooled on how to deal with intense situations. And on this dark Sunday morning, Morgan's desensitization training had betrayed her as well.

"Where's Boo?" John's voice trembled.

Morgan stepped forward and gently squeezed his hand. "Mr. Williams, I'm Ann Morgan. We spoke on the phone."

"Where's Boo? Where's my little girl?" He frantically asked.

"She's in a treatment room down the hall," Morgan answered.

"I want to see her now!" John demanded.

"Dr. Roland wants to speak with you. I'll have to take you to him first."

John wanted to argue, but he didn't. Instead, he swallowed hard attempting to clear his mental circuits for the meeting with the doctor. He understood hospital procedure. He had experienced the same formalities when Rebecca was treated. The doctor always comes first.

The walk down the hall seemed to last forever. His movements felt slow, as though he was weighted by an enormous gravitational pull. Yet, he pushed forward, never noticing the wheelchaired patients, the rolling stretchers, or the bustling staff of orderlies, nurses, and doctors. He just stared vacantly ahead down the gray hallway as the disjointed thoughts rolled through his head. *Maybe it's just a virus or, at worst case, the flu. Maybe.* But he knew it wasn't. He could sense it. Too many tears.

Ann Morgan opened the door, allowing the room's antiseptic odor to shake John from his broken thoughts. Both stepped inside to find Dr. Roland furiously scribbling on what looked like a patient file affixed to a metal clip board. John was surprised. Roland looked more like a rock 'n roll star than a medical doctor. A shock of unruly red hair and a scraggly beard covered his young face. He appeared wild eyed and agitated, more suited for a leather jacket and a bass guitar than a white smock and a surgeon's scalpel. John stood in disbelief. He had expected to find an experienced practitioner with graying temples and a square jaw. That was the type of doctor he wanted treating his daughter. Instead, he found a cocky second year resident.

"Mr. Williams, when your daughter came in this morning, she had a very high fever, and she was having difficulty breathing. She had very rapid and shallow breaths, like an asthmatic. Has your daughter ever been diagnosed with asthma or any other bronchial disease?"

"No, never. Is she okay now?" John nervously asked.

"Has she been taking any medications?"

"No, nothing," John quickly responded.

"Has she ever had pneumonia or any other respiratory infection?" Roland asked, not bothering to answer John's question or return his gaze.

"Nothing more than a cold or sore throat. She's always been healthy."

"Has she ever been diagnosed with tuberculosis?" Roland continued.

"No, I told you, she's never had anything more serious than a stomach virus. Why are you asking me all of these questions? Is my daughter all right?" John bit his lower lip as heat filled his face and nausea squeezed his stomach.

"I need her medical history for the records. Has she ever been tested for the HIV virus?"

"HIV virus?! Look, I told you that she's always been healthy. I want to see her now!" John demanded as the frustration mounted.

Roland quickly glanced at his notes. "Your daughter fell into a coma about fifteen minutes after she arrived this morning. About twenty minutes later, at 6:10, she stopped breathing. We still don't have any test results so all I can do is give you a preliminary guess. Could be a congenital malformation of the lungs, or maybe an allergic reaction to some foreign substance. It may even be a rare parasitic disease similar to pneumocystis pneumonia. I've sent a blood sample to CDC for testing so it may take—"

"Whoa, wait a minute! What do you mean she stopped breathing? What are you talking about?" John interrupted

Roland continued his unfeeling prose. "As I said, at 6:10, she died from respiratory failure. Now, it may take a couple weeks to get the CDC results, but in the meantime, I would recommend an autopsy. That way, we can cover all the bases. All I need is your signature on—"

John lost his sense of balance. He was torn between a feeling of sweeping anger and that of complete despair. He wanted to slap Roland's arrogant face into the next county, but the crushing weight of the doctor's announcement left him in a state of paralysis.

"You must be mistaken. My little girl has never been sick. You're wrong," John said the words, but he knew they had no meaning. He longed to simply walk down the hall, pick up his exuberant daughter, go home, and get his life back to normal. But his wish would not be granted.

John couldn't remember turning his back on Roland and walking out the door, nor could he remember the wobbly trip to the ICU treatment room. A drowning tide of emptiness had muddled his senses, leaving him weak-kneed and bewildered. Fortunately, Nurse Morgan was there; she allowed him to lean on her slender shoulder as she guided him down the hall. When the door finally opened, he staggered inside and inched closer to the bed.

At first, he refused to look. He merely sat at her side, softly calling her name, telling her what they would do when they got home. He talked for two hours before he finally summoned the courage to pull back the snow-white sheet. It was then that the tears began to fall. Like crestfallen rain they poured. The sight of her expressionless face sent a spiral of pain to his broken heart. He couldn't think straight. All he could do was beg God to bring his baby back, to make her eyes shine again, to take him instead. Over and over, he pleaded as he held her little body against his chest.

PART THREE

38

Take heed that ye despise not one of
these little ones; for I say unto you,
That in Heaven their angels do always,
behold the face of my Father....
                    Matthew 18:10

Sorrow does not discriminate among the young or the old, nor does it favor men more than women. It does not cast judgment or consider its harmful effect. It is a living death that is simply indifferent. One day its consuming face appears at your heart's doorstep and invites itself in. And when that mournful day arrives, you are left with heartbreaking grief and disillusionment, a lack of self-worth that leaves you disconnected with the rest of the world.

And so, that was how John's pain began. He was left a broken man without a soul. He no longer hungered to watch another rising sun or astral moon, nor did his heartsick body feel a need for nourishing food or quenching drink. Life's harmony was stolen from him when the thing most precious in his life was taken away. His initial reaction was to surround himself in silence. The house had become tomblike, isolated and dark. And he had become a living zombie, withdrawn from the world, content to drink himself into drunken stupors. That was the only way he could cope, the only way he could find any semblance of peace that would allow him to sleep. And so, for over four days, that was how it went.

39

The memorial service was scheduled for mid-afternoon. Lori and Tina had had met with the funeral director and chosen a brief chapel ovation without the typical grave-side ritual. Both had handled the arrangements since John was unable to effectively express his thoughts. They had also made a crude attempt at grooming and dressing him for the funeral. Although they had done their best, he still wore the signs of anguish in his empty eyes, tangled hair, and half shaven face. He also looked anemic. The terrible grief had him skipping meals and drinking instead. The smell of whiskey on his breath announced that he was not ready to make the pilgrimage to recovery. The booze had racked his senses, dulling the pain and prolonging his unwillingness to communicate with anyone.

Tina knew he was on the path of self-destruction. She had discovered two half empty bottles of Jack Daniels in his bedroom. One bottle was on its side on the carpeted floor while the other was placed on top of Rebecca's Bible on the nightstand. She gathered them up and poured the alcohol down the bathroom sink. Then, she searched the house for any additional stash. Meanwhile, Lori ushered John down the stairs to the kitchen and prepared a turkey sandwich and chips. The food remained mostly uneaten, but he did manage to drink two cups of strong coffee.

Within minutes, Tina joined them with Azriel following closely behind. The cat had been outside for three days subsisting on a meager diet of two slow footed chipmunks and an inattentive robin. The feline's belly was swollen from the incidental fur and feathers. Tina had the answer to Azriel's problem. She opened a can of chicken and tuna mix and fed the half-starved animal. Afterwards, she gave John a mild rebuke for ignoring the cat and made one last attempt at prodding him to finish his own meal. His refusal signaled that it was time to leave for the funeral home.

Tina's beat-up Buick rumbled down Roswell Road as the engine sputtered and the front-end shook from the lack of alignment. The steering wheel quivered like a vibrating bed at a cheap motel as she goosed the pedal, urging the old clunker up the next hill. She gave little thought to the impatient drivers who blew their horns and flicked their obscene gestures. She just plowed ahead and made idle chat with Lori while John, seated in the back, stared vacantly into space. He remained lifeless until he overheard Tina talking to Lori about Boo.

She was describing the strange events on Friday night and early Sunday morning. Tina gave a chilling account of the peculiar sounds beginning around midnight on the first evening. The disturbance began when she woke up to the noise of opening and closing doors and the soft patter of footsteps. She rose and followed the sounds to the bedroom where her granddaughter and Boo were sleeping. She stood outside the closed door and listened intently as two strange, disembodied voices broke the stillness of the night. For some reason she froze. It was as though she was mesmerized by the unnatural tone. She knew it wasn't her granddaughter or Boo, but she still couldn't lift a hand to turn the doorknob. Perhaps it was fear. Yes, it had to be fear. That was the only explanation that made any sense.

"That's when I hear the scream," Tina said.

"What scream? What did you hear?" Lori asked.

"It was loud. It sounded like someone was yelling "low tire shoe!"

"Low tire shoe. That's weird. What did you do then?" Lori questioned as John leaned forward. He wanted to overhear the conversation.

"The door was locked, I couldn't get in, so I went to get my husband. When we get back to the room, the door was open."

"Oh, my god!" Lori gasped. "You must be kidding?"

"No, it's true," Tina answered.

"Were the girls okay?" Lori asked.

"Yes, they were asleep. So, we looked in the house and find nothing."

"What did you do then?"

"My husband says one of the girls was talking in her sleep. He didn't believe me when I tell him it wasn't. So, he went back to bed and sleep."

"What did you do?" Lori asked.

"I go back to bed with him, but I couldn't sleep. I still hear someone walking in the house later on—two or three times."

"Did you wake him and tell him about that?"

"No, no! He thinks I'm crazy, so I didn't tell him," Tina answered.

Tina continued the story by describing the faint rustlings she heard throughout the night. When the sun rose, she questioned the girls about the voices and sounds, yet neither had awakened nor heard anything all evening. So, with the help of her husband, she managed to convince herself that she had imagined the unearthly footsteps and strange voices. She was certain she had conjured it all up until the unimaginable occurred during the wee hours on Sunday. Once more, she was stirred from a restless sleep by an eerie scream from her granddaughter's bedroom. But this time, her husband heard it as well. Both jolted upward at the horrible sound.

"We got to the bedroom, but no one was there."

"What about the girls? Were they gone?"

"No, they were still there, but Boo was very hot, she had fever and was talking in her sleep. She was calling for Mister John to help."

"Was your granddaughter sick, too?" Lori asked.

"No, she was okay. But Boo began to shake and yell for her mother. And the room, it smelled very bad." Tina gave a nervous twitch of her nose as though a foul odor had entered the car.

"What kind of smell?" Lori asked.

"I don't know. Nothing like I ever smell before. It was in the air, in the bedroom and some in the hall. And Boo, she had the bad smell on her. And she just kept on crying for her mother and father, and she was shaking...."

Tina burst into tears. She was deeply attached to Boo and her memories had brought a shower of emotional pain. Her cutting words had also reopened John's painful wound as he recoiled back in the seat, fighting off his own tears. The pain had, again, gathered on his pale face. His listless appearance warned that he had, most likely, dismissed Tina's story as an overworked imagination. This was just one more weird incident that could be logically explained. He had withdrawn back into silence, feeling betrayed, unable to come to terms with the tragedy.

Tina slid the big Buick into a reserved parking space at the back entrance to the funeral home and gathered her composure. John, still in a daze, was an emotional mess and Tina knew she needed to be strong for him, to provide him a comforting shoulder to lean on. Lori knew that as well. So, the two of them helped John from the car, escorted him inside and down a narrow hallway to a private side door to the chapel. He took a seat in the front row that was reserved for family and special friends. Their plan to avoid the people milling about in the larger foyer and in the back of the chapel had worked. With shoulders hunched and eyes tightly closed, he sat in solitude, away from the grave faces and solemn voices. But it really didn't matter. He couldn't hear the mourns, nor see the tears or smell the perfume of the circled flowers.

He never even heard Pastor Sims's profound words about how Boo's death was part of a greater plan, and how she was in a better place now. It was best that he didn't, for he wouldn't have embraced his words anyway. His mind was closed, withdrawn into the breeches of a helpless void, unwilling to receive any measure of solace from the outside world. He was sitting in repose as those around him remembered his beautiful daughter in a tearful rite.

After the service, Lori moved John about the chapel and foyer like a puppet, making him available to greet the many consoling friends. At that point he began to notice his surroundings, to break just a little from his muted shell. The sight of his fellow officers along with their warm handshakes and tender hugs had a therapeutic effect. He needed it. It reminded him that he had many friends that cared deeply for him and Boo, that maybe there was a breath of hope that could help him recover. For a brief moment, he actually felt human.

But the comfort quickly left when Victor arrived with a clumsy remark about Boo's death being God's will. Lieutenant Milligan's comment that it was good that Boo didn't suffer was more than he could stand. To John, the thought that God would abandon his baby, let alone knowingly sponsor the taking of his innocent lamb was totally unacceptable. And the notion that Boo's passing occurred without pain certainly did not mitigate the fact that she was gone. Both tenets were reprehensible to a grieving father, but the mere thought that a divine being would place lethal sights on his little girl made his heart burn bitter with hate. It implored him to instantly reject all of his religious teachings. His face had hardened into twisted muscle, hewn from anger and grief. He had heard enough. Lori and Tina recognized his angst and quickly dismissed him from the encircled voices, thanking the surprised friends as they spun him toward the exit. They urged him through the remaining crowd and out the side door. Only Charlie Connors was able to intercept him in the parking lot before they reached Tina's car.

"John! I've got to talk to you about Boo," Connors said in a beseeching voice.

John could only guess that Connors was about to add to Victor's and Milligan's insensitive remarks. Maybe something about everything being okay because Boo was now with her mother—words he simply didn't want to hear.

"I've got to go, Charlie. I can't talk," John brushed aside his friend as he opened the Buick's rear door.

"John, I know this is a terrible time, but I've got to talk to you about the lab tests on Boo. It's important."

"I'm not in the mood to talk about it. I just don't care right now." John slammed the door and sank into the seat as Tina cranked the sputtering engine.

Connors was determined. He walked, almost at a trot beside the big car, yelling through the closed window, insisting on getting in one more plea. "John, please! Give me a call. I've got some important information that you need to hear."

John was stunned. Until now, he hadn't noticed the look on Connors' face. But as he glanced over his left shoulder, he caught a glimpse of a stare, a look of precarious concern that made him wonder what deep, dark secret Connors was holding. He wondered, just for a second, and then fell back into his indifferent trance.

40

The next twenty-four hours provided John one more day to
harden his heart and deaden his senses. Tina's booze raid
had failed to uncover a bottle hidden inside the cabinet under the kitchen sink. After the funeral, John wasted no time
refueling his agony with the liquor. Resting on the den recliner, he methodically filled glass after glass, drinking and
thinking of the future that could have been. It was his way of
continuing the solemn withdrawal. Finally, the whiskey took
hold, sending him into a deep, hypnotic sleep. In this unconscious state, he was able to follow his daughter's footsteps
through a reborn time as though her tragic death had never
occurred. It allowed him to measure his own fatherly role in
this make-believe world; through her loving letters, he found
a temporary peace.

Dear Daddy,

*Today we went swimming in the lake. They let
the boys swim with us but mostly they teased
us. I think its cause they like us. I met one boy
who was nise. Hes ten years old like me. His
name is Mark and this is his third time at summer camp. He was on my team when we
played soft ball. I fell and scraped my knee
and my countseler let me watch for the rest of
the game. Shes nise. Her name is Donna. We
had a campfire tonite and got to roast hot dogs
and marshmellows. Mark sat next to me. It
was fun but I miss Tinas cooking. Tomorrow
we get to go canoeing and make something in
arts and krafts. They are about to turn off the*

lights so I better end this letter. I miss you and love you very much. Hug Tina and Azriel for me. Ha, Ha, like you would do that.

Love you lots,
Boo

Dear Dad,

After three weeks at college, I've become an incurable football fan. I never realized how exciting a game could be until this past weekend. A stadium filled with 90,000 Bulldawg fans is a sight to behold and hear. The barking goes on forever. I know you're not a big football fan, but I wish you would come see a game. And, don't get worried, I'm studying in between games, dates and parties. Ha, Ha, just kidding. Actually, I'm studying a lot. I like all of my classes except one. My English professor acts like a real stiff, I mean, no personality. There is a real cute guy in the class though. His name is Wes and he asked me out for Saturday night. I think you would like him. Oh, I think I may get a part-time job answering the phones at the Campus Security Office. I told them my dad was a cop and they seemed to like that. The money you put in my account doesn't seem to go very far so I really need the work.

Got to close, hope to come home in a couple of weeks. The football team has an away game.

Love you,
Lisa Beth

Dear Papa,

Wesley has an interview next week in Atlanta. It would be great if he got an offer and we were able to move back to the South. We have some wonderful friends in Chicago, but I sure miss the warm weather and Southern hospitality. I'm sure I could find a job teaching in the Fulton County school system and the company that's interested in Wesley is really solid. Besides, I know you'd like to spend more time with Johnny. It's hard to believe he's already five years old. We tell him he looks more and more like his Papa every day. And he runs to the phone every time it rings, hoping it's you. He's really crazy about you. You must of brainwashed him on your last visit because he's been telling all of his little soccer friends that he wants to be a policeman when he grows up. I think Wesley is jealous of the influence you have on him, but I think it's great. Well, the reason I'm writing is to let you know that we're coming next week with Wesley, and Johnny and I want to stay with you, if we can.

Wesley is going to visit his parents in Macon after the interview. I'll call you this weekend to let you know our plans.

Love,
Lisa

John woke up to the sound of thunder at ten o'clock in the evening. It was at that moment he realized his dream was just that, only a dream. He knew that the mail from his daughter would always remain unopened. Now, he understood why the death of a child was the ultimate tragedy. Unlike a parent whose son or daughter dies on a battlefield, or an elderly parent who loses a middle-aged offspring, or even parents who suffer through the death of a newborn, nothing could be more painful than the loss of a growing, full-of-life adolescent. It was Boo who had briefly experienced the joy of life, yet it was Boo who would never learn of life's beauty.

John's pain was knowing that she would never tingle from the thrill of her first love, nor hold her head high on graduation day. He understood too well that she would never whisper, "I do," or swell with pride from a much-deserved promotion. But the harshest pain was knowing that Boo would never feel the innocent arms of her own child wrapped tightly around her neck. John knew what it was like to experience that feeling, to be uplifted in spirit by that tender embrace. And he knew that to lose that loving touch was to leave a person without hope. And without hope, one cannot live. That was where he found himself, lost without direction in an incomplete world. He opened his eyes, stared upward at the off-white ceiling, and issued a soft prayer.

"Please, I just wish she could come back. I just want her back at home where she belongs. I'd do anything to get her back. Anything," he cried.

He groped for the over-stuffed arms of the recliner, lifted himself upward, and swayed to his feet. There was nothing quite like watching a drunk attempt to maneuver through a house. With hair looking almost Medusa-like, John walked at a tilt as he stumbled to-and-fro, tripping over his own clumsy feet. When he reached the bedroom, he didn't bother to remove his untucked shirt or wrinkled trousers. He was just too exhausted. Instead, he took one last swig of the hooch and collapsed on the bed. He rolled to his side and coiled his arms and legs into a fetal position. His willingness to resort to wishing and praying for something he knew would never be granted showed just how desperate he felt. But when you are powerless, magical thinking may be your only option. So, he softly repeated his prayer.

"Please, God. Please bring back my baby." He wept, and then fell to sleep.

The night offered no horrible nightmares or unwanted flashbacks. As a matter of fact, it was the first time since Boo's death that John slept without interruption. That was, until about five in the morning when he felt the piercing jab to his lower back. His face scowled as he partially woke and issued a familiar admonition.

"Boo, sweetheart, you need to scoot over. You're kicking me in the back," John whispered.

Again, the poke came, but this time, with more punch. "Boo, move over or you're going to have to sleep in your own bed," John's voice grew louder.

Reality hit John ten minutes later. It took that long for his drowsy mind to calibrate and rationalize what he had felt. Quickly, he sat up in bed as his head pounded from the hang-over and his heart raced from the spine-tingling feeling. His eyes searched for his missing daughter. Of course, she wasn't there. It was simply a dream—nothing more than a subliminal trick of the mind. He attempted to slow the throb in his aching head and the beat of his racing heart as he listened to the patter of the rain on the bedroom window.

The strategy worked for a moment, until he felt it. With lightning speed, he sat up and flung the sheets to the foot of the bed. Underneath, he discovered something that made his heart speed at an out-of-control rhythm. It was Boo's favorite toy, the white stuffed bear she treasured so dearly, the bear she clung to every night in her sleep. John lifted the inanimate bear as though he was checking for a spark of life. For a long time, he held it, staring at its brown glassy eyes as though it held some hidden secret, a hidden truth about his daughter. And for a long time, he tried to rationalize the bear's sudden appearance in his bed. But like an un-programed computer, his brain held no answers. He had been drunk for a week and his fermented memory could recall only brief flashes, fuzzy pictures without method. He, of course, chose the sane explanation. Last night, in his drunken stupor, he had visited her room, gathered the bear and returned to sleep. He just couldn't remember what he had done. It was as simple as that.

John returned the stuffed animal to its resting place on Boo's bed. Supernatural thinking has no place in the real world.

41

"I'll be there in twenty minutes, John. I promise."

It was Charlie Connors. The call had wrenched John from a mid-afternoon respite. These semi-conscious binges of alcohol mixed with depression had become routine for him and today was no different. He understood very little of what Connors had to say, other than needing to talk to him about Boo's death. He would have refused his visit, but he never got the chance. Connors hung up the phone too quickly. It was an effective strategy. It forced John to momentarily leave his dismal thoughts of emptiness, hopelessness and worst of all, self-destruction. Yes, suicide, the most dreaded impulse, had now entered his mind. He had given up on wishing and praying for it was childish to think that magic would bring Boo back anyway. That sort of hope is reserved for kids who believe in Santa Claus and the Easter Bunny. His contemplation had progressed to something far more certain, something rooted in deadly reality—the unrefuted fact that a 10mm silvertip from his Colt couldn't bring back his daughter but, if God would forgive him, it could take him to her. But the urgency John felt in Connors' words made an imprint. He would suppress his forbidden thoughts and wait on his friend to arrive.

To Connors, a promise given was a promise kept. He was a man of few words who held truth to his bosom as a loving mother holds her newborn. His character was unreproachable, and John knew it. John opened the door, permitting Connors to enter. Once he stepped inside, he was virtually blind. His dark, brown eyes squinted, attempting to discern the features of the open room. John failed to offer any assistance, so Connors shuffled his feet, feeling his way until he found a light switch on the wall. He had anticipated finding a switch in that location, yet he had not anticipated what the vivid light would reveal.

What he noticed first was John's face. His complexion was white, corpselike, and haggard. And his hollow cheeks and reddish eyes made him look sickly and frail like an emaciated drug addict. Connors was stunned at how his friend's appearance had changed so dramatically in such a short period of time. And the smell was foul, very foul. Connors didn't need illumination to unveil that surprise. He caught a snoutfull of the sweat and urine as he walked over to greet his friend. But Connors said nothing about the odor or John's misshapen appearance. Instead, he kept his focus on the reason he was there.

"Mind if I sit down, John?" Connors asked as he moved to the sofa in the den.

"No, go ahead, Charlie, have a seat." John responded indifferently. He followed Connors to the den and returned to the recliner that had been his asylum over the past days.

"Are you okay?" Connors asked.

"Yeah, I'm all right. All right as I can be. I just need a drink."

"Before you have that drink, I've got to talk to you. It's important. That's why I tried to stop you at the chapel."

"You sounded strange on the phone," John said.

"I wanted to tell you how sorry I am about Boo. I know how much she meant to you. I know it hurts and that you miss her badly."

"You don't know, Charlie. You don't know how it feels," John answered quickly as tears welled in his eyes.

Connors disagreed, "I lost my first daughter in a car accident when she was four. She struggled to stay alive for two days. She never regained consciousness and I never had the chance to say good-bye or to tell her one last time how much I loved her and how much joy she brought to my life. So, I hurt. I hurt so bad that I didn't care about my friends, my family, and even my wife. I hurt so bad I didn't think I could stand it. So, I do know how you feel, John, and I do know what you're going through."

John didn't reply. He looked down to his feet and lifted a white shoe box off the floor. The box was filled with photographs of Boo. It was the treasure he had carried with him everywhere in the house. He had taken it from room to room, to bed, and even on his occasional trips to the bathroom when the booze sent him in search of the toilet. John reached inside and lifted the photo on top. It was the last one taken, the one of her dressed in baby doll pajamas, holding Azriel in her arms. He was silent for a moment as he stared at her blonde hair and deep blue eyes. At that precise moment he finally understood. Connors had confirmed the truth that no amount of wishing and hoping would bring her back. As the tears rolled down his cheeks, his eyes drifted upward to find the face of his friend. The time had come for John to say the painful words that proclaimed he wondered no more.

"She's not coming back, is she, Charlie?" John cried.

"No, John. Boo's not coming back," Connors broke down as well.

Tears flowed like a wellspring from the eyes of a man who had just peered into his own wounded soul, a man who trembled with the knowledge that a part of him was forever gone. It was life's cruelest lesson and the enormity of its impact was impossible to mark; the scars were invisible and the void was without scale. It was a feeling that was indescribable to someone who has never been touched by the pain. But Charlie had suffered through the grief and had felt the same pain.

And so, he rose to console his friend and to share in the sorrow. It was a closing of lives between two men who had little in common outside of their work. They embraced and cried. The loss they shared allowed them a special, unforgettable moment. When the two finally regained their composure, they sat and talked about their daughters' brief childhoods, their hopes, and their dreams. A hint of relief appeared on John's pallid face. He was actually beginning to feel human again until Connors told him the other reason for his visit.

"John, I have a good friend at North Lake, at the hospital."

"Yeah?"

"I stopped by there the other night and read Boo's patient file. My friend arranged it. I told him it was part of our investigation into her death."

"Why?" John asked.

"I did it because I was suspicious. Suspicious that the doctor didn't give you all the facts about how she died."

"What are you saying?"

"I'm saying that there were some unusual circumstances about her condition that you weren't told," Connors continued.

"Like what?"

"Well, first of all, one of the emergency room nurses recorded that Boo had rigors."

"What's that?"

"It's an involuntary shaking of the upper body," Connors stated.

"Tina said she was shaking when she took her to the hospital," John replied.

"Yeah, but Boo was shaking violently, and she never stopped. Usually rigors will come and go, but not with Boo. Plus, her breathing was very short and rapid… and the nurse recorded that her mouth and throat were raw and bleeding."

"Nobody told me she had rigors or that she was bleeding."

"Did anybody ask you if she'd been sick?" Connors asked.

"That piss-ant of a doctor asked me and I told him no," John snarled.

"That's what's so strange—that she would have those types of symptoms so suddenly without warning. It just doesn't make sense."

"No, it doesn't. What else did you find out?" John asked.

"Extremely high fever. And Roland, your piss-ant of a doctor, reported a toxic, unidentifiable odor emanating from her respiration and sweat. The odor was so strong that one of the nurses collapsed from being overcome. He described it as smelling of phosphate or sulfur."

"Doctor didn't say anything about that. He just said she may have had an allergic reaction or maybe pneumonia," John responded.

"Wasn't pneumonia. Sample taken from Boo's lungs was sent to toxicology for analysis. It came back negative, yet Roland recorded her cause of death as hemorrhagic pneumonia. That's how he explained the bleeding. He said that it was coming from her lungs, but remember the nurse reported there was hemorrhaging from Boo's mouth and throat, not her lungs?"

"Couldn't the nurse have been mistaken? Maybe it just looked like it was coming from her mouth?" John asked.

"Maybe, but the lab said it couldn't have been pneumonia. So, I tend to believe the nurse," Connors continued.

"Are you saying that the doctor is trying to cover something up?" John asked.

"I don't think it's a cover up. I just think they don't know what happened and why she died. So, they are being very careful about what they say and report. They're afraid of the liability if they misdiagnosed her condition."

"Do you think they screwed up, Charlie? Do you think Boo could've been saved?" John asked as his eyes widened with expectation.

"No, John. There was no way they could save her."

"Why do you say that?"

"The hospital sent a vile of her antemortem blood to the CDC for analysis. I read the report. It said that there was a powerful toxin in her blood, something similar to phosphorus but it had a different chemical make-up."

"How in the world did something like that get in her blood?"

"I don't know, John, but hang on to your seat for what I'm about to tell you." Connors leaned forward.

"What is it?" John leaned closer.

"Remember Sugar Bear?"

"Yeah, what about him?"

"Remember, I sent hair samples to the FBI lab for DNA analysis?"

"Yeah, I remember."

"Well, I also sent tissue samples from his wounds and samples of his blood, liver, and lungs for chemical analysis."

"And?" John asked.

"The DNA results aren't back yet, but I did receive the report on the other samples this morning. They reported that there was a poisonous toxin in Sugar Bear, a venom they couldn't identify, but they gave me the chemical make-up. It had the exact chemical profile as the toxin in Boo. The odds of that happening are a million-to-one, John. A million-to-one."

"Charlie, you're not saying what I think you're saying!"

"I know it sounds crazy, but I think their deaths are somehow related."

"No, it can't be. Boo had no connection with Sugar Bear."

"Yeah, but you do, John." Connors pointed at John.

"It just doesn't make sense," John shook his head in disagreement.

"Hell, none of these murders make sense, but I believe they are connected. I'm going to push for a court order to exhume Price and Rimmon. I want the FBI to run the same tests on them."

"Good luck with that. I'm sure you'll get a fight from their families."

"You're probably right, but I'm doing it anyway. And, John, I know you're not going to like this, but I—"

"Don't even say it. It's not going to happen!"

"But if I could take some samples from Boo and do an autopsy, then we could narrow this thing down."

"No way! Forget it. I've seen too many autopsies. You're not going to butcher her. You're not touching her," John yelled.

The heartfelt bond between John and Connors ended as quickly as it began. Connors' request was shocking, and it hurt John badly. It was a clear indication that he was thinking as a county medical examiner and not as a forlorn father. His hard words had, again, awakened John's bitterness. John immediately escorted him to the door. On the way out, he made it clear that if Connors tried to pursue the matter, he would perform an autopsy on him...a living autopsy. After John watched Connors back out of the driveway, he returned to his recliner, his bottle, and his pain.

42

It was nine o'clock in the evening when Lori called. The shrill ringing broke the silence in the house, forcing John from the den recliner. He rejected Lori's request to drop by. After the visit from Connors, a bitter uneasiness had dropped into his gut like a gallon of sea water. A visit from her tonight was simply not in the cards. Still feeling sick, he just couldn't stop thinking about his meeting with Charlie and his suspicion of foul-play. And Connors' request to perform an autopsy on Boo kept the knot in his stomach tied even tighter. Lori was smart. She didn't push it. Instead, she accepted his excuse and agreed to postpone her visit until the following evening.

Even though John was rankled by his physical illness, he had made a tremendous step toward improving his mental health. He had stopped drinking for the past twelve hours and it allowed his brain to regain a semblance of reason, and his desire to explain away Connors' illogical theories forced him into a frenzy of non-stop brainwork. There were still too many missing elements, too many for him to give factual credibility to his friend's speculation. Yet he knew that Connors was a man of reason, and that knowledge was enough to heighten his own curiosity.

He continued to ponder Connors theory until he walked upstairs and stopped by Boo's vacant bedroom. When he entered the room, he was struck by a faint, sweet scent. He tilted his head upward and flared his nostrils. Could it be jasmine? No. Perhaps the perfume of an orchid? No, it was neither. He inhaled deeply but did not recognize the bouquet or its origin. The only thing certain was that the scent was lovely, intoxicating, and comforting as though he were lying in a bed of roses. Yes, it could be the scent of a rose. And then, it disappeared into the darkness.

John thought it was strange that the smell seemed to materialize from nowhere and then vanish. He turned on the light and scanned for any additional clues. Nothing there, only the fastidious room of a four-year-old girl—and that was another oddity. The bed was neatly made, the stuffed animals were lined in two ranks on the dresser, the marker board resting on the easel was cleaned and unused, the floor was vacuumed, and the bookshelves were dusted. Unknown to John, Tina had cleaned Boo's room the day of the funeral. She had also aligned her toys in meticulous fashion as though she were arranging treasures for a hallowed shrine. He had been in the room since her cleaning spree but he was too drunk to notice, almost too drunk to even remember being there. Now, everything was clear to his sober eyes. It was unnatural to see such order in a place that earlier held such little-girl excitement. He missed the array of broken Crayolas, strewn coloring books, scattered animals, and loose clothing. The stillness made him feel sad, and a new surge of hopelessness found his heart. How could anyone harm his beautiful little girl? Why would anyone do such a horrible thing?

John lingered for a minute and then left the room, pulling the door tightly closed behind. Much like the stormy sky outside, a shadowy cloud of his own had propelled him back into the booze for a heavy nightcap. After a single and a follow-up double, he curled up in bed and fell asleep listening to the wind howling around the eaves. He slept soundly for an hour, ignoring the loud thunder and bright lightning until the slightest whisper of a sound woke him up. It was an unmistakable voice that he could barely discern between the thunderous claps of the rainstorm. At first, the sound seemed to come out of the walls like a wistful echo. But then as his mind cleared, he determined that the voice was coming from

Boo's bedroom. He heard it again, but this time with more clarity.

"Daddy," it whimpered.

John sat up in bed, looked to his left in the darkness and carefully listened. This time, for certain, the cry came from her bedroom.

"Daddy, please help me."

A panic-stricken grip of terror tightened around his neck, making it very difficult for him to breathe. Here was a man of enormous strength, a man who feared nothing of flesh and bone, a man untouchable by even the fiercest of men. Yet, the grit of his muscle and the skill of his hands were useless against something he could not see or touch. He was scared. He switched on the lamp on the nightstand, rose from bed and moved cautiously toward her bedroom door. When he arrived, he heard the voice one last time as it faded to silence.

"Daddy. Help meeee...."

John stood there breathless, his heart thumping wildly. For an instant, he thought of walking away, of accepting the voice as an illusion of his overwrought mind. But his need to investigate was too great and he was certain that the plaintive voice was not a figment of his imagination. Slowly, he turned the doorknob until the latch released. He then pushed the creaky door with his fingers, exerting just enough force to swing it open. Cautiously, he slipped into the shadowy room and looked from right to left. Unable to clearly see, he reached for the wall switch and turned on the ceiling light.

His eyes nervously scanned from left to right, desperately searching for the source of the voice. He saw nothing, so he explored the closet. Nothing there, so he looked under the bed. Nothing again. *Perhaps my mind has snapped*, he thought. *Perhaps the depression has clouded my senses.* He had arrested many homicidal maniacs that blamed their actions on a little voice inside their heads. Perhaps it was happening to him.

Maybe he was turning into a deranged madman, unhinged by his terrible grief. But when he rose from the floor after searching under the bed, he saw an unnerving sight, a sight that made his eyes swell like saucers and his heart burn with dread.

Boo's properly made bed was no longer properly made. An indentation in the covers revealed that someone or something had been resting on top of the bed. John's first thought was to point an accusing finger at Azriel, but the bedroom door had been closed and the cat, afraid of the storm, was doing her nocturnal resting under the sofa in the den. Besides, the furrow in the covers was too large for a cat. It was more the impression of a child.

"What the hell is going on?" John murmured.

He had seen and heard enough. He quickly left the room, closed the door, and double checked the knob to make certain it was secure. Then, he walked back to his own bedroom. Until then, he had never considered the possibility of any kind of existence after death. Yet he was certain that the voice pleading for help belonged to Boo. He was also certain that the bed was neatly made when he had earlier visited the room. He struggled for a rational explanation for what had happened. He couldn't conjure one up, so he settled on formula raison d'etre—shock plus depression plus grief plus alcohol equals hallucination. Back to logic, that was the cop in him, still unable to fully embrace the unearthly.

The weird episode convinced John that he needed to return to the booze. He opened the bottle of Jack Daniels and took several long swigs before he returned to bed. It didn't take long for the alcohol to pool in his empty stomach then seep into his frayed nerves, making him less wary and more receptive to sleep. And sleep he did. He even dreamed about Boo. For a short time, he was peaceful, without apprehension, until the terror returned in the cast of a haunting silhouette.

BAAAAAM!

The explosive sound of the lightning bolt caused him to instantly sit upright, eyes flying open and mouth agape. Not prepared for what he saw, he screamed at the top of his lungs.

"BOOOOO!"

The vivid light from the thunderbolt streaked through the window blinds, turning his tranquil dream into a wakeful nightmare. It was Boo. No doubt about it. It was her standing beside the bed, dressed in blue baby doll pajamas, clutching a stuffed teddy bear, her eyes fixed intently on him. Aided by the flash of light, he saw her for only an instant, and then the bedroom was enveloped in blackness. A charge of primal fear sent a turgid flow of adrenaline coursing through his veins. His frantic attempt to turn on the lamp sent it crashing from the nightstand and to the floor. He leaped from the bed away from Boo's ghostlike image, and stumbled into the wall, cracking his head on a hanging picture in the process. The force of the collision rocked him senseless and dislodged the picture to the carpet. He would have been a worthy imitation of a slapstick comedian had the circumstances not been so dire. But this was no vaudeville act; it was an act of sheer panic. He clawed at the wall switch, finally turning on the fixed light on the ceiling. His bulging eyes blinked wildly as he grabbed his pounding chest, now afraid that his heart might explode. He saw nothing, no mysterious shadows, no haunting apparitions—no Boo.

He slowly caught his breath and began to rationalize. It was a nightmare, just a bad dream ignited by the thunderstorm. Boo had subconsciously been on his mind, and he was still in a semiconscious, dreamy state when the storm woke him. Boo's appearance beside his bed was simply the conjecture of a quiescent mind, after all, she had often times sought refuge in his bed on stormy nights.

John caught sight of something that made him break into a cold sweat. On his bed was something that could not be explained, something that sent a chill to the core of his soul...it was Boo's white teddy bear.

He found no sleep for the rest of the night.

43

John had always loved the house. He had felt comfortable there, at ease with the surroundings, always able to unwind after a stressful day on the job. But now, there was something frightening about it, something haunting that drove him back to work to find the peace that his home once afforded. His fellow detectives didn't notice him enter the squad room. They were too busy listening to the verbal antics of Mouse Curtis. John paused just beyond the circle of cops and watched and listened. It was impossible not to see and hear him. With a name that belied his size, Mouse stood at six feet ten inches. And although he was forty years old, he still held the frame of a young man. He was bull-necked with a black-smith's shoulders and a boxer's waist, an imposing three hundred pounds of menace that struct fear in every criminal he had arrested.

There was nothing small about him, even his private parts were of superhuman repute. He often boasted of his youthful stamina in bed. As a matter of fact, the only feature that un-veiled his real age was a wrinkled, skin-burned face that was hard-bitten from too many hours in the tanning bed. But that was the result of an overblown ego and a reputation for being a ladies' man.

Phil Sayers, the office clown, was the perfect straight-man for Curtis. Both viewed the world as a place where women were sexual objects, here on earth to remain unseen until the detectives' trouser pythons beckoned their appearance.

"So, what happened next, Mouse?" Sayers asked, as he handed Curtis his morning cup of coffee.

"Up to then, nothing unusual. She told me her name was Peaches, that she worked downtown, you know, the usual crap before you get down to business." Mouse replied matter-of-factly, sipped his coffee, and waited for his straight man to reply.

"Oh man, Peaches. What a name, huh, Mouse? Peaches from downtown. So, what next?" Sayers took pleasure in making fun of her name while completely ignoring the absurdity of a three-hundred-pound tank named Mouse. He would never ridicule Mouse anyway because if he did, Mouse would crush him like an empty beer can.

"Well, we had a few more drinks and then I popped the question. That's when she unloaded the surprise. Said she would go back to my place, but a girlfriend had ridden with her to the bar and she couldn't leave her by herself. So, I told her to bring her friend along, and she said okay."

"All right, all right! I get it. So, you cooled both the bitches, right, Mouse?" Sayers wheezed with laughter, certain that he knew the coup de grace to the story.

"So, she brought her friend over and introduced her to me. Her name was Bunny. She and Peaches worked together," Mouse continued.

At this point, Sayers' skinny body convulsed with hysteria. His brain was teeming with at least five wise-cracking lines that would surely rock the station with laughter. But he would have to insult Mouse to deliver the punchline and offending a chauvinistic rat with that hefty body was a bad idea, especially when you counter the scale at one hundred thirty-five pounds. He thought better, and instead, gathered his composure.

"Hot damn! So now we've got a Mouse, a Bunny, and some Peaches…all going back to the ole' Mouse trap. How 'bout that guys? How many of you ever been with two broads at one time?" Sayers high-stepped among the detectives like a drum major leading a one-man band. But little did he know, the climax to the story was anything but a confirmation of Mouse's sexual prowess.

284

"Cool it, Phil. It's not what you think." Curtis retorted, still sipping his coffee.

"Sure, sure, Mouse. So, what is it?"

"We got back to my place and I asked Peaches and Bunny if they wanted something to drink. They were both pretty ripped already, but they said they'd drink some wine if I had it. Told 'em all I had was beer, but that I'd run down to the liquor store if they really wanted wine. They said it was okay, that they'd probably had enough to drink already. But they were acting a little nervous, so I decided to go anyway. I told 'em to make themselves at home and I'd be back in fifteen minutes."

"What'd they look like, Mouse? Did they have big boobs?" Sayers asked, as he reached down and tugged at his crotch, readjusting his stunted brain.

"Peaches was average, about a 34B. But now Bunny, she had some sneakers. Probably a 34 DD." Mouse answered, unable to resist the chance to showcase his own intelligence. All the detectives were familiar with Curtis' genius for accurately guessing a woman's bra size. And, of course, sneakers were a well-known term of bimbo endearment used by male chauvinists like Mouse. It was used to describe an enlarged bosom, hidden by overly loose clothing and restrained by an extra tight brassiere.

"All right, all right! Some jumbo sneakers! Man, I'd love to have seen those babies slingshot from that bra when you took it off. So, you got back with the wine, had few drinks and then you nailed 'em, right, Mouse?" Sayers continued to strut and crow. In his mind, he was certain he had properly set up Mouse for the knock-out punch.

"I got back with the booze, but I couldn't find the girls. I looked in the den and the kitchen but couldn't find 'em."

"Oh, hell. Don't tell me they skipped out on you, Mouse," Phil had a look of disappointment.

285

"I thought they had until I heard some noises coming from my bedroom," Curtis said.

"So, they were in there waiting on you, Mouse?" Sayers asked with a tinge of uncertainty in his voice.

Curtis paused for a moment and took another sip of coffee before answering. At that moment, an incredible stillness fell on the squad room like a ton of muted bricks. All of the normal clamor and usual bustle came to an instant halt. The detectives were staring at Curtis in wide-eyed wonder, holding their breath in anticipation of his explanation.

"They were in there all right. As I got closer, I could hear moaning, you know, good moaning, not like when someone is hurt. I slipped down the hallway and looked around the corner. At first, I thought maybe the television was on in there, but then I saw them. I saw them both in my bed, buck naked, all over each other." Mouse took the final sip from his cup.

The explosion of laughter was deafening. Even John had to snicker at the look on Sayers' face. He was crushed, absolutely devastated by the ending to the story. Even though he had played no role in the evening, his credentials as a lady-killer had been seriously damaged given his close association with Mouse.

"You mean, they were gettin' it on with each other, Mouse? Like, they were lesbians?" Sayers asked, devastated by the thought of two women preferring each other over his hero.

"Well, they said they were bisexual. You know, they liked men and women. They asked me to join them, but I kicked 'em out. I wanted no part of that stuff."

The horseplay quickly ended when Bob Counch announced that Captain Reid was on his way in. The men noticed John as they scattered to their desks. Each detective welcomed him back with a few kind words or a cordial pat on the back. Mouse extended the same nod of respect along with an extra surprise.

"Did you hear the whole story, John?" Mouse asked.

"Yeah, Mouse. I heard it. It was pretty funny," John replied with a smile.

"Well, let me tell you something funnier, or better yet, something strange."

"What's that?" John asked.

"You know these girls I was talkin' about? When they left my place, one of 'em left her purse. I was curious about 'em so I looked through it. It was Bunny's. She had a pay stub in there from The Foxes Den. Isn't that the place where you and Victor had the scuffle? The place where that dead bouncer worked?'

"Yeah, it is," John answered with a straight face.

"Well don't you think that's kinda weird?" Mouse asked.

"I don't know. Maybe it's just a coincidence."

"Maybe. But when I told 'em I was a homicide detective when I first met 'em at the bar, they started asking a lot of questions about these recent murders. Even asked if I knew you," Curtis said.

"They probably read about the murders in the newspaper or heard it on the TV reports," John explained.

"Yeah, I thought that too. But when Bunny came back for her purse, I asked her where she lived and worked. She didn't answer. Didn't even look at me. She just grabbed her purse and high-tailed it out of there. She acted really weird, sorta scared. I have a bad feeling about this, John." Mouse looked grim.

"Did you tell 'em anything about the cases or me?" John asked.

"Hell, no! Just told 'em the murders were under investigation. Nothing about you either."

"Have you said anything to Victor about this?"

"No, but I will if you want me to," Mouse said.

"No. No, I'll do it. Just leave it to me." John had the final word as he turned to walk to his desk.

Rumors had been circulating in the department about John, that he planned to resign, that his spirit was so damaged he had accepted life as a useless pilgrimage without meaning. It was common to fall victim to such tendencies when tragedy struck, and the detectives knew it. But after the mysterious episodes John had experienced at home, he had begun to respond in a different way. Now, a silent voice inside his head begged him to embrace the living by seeking answers for the dead, and the reassuring voice of Captain Reid offered him the chance to begin a new journey. Reid intercepted him on his way to his desk.

"John, I just got word that the body of a young kid was discovered in an alley downtown. Looks like a homicide. Patrol officer identified him as Roger Baneda. Does the name ring a bell?" Reid asked.

"Yeah. He's the guy Victor and I interviewed while he was in jail. We thought he might know something about the murder of the bouncer from the strip joint," John replied.

"I thought the name sounded familiar. Thought you'd like to know." Reid was a shrewd man, and his comments were a well-planned approach to gauge John's state of mind, and his willingness to return to work without asking him directly. Reid knew that returning to duty was the best medicine for him. John responded before Reid could continue the conversation.

"Captain, I'd like to go to the scene."

"Are you sure you're ready for this? I don't want you to come back too soon."

"Yeah, Captain. I need this. I think it will help if I stay busy."

"All right, John. Check with Tombrello at the desk, he's got the address." Reid smiled and gave John a supportive pat on the shoulder.

"I'll get Victor and head out," John said.

"He's already at the scene. Got there right after the patrol officer," Reid said. "You'd better get going."

In the back of his mind, John still carried a lingering suspicion of Victor. As he drove the car, he listened to the communications on the police radio and wondered how Victor arrived so quickly at the scene. Maybe it was just coincidental, but as far as he was concerned, there had been too many unexplained coincidences.

As he stepped from the car, he felt a familiar surge of adrenaline sweep through his body. It was the energy, the sheer excitement of being back on the job that triggered the reaction. It was good to feel alive again. John dipped under the yellow crime scene tape that cordoned off the alley entrance and walked toward the busy activity some twenty yards away. Along the way, he passed several uniformed officers and two technicians working hard at controlling the scene and gathering evidence. As he neared the individuals clustered at the dead-end of the alley, his excitement fell prey to apprehension. It was a feeling of uneasiness; the same anxiety he had experienced each time his mind was shattered by the unwanted flashbacks. He remembered how realistic the sensations had been and he fought hard to prevent their arrival by staring at Victor, focusing on him as though he were a bullseye in a target. For a moment he felt misty, as though he might lose the battle. But suddenly, the strategy worked, and the sensations disappeared. By the time he arrived at the dead body, he had regained his balance.

The stillness of death had found its way to a dim, filthy side-street in downtown Atlanta. Today, it was in the shape of a battered young man. John kneeled between Victor and

Connors to gain a closer view of what could only be described as gruesome. Both men drew back as though John was a ghost. For a moment, the grisly business of examining the corpse was temporarily suspended while the men tried to marshal the right words to say.

"Gosh, John. I didn't expect to see you here," Connors said with a look of amazement.

"Yeah, I'm a little surprised myself, but I just needed to get out of the house and back to work," John responded.

"I'm glad you're back, John. We really need your help on this one," Victor sounded sincere, yet John was still cautious.

"Lab techs finished?" John asked.

"Yep. Photos taken too," Victor answered.

"Does this guy look familiar?" Connors pointed his index finger at the mangled body.

John's face puckered as he stared at Baneda's twisted visage. The body was sprawled on its back in a pile of loose trash, next to a dark green dumpster. The body was stripped and badly disfigured. The nose was twisted, curled upward and out, obviously broken in two distinct places. Below, an open mouth revealed not a single tooth intact. His normal hollow cheeks were swollen from a beating that broke his jaw and bruised his eyes. Fingers and knees were broken, and the torso was singed by what appeared to be cigarette burns. The scrotum and testicles were pockmarked from puncture holes inflicted by a needle-like instrument.

"Damn! If I didn't know he was Bandea, I'd never identify him. He's been through hell." John winced.

"Tortured for hours before he died. It was done someplace else and then he was dumped here," Connors said, as he studied the boy's battered face.

"No doubt about it," Victor said. There's no blood. The ground would be saturated if it happened here. But there's not a drop anywhere."

"Yeah, plus look at the bruises around his wrists and ankles. Looks like he was tied up when this happened," John asserted.

"Damn, you're right, John. Had to have been tied up and beaten. But for what reason?" Victor asked.

"I think he was killed because someone thought he knew something. Maybe whoever did it thought he could identify them at Sugar Bear's apartment the night he was killed. Maybe he was tortured to find out what he knew," John surmised.

"You think the same person who killed Sugar Bear killed this boy?" Victor asked.

"Not likely," Connors joined in. "The person who murdered Sugar Bear was very strong. Wouldn't need to tie up this skinny kid to torture him. Besides, I don't see any of the deep lacerations that were on Sugar Bear. And there's something else missing."

"What's that?" Victor asked.

"No smell." John said as he leaned forward to sniff the body. "Not even an odor from decomposition."

"Bingo." Connors smiled. "No cuts. No smell. That's what's different from all the other murders."

"You talking about Rimmon and Pierce?" Victor asked. "You talking about that stench?"

"Yes, same smell. Same smell on Sugar Bear," Connors answered.

"But there's something else missing or, should I say, not missing," John piped in.

"I'm reading your mind, John," Connors said.

"Okay, I get it. Roger, here, still has his dick," Victor said. "But doesn't that mean that his murder may not be related to the others. This may just be payback from a drug dealer that Roger owed money to."

291

"A drug dealer would've just shot him in the head if he wanted him dead. Quick and clean. No muss, no fuss! No, this kid was tortured for a reason and looking at his body, I'd say the person who did this didn't get what he wanted," John said with authority.

"You're right, John," Connors confirmed. "If this boy knew anything, he would've talked long before he endured all of this pain."

It was rare for all three of these men to agree on anything. Sports, politics, you name it, anything. Yet in Baneda's case, they were in total concert. Their teamwork continued with the hideous job of searching every square inch of the corpse.

After they finished, they rose in unison, moving back carefully to avoid disturbing any evidence around the body. Their departure was a cue to the technicians that it was time for them to move in. Time to finish the dirty job of picking over the dead boy before transporting him to the morgue. John and Victor went about the business of managing the crime scene, directing the uniforms to canvass the area in search of anyone who may have seen any suspicious activity. They also instructed the officers to keep the unavoidable newshounds clear of the scene. For another hour, the investigation continued in a routine fashion until a late-summer thunderstorm washed away any more would-be evidence. The driving rain added to the detectives' frustration. By the time the storm subsided, the alley was inundated with two inches of water. Not even the chalk-line that outlined the body remained. It was time to call it a day.

With some hesitation, John returned home. His fervent emotions divided between a loneliness evoked by the past and an anticipation of the future. Of course, he missed Boo, and everything about the house reminded him of her. But at the same time, he hungered for answers to the strange happenings within this same house and he knew drowning

292

himself in sorrow would not expose the truth. He also longed to see Lori, to learn if her presence would cleanse his wounds and help him heal.

Perhaps his return to work started this new beginning. It forced him to concede that he was still alive, still able to function in society. And so tonight, he would face the next test, the most important decision. Tonight, he would stand at the crossroads of existing in the past or living for the future. As he sat in the den recliner waiting for Lori's arrival, a familiar sadness pierced his lonely heart. The grief was an acknowledgment that regardless of the path he chose, Boo would always be a part of the journey. For one did not bury the memory when one buried the child. Once more, the sadness sent him to the whiskey in an attempt to erase the pain.

John didn't hear the knock at the unlocked door, nor did he hear her soft footsteps once she was inside. He simply smelled her sweet perfume and looked up to find her standing before him. In a single glance, her vision released him from the heavy emptiness that engulfed his soul. John had never seen a more beautiful woman, still perfect in face and figure as though sculpted by the gods. Speaking no words, she knelt in front of the chair, took the glass of whiskey from his hand and placed it on the floor. Then, she clutched his hands and gazed into his eyes.

Her dark eyes softened, begging him to share his pain. And so, he did. He accepted her soulful invitation by burying his head against her shoulder and weeping. She responded by stroking his hair, clinging to him, murmuring soft words. She had seen the hurt in his eyes, the powerful need to be loved, to feel alive once more. And for a very long time they embraced, passionately kissing until they finally made love. And for a very long time, John forgot about his suffering and pain.

44

The harsh erosion had temporarily ceased in John's life. Lori had seen to that. She had revived his soul by convincing him that she would always be there for him, that she would never allow the haze of loneliness to blind his way. And for two days, he lived in a world bright and pure, a perfect world not clouded by anguish and desolation. Over the weekend, he had found a replacement for his lost daughter, a surrogate that fulfilled his grown-up needs with a furious passion.

For hours, she had listened to his stories about Boo. She had cried and laughed, sharing his deep emotions as though she had lived each of those wonderful days herself. By holding him tightly and drying his tears, she had provided the comfort and strength he so desperately needed. And yes, she had been a garden of pleasure that resurrected his once lifeless body. In doing so, she had become his needful crutch. He could only pray that nothing would ever happen to her, that she would never forget her promise, that her loving arms would always welcome him back again and again.

Before she left on Sunday night, John gave his own pledge of undying love and commitment. His tender words made her weep with joy. Entangled in her arms, he then returned her solace by drying her tears. He was in heaven, touched by her warmth until finally, she had to leave. It was then that the hurt returned, leaving him in a hellish state of bitterness, confusion, and betrayal. Even though the weekend had been therapeutic, he was alone again, dwelling on the past. Still a prisoner to her memory, he just couldn't forget about Boo—especially that dreadful morning at the hospital. So, he returned to the booze to try to find some semblance of peace. But all he found was a blind numbness, a drugged stupor that allowed him to forget his pain and sleep until morning.

45

Dr. Susan Brown was an extremely busy woman, but after hearing of Boo's death, she extended her sympathy and agreed to meet with John before her Monday morning class. He had sounded so desperate on the phone; she would have been remiss to ignore his plea for help. After his call, she was prepared to deal with his emotional trauma, but not at how much his physical appearance had changed since their last meeting. It was a complete metamorphosis. An angular body, that once stood as erect as a powerful tree, was now bent, hunched from the shoulders. His blue jacket and khaki trousers hung loosely on a frame thin from weight loss, and his once wavy hair was now matted with oil.

But the thing that Dr. Brown noticed the most was his face. She remembered a man who was fine-featured, glowing with a boyish grin. The face before her now had the look of a shriveled apple that had partially rotted on the ground. She was startled, shocked at his pinched skin, hollow cheeks, and veiny red eyes. Dr. Brown had counseled many heart-stricken individuals who wore their grief on their faces, but she had never seen this kind of transformation.

Unable to stop staring, she asked him to sit down and tell her about Boo. John slouched in the chair and recounted the events including his foreboding dream on the night of Boo's illness. For an hour, Dr. Brown intently listened without interrupting until John recited the strange words Tina heard on that same night. The sound of the phrase had a chilling effect on Dr. Brown, sending her scrambling for a much-needed cigarette. She waved her hand, motioning him to stop while she nervously lit her smoke and deeply drew several puffs. John noticed she was jittery; her trembling hands made that very clear.

"Is there something wrong, Dr. Brown?" He asked, pulling his chair to the front edge of her desk.

"Were those the exact words?" She asked, exhaling a cloud of smoke.

"Yeah, I'm sure that's what she said. It was 'low tire shoe.' She said it was loud, and that it was said over and over," he answered.

"Low tire shoe...Lo tir sho...Lo tirsah. Could she have heard lo tirsah and mistook it for low tire shoe?" Dr. Brown asked.

"It's possible. Her English is not the best and she sometimes mispronounces words. I can see how that could happen. What does low teersha mean? I've never heard of that." John cast a quizzical look.

"Lo tirsah, its Hebrew." Dr. Brown looked as though she would prefer to seal her lips and end the discussion, but John was too curious.

"So, what does it mean?" He repeated.

"It's Hebrew for thou shalt not kill," she sternly said. She extinguished her cigarette in a glass ashtray on her desk and dipped into the pack for another. The office was already filled with smoke and tension and it was about to get worse.

Meanwhile, John's heart hammered his chest, signaling his own bout of anxiety. "Thou shalt not kill? How could she hear...I mean...Hebrew...why would anyone say....it doesn't make sense, does it?" John's mind was as haywire as a short-circuited computer.

It would have been easy for Dr. Brown to take the Freudian way out. She could pronounce him neurotic, or perhaps diagnose his condition as a functional disorder linked to something he heard while in one of his dream-like states. But her instincts would not allow her to dismiss his words as the conjecture of an over-racked mind. She truly believed him and so her response was direct and honest.

296

"John, I've got a really bad feeling about this," Dr. Brown said looking concerned.

"Why do you say that?" John asked shakily.

"My senses tell me that there's something evil that has targeted your family. Remember when we first met, we talked about evil, about demons? You and Victor made fun of the idea that there could be a devil."

"Yes, I remember," John answered.

"Well, hang on because I want you to know something else. There are also angels. Angels, I believe, that are trying to deliver a message to you. Did you know that the Greek work *angelos* means messenger?

"No, I didn't."

"Did you know that angels can also act as guardians for humans? Dr. Brown asked while exhaling another drag from her cigarette.

"When I was a boy, I used to hear my foster mom praying for angels to protect me. She'd ask them to surround me and keep me from harm. But what would angels have to do with Boo?"

"I don't know. I just believe that all of these strange events are somehow connected—the Bible mysteriously appearing from nowhere, your visions, a bizarre voice yelling in Hebrew, and Boo's sudden death. None of these things seem rational, yet they all happened. And I think they happened for a specific reason," Brown rationalized.

"What reason?" John asked.

"I don't know for sure, it's just a guess."

"Please just tell me. I just need to understand."

"It's got to be you, John," Dr. Brown answered.

"Me?"

"Yes, you. It all started with your flashbacks, didn't it?"

"Yeah, I guess so," he answered.

"I think your visions are a message. A message that has meaning for you and your future," Dr. Brown explained.

"You know I have a hard time accepting that stuff."

"I know you do, but you've got to believe and open your mind. Did you know that God gave Daniel a prophetic vision that he couldn't understand?"

"No, I didn't."

"Well, he did. And when Daniel prayed that its meaning would be revealed, an angel was sent, an angel that appeared before him and explained the message."

"I don't know...." Doubt appeared on John's wrinkled face.

"Tell me, John. Have you had any visions since Boo's death?"

"No. None."

"Has anything strange happened at your house since Boo's death, like the appearance of the Bible or any unexplained voices?"

Her poignant question sent a wave of coldness through John with the force of an arctic blast. Goosebumps rose on his flesh as he panted in an attempt to curb the nauseous feeling. She had just hit the most maddening nerve in his body. She immediately rose from her chair and scurried down the hall. Moments later, she returned with a glass of water and a barrage of soothing words to ease his anxiety. Her comforting voice and soft eyes reminded him of his foster mom. Perhaps that is why he returned to Dr. Brown, a woman with motherly features who quoted the Scriptures. But, for whatever the reason, it worked; he slowly regained his balance and began to speak. He answered her question by detailing the ghostly sound of Boo's voice emanating from her bedroom and her spectral appearance at his bedside. He recounted everything from his recent past with exception of his intimate weekend with Lori. When counseling with your substitute mom, some things are best left unsaid.

"Rebecca came to Boo," Dr. Brown said, analyzing the strange events. "She appeared to her with a warning. Then, someone or something was at Tina's the night Boo got sick. I believe that someone or something was trying to protect your daughter. Could it have been an angel? I don't know. But there's no way Tina could have just dreamed up those words. And now, Boo has appeared before you. I think her spirit is restless because she knows what's going on. She knows and she is trying to communicate with you."

"I don't think I can handle this," John said with exasperation, as he gasped for air.

"You don't have a choice, John. It's happening and you don't have any choice in the matter. You've got to get a hold of yourself. I remember two verses in Hebrews that I think are relevant. It reads, '*Wherefore lift the hands that hang down and the feeble knees; And make straight paths for your feet lest that which is lame be turned out of the way; but let it rather be healed.*' The Scriptures are telling us not to give up, John. In order to heal, you can't give up!" Her voice rang with determination. She sensed there would be grave consequences if he surrendered, repercussions beyond even her imagination.

"There are forces at work here, John, good and evil forces. And like it or not, you're right in the middle."

"So, what are you sayin' I should do?" John labored.

"You've got to seek out the answers to these questions. I don't think you or Boo will ever find peace until you do. Go back to work. I believe the source of the murders has a heavy hand in this, and your investigations will help. There's still a satanic coven out there. I know there is. Find it, and you'll find the source. They're deriving their power from somewhere," Dr. Brown said beseechingly.

"Anything else?"

"Yeah, keep an open mind, and get some rest; you need it. Oh, and pray—pray a lot."

Dr. Brown rose from her chair, rounded her desk and clutched John's left hand in a clasp of reassurance. Lastly, she advised him to trust his heart, to keep in touch, and then she departed for her morning class. He remained seated for several minutes, feeling fatigued as though he had just fought fifteen rounds with the heavy weight champ. He was also confused. Dr. Brown had just confirmed that the physically impossible was possible, that the dead weren't necessarily dead. Even though she believed his unnatural stories without question, he still carried a seed of doubt given her own uncommon explanations.

It was the booze he thought. If you drink enough whiskey, you can see and hear anything. Ghosts, pink elephants, flying saucers...anything. And yes, there probably is a satanic coven out there. But the actions of the cult's members were no different than the acts of other emotionally disturbed criminals who conveniently blamed their heinous crimes on some unclean force outside of their control. He had heard *the devil made me do it* more than once and, every time, he had dismissed the excuse as nothing more than that, an excuse. But her advice about returning to work was something he could wholeheartedly accept. He gathered himself and left.

John found his desktop covered with paper when he returned to the squad room later that morning. He meticulously arranged his work in neat stacks consisting of phone messages, incoming mail, and internal memos. He started with the phone calls; he returned all except the ten urgent messages from Felix Lovelady. Mouse Curtis had tipped him off about the calls from the insidious barrister. Lovelady, the consummate pariah, had smelled blood in the form of a wrongful death action and he was trying desperately to make John his client. In keeping with his obscene character,

Lovelady had shifted his loyalty from Marty Lococo who wanted to sue for police brutality, to John, who had lost a daughter to a possible misdiagnosis by a deep pocketed doctor who worked for a financially loaded hospital.

To a bloodsucking lawyer, ·it made perfect sense—the medical profession simply had more money. To John, it was unconscionable. How could anyone think of extorting money when nothing could make his daughter come back? But then, he remembered that he was dealing with the shifty-eyed Lovelady. This was the same gold-chained vermin whose middle name was Weasel, a man who paid finder's fees to ambulance drivers for referrals. Lovelady had no scruples. Neither did he possess any skill as a litigator. The local lore was that he once asked a judge to have mercy on his client, a despicable young man who murdered his parents with an axe. Lovelady pleaded that his client deserved leniency since he was now an orphan. But what Lovelady lacked in integrity and courtroom skill was entirely offset by his willingness to harass. Grinding harassment, heavy-handed, and unyielding until he got what he wanted. He would harass anyone including his own client as John discovered when he answered the phone. It was Lovelady, calling again, begging for a meeting. John slammed the phone down. He had no time, patience, or desire to hear the attorney's vulgar pitch.

John spent the remainder of the day completing overdue progress reports on his cases. Victor would normally help with the paperwork, but he had called in sick with a fever. At five-thirty in the afternoon, John finished the last form and then left for home. At least he started home, but then decided to stop by the morgue in hope of finding Connors still at work. He was curious to know if the autopsy on Roger Baneda had been completed.

John drove past the front of the county building, turned the corner, and parked at the back entrance. He exited the car and for a moment stared at the gothic-like structure. No matter how many times he had visited the place, he was always struck by how irregular the sooty brick building appeared among the surrounding glass skyscrapers. But then, he remembered all the uncommon activities that took place within the unfashionable walls and decided that the architecture was true to form. The out-of-date, three story, edifice was the home of the morgue, the crime lab, the DNA unit, the Serology unit and the Medical Examiner's office. It was an asylum for bodily fluids and withered flesh. That's what made his skin crawl.

He entered a narrow hallway engulfed in dimness and the faint, antiseptic smell of alcohol. The odor emanated from the morgue, just thirty feet down the corridor. He stopped by Connors' office which was located just off the hallway. The lights were off, and no one was in, so he followed his nose until he arrived at a set of double metal doors. The doors swung inward to an open room adjacent to the morgue. This was the back entrance to the examination room. It was also the receiving area for any corpse that had to be checked-in, weighed, and X-rayed. Continuing his search, John passed through the heavy doors and walked toward a single doorway straight ahead. This smaller entrance led directly into the huge examination room where the autopsies were performed. He ignored the *Authorized Personnel Only* sign and kept moving until he stood in an open area between four autopsy tables. Two to his right and two to his left.

The air was cold, and the lighting was obscure, but he could see that the room was vacant with exception of one slender corpse. The partially covered body of Roger Baneda rested on one of the stainless-steel tables to John's right. John wanted to leave, but he didn't. He just remained motionless until suddenly, he felt an uncontrollable need to move forward. Like a strong magnet, some unknown force was pulling him to Baneda. It was a powerful feeling, almost omnipotent. Unable to resist, he found himself standing over the boy's rigid body. A body that had been untouched by the M.E.'s bladed instruments. It was then that he smelled it. No, it wasn't the wretched stench of decomposition nor the sterile scent of alcohol. This aroma was completely opposite. It was the same sweet, rose-like odor he had experienced in Boo's bedroom.

As he stared at the boy's emaciated frame, he felt compelled to touch him, to hold his delicate hand. Perhaps it was the intoxicating odor, or the innocent look on the boy's gray face. Maybe he felt he could still provide Baneda some measure of comfort. Whatever the reason, every fiber in his body told him to do so. And when he did, when he clutched Baneda's hand, the blinding visions returned.

BAAMM!

He was wobbled. Unable to feel his arms or legs, he could see only the menacing image of a Minotaur standing in a burning inferno. As he watched the lake of flames licking about the animal's hideous legs, he recognized its face. It was Victor. Victor the beast. Victor the wicked. Victor charging at him.

"NO!" John's scream was sharp and loud. It echoed about the shadowy room like a church bell on a frosty morning. The earsplitting sound broke him from the daze, allowing him to regain his normal vision and balance. He felt relieved until he realized he was still grasping the boy's lifeless hand. At least he thought he was grasping Baneda's hand. Instead, it was the boy who was applying the squeezing pressure. The terror was stark, raw in the way it surprised him. Frantically, he struggled to release the powerful grip, his eyes bulging, his hair standing on end. Again, his shrieking voice racketed throughout the room.

"NOOOO!"

The scream was still in his throat when suddenly, the dead boy let go. John staggered back several feet and stared at the motionless body. He had heard Connors talk about the dead having unexpected muscle contractions, but he never thought he would experience one firsthand. It was as frightening as the vision. Scary enough to make his hands shiver. But the real horror was just beginning. With no warning whatsoever, Baneda's lifeless body snapped forward as he sat upright on the metal table. John recoiled backward, tripping on his own panicky feet.

He didn't notice the sharp pain as he landed hard on his rump, nor did he realize he had knocked over a tray of surgical instruments on his fall to the floor. He was too much in awe of something far more awful. Baneda's distorted head cocked downward, and his muscles tightened across his livid face. In an instant, a pair of solid white eyes opened, staring at John as though they could witness his presence. And his thin, bluish mouth fell agape delivering a horrible message.

"You must stop it! You must stop the beast!"

The sound was deep like thunder, nothing like the adolescent pitch of Baneda's normal voice. This was no after death muscle spasm.

John scrambled to his feet in time to watch the boy collapse back against the table.

THUD!

Just like that, it was over. Baneda's eyes instantly closed and his mouth stopped twitching as a rush of cold air blew through the room. John just stood there shivering in disbelief. Could it be that he had just witnessed the passage of a soul? Roger Baneda's soul? Or was it something else? And what about the beast? This was the second time he had seen Victor in that awful form. Could Victor really be the culprit behind all of this madness? He had questions, lots of them, but this wasn't the time or place to ask them. It was the time to leave immediately.

The only sound was the whacking of the double doors swinging back and forth. John had bolted from the examination room and walked briskly down the hallway, still looking over his shoulder as though he expected Baneda to be in hot pursuit. As he neared Connors' office, he slowed his pace. He could hear someone talking inside. At first, he was excited, thrilled that Connors might be in. He desperately wanted to question his friend about the hair-raising incident. But then he heard his name being spoken, so he stopped in the darkness, gathered his breath and listened.

"Don't worry about John Williams. He'll never find out." Connors spoke sternly into the telephone. "Look, you worry too much. I'm the chief M.E. and no one at the department will find out. I'll write the report, and no one will know about the kid, especially Williams."

John considered walking into the office and confronting Connors. Yes, in his mind, it had to be Victor on the other end of the call. Although Connors had not mentioned Victor by name, John was certain that his partner was somehow involved. However, after his vision and the unnatural episode with Baneda, John wasn't certain if he really heard what he thought he had heard or saw what he thought he had seen. He was no longer certain of anything. So, in the darkness, he silently walked away. Bewildered. Frightened. Confused.

46

John was like a man unable to awake from a nightmare, a man unaware of who he was or why he was still alive. Especially since the ones he loved so dearly were no longer with him. The department had granted him a leave of absence. For the time being, he had ignored Dr. Susan Brown's advice on returning to work. He regretted that decision because he knew it was a step backwards. A week of solitude had only intensified his doubts, his pain, and confusion. Watching old videos of Boo was his only reprieve from the anguish. How long he had been curled on the couch, eyes riveted on the television, he didn't know. He simply watched, drinking heavily while slipping in and out of sleep. Deeper and deeper, the blackness grew until his agony was abruptly interrupted by a loud noise coming from his bedroom upstairs. At first, he thought it was Azriel running and leaping from the floor to the furniture in a game of feline high jinks.

But then, he heard the creaking noise of an opening door followed by the haunting smell of roses. After that, he swore he could hear the faint sound of footsteps running about from room to room—footsteps, along with an indistinct giggle, a child's titter for sure, he thought. John rose and warily walked up the stairs. Not knowing what to expect, he cautiously moved from bedroom to bedroom, skulking around corners, peeking into dark closets. The search finally ended in the master bathroom with nothing found disturbed, so he placed the incident in the back of his mind with all of the other Jack Daniels delusions.

He thought for a second about returning downstairs to his videos but opted instead for a soak in a tub filled with piping-hot water. Feeling a little ill, he hoped a soothing bath would help wash away his disorder. He relaxed as the faucet dripped and the steam rose, filling the room with a thick fog. He lay quietly in the tub with his eyes closed while listening to the steady drip from the faucet and his slow breathing.

Then he began to think about Boo, to wish that somehow, some way, she could come back. He even said the words over and over. *I wish you'd come back, Boo. I wish you'd come back.* The calming effect of his prayerful chant and the soothing hot water had almost placed him in a trance when he smelled the sweet fragrance and heard the shrill creaking of a closing door. And this time, it was nearby, really close. John instantly sat up and turned his head in the direction of the odd sound. What he saw was impossible, or at least he thought was impossible. Trembling, he watched in amazement as the bathroom door slowly swung shut.

"What the heck…." John spat the words as he hung on the edge of the tub. He half-expected Azriel to appear from behind the door. That would have surely explained the door's movement. But there was no one there, or at least no one to be seen. Yet, he could sense some eerie vibrations in the room, that he was being watched. Suddenly, the smell of roses grew heavy, as heavy as the steam that filled the air. And then the horror really began. John's eyes were drawn to a full-length mirror attached to the back of the closed door. As he sat paralyzed, letters appeared on the mirror as though someone was writing on the heavy mist. Slowly, letter by letter, the words took shape, sending a bone-chilling message that made him helplessly shudder. He recognized the handwriting, the spelling, and the undeniable message.

Hid n Seek

"Boo," John's voice quivered. "Boo, are you there?" There was no answer, only the giggle of an adolescent coming from outside the bathroom. The laughter was rompish, energetic, as though a bored child had just been given permission to play. The sound was followed by the pitter-pat of footsteps, running in the direction of Boo's bedroom. With the dexterity of a bull in a china shop, John slipped twice before he managed to lift himself from the tub. Water exploded in every direction, splattering the wall and the tile floor.

Frantically, he wrapped a towel around his waist and burst from the bathroom in dripping pursuit of the noise. He crossed the hallway and arrived at Boo's bedroom. With a violent pull, he yanked the door open, expecting to find his lost daughter. Instead, he found Azriel. With a wild jerk, the cat exploded from the room, running, hissing, fur flying in all directions. The animal was obviously very frightened. and so was John.

The surprise sent him two feet in the air. *How the hell did that cat get into the room?* He thought. The door had been closed for days and he knew that he had seen Azriel in the kitchen at least twice that morning. He flicked the light switch and made a quick inspection of the bedroom. He knew that his search of the open room would be unproductive because he knew that Boo's favorite hiding place was not under the bed or beside her dresser, but in the closet. With only one exception, every game of hide-and-seek had ended at that closet. She would leap from the darkness and jump into his arms.

John moved to the closet door. He desperately wanted to see his daughter, to hold her and to tell her how much he loved her. But he was stone-cold scared of what he might find. Would it be a little girl of flesh and blood? Would he be able to see her blue eyes and feel her soft hair? Or would he find something entirely different? Perhaps there would be some hideous paranormal creature that had no resemblance to anything human. Slowly, John slipped his fingers around the doorknob and issued a precautious query.

"Boo, are you in there?"

No answer.

"Boo, if you're in there, you need to come out." John spoke softly as the water dripped from his hair, streaming down his face to his chest. No answer.

"Boo, the game's over. Answer me if you're in there," His words grew stern. More silence.

His burning need to know outweighed his fear to walk away. He turned the knob and opened the creaking door. Holding his breath, he peered into the dark shadows. He found nothing but a rack of hanging dresses above a floor covered with a little girl's toys. No Boo, no monster, just the closet's normal contents. The only abnormal finding was the fading smell of flowers.

"God help me," he whispered.

John closed the door with one last thought passing through his mixed-up mind. *I must be going insane.* A man who couldn't remember his last lucid moment had to be going insane.

47

The following two weeks had been a roller coaster ride, a crossing of Heaven and Hell. John felt hope each time Lori visited. She continued to be his best friend and lover, listening to him speak of his sorrow, awakening his passion with lovemaking that reached a new intensity each time they undertook the act. When the two of them first met, Lori had been straight-forward in her actions. Yet she had always retained a demure plumage that was fascinating and attractive. It was a sexy combination. But now, those feathers had been plucked and replaced by a plume that approached tawdriness. Perhaps she felt that sex was good for him, that it was the antithesis of death, and therefore, the exact medicine he needed to heal his wounds.

Whether it was or wasn't didn't matter. He never complained, so she kept coming back. Without mercy. And he just kept being astonished by her sexual prowess, her unbelievable gymnastics. John was always amazed at how good it was when she played that rough and risqué role in the bedroom. But every time she left him alone, the hell returned and so did the hauntings.

Clattering footsteps and a disembodied voice became the norm. It was a sweet voice, a frightened voice that John knew belonged to Boo. And the footsteps were soft like those of a little girl. At all hours, she would roam from room to room, calling out over and over. "Daddy," she would cry. At times, it would sound so close he could almost reach out and touch her. But other than the stormy night when she appeared at his bedside, he never saw her again. No apparitions, no misty silhouettes, no balls of light, no anything.

He may not have made visual contact, but he knew without a doubt, it was her. The telltale signs were always there. It didn't matter if it were night or day, she left her autograph on everything. Upon arriving home from work one day, he found Azriel wearing a tiny bonnet that belonged to one of Boo's toy dolls. When Boo was alive, she had placed that same hat on Azriel, pretending that the cat was her own baby. Once, he found the drawers to her dresser open and her clothes strewn about the room. On yet another occasion, her linens were pulled from her bed and a small table lamp was overturned, broken on the floor. It was as though she was upset about something and decided to throw a tantrum. And there was John in the middle of it all, not knowing whether to be glad that he could still feel her presence, or sad that she was without peace and unaware that she was no longer alive. He had no interest in dealing with this emotional tug-of-war, so he remained indifferent, listless, usually drunk, not giving a damn about anything. But then, Boo did something that rocked him from his stupor. She sent him a message from the spirit world that he couldn't ignore.

It was Wednesday. Lori was still in Connecticut. She had been there two days visiting relatives. John was going through the motions, finally back on the job and in the work routine with Victor. It had been an uneventful day other than a quick investigation and arrest in a gang related drive-by shooting. Unlike most murder investigations, the cops lucked out on this one with two eyewitnesses identifying the shooter. With no leads on their other cases, it felt good just to close one file. His workday ended at seven-thirty in the evening when he finished the investigative report and left for home.

The bad weather and resulting fender benders prolonged John's commute. The thought of slowing down on rain slick roads was unthinkable to Atlanta's drivers. Most just kept motoring along, tailgating while doing twenty miles an hour over the speed limit. But John didn't mind. For thirty minutes, he chugged along as the manic cars and trucks zipped by. Boo's next surprise was always on his mind when he got in the vicinity of the house, and he was in no rush to discover if she had been dressing the cat or rearranging the furniture.

He walked uneasily from room to room until the search ended in her bedroom. Glancing from left to right, his eyes found nothing out of place. He thumbed off the light switch and backed from the room, feeling relieved that she had not dealt his psyche another blow. He was also feeling exhausted, so he decided to go to bed early. But first, he prepared a peanut butter sandwich for himself and a bowl of dry cat food for Azriel. He then followed his usual routine of drinking enough stiff bourbons to get half-crocked before heading to his bedroom.

Light-headed and wobbly, he carried the booze with him and quaffed down the last two drinks before dropping the empty bottle on his bedroom floor. He stumbled to the bathroom, relieved himself, and then undressed in front of the mirror above the sink. Perhaps he could have seen his faded body had his vision been clear. But it wasn't, so he never noticed that twenty pounds had been subtracted from his bones. Nor did he notice that the vibrant hue had been bleached from his face. **The** effects of too little food and too much alcohol had left him poisoned and weak. But then a strange thing happened.

Like a camera lens finding its focus, his vision cleared. Why and how it happened, he didn't know. Perhaps it was a remedial touch from Heaven, a wakeup call that he would soon be lost if he didn't restore his faith. The reason really didn't matter. What did matter was his reaction. He couldn't believe the person in the mirror was him. He just gazed at his reflection, almost catatonic. He looked at his hollow eyes and rib-bare chest. He would have remained there longer had a clap of thunder not snapped him from the trance. Slapping some cold water on his face was a vain attempt to return some color to his cheeks, but he did it anyway. It was the last thing he remembered before he passed out on the bedroom floor.

The first seven hours of sleep were peaceful. Warm memories of Boo and Rebecca filled John's dreams with a soothing calmness that provided his weary body some much needed rest. But the serenity abruptly ended just before dawn when his dreams turned fateful. It was an odd sensation. He knew he was dreaming—that is, he knew he was asleep, and he knew that the vision was a dream. That was what made the sensations so real, the images so clear.

The first thing he noticed was the music. He could hear singing from all directions, sweet heavenly songs from a choir of an untold number. He knew that he was being watched by thousands upon thousands, millions upon millions, yet he could see no faces. His eyes were screened by a body of thick, white clouds that slowly swirled about in rhythm with their songs. It was beautiful. In vain, John squinted as the surreal sensations continued.

He tried to move, but couldn't. His mobility was tied to a giant white steed upon which he sat. Surprisingly, he found himself stroking the horse's muscular neck with his right hand as the animal snorted and pawed. The horse seemed very impatient, as though it was about to start an important race. But John wasn't dressed as a jockey. He was equipped in attire of a far more serious calling: a uniform—a military uniform at that. The leather breastplate extended up and over his shoulders. The outfit also included a white knee-length skirt with deep pleats, and brownish leg protectors and sandals. It was military, maybe Parthian, for in his left hand he held a powerful hickory bow.

Suddenly, the singing stopped, and the horse grew calm. The clouds parted, issuing forth a narrow path like those found in the deepest woods. Somehow, John sensed that the path was for his use, so he kicked at the horse's sinewy flanks. But the animal remained steadfast, not flinching from even the hardest of his blows. It was then that John realized the billowy path was meant for someone else. At a distance down the way was a glowing silhouette, a small profile that was slowly moving along the path in his direction. He felt no fear as he stared at the indistinct light, only loving peace. As the shape drew closer, the wind began to rise and the light became brilliant, making it difficult to see. But for John, the image in the glow was unmistakably clear.

The shimmering blond hair, the vibrant blue eyes, the resplendent skin, and the diminutive arms and legs. It was Boo, adorned in a white linen dress that blew about with the heavenly wind. She was beautiful. He gasped at her radiant appearance and the intoxicating smell of roses that emanated from her aura. He wanted to run to her, to hold her in his arms, so he attempted to dismount the steed, but his legs refused to move. Desperately, John pulled to free his feet from the stirrups, but it was to no avail. Neither could he free his hand from the hickory bow. It was as though a powerful glue had sealed his limbs to the horse and weapon. Finally, John gave up and turned his attention back to Boo.

She had stopped within several feet of the horse and stared up at her bewildered father. He studied her features from his own vantage point. She didn't appear afraid, nor did she express excitement or remorse. Instead, she seemed at peace, in perfect harmony with her surroundings. But then something happened that made him wonder if things were as perfect and harmonious as they seemed.

Boo's expression turned serious, focused, as though her role in this vision was gravely important. She extended her right arm upward, attempting to bestow a golden crown upon her father. It was a crown of exquisite beauty encircled with incandescent jewels. He wanted to ask why she would offer such a precious ornament to him, but he found himself unable to utter even the faintest of words. Much like his extremities, his lips had been sealed by the same mysterious force. He took the crown from her hand, and when he did, Boo smiled with heavenly contentment. As he lifted the crown and fixed it above his brow, he felt an incredible sensation. It wasn't peace or fulfillment. It was something quite different. The surge he felt was one of power. Raw and invincible. The energy was beyond belief. It was as though he was baptized in fire and about to declare war on the world.

A great undertaking was about to happen, and the darkening sky signaled its beginning. A passage to the land below appeared beneath the horse. Once more, Boo stepped forward and held forth another gift—at least, John thought it was a gift. It wasn't. It was an ancient book. A timeworn book that looked very much like Rebecca's Bible, only much older. A blood-red seal had bound its pages to prevent it from opening. No, Boo didn't offer the book to her father. Instead, she pulled it to her bosom and then broke the seal with ease. A simple movement of her tiny finger was all it took. And then the fireworks began. Sparks erupted from all directions and thunder roared through the Heavens. All the while, John's energy grew to an almost unbearable level. The horse felt the energy as well. It whinnied and reared in anticipation of the upcoming journey. And then a deep voice above echoed a resounding command.

"COME!"

The booming exclamation was enough to break John from his deep sleep. The dream had been so real, so frightening that he vaulted from the floor as though he were launched from a trampoline. His skin was dotted with goose bumps, his breath was short and sporadic, and his chest pounded as he rubbed his eyes. After looking all around the room, he convinced himself that he had left all the unnatural specters behind. He then cleared his throat and blurted out a few words to ensure his tongue had returned as well.

"It was all a dream," he said, "just a dream."

Mama Ruth had read him the Book of Revelation when he was a boy, and even back then he had dreams about the four horsemen. Dreams that at times seemed more like nightmares. Even though tonight's illusion seemed incredibly real, it was still just a dream. But then, the terrible anxiety returned when he heard that word again. That same command he heard in his sleep.

"Come."

But this time it wasn't loud or commanding. It was spoken like the whisper from a baby bird.

"Come here."

John was sure the plea was coming from Boo's bedroom. And he was certain that the angelic voice belonged to her.

"Come here, Daddy," She begged softly.

John moved through the darkness to Boo's bedroom. He stopped outside the door and listened for several minutes, yet he heard nothing else. The soft, plaintive words had ended. They had been replaced by something equally disturbing. It was the sweet smell of flowers. By now, the scent was so common to his senses; he knew instantly what it meant. His whole body tingled with apprehension; he momentarily thought about turning around and walking away, but his need to know urged him forward. He slowly opened the door, stepped inside, and flipped on the light switch. No ghosts there of any kind. But someone had been there. His eyes were drawn to Boo's marker board and easel across the room. She loved that board, and had spent hours drawing and writing with every colored marker pen in the box. John was certain that the board had been as clean as the rest of the room, yet to his horror, a message had been left. He stared in shock.

It killed me

48

Grief was always part of losing a loved one—a harsh, merciless anguish that filled your heart each waking hour. But so was bitterness. Unlike the story of Job in the Bible, John had allowed his resentment to fester, to boil to the point of ignoring all of his Christian upbringing. He had blamed God for Boo's death. His foster parents' untimely passings along with the deaths of his wife and daughter had led him to believe that God wasn't watching over anything. John believed he was a blameworthy victim that was being punished for sins he had committed in the past. The fact that his prayers for his daughter's return had been unanswered convinced him even more. God was his only reproach. That was, until Boo implicated someone else in her message… "it."

His daughter would never refer to God as *it*. Rebecca had taught her otherwise. She had responded to Boo's curiosity throughout her brief childhood with frank and open discussions about God, tutoring her daughter on his love and compassion for all of his children. Even at a very young age, Boo had absorbed her mother's teachings and every night she expressed her understanding with a sweet bedtime prayer to God—never to *it*. *It* was the culprit, and her revelation was his cue to focus his efforts on something other than heavy doses of bitterness and booze.

He was certain he could find what took his precious daughter. After all, he was a homicide detective. Apprehending murderers was what he did for a living. But he wasn't sure if he could endure the ordeal of communicating with Boo, a child who, by all laws of science, was dead. That frightened him. He just hoped that he could maintain his sanity until he found the answers.

John spent the morning and afternoon with Victor at the department. They painstakingly reviewed the evidence gathered at the murder scenes in hope of finding a common thread, a lead that would point them to the killer or killers. They found nothing of the kind. The only thing that had touched each of the victims was a connection to The Foxes Den. So, with no other leads to pursue, the detectives decided to revisit the strip joint for another interview with their favorite victim, Marty Lococo.

The drive to the club would normally be a short one, but in rush hour traffic, it took all of half an hour. Victor handled the driving, as well as all of the talking. John sat silently, occasionally issuing a nod while wondering if his partner was a friend or foe. He wanted to question him about Connors and the telephone conversation he overheard at the morgue. He also wanted to ask him about the stun gun and Freon in his desk. In fact, John wanted to interrogate Victor about all of his suspicions. But doing so would alert him and Connors about his distrust, and without solid proof, that was the worst thing that could happen. He kept his distrust to himself.

By the time they arrived, the sun had disappeared on the horizon and the sky was dark. It provided a stark backdrop for the red and white neon sign that flashed in the darkness, beckoning the soon-to-arrive patrons who would stare, hoot, and stuff their hard-earned cash in the garters of the swaying dancers. But John and Victor found none of that when they entered the club. It was too early. Instead, the bar stools and tables were empty. The venue was silent. The only movement and sound came from a muscle-bound bartender, named Apollo, who intercepted the men as they walked toward Lococo's office.

"Club's not open yet. Won't be for another hour. Y'all come back then," Apollo forcefully said as he pointed his finger at the exit.

The detectives couldn't believe the size of this bartender. This specimen was even larger than Sugar Bear and far more muscular. His huge neck, chest, and arms stretched the undersized red T-shirt to its limit. And unlike Sugar Bear, he was beardless with a polished head and hairless arms. He lacked all of the Bear's heavy fur. However, he did have the same wild-eyed look and snarling thin lips. And the bad temper and short fuse were there as well. Perhaps it was even worse due to the angry steroids he popped every day to maintain his swollen body. Apollo seemed even more annoyed when the men failed to immediately execute an about-face and leave the premises.

"You guys hard of hearing? The club doesn't open for an hour. Now, turn your asses around and get out."

John was unruffled by the young man's countenance and so was his partner. Victor calmly pulled his detective's shield from his jacket pocket, held it in front of the man's hostile face and issued a command of his own.

"No, we're not hard of hearing. Are you hard of seeing? We're homicide detectives and we're here to see your boss. So why don't you turn your ass around and tell him that Detective Lechman and Detective Williams are here to talk to him." Victor barked in his best New York accent, returned the badge to his jacket, and waited for someone to make the next move.

It wasn't going to be John. He was frozen stiff. A cutting sense of impending danger had hit him as though he were surrounded by a pride of hungry lions. But the threat was not the neurotic bartender or anything material in the club that he could see or touch. It was intuitive, like a sixth sense telling him that he was destined for a confrontation, a battle with a close by evil force. John was wary, but he had not taken his eyes off Apollo to search for this unknown demon. He was wise not to do so; the fuming bartender doubled as a bouncer

320

and was giving serious thought to bouncing both detectives out the door. John and Victor stood firm, waiting for Apollo to make the next move. Both detectives watched as the big man's eyes narrowed and a tangle of rope-like veins bulged from his neck. The bartender continued to swell, moving in half-circles as though he were stalking his prey. He was ready to launch a powerful fist at Victor when a shrill voice stopped the attack.

"APOLLO!" Lococo screamed. "Don't do it!"

Hatred had arisen in Apollo's eyes. He may have been undisciplined in the fine art of pugilism, but it would take only one wild blow from that sledgehammer fist to send Victor to the Promised Land. Again, he cocked his right arm in preparation when, once more, Lococo demanded his retreat.

"APOLLO!" Lococo screamed. "BACK OFF, NOW!" Lococo scampered from the direction of his office where he had been watching the showdown. He slid between the bouncer and the detectives.

"Aren't these the cops you been talkin' about, Marty?" Apollo asked, still gritting with anger.

"Yeah, they're the ones. But you've gotta back off. This isn't the time or place to start something," Lococo exclaimed.

"But you said that we were gonna take care of these chumps. You said—"

"I know what I said, Apollo. Now, back off and get behind the bar. I'll take care of this."

By comparison, Lococo was a Lilliputian next to Apollo. Yet, Lococo appeared to have some strange power over this man who was three times his size. Still fuming, the bouncer obeyed his master and reluctantly walked away, but his temper and ego wouldn't permit him to cower behind the bar. Instead, he stopped halfway to the counter and took a position some fifteen feet behind Lococo, standing ready should

321

his strength be summoned into action. Lococo didn't notice that Apollo had followed only half of his order. He was too focused on John and Victor, too angry himself to notice anything but the detectives. He stood with his hands resting on his narrow hips, his eyelashes twitching, and his face seething with disgust. Finally, he opened his pursed lips and spoke.

"What do you two want?" Lococo's fluty voice had turned as off-key as an out-of-tune piano.

"Good lord, man. Where did you get that outfit?" Victor chuckled. He knew it was the wrong thing to say, but he was a New Yorker, and by New York standards, his comment was a statement of fact. Besides, Lococo deserved the rude prod. His lavender bell-bottom trousers looked like a flashback from the sixties. And the huge open collar on his white ruffled shirt brought back a glimpse of disco fever. Even John had to grin when he caught sight of Lococo's Nehru jacket and crushed velvet hat. But then, he saw the satanic necklace hanging from Lococo's neck, and his grin turned to a scowl.

"You look like a little pimp I used to bust when I worked vice in Brooklyn," Victor continued.

"You can keep your insults to yourself," Lococo retorted. "Someone who looks like a fat man dressed in a blue light special has no room to talk."

"You little twit," Victor snapped. Lococo's comeback, along with Apollo snickering in the background, wiped the sneer right off of Victor's sneering face. John realized that the conversation was about to get out-of-hand and wisely interceded.

"Cool it, Victor," John said.

"That's right. Cool it, Victor, or I'll sic Apollo on you." Lococo's skinny body swelled with contempt.

"You threatenin' me, pipsqueak?" Victor snapped back.

"You heard me, fat man!" Lococo pointed a scornful finger at Victor.

322

The harsh words were about to escalate into violence. Apollo crept up from the rear and even though Victor's shirt size may have been a double-tubby, John had seen this fat man in action and knew he possessed incredible strength. There would be no winner if these two tangled. John stepped forward and brushed back the two men like a referee separating two boxers. Fortunately, his tactic worked. Apollo stopped and Victor and Lococo stepped back, allowing the tension to temporarily ease.

"Look, we're just here to follow-up on the Pierce investigation. We just want to ask a few questions, and then we'll leave." John spoke in a tranquil tone, hoping to placate the tempers. But Lococo fired back with venom.

"The two of you can take your investigation and shove it up your asses! Besides, what are you doing about Sugar Bear? Are you investigating yourselves? Because I think the two of you killed him!"

"We had nothing to do with Sugar Bear's death, but our investigation is on-going and—" John tried to explain but Lococo interrupted.

"On-going my ass! You haven't done anything except cover up your involvement. That's what cops do for each other, isn't it? Cover for each other!" Lococo spat.

John remained focused and calm, refusing to exchange barbs with Lococo. "Just a few questions for you and some of your employees and we'll be out of here."

"You're not talkin' to anyone here and if you have any questions for me, contact my attorney. I believe you know Felix Lovelady!" Lococo shot back.

John knew he and Victor weren't going to get a productive conversation with Lococo during this visit. He tugged at Victor's shoulder to pull him towards the exit. Victor resisted at first but yielded to good judgment and turned to walk away. Their departure would have been uneventful had Lococo kept his mouth shut, but his mouth was his enemy and his words stirred a rage, a rage of violence that would have been best left undisturbed. His voice echoed across the vacant bar just before the men reached the exit door.

"Hey, Williams! How's that little girl of yours doing?" Lococo blurted in a high pitch tinge.

The outburst took John by surprise and froze him in his tracks. Victor was shocked as well, unable to believe that Lococo would be so daring as to say such a thing.

"What did you say?" John turned and asked, thinking that perhaps he had misunderstood the question.

"Now you know what it's like to lose someone close to you. Now you know how I felt when you killed Sugar Bear."

Whether or not Lococo had blood on his hands didn't matter. The mere implication that he played some role in Boo's death was enough to ripen a rage in a man who would never act with malice. It brought forth a transformation that temporarily stunned Victor as he watched his partner's face morph with hatred. John's eyes became transfixed, turning as dark as a storm on the horizon. They had a terrible hardness about them. No one could cool John, and no one could stop him. Lococo realized he was in jeopardy and he did the only thing he could.

"Apollo!" Lococo yelled.

The big bouncer responded with breakneck speed He charged like a wild bull hell-bent on trampling John with his heavy body. But Apollo was not dealing with a mortal man of average skill and demeanor. His contender was a man possessed, a man who had lost reason, a man who didn't care. This man knew how to maim, and worse yet, he knew how to kill. Apollo never knew what hit him. The technique John used was impossible to depict. The naked eye couldn't follow the rapid-fire moves. John never made a conscious decision about using the minimal force. The sound of pounding flesh and breaking bones that echoed throughout the empty bar signaled he had done the opposite. His assault was punitive and unfeeling. Fortunately for Apollo, it wasn't deadly. The bouncer's thick body shook the barroom floor when he landed squarely on his back. Thud! Apollo's unmoving eyes disclosed his unconscious state while John's eyes never left Lococo. Still in a vortex of blind rage, he continued to briskly walk towards him. Meanwhile, Lococo stood frozen like a mouse facing a deadly snake. The only movement he could muster was another cry for help.

"I've got a surprise for you, Williams," His voice cracked with fear. "Yuko!"

For some unknown reason, John stopped dead in his tracks. Perhaps he felt the presence of someone moving toward him from the shadows. Could this be the force he sensed earlier? Was it the horrible demon that he was to confront? His eyes told him otherwise. It was just another thug Lococo had enlisted for protection. But this bodyguard was not from the mold of Apollo or Sugar Bear. Except for The Foxes' Den T-shirt, he was just the opposite. At one hundred sixty pounds, he was short and stocky. His other features hinted at an Asian descent. Unlike Apollo's wild charge, this smallish man moved with an air of confidence. He slowly moved forward until he stopped within an arm's length of John. Next, with careful deliberation, he rolled his head from side to side as though he were releasing some pent-up tension. And then he smiled. Lococo broke the silence before anyone else could speak.

"Williams, meet Yuko. I hired him after you killed Sugar Bear."

"When are you going to get it through your feeble head that I didn't have anything to do with his death?" John asked Lococo, but his eyes never left Yuko.

"You hurt Sugar with all of that kung-fu shit, so I found someone who knows how to hurt you with that same stuff," Lococo squealed.

"You tell Yuko here to back off and he won't get hurt," John's voice was steely. He was still seething, but he sensed this undersized bouncer shouldn't be underestimated.

Lococo burst into a shrill laughter that momentarily broke the heavy tension.

"You're the only one who's going to get hurt," Lococo scoffed. Yuko's presence had obviously allowed him to regain a pinch of bravado.

"If I find out you had anything to do with my daughter's death, you'll wish to God you'd never been born," John snarled.

John was on the verge of a violent outburst. The only question left unanswered was, who would be the unlucky recipient? Lococo or Yuko? The answer came quickly.

"Yuko! Show this cop the door, and kick his ass on the way out!" Lococo yelled.

John had no time to negotiate a non-violent departure. He really didn't want too anyway. He wondered if his partner Victor, the man he suspected of wrongdoing, was backing him up. Yuko cut his contemplation short. The bouncer lodged a series of high kicks at John's head. One by one, John slapped away the kicks until he dipped under the last attempted blow, sweeping Yuko's pivoting leg from under his whirling body. The takedown maneuver sent the bouncer flying through the air like the Fuji blimp until gravity pulled his stout body to the hard linoleum floor. But unlike Apollo, who was unable to rise, Yuko sprang to his feet, ready to spar again.

His next barrage was a flurry of hand blows that John parried away much like the high-flying kicks. It was as though John knew what was going on in Yuko's mind, what punch was coming before it was thrown. Without thinking, he blocked an ineffectual jab with his left forearm. He then used the same left hand to grab Yuko's arm and pull him into a violent punch from his own right hand, a punch that landed squarely on Yuko's throat.

The powerful blow struck his Adam's apple, smashing the thyroid cartilage, causing the surrounding muscles to constrict and spasm. It forced a helpless hoarse-like moan from Yuko's mouth. As the defenseless bouncer dropped to his knees, a disturbing thought entered John's mind. He remembered that the same type of blow was used to crush Sugar Bear's larynx, to silence and incapacitate the big man. An awful vision of himself inflicting the violent blow flashed in his psyche like an instant snap from a camera. With all that had happened to John, he never considered the notion that he was involved in Sugar Bear's death. How could he be? He wasn't there when he died—or at least he didn't remember being there. But he couldn't recall much of anything that had happened over the past few weeks. For a moment, he stood with his hands at his side, confused by the strange sensation. His brief contemplation ended, however, when he felt someone hitting him on his back. At first, he thought Apollo had risen from the floor to engage him once more. But the jabs were too soft to come from the muscular man. It was Lococo.

He was crying and screaming something about how he hated John for what he had done to his boys. He continued the salvo as John turned to face him. It was a mistake, a bad mistake. John still held too much unbridled anger to ignore the assault. He was filled with so much hate. He delivered a straight right fist at the wildly swinging Lococo. It landed squarely on Lococo's mid-torso, knocking the wind out of him, and propelling him backward to the floor.

It was an incredible scene. Lococo flopping around like a fish gasping for air, Yuko on his knees clutching his spasmodic neck, and Apollo lying on his back still out like a light. But where was Victor? John found him some thirty feet away in the shadows, standing with his gun drawn from its holster. Victor had taken aim at three barrel-chested bouncers who made up the rest of the goon squad. John's partner had covered his back again and he appreciated the loyalty. But Victor's loyalty was also confusing.

John had pegged him as one of the co-conspirators. Was Victor really conspiring behind his back, entangled some way in the murders? Why would he protect John from attack if he were guilty? And was John himself somehow involved in Sugar Bear's death? In his mind, it was impossible. Lococo had simply planted that seed with his incessant accusations. All of these crazy ideas were just madness.

"You want me to call in for back-up?" John asked as he exhibited a smile that said, "Thanks for covering my ass," to Victor.

"Yeah, and better call in an ambulance for your pals over there on the floor." Victor answered John and then posed a question to the three bear-like bouncers still standing. "You guys gonna be good boys or do you want to go to jail with your boss and your other buddies?"

The three men wanted nothing to do with the city jail, so they turned and walked over to help their wounded comrades. The fight was out of everyone, including John. He was beginning to have second thoughts about his actions. Thoughts about his use of excessive force. After he made the phone call, he returned to find Victor kneeling over Apollo, checking the bouncer's neck for a pulse.

"God, don't tell me he's dead," John voiced his concern.

"No. He's still alive. I don't know how after what you did to him, but he's still alive," Victor answered as he rose from his knees.

"What do you mean, after what I did to him? The guy attacked me!"

"Yeah, I know. I was here, remember? But I've never seen anyone fight like that. And the look in your eyes. I mean, it was scary!" Victor appeared worried.

"You saying you're not backing me on this?" John was now face-to-face with his partner.

"Of course, I am. I'm behind you one hundred percent."

John could sense hints of doubt and fear in Victor. The eyes of this tough, street hardened New York cop revealed that he was genuinely afraid of provoking his partner, and he would say anything to avoid it. And John knew why. He couldn't remember the horrible blows that he delivered to Apollo's body, nor could he explain why he had dealt the crushing blow to Yuko's throat. It was as though the person inflicting the damage was not him, but someone who was possessed by a force that he could not control.

"You think I was out-of-line here, Victor?" John asked.

"Hell no! This guy is twice your size." Victor pointed to Apollo on the floor. "And Bruce Lee over there was throwing all of that karate shit at you. You had to defend yourself!"

"So, you're backin' me on this?" John asked again.

"I told you I was," Victor answered.

John heard the words, but he still felt sick at his stomach—not because of his doubt in Victor, but because he was hit by the realization that he had added one more person to his list of suspects. Himself.

49

He could only wonder when it would end. He still desperately needed help, so he stopped blaming God for Boo's death and had prayed for his life to get better. But this new day would not bring about the fresh start he so badly needed. Instead, it ushered in more pain and despair. Milligan was waiting for him when he arrived at the department. Like a loaded shotgun, the lieutenant sensed that the opportunity to cut John in half had arrived and he was prepared to pull the trigger. John anticipated a verbal assault from the brass. What he had not anticipated was the silent treatment he received from his fellow officers. No one acknowledged his presence when he entered the office. It was as though he had leprosy, and no one could bear to cast their eyes on his diseased body. All heads turned the other way. All but Milligan's.

"Williams! In my office...now!" Milligan shouted the order. He wanted everyone to know that he was about to hold court.

John turned away from his desk and reluctantly entered the lieutenant's office. He knew what it was about. Lococo and the two bouncers had filed formal complaints. Felix Lovelady had done so immediately after the confrontation. John sat in one of the two chairs in front of Milligan's desk and waited while the lieutenant nervously paced outside the office door. Milligan was waiting on someone else to join the inquisition. John was relieved when he saw Captain Reid approaching. Reid was the friendly face that he needed, the comrade who would surely take his side. When the captain arrived, he motioned for John and the lieutenant to follow him to his office. It was his way of usurping Milligan's authority. It was his statement to the troops that he was the commanding officer, not the lieutenant. The informal hearing would take place on his turf and on his terms. Milligan didn't object. It was the only smart thing he had done all morning.

Once inside Reid's office, John and Milligan took seats in the two armchairs that flanked the desk. It was a typical office for a captain. The walls were covered with plaques, pictures, and certificates of recognition for his years of sterling service. The desktop was neat with progress reports stacked on one side and manpower reports on the other, and a large bookcase filled with memorabilia stood behind the desk. It was an impressive panorama. The captain took his seat and opened a manila folder placed in between the two larger stacks of files. He stared at the briefing memo from Victor regarding the melee at The Foxes Den. As he reviewed the report, a frown slowly developed across his face. And when he closed the file a few minutes later, he exhaled a long sigh. John knew he was in deep trouble. The captain could no longer hold him with favor.

"I'm sure you know why we're here," Reid said while looking at John.

"The scuffle at The Foxes Den," John answered.

Milligan couldn't restrain himself. "Scuffle! You call that a scuffle? You put three people in the hospital."

"Be quiet, Harold. I'll handle the questions." Reid rebuked the lieutenant and then turned back to face John. "Dammit, John. Couldn't you've just walked away?"

"They came after me, Captain. Every one of them."

"That's not what the report says. That's not what your partner said either." Milligan barked.

"Shut up, Harold. I said that's enough from you!" Reid gave no quarter.

John couldn't believe what he had just heard. "What do you mean, that's not what Victor said? He was there. He saw everything."

"Look, John. Harold's right about that. Victor stated in his report that you made the initial move at Lococo. He said you charged at Lococo when the big bouncer jumped in."

"Yeah, well, did he say that Lococo provoked me? That the little weasel may have had a hand in Boo's death. Did he say that?"

"He said that Lococo made some remarks about Boo. And I understand what you've been through, but dammit, John, you know that a police officer can't take stuff like that personal. You're trained to ignore comments like that."

"You don't understand, Captain."

"I know you've been through a lot. I know how much Boo meant to you."

"No, you don't! Nobody understands what I've been through."

"John, I'm sorry. I'm really sorry, but this is over my head. You've got to get some help. You're scheduled to attend the conflict resolution program. First class begins two weeks from today," Reid shook his head dejectedly.

"Don't you want to hear my side of what happened?" John pleaded.

"Internal Affairs has been assigned to investigate your side," Milligan piped in for the last time.

"Harold, get out! I told you twice to keep quiet." Reid's order was emphatic, and Milligan left without saying another word. His departure allowed John and Reid to speak as two friends without the air of formality.

"John, I wish I could do something, but this has gone all the way to City Hall. Hell, I've even had a call from our local senator. Right now, I don't have a say in these decisions. Internal Affairs is in charge until they report their findings."

"I'm going to find out who killed her, and I'm going to find out who killed the others, too. It's all got to be related"

"John, I've got some more bad news. It kills me to tell you this, but I have to," Reid dejectedly said.

"What is it?" John asked.

"You're being suspended with pay until the investigation is over."

John was stunned. He had always been a proud man and now what little pride he had left was being stripped away. His shoulders slumped as though his body had been drained of all its energy.

"It's just until the investigation is over. You could use the time to recover, to rest up. After what's happened, you need it."

"They can't do this to me. I was just defending myself." John's argument was useless.

"The decision's been made. There's nothing else I can do. I need your shield." The captain held out his hand.

John sighed heavily and, for a moment, thought about making a plea for reinstatement. But then, he handed Reid his badge. He knew how the system worked and he knew that no matter how much he pleaded, his request wouldn't be granted. It was a devastating feeling, especially when compared to all the good times he enjoyed when his career was spiraling upward. In his mind, he had now lost everything. His family. His career. His will. His whole life had been a devotion to family and work, and for all of his dedication, he had little to show for it. Now, he was left only with a father's broken heart and a cop's bitter memories.

The only reason he still clung to the faint flame of life that burned within him was Lori. He still had her to lean on. John refused to speak another word as he left the office. When he walked from the homicide room, he never responded to the captain's soft apologies or the lieutenant's dirty looks. In the past weeks, he had witnessed his life completely unravel and, today, he dreamed of knowing only one thing. Who was responsible for filling his life with such misery? He never looked back.

50

John was too stubborn to seek professional help, so he lay on the bed and vainly attempted to find the answers himself. Fully clothed, including his shoes, he took slug after slug from the Jack Daniels bottle as the whiskey dripped from his lips to his stained white shirt below. Why had he been singled out to live this horrible nightmare? Why was this madness all around him? He didn't know and he had no bona fide plan to find out. At least no plan other than these mind-numbing drinking binges. And he certainly couldn't resolve his problem by sloshing down more booze. But he was depressed. Rocked by the news of his suspension, he had little to do other than simmer in his own pity. He occupied a place in no one's life other than Lori's and she was not due back from her trip until tomorrow night. So, he took another drink, closed his eyes and mumbled something about how he hated Milligan, Lococo, and all the others who had failed him. He would have continued dwelling in his bitterness had the doorbell not rang. In rapid succession, someone was pressing the button with one hand and rapping on the door with the other. He stumbled down the stairs and through the den; he arrived at the front door, still clutching the half empty bottle of whiskey.

When he opened the door, his neighbor Carl Otto rudely greeted him. The expression on Otto's face was one of harsh resentment. He was upset, angry at John for allowing his yard to go unattended for over a month. He kept yelling something about the grass being deep enough to hide a Bengal Tiger. In Otto's mind, he had allowed John plenty of time to mourn and tonight was the night to reprimand his neighbor for his sloppy yard work. He attempted to make his point by jabbing one stubby finger on John's chest while pointing another at the weed infested grass.

Had John not been so drunk, he would have thrown a fist into Otto's pug nose, or perhaps snapped that jabbing finger like a matchstick. But he was queasy drunk, sick drunk. So, instead of launching a right-cross, he let go a spew of vomit that landed squarely on Otto's sandals. Otto frantically backed away until he lost his balance and landed square on his backside in the middle of the yard, he so vehemently despised. He was furious. His face hardened, and his eyes narrowed as he prepared to rise and return the favor with a punch of his own.

"You son of a bitch!" Otto yelled.

To add insult to injury, John stood outside the front door, swaggering and laughing like an over-tanked clodhopper. He couldn't help it. Otto looked so funny stumbling and crashing on the lawn. The comic relief was a welcome change from his depression, so he continued guffawing until something very strange happened. As Otto scrambled to his feet, his demeanor dramatically changed. His ruddy face turned as pale as the undershirt he was wearing, and his eyes bulged from their sockets. The sky was overcast with only a streetlamp and a sliver of moonlight, yet John could see the fear in Otto's eyes. They were tracking something in the direction of John's house, something on the second floor.

John may have been drunk, but his mind was sharp enough to recognize panic. He watched as Carl stepped back in the yard, tripping again on his own clumsy feet. Despite the hard landing, Otto pointed upward at the house.

"Up there!" Otto muttered as he sprang to his feet and bolted toward his own house. He sprinted like a twenty-year-old running back at the University of Georgia and never looked back.

John took a heavy swig from the bottle. The booze hit his stomach hard, bringing back the unwanted queasiness. He tried to fight off the nausea, but his effort was useless. In one long purge, he threw up the whiskey and the remainder of his evening meal as he clutched his knees for balance. He staggered over to a small oak beside the driveway and leaned against the trunk. The slender tree provided little support, although it was better than nothing and it afforded him the opportunity to turn back toward the house in search of the source of Otto's trepidation.

John noticed what appeared to be a white glow coming from Boo's bedroom window. The light was off; he knew that for sure. He had checked the room earlier in the evening. But he was uncertain about the blinds. He thought they were closed, but the radiance emanating through the window implied that they were drawn. He deduced that the reflection from the nearby streetlamp caused the strange glow. *Not bad reasoning for a drunk*, he thought. But as he staggered closer, he saw what Carl Otto had seen and it wasn't the reflection of a streetlamp, moonlight, or anything else.

To his horror, it was the vivid silhouette of an iridescent face. A misty face that was unmistakable to a grieving father. He blinked once, and then again. She was still there. It was Boo. John stood frozen, breathless, and immobile. He could only stare as her face and hands became more visible. John thought that he had watched her for at least a minute, but it was more like ten or fifteen seconds before she vanished. It was long enough for him to discern the worried look in her eyes and to read her trembling lips.

She was calling out *Daddy. Daddy. It's here.* He couldn't hear her voice, but he knew she was trying to warn him. And yet he sensed that she wasn't in real danger. After all, she was a spirit, an apparition not threatened by anything human. But he did know that she wanted to tell him a secret. He dropped the bottle and wobbled into the house and up the stairs. Boo's bedroom was dark, no spiritual glow to be found. So, John turned on the wall switch for the ceiling light as he swayed drunkenly just inside the bedroom entrance. He tried his best to focus his eyes to scan the surroundings when the marker board caught his attention. Boo may have been missing, but her frightful message was not.

MonStr

The faint scent of a rose was gone, and a nightmare had taken its place.

51

John had not slept a wink all night. He was still confused and disturbed by the word on Boo's marker board. Nevertheless, he dozed off the next morning at six—after he blamed himself for the message and explained Boo's visage as the blurry eyed hallucination of a drunk. He was just too intoxicated to remember writing the letters and his daughter's appearance was the consequence of an inebriated father. It was much like seeing a pink elephant or flying pig. After dismissing the crazy events of the prior evening, he remained asleep for a solid twelve hours. The rest was badly needed but he was glad he had awakened. Lori would be arriving soon, and he needed to get ready for her visit. He sat on the edge of the bed, took several deep breaths, got up, and walked slowly into the bathroom. Instead of taking a shower, he filled the tub with warm water and soaked for about fifteen to twenty minutes. He wanted to spend more time in the soothing water, but time was short, so he got out and dried off. He searched for one clean shirt and a pair of trousers that didn't stink to high heaven.

The search proved to be a difficult challenge. Without Tina around to handle the laundry, his meager wardrobe had grown grimy. She had called many times offering to stop by to help with the cleaning, but he had refused on each occasion. So, he was left to sort through a pile of clothes, sniffing their aroma in hope of finding something that smelled of anything but a football locker room. And the house had grown stale as well. It had become the indoor equivalent of the front yard, an inside jungle that smelled more like the home of a goat rather than the abode of a human being. Dirty clothes, dirty dishes, dirty carpet, dirty bathrooms, and the cat's unattended litter box had fused to create a distinct, smelly musk. But John was too preoccupied to worry about matters such as cleaning. Besides, he had just found a wrinkled polo shirt and khaki trousers that didn't offend his nose.

He rambled to the kitchen and sat at the table while drinking a whiskey shooter followed by a beer. And then he had another. And another. Thoughts of Rebecca and Boo fluttered through his head like a slow-motion picture show. Frame after frame, the images were very clear. His eyes softened as he remembered the many times he had stood outside of Boo's bedroom door, listening to Rebecca read her a bedtime story. He remembered how lucky he felt to be a part of their lives, to be able to witness the special love that they shared. Those visions would be with him forever. He just wished they were still alive so he could tell them how much he loved them, and how he missed them so very much. But then he heard the doorbell and his retrospection quickly ended. It was Lori. He stashed the bottle of whiskey in the kitchen cabinet above the sink. He was uncertain about how she would react to his heavy drinking, so he decided to err on the side of caution. Given the strong smell of whiskey on his breath, it was a wasted effort, but he did it anyway.

When he opened the door, he saw her beautiful face, those stunning eyes, and a warm smile that welcomed him back into her arms. He accepted her invitation the instant she stepped inside the doorway. Their loving embrace was followed by a long, deep kiss and a gasp for air.

"I missed you. I missed you a lot," Lori softly said between breaths.

"I missed you, too. It's been awful around here for the past few days," John replied.

"Let's go sit down and you can tell me about it."

Lori clutched his hand and led him to the kitchen. The two of them sat down in chairs on each side of the small table. John wasted no time with idle chitchat. He began the discussion by telling her about his job suspension, about how unfair the department had been, about how the captain and Victor had failed to back him in his hour of need. But he quickly moved to the real drama, his sightings of Boo. He leaned forward and squeezed her hand as he spoke in a whispering voice that cracked at times with emotion—emotion so deep it drove him to cry. It also drove him back to the bottle he had hidden in the cabinet. He didn't care if she knew. In those hard weeks after Boo's death, he had become a hard user. In truth, he was an alcoholic. He wouldn't admit it, of course, but he was. And after hearing of his unnatural experiences, Lori began to understand why. She needed a drink herself, so she helped him search for two glasses before they returned to the table.

For an hour, they poured glass after glass of whiskey as John poured out his heart. Lori listened intently until finally the alcohol numbed John's tongue and muddled his brain. His broken sentences and slurred words were followed by a long pause. It presented Lori with the opening she wanted. It was her chance to counsel him, to give him advice on what he should do. Even though she had matched him drink for drink, she seemed unaffected by the booze and her words made sense.

"Consolation could be found in Boo's bedroom," she said. "You must face your fear," she said, "and the best way to do that was to visit her bedroom, to speak of her there, to release your emotions in her most familiar place."

John was reluctant at first, but his reluctance gave way to her insistence and his inebriated condition. He followed her up the stairs and into the dark room. After turning on the small lamp on the nightstand, they surveyed the surroundings before they settled on Boo's bed. John was so boozed-up, he didn't notice the ruffled bedspread or the small indentation in the middle of the bed. He didn't notice that the air

341

had grown chilly either. And if Lori did, she certainly didn't mention it. She seemed more concerned with his therapy than the chill, so she pushed the dialogue along by asking more questions.

"How do you feel about being in this room, John?" She asked.

"It makes me uncomfortable, sad," John replied.

"Why is that?"

"It brings back all the memories; all the emotions come back when I'm in here."

"Do you ever feel anger?" Lori asked.

"Not when I'm in here. But I have felt anger before," he answered.

"When?" She asked.

"When I try to understand why she died—why she was taken away from me."

"Do you ever feel betrayed?" Lori's questions continued.

"Yes, I've felt that way…. I've felt that way a lot of times. I know that for sure." John's face grew stern.

"When you feel that way, do you feel like God betrayed you?" She asked.

"I don't understand how God could let this happen. He's supposed to look out for little kids. He's supposed to protect them.

"God may have a purpose for what happened, a reason that we don't know about or understand," Lori explained.

"There's no good reason for letting a little girl die. NONE!" John shouted.

Lori had struck a nerve and she knew it. The questions stopped as she allowed John the chance to vent his frustration. And sound off he did—about everything, not just Boo. The job, Milligan, Victor, the murders, Connors, Lococo, Dr. Brown, everything. He talked for two solid hours as Lori's eyes held fast to his troubled face. She absorbed his every word. She was much more than just his therapist. She was truly the one he loved, his confidant, his lover. And when he finished, he was exhausted. All of the bitterness had flowed from him like the surge of a wild river.

He would always mourn the death of his daughter, but at this very moment, the virulence had left his frayed body. He had no tears left either, but Lori shed enough for them both. She fell into his arms and cried for a very long time until finally his memories and her tears gave way to their passion. Raw, unadulterated passion. It started with a simple murmur, a whisper that she loved him very much. In return for her avowal, he kissed her again and again. Long, slow kisses that were followed by fast breathing and stimulating caresses. Unable to wait, he groped at her dress in an awkward effort to peel it back when suddenly she pulled away and rose from the bed. It startled him at first. *Could she be upset about something I did?* He thought. He trembled at the notion that she might refuse his affection, but it was nothing like that. Her move from the bed was one of carnal provocation, to allow him to study her body. It was a very effective approach.

She gasped for air as she prepared to tempt him, to make him ache for her, to beg for her favor. Her first move was to loosen the buttons about the collar of her ankle length dress. This allowed the black, loose-fitting garment to stretch outside of her round shoulders. It slowly, sensually slipped downward until it caught for a tantalizing second on her breasts. John had anticipated her braless condition. He had felt as much in their warm embrace. What he had not expected was the surprise when the dress slid over her hips and thighs. The bra wasn't the only undergarment missing. Beautiful and sexy, that's the only way he could describe her.

Her plan had worked to perfection. He wanted her so badly he thought he would scream, but Lori hadn't finished her erotic performance. When he tried to rise to meet her, she shoved him back to the bed and in a hoarse voice, told him to stay. Like an obedient puppy, he obeyed and stared as she stepped out of her dress and shoes. So close now, she was so close to him. Her fragrance was so sweet he couldn't resist. His arms reached out to feel her smooth flesh and again she quickly shoved them back to his side and shook her head, telling him no.

He started to question her motive, but she quickly shushed him. He complied with her wish by remaining silent and intently watching as she steadied herself by spreading her legs shoulder width apart. She continued moving her hands across her flat stomach, slowly stroking her skin. With her head slightly tilted backward and her eyes partially closed, she allowed her hands to drift upward, finding her breasts. They covered every square inch. Caressing and squeezing, over and over. The contrast of her small hands against her large bosom was sexy, very sexy.

John was ready to explode. He could feel an uncontrollable pounding in his ears and worse yet, in his groin. Lori sensed his arousal. It excited her. She responded by moaning low at first, and then a little louder. John continued to watch and listen as her mouth slightly parted, allowing her tongue enough room to lick those sensuous lips. It was then that the moans grew even louder. Then, one hand drifted downward and the moans were mixed with talk. Dirty talk. John was certain she was about to have an orgasm on her own, leaving him rock-hard and frustrated. He could stand no more. Springing to his feet, he grabbed her and attempted to pull her to his bedroom. She resisted.

"Take me right now. Here!" She demanded.

"No. Not here. Let's go to my bedroom," he pulled again.

"I can't wait, John. Right here. On the bed. I can't wait!" She pleaded as she fell backward on the bed.

It was the ultimate indignity. This bedroom was Boo's. It was her special place, the room where she played and slept, the retreat where she always felt safe. Since her death, John had declared the area hallowed ground. Other than tonight, it was rare that he ever spent more than a few minutes inside the door. It was one thing for him and Lori to speak of Boo there, but now he was ready to desecrate her memory by having sex on the bed where she slept. But Lori was unwilling to compromise, and he was without the power to resist.

And so, they met for a brief convulsive moment. The culmination was fierce, almost violent. Lori screamed so loudly that John was certain Carl Otto could hear her next door. He was stunned at first, unable to believe he had done such a thing. How could he think of only himself, of ignoring his true feelings just because of his lust, his wanton hunger? And then, the guilt came as quickly as his climax. As he was lying on Lori, propped on his elbows, it hit him full force. So full of shame. She noticed the concern on his face and stiffened beneath him.

"John, what is it? What's wrong?"

"Nothing. Nothing's wrong." His answer was not convincing.

"Something's wrong. I can tell. What is it?" She asked again.

He wanted to tell her that he regretted what they had done, that he now felt so sick he thought he might throw up. He had almost found the courage to reveal his true feelings when without warning, the bedroom door slammed shut.

BAMMM!

It was hair raising. John was so surprised he recoiled a foot above Lori before he crashed down on her nude body. And when he landed, she screamed to the rafters. It was almost as shocking as the slamming door. John reacted to her scream by recoiling again, only this time he landed squarely on his feet before he bolted for the door.

"What in the world!" John called out as his trembling hand turned the knob. He yanked open the door and stood, peering outside as though a monster might be waiting in the darkness. The first chill was still spreading through his body when he was shocked again. No, not by some unknown monster, but by Lori. Curious about the commotion, she had slipped up behind him and touched his jittery shoulder. From a flat-footed stance, he leaped two feet in the air.

"Good god, Lori! You scared the crap out of me!" John's eyes widened with fright.

"What's the matter with you? Get a hold of yourself."

"Get a hold of myself? You saw what happened. It was Boo! She's upset about what we just did in her room."

"I didn't see anything." She drew back.

"You heard the door, didn't you? You saw it slammed shut."

"Yes, I heard the door slam, but I didn't see how it happened."

"It was Boo. I'm telling you; it was Boo. There's nobody else here, but us. So, it had to be her." John's voice was absolute.

Lori stepped to John's side and strained her eyes, looking down the dim hallway and into the entrance to his bedroom.

"There's your ghost, John. Right by your bedroom door." Lori pointed at the small creature that exploded from his bedroom and dashed down the stairs. It was Azriel. It was unusual for her to growl and hiss that way, but it was her.

"There's no way that cat could've done that. That door shook the whole room when it closed. Hell, it shook the whole house!"

"Well then, if it wasn't the cat, how about the air conditioner? It could've sucked the door shut when it kicked on. I felt some cold air about the same time it happened." Lori presented her second explanation.

"I'm telling you, it was Boo. The air was off and that cat didn't have anything to do with it," John insisted.

"Okay, okay. It was Boo. She did it. It wasn't the cat. It wasn't the air. It was her!" Lori said it, but she didn't mean it. Her voice was tainted with disbelief and John sensed it.

"You don't believe me, do you?" He appeared astonished at her reaction.

"I need to go." Lori turned, found her clothes on the floor and began dressing. Her avoidance of his question confirmed what he already knew. She didn't believe him.

"I need to know, Lori. I need to know if you believe me or not," he pleaded.

Her face and eyes softened as she fastened the buttons on the dress. It was his distress that moved her, his dire need to have her believe.

"John, I know you believe Boo did it. You've been through so much and I know you miss her. It's normal to want her to come back—"

"You think I'm nuts!" John interrupted.

"No, I don't think you're nuts! But let me finish. I was about to say that I believe that *you* believe it's her. And if you believe it, then so do I.

"That's the biggest bunch of mumbo jumbo I've ever heard. You think I'm crazy, don't you?" John looked incredulous.

"No, I don't, but you're acting silly."

"Oh, so now I'm crazy and silly," his face turned red with indignation. "I've heard enough!"

Distress or no distress, he had pushed her too far. Lori grabbed John's trousers and threw them at his face. They hit him squarely between the eyes before they fell into his arms. Furious. She was furious and her cold gaze confirmed it.

"I think it's time for me to leave." She said angrily.

Lori brushed him aside, leaving him unclad, confused, and wishing he had kept his mouth shut.

52

John had returned to Boo's bedroom, the scene of his indis-
cretion. He wanted to make certain that everything was back
in order. It was his way of apologizing to her for his immoral
behavior. Regardless of Lori's explanations, he was sure that
Boo had slammed the door, sure that she was upset and
wanted him to know it. Returning the room to its untainted
condition seemed the proper thing to do. So, he diligently
worked on the bed, straightening the covers and tucking the
pillow. With it properly made, he was satisfied and ready to
leave when he noticed an oddity in the corner of the room.

Boo's marker board was face down on the floor. Even
though John had been drinking last night, he didn't remember jarring it from the easel, and he knew he hadn't accidentally bumped it this morning. Today, he was sober as a
judge. Shrugging his shoulders, he turned from the bed,
walked over, and picked up the board. He only wanted to
return it to the easel until he saw the picture drawn on the
front.

At that very moment, his puzzlement turned to shock. He
dropped the board as though he had grasped a prickly rose.
Then, he staggered backward and watched as it bounced on
its side before it landed face-up on the carpet. He couldn't
believe his eyes.

All sorts of crazy thoughts ran through his mind as he
stared at the drawing, trying to understand how it got there.
But his deliberation was a waste of time. He knew who had

drawn the eerie sketch. It was the handy work of a four-year-old little girl. It was Boo. This picture was too simplistic to have been stenciled by anyone else. But there were other unanswered questions.

What in the world had she drawn and why? Yes, the artwork was simple, but it was horrid as well. The forked tongue, evil eyes, and barbed tail had all the markings of some devilish-like animal. But is that what it really was? And why had she drawn it? Could it be that this was a chilling scream from the grave? Was this a message that this horrible creature played some malevolent role in her death? Was this the *Monstr*? She would never have drawn such a fiendish beast if this were not so. And obviously, she wanted her father to know. But instead of studying the picture in an effort to understand her message, John did just the opposite.

He placed the board back on the easel, grabbed the felt eraser off the floor, and quickly rubbed the drawing from existence. His instinct told him to do it. Instinct and his queasy gut. If the picture was erased, he could declare it null and void. He was still rooted in reality and he had never seen a beast like this in the real world. It was something untouchable, outside the realm of normalcy. Although he had accepted his daughter in the form of a spirit, his rational side refused to let him acknowledge the picture as anything but a cat—an angry cat perhaps—but a cat just the same. That was what the little voice inside his head told him and that was the explanation he accepted. He had spent the last few weeks swimming in a sea of insanity and to embrace any other argument could have taken him down for the count. "It's just a cat," he said as he left the room and closed the door behind. "Nothing more."

John made his way to the kitchen and back to the bottle. He may have conjured up an intellectual explanation for the drawing in his mind, but his heart begged him to reject the

350

rational and to take cast of her picture as the message he knew it to be. That was why he needed the booze. It would dull his mind and harden his heart so he wouldn't have to cope with either interpretation. After several drinks, he tried to call upon his second line of defense. Lori. He called her number repeatedly, but she never answered. Finally, he lost hope and left a message on her voice mail. It was a pitiful, apologetic message. His loneliness prompted him to swallow his pride and ask for forgiveness. He felt totally unconnected to anyone but her and the thought of letting a disagreement come between them was simply unacceptable.

"I need to see you, badly," he said. "I've got something very important to talk to you about, something to ask you," he said. The thought hit him as he was about to hang up. Marriage. Yes, marriage. The nuptial knot would cure his loneliness forever. As to his other problem, the ghostly one, moving out of the house would solve that as well. Surely Boo's restless spirit would not follow him to new quarters, a new wife, and a new house. Everyone would be happy, and everything would be back to normal.

Problems solved. It was a bold move, especially since he had known Lori for such a short time. He had never met her parents, nor did he know if she had brothers or sisters. He barely knew what she did for a living, although he thought she was an unemployed schoolteacher. He had been so souped-up on alcohol; he had lost much of his short-term memory. *Oh well*, he thought, *there would be plenty of time to catch up on her family and career if she would just say, "I do."* However, unknown to John, he had another problem—a problem that was brewing at his favorite night club.

351

53

Even though the sky was clear, the sun's cutting rays could not penetrate the thick, black walls of The Foxes Den. It was probably best that it couldn't because in a dusky room next to Marty Lococo's office, a dark ritual was taking place. A ritual undeserving of Heaven's warm light. It was a black mass. All of the makings were there. Four walls were beset with all sorts of satanic symbols. A ram's head along with an array of inverted crosses and stars were just a few of the demonic ornaments on the walls. An even more ghastly assortment of laboratory jars containing formaldehyde and human body parts was arranged in a half circle on a wooden table that served as an alter in the middle of the obscure room.

Six hands, six hearts, six penises, and the most coveted prize of all, a man's head. This human head was the "Hand of Glory," the ultimate sacrifice to Satan. It was also grotesque. The tongue protruded from its mouth, the cheeks bulged in all directions and the skullcap had been removed with a surgeon's precision. But the cult needed it because, today, the members were making an unusual request of their master and all of these gruesome offerings were required for appeasement.

The twenty-four cult members stood in a circle around the table, holding candles while chanting in monotone voices. They were calling upon their god for psychic energy. This unholy energy was to be directed toward John. His name was written in blood on an unrolled scroll on the table with the severed body parts. What was not obvious was the identity of the cult members. Each was dressed in a dark, hooded robe that shielded their faces from view. The rhythmic chanting continued for twenty minutes until suddenly it stopped.

Out of the shadows stepped an individual dressed in a bright, orange gown that lacked the traditional color and markings of the other robes. Like the other cult members, it was impossible to identify who it was, although there was no mistaking the person's role. This was the shaman. The high priest. The evil current that followed him as he stepped past the gathering and toward the altar in the middle of the room confirmed it.

You could almost smell the malevolent power that surrounded him. But this raw energy wasn't the only thing that he brought to the ritual. In his right hand, he held a ceremonial dagger, and in his left, he clutched a writhing black cat by the nape of its neck. The cat was a portent, an omen of something momentous that was about to happen. The animal was to be a living sacrifice, a gift in return for the called upon psychic energy. It was this energy that was to influence John and make him part of the upcoming calamitous event. The shaman wasted little time in fulfilling his role—an intonation in Latin, a slitting of the animal's throat, and the draining of its blood upon the scroll on the altar. There was nothing left to do but wait. Wait and see if the prophesy would come true.

54

*We are pressed on every side by troubles, but
we are not crushed; we are perplexed, but not
driven to despair; we are hunted down, but never
abandoned by God; we get knocked down, but we
are not destroyed.*
II Corinthians 4:8-9

Victor had called three times. He desperately wanted to meet
with John to tell him about the new evidence he had uncovered in the murders. But on each occasion, John had re-
buffed his calls. In his mind, Victor was a Benedict Arnold,
a traitor of the worst kind and he held no forgiveness in his
heart for his one-time partner. Yet there was a flicker of uncertainty on his face when he hung up the last time. It was a
tinge of doubt that begged him to listen. And he should have
listened, for on this day he would learn the truth. On this
day, a blackness would be unveiled that would make John
question his sanity, to wonder why his life had been infected
with such horror.

The foreboding signs were all there. The rustlings in the
house had reached a new, unbelievable level. Closing doors,
footsteps and strange noises grew louder by the minute as the
sun fell on the horizon. And the sweet smell of roses drifted
from room to room as though Boo were patrolling the house
like a street wise cop. Yet John held no clue about the biggest
omen. He had lost track of the calendar and didn't realize
that it was the eve of all Saints Day. Yes, it was Halloween,
the time when the dead come back to visit the living. At least
that was what the Druids of ancient Britain thought when
the holiday was first dated. John would have been better

served to respect that old superstition rather than to have lost sight of the date.

If Boo were still alive, he would have never forgotten. Just one year ago, he had dressed her as an impish ghost. It was the simplest ensemble, a scissored white sheet with two small openings for eyes. Door to door, he walked with her until her bag was filled with candy. She loved the occasion. And today, she threatened to return in kind, but she wouldn't need a costume to fulfill that same ghostly role. And she certainly wasn't in search of candy. It was the purest of ironies.

But tonight, John had other things on his mind. He no longer wanted to be the centerpiece in this drama. First, he would tell Lori that he was going to sell the house. When asked why, he would explain that he needed a change. It was not the complete truth, but in his mind, there was no need for further detail. Yet in his heart, he knew that he was running. But to disclose the truth would be admitting that he was a coward, afraid of staying in his own home. John's persona had been fashioned in Southern tradition where a man was always strong and fearless, always the protector. Therefore, to admit his anxiety would be a sign of weakness. So, he decided to dance around his true feelings and hope that Lori wouldn't probe for the real reason.

After that issue was behind them, he would turn the conversation to more important matters. He would pop the big question. *Will you marry me?* The thought made him shudder. Not so much the question, but the uncertainty of her response. That was what troubled him. John didn't see himself as the confident, strikingly handsome man that he once was, a man that any woman would love to marry. Today, when he looked in a mirror, he saw a sallow face that had been hard-bitten by the emotional strain of losing everything. Uncertain. Sad. Troubled. And very lonely.

The thought of being without a mate for the rest of his life overpowered any fear of rejection. He knew he could declare his love to Lori, yet he also knew in his heart that his whispers of affection would be shallow; his words would only prove so much. Even though his passion for her was real, it was not the deep-felt ardor that he shared with Rebecca. But given time, perhaps she would touch him in that special way, perhaps their walk together in life would allow him to feel that special feeling.

For now, loneliness was driving him, and it was a merciless force. He had decided that a romantic dinner would set the mood, a few drinks would soften her heart, and then he would ask for her hand in marriage. That was the plan, and he thought it was a good one until she returned his phone call. She insisted on meeting him at the house. She sought privacy for the evening. Lori said she had something very important to tell him. Her request ambushed him. It made his uncomplicated plan complicated. He could only imagine that her revelation would be something horrible. His wounded soul demanded it. He had jettisoned all of his self-esteem and could anticipate nothing but bad news. *She was going to end their relationship.*

Outside, the sun had set, leaving the sky as black as a bottomless pit. The evening remained in darkness until the moon began darting between the ragged edges of some drifting clouds. Like a slow motion strobe, the short bursts of light created some eerie shadows for the trick-or-treaters. And the howling wind added to the chilling ambiance by forcing the trees to sway like a mob of angry monsters. It was spooky. Perfect for Halloween. Inside, John was oblivious to it all. But not for long. He had just showered and shaved when the doorbell rang, sending him into a panic. He half-dressed by yanking on a pair of Chino trousers. Certain that Lori had arrived early, he ran down the stairs, skipping every other step. Much to his surprise, when he opened the door, he found something entirely different.

"Trick or Treat!" The squeaky voices rang in unison.

John had forgotten the occasion; he stood and stared at three undersized goblins standing on his porch. Two diminutive ghosts were covered with sheets just like the one Boo had worn. And the third little girl was dressed as a witch. Fully equipped with a pointed hat, black dress and miniature broom stick, she was the cutest witch you have ever seen. But she was an impatient witch as well. She led her ghostly friends in another greeting.

"Trick or Treat!" They screamed as they rattled their half-empty bags.

"Oh, my gosh," John's face was red with embarrassment. "Is it really Halloween?"

"Yeaaah!" The kids screamed.

"Just a minute. I'll be right back."

Quickly, John turned and bolted for the kitchen. He kept muttering something about how in the world could he forget Halloween while he ransacked the cabinets for anything that resembled a treat. Crackers, cat food, stale bread, he found everything but candy. Being the good father, he had always discouraged Boo from eating the sugary stuff. So, there was no candy in the cabinet, but he got lucky and found a good substitute...Kool-Aid. All the flavors were there including cherry, grape, and lemonade, so he grabbed one of each for the little gremlins and scooted back to the door. By the time he returned, the two ghosts were bickering about who had the heaviest bag. Must be two sisters, John thought.

"Okay, I've got Kool-Aid for everyone," John announced, feeling proud that he had rebounded from disaster.

"Booooo! We don't like Kool-Aid. We want candy."

His pride left him as fast as the air from a punctured balloon. "I'm sorry. That's all I have," John replied as he

357

noticed some movement on the street. Two nervous parents stepped from a car parked next to the curb and walked up the driveway. Their concern was understandable. A bare-chested man was doing something to agitate their kids and they wanted to find out what was going on. John recognized that the situation was about to get dicey, so he bent over and dropped all the packets into the bag held by the little witch.

"Sorry about that." John apologized to the ghosts and quickly closed the door. He could still hear the kids arguing outside as he walked back up the stairs. The spooks had decided that Kool-Aid was better than nothing and wanted the witch to share the booty. The determined witch resisted. The parents intervened to settle the dispute as they tugged their kids back to the car.

John returned to the bathroom, dried his hair, and finished dressing in time to answer another knock at the door. He carried the box containing the Kool-Aid with him this time. It was a good plan since a pint-size Dracula and a knee-high clown were waiting for him to answer. And this time, there were no complaints about the treat.

John answered the door a half dozen more times to greet a new group of trick-or-treaters and on each occasion, he noticed a bank of rolling thunderheads slowly approaching from the west. A nasty storm would be there soon. The air was so thick with humidity you could feel the building pressure against your face. Finally, thunder boomed, and a heavy rain began to fall seconds after he pitched his last packet in the bag of a dwarfish Superman. Surely, the bad weather would discourage the trick-or treaters and he would need no more. Although, he began to wonder when the doorbell rang only minutes later.

This time, the person waiting was not shrouded in a make-believe costume to entertain for a chocolate bar or pack of soda. No, this person was of age and her motivation was certainly not candy. John opened the door to a gusting wind, a driving rain, and a dripping-wet Lori. A woman who looks good when drenched from head-to-toe is truly exceptional, and Lori looked fantastic. Her exposed skin glistened from the dampness, and since she was adorned in the same low-cut, black dress she had worn on their first date, there was plenty of wet skin for John to ogle. And ogle he did. So much so, he momentarily forgot to invite her in.

"Are you going to make me stand out here until I catch my death in a cold?" Lori smiled while brushing a few strands of windblown hair from her face. She seemed to welcome his close observation.

"No! Sorry about that. I was a little surprised. I thought you were a trick-or-treater." It was the only thing he could think to say. He was embarrassed at being caught gawking.

"Oh, so I must look like a witch to you, then." She smiled again as she stepped inside the doorway.

"Gosh, no! Of course not. You're not nearly as ugly as a witch." John was still tongue-tied, abashed at how the wet dress clung to her figure.

"Okay, so how ugly am I?" Lori asked, stopping long enough to give him a wet peck on the cheek before she walked by.

His plan to appear composed and suave was falling apart. The scent of her perfume and the priapic heat in his groin took care of that.

"No! No, I didn't mean it like that. I meant that you don't look anything like a witch."

"So, who do I look like? Maybe some mean ole´ creature from the black lagoon? I'm wet enough, you know," Lori teased as she attempted to smooth the tight dress around her hips.

John's heart skipped a beat and his face softened. "You don't look like a witch or a creature from the black lagoon, or any other monster. You look terrific." He reached for her waist.

She and John embraced in a long passionate kiss, separating only because they needed a breath of air.

"I really missed you," she said, gasping.

"I missed you, too," he replied.

"Come on. Let's go upstairs. I need to get out of these wet clothes." Lori stepped from her heels and reached down to pick them up from the floor. She then grabbed his arm with her free hand and led him to the bedroom.

John never gave one thought about his marriage proposal. He never thought about the important news she wanted to tell him either. For the moment, he was lost, consumed by his desire. He never gave Lori the chance to change into the flannel shirt he found in his closet. The instant her wet dress hit the floor, he pounced on her like a love-sick lion. Not a real cool move, but he felt wild, totally out of control as though possessed by some outside force.

Lori returned his passion with the same fervor. So intense was their lovemaking, they barely noticed when lightning struck a nearby power pole. The bolt hit a transformer causing a loud boom, a burst of sparks, and a neighborhood power outage. Their fantasy simply continued in the dark until it culminated with a fireworks' display and a loss of power of their own.

John hadn't noticed that the rain had ended until he heard a loud pounding on the front door. His first inclination was to ignore it, but Lori prodded him to get out of bed since their appetite for sex had been more than satisfied. He quickly complied by slipping on his trousers and grabbing a flashlight from the bedroom closet. As it turned out, the flashlight wasn't needed. The moon had reappeared between the rolling clouds, providing enough light through the window blinds to make his walk down the stairs a safe one.

Fortunately, he did arrive unscathed and upon opening the door, a pucker of surprise appeared on his face.

Two teenage boys that lived down the street were impatiently waiting on the stoop. John didn't notice that they weren't in costume since their day-to-day appearance and clothes were costume enough. Dyed green hair, pierced noses, low-rider jeans and shirts large enough to conceal the Incredible Hulk gave them a Halloweenish look without the official Halloween stamp. John switched on the flashlight and pointed the bright beam at their faces. He wanted to make certain his eyes weren't playing tricks on him.

"Trick-or-Treat!" The two held out two ordinary lunch-bags.

John squinted. "Aren't you guys a little old for this?"

"No way, man!" One boy said, "You're never too old to trick-or-treat."

"Yeah, man!" The other said. "We like candy as much as the little nerds running around the neighborhood."

Had John not been in such a good mood, he would have dressed them down and sent them on their way. But the evening was going extremely well, and he was in good spirits, so he went to the kitchen to search for a treat. Of course, he had no candy, but he did find two substitutes. A badly bruised apple and a banana that was black from partial decomposition. From the kitchen, he could hear the boys laughing, joking about how stupid adults were to buy into their inane scheme. John grinned, knowing that he was going to play a practical joke of his own. He returned to the door and found the boys as he left them, arms outstretched with their brown bags held open.

Bap! The brown apple dropped from his hand into the first bag.

Bap! The black banana made a similar sound when it landed in the bottom of the other sack. From the expression on the teenager's faces, you would have thought that he just filled their bags with cow manure.

"That's it?" The boy with the darker green hair spoke first.

"Yeah, it's fruit. It's good for you, a lot better than candy," John answered and quickly closed the door before the boys could respond, but he could certainly hear their reaction from his vantage point inside the house: language so foul it would make a sailor blush, and talk of revenge, a disgusting plan of getting even with the old codger inside. John chuckled at their threats of rotten eggs and water balloons filled with anything but water. He could still hear their loud voices as he walked back to the kitchen.

Their tomfoolery reminded him of his own teenage shenanigans on Halloween. He had done far worse than toss a few balloons. But his memories faded as quickly as they arrived when he remembered his real objective for the evening. The proposal. For that, he would need a shot of liquid courage, something to take off the edge. Here was a man who feared no mortal being, a man who had been shot and stabbed, a man who had bravely fought for his country, yet a parlor room proposal scared the devil out of him.

If she said no, how would he live without her, how would he ever shed his grief? That was all he could think about as he yanked the whiskey from the cabinet, unscrewed the cap and lifted the bottle to his lips. Two huge gulps should be enough to loosen his tongue and make him sound coherent, maybe even romantic. No, that would take three. Hurriedly, he swallowed the last mouthful and returned the bottle to the shelf just as he heard footsteps coming down the stairs. It was Lori. His quick actions saved him from the embarrassment of explaining why he needed a nerve soothing cocktail. Subterfuge was needed, so he emerged from the kitchen with two candles and a small box of matches.

"Hey, what 'cha doing?" Lori asked.

"Just getting some candles from the kitchen. Thought we might need 'em until the electricity comes back on," he answered.

"Good idea. It'll be romantic." Lori moved closer, wrapped her arms around his waist and snuggled against his bare chest. He could feel her body heat through the plaid flannel shirt

"Or spooky."

"Spooky! That's not very romantic of you," she simpered.

"I guess I'm not a real Don Juan sort-of-guy." John chuckled.

"Well, we'll have to work on that. By the way, who was that at the door?"

"A couple of pimpled-faced teenage boys looking for candy. Way too old to be trick-or treating. Not even dressed up for Halloween."

"What did you tell 'em?" She asked.

"Nothing. I gave them a rotten apple and banana and sent them on their way."

"Oh…aren't you the meanie."

"You should've seen 'em. Green hair and pierced noses. Really weird looking cretins," John laughed playfully.

Lori drew back, allowing them a little space, and laughed with him until a more serious thought suppressed her jubilation. Her smile slowly dissolved as she stood on the tips of her toes, pressed against him and gave him a warm kiss. His effort to hide his drinking was a waste of time. The taste of whiskey still lingered on his lips. Again, she drew back and gazed into his eyes.

"When we talked on the phone, you said you had something to ask me," she said.

"Yeah, and you said you had something important to tell me." John's face grew earnest.

"So, let's go in the den and talk." Lori smiled.

"Good idea," John replied. "I'll take care of the candles."

"No. I'll light the candles." Lori seized the slender candles from John's hand. "You go back in the kitchen and fix me a drink. I think you've had a head start." Lori smiled, turned, and walked away, leaving him red-faced and embarrassed.

Within a few minutes, John shuffled into the den with both hands full. Lori had positioned the lighted candles on the coffee table that was situated in front of the sofa, so there was ample light for him to see. But lucidity was not the problem. His pressing dilemma was the over-filled glasses of whiskey and ice. Painstakingly, he tried to balance the two drinks as he slowly stepped around the table, hoping to avoid a disaster. Once he managed that task, he leaned forward and gingerly handed Lori her drink before sitting beside her on the sofa. Both hesitated long enough to sample the spirits. Lori took dainty sips, while John guzzled down half the glass in one long slurp. It burned—a lot. It also made him light-headed, but not so much that his eyes couldn't focus in the flickering light. Wearing only a half-buttoned shirt, Lori looked seductive, and even in his state of sexual recovery, she still stirred his libido, especially in the shadowy light. But he wanted to discuss their future before any more time was lost to sex.

"Lori, I—" John attempted to begin the conversation.

"John, I—" Lori started at the same time.

"You go ahead!" John said.

"No, you go first!" Lori replied, and then laughed a nervous laugh.

"Okay, okay. I'll go first." John paused for a few seconds to catch his breath and take another drink of courage. "I just wanted to talk about the future, you know, you and me, the house... us."

"Yes, I wanted to talk about us, too." Lori took another sip and looked directly at him.

364

"I'm thinking about selling the house. I think it would help me get on with my life if I moved somewhere else," John said.

"That's a good idea. A fresh start is just what you need," Lori agreed.

"It's not just that. It's Boo. I know you don't believe that her spirit is still here in the house. But I swear to you, Lori, she is. And she's really been active lately. It's as though she's restless, you know, not at peace and I think I may be the problem."

"John, I'm not sure we should talk about her. Remember the last time we did? We had a fight." Lori lifted her glass and took a heavy swig instead of her usual light sip.

"I need you to believe me," John appealed for her support. "I know I must sound like a lunatic at times, but I'm telling the truth about Boo. I know it's her."

Lori reached over and clasped his free hand and squeezed. "John, I do believe you. I really do. And I love you very much. I'll support whatever decision you make."

"Thank you. Thank you so much. I really needed to hear that."

"Is that what you wanted to tell me?" Lori asked.

For a moment, John thought of backing out, of not bringing up the most important reason for her being there. He felt somewhat trapped by his own plan, by his earlier announcement that he had an important question to ask. The ice cubes jiggled in his glass, making a nervous clinking sound. He was trembling, but he still forced the words from his lips.

"No, there's something else." John placed his glass on the table and gazed directly into her dark eyes. "Lori, I know we haven't known each other that long. But I also know that I care about you very much. The time we've spent together has been very special. So, I'll get right to the point."

Lori slid closer to his side.

"Also, I don't want you to think that my decision has anything to do with what happened to Boo or my job or anything else. It's just about you and me and how I would like the future to be. And how I feel about you." John continued rambling until Lori grew impatient.

"I thought you were going to get right to the point."

"Okay, okay. I will." John's eyes were fixed on hers.

"Lori, will you—"

BAAAMMMM!

The slamming door shook the house. The unexpected sound sent John's heart racing. He sprang to his feet and turned in the direction of the noise. It was definitely Boo's bedroom.

"What the hell!" His face was filled with shock.

Lori grabbed his arm and pulled him back to the sofa. Her eyes glittered with displeasure. He stood again, but she pulled him back harder this time.

"I'd better go check and see what's going on up there." His voice was laced with concern.

"Don't leave me, I'm scared. Besides, you were about to ask me a question," she said.

"But you heard that! And that wasn't the cat or air conditioner."

"I know. I told you that I believed you. But I think it's important that you ignore her. Remember you said it yourself. You want to sell this house and move. A new start. Remember?" Lori's voice was adamant.

"Yeah, I guess you're right. Maybe if I ignore her, she'll stop." John settled back on the sofa, but only a little. He was still very apprehensive.

"So, where were we before this happened?" Lori smiled.

"I was about to ask you a very important question."

"Yes."

Before John could respond, a whiff of icy air blew across the room. The sudden breeze whipped the candle flames about, yet it didn't blow them out. The unexpected draft also carried with it a heavy scent, a very familiar scent to John. He had smelled it many times before but never had the sweet smell been so strong. Boo was close, really close. The touch of an invisible hand on his jittery shoulder confirmed it. John was gripped in a cocoon of fear; his eyes bulged, his hair stood on end, and his face turned as pale as the Halloween moon.

"She's here, Lori. She's right here. I felt her touch me." John flinched.

Madness was about, yet Lori didn't speak or move. It was as though her body had been frozen by the chilly breeze. However, John wasn't idle. His head swiveled back and forth like a marionette until his gaze was drawn to a dim aura that appeared directly in front of the coffee table. It was a misty, white glow that he saw, a diffused glow that started to slowly take shape. As though inspired by some unforeseen power, second by second the image grew sharper until it was in focus. John's fear turned to agony as the tears welled in his awestruck eyes. It was Boo. His little girl had returned.

"Lori! Can you see her?" John's voice quivered.

Lori remained silent and motionless. Meanwhile, Boo stepped closer, allowing her father a better point of view. Her face, body, and hair lacked any color other than achromatic white. Yes, she looked ghostly, but she also looked radiant, beautiful in her ivory nightgown. And although she appeared three-dimensional, she was not solid. In the shadowy room, he could vaguely see the wall on the other side of her wispy image. Yet, he could distinctly make out her features, especially the concerned expression on her face. He wanted to leap from the sofa and sweep her into his arms, to calm her worries and tell her how much he loved her. But in his heart, he knew that it was impossible. Besides, Boo seemed more interested in communicating than embracing. Straight into his eyes, she stared as he followed the movement of her lips. No words were spoken, but like a radio signal from beyond, he understood what she was attempting to say.

"She's trying to say my name. Look, Lori, she's trying to get my attention."

Lori remained speechless. Meanwhile, John panted and watched as Boo moved two steps closer. She attempted to say his name again and this time her voice was audible. It was a mere whisper.

"Daddy," She wistfully cried.

"Yeah, baby. I'm right here." His heart ached so much. "What is it? What's wrong?"

Boo's face grew even more troubled as she attempted to speak again. John's face was contorted as well. He wanted to understand her message so much, yet her voice was still just a murmur. Just the same, her lips continued to move as she slipped closer, but the sound was still barely audible.

One step closer.

Nothing yet.

Another step.

The words finally broke from her lips.

"It killed me," she whispered.

Yes, she finally told him what she so desperately wanted him to know. And to make certain, she seemingly pointed in his direction. John was horrified and in disbelief. It was the pungent smell that he noticed first, the same stench that singed his nostrils at the murder scenes. It was the antithesis of the heavenly perfume that Boo brought to the room and it seemed to be gaining strength with each passing second. But how could it be coming from him? Then, he heard her speak again and now, it was much more than a whisper.

"MONSTER!" Her hollow scream echoed throughout the room.

John looked to find his ghostly daughter pointing her finger again. Boo sensed that her father had misunderstood her first message. This time, he was more attentive as his eyes carefully followed her finger in another direction. Right to his lovely Lori, the one he wanted to marry. The goatish odor confirmed it. It was emanating from her, not him. Lori stared back, at first assuming a normal appearance, but as he squinted, he took note of her hair. It appeared to have coarsened and turned somewhat unruly. Could it be that way or was it just the flickering light that gave it that semblance? Confused and scared, he was unable to answer that question. He rubbed his eyes before he shifted them to her again.

"Lori?" He asked.

"John." She made a guttural sound and smiled.

Whatever doubt he had about her strange appearance was instantly compounded by that smile. It was dark, but he could see well enough to make out two rows of jagged teeth; pointed, razor sharp teeth between those grinning lips. And the stink was her breath wafting from that hellish mouth. He recoiled until the arm of the sofa stopped his retreat. An awful feeling swept through him, so awful it made his stomach spasm with dread. He had just seen and smelled evil of the worst kind and his mind had registered what no human mind should ever have to acknowledge. *How could this be happening? Is she playing some sort of trick on me?*

"Lori...." his voice quivered. "You look like—is this a Halloween joke?"

"Don't you have something you want to ask me, John? Don't you have an important question for me?" She interrupted him and smiled even wider, allowing a yellowish spittle to secrete from the corners of her mouth.

"Your face, it's changing! What's going on?" He pleaded as he continued to witness her facial undulations

"I believe you were about to ask for my hand in marriage. Weren't you? I'll give you my answer as soon as you ask." She slid over, closing the distance between them.

Boo screamed again. "MONSTER!" She was now within three feet of Lori, pointing directly at her transforming face.

"Shut up you little twit. I'm talking to your daddy." Lori growled and then slung the remaining ice and booze from her glass. The contents flew through the air, wisping through Boo's spirit and splattering on the opposite den wall. Her action had no effect on Boo. She remained steadfast and continued pointing. However, it did affect her father as it would affect any father who witnessed his sweet child being threatened, spirit or not. For it was in those moments of menace that every parent becomes an angry guardian. No matter how lopsided the odds, a person draws a ray of strength from Heaven that transforms the weakest of the weak into a cyclone of fight. And it is that strength from above that sends shivers into the heart of the oppressor. For God surely frowns on those who wage abuse against the meek. John felt eclipsed by that special power as his fear fell prey to intense anger. He was fuming mad. He felt his whole body swelling. Literally getting larger.

"YOU STAY AWAY FROM HER, YOU BITCH!" John sprang to his feet.

"Oh! Is that anyway to talk to your lover? And besides, the little twit can't feel anything. She's nothing but an irritating vapor, an insignificant spook that you want to get away from anyway." Lori rose from the sofa, unimpressed by his newfound brawn. "Now don't you want to ask me a question?"

"The only question I have is, did you kill my little girl?" John's eyes narrowed as he squared his shoulders.

Lori was annoyed by his reply. "No! Are you that stupid? The question is, 'Lori, will you marry me?' And my answer is, yes, I will. Yes, I'll marry you." She attempted to smile but her lips now appeared desiccated, shrunken back from her prominent gums and teeth. It was impossible to believe that those lips were once full and sexy.

"Fuck you!" John snapped back

"I believe you've already done that, Johnny. You want some more now, or do you want to wait until the honeymoon?" Lori rolled her head from side to side and grabbed her crotch with her bony fingers.

The candlelight was dim, but not so dim that John didn't notice the continuing transformation of her body. Her skin seemed to be rippling, quivering as though the underlying bone structure was undergoing a metamorphosis. Her nose flattened against her rising cheekbones and her eyes sank deep below a jutting forehead.

"My god. What are you?" John asked as he stepped back several more feet.

"Why don't you ask little Boo? She's got all the answers." Lori cocked her head toward Boo and acted surprised to find her missing. "Oh, the little spook is gone. It's just as well, you know. If it weren't for her, you and I would already be married. But she keeps coming back, doing her best to spoil all of my master's plans. I'd kill her again if I could," Lori laughed hideously. It exposed a flicking tongue much like the bifurcated one Boo had drawn on the marker board. "But no matter, back to business. This is the last time I'll ask, Johnny. Are we getting married or not?"

"You must be kidding. Hell no!" John stepped back two more steps.

"Well, that's too bad. After all, we've got a little one baking in the oven and I know you'd want to do the right thing by

371

getting hitched before it's born." She rubbed her belly and grinned a wicked grin.

"My god! Why are you doing this to me?" John pleaded; his eyes filled with incredulity.

"Why? You mean you really don't have a clue?" She sneered.

"No!"

"Even after all the hallucinations?"

"No!"

"The master thinks you're the orphan spirit, the chosen one. He wants you on our side. And I came close, real close. If it weren't for that little snot-nosed kid of yours, you'd be over to us." She reached for the open slit in the flannel shirt and ripped the garment from her pulsating body. Buttons exploded in all directions.

"What do you mean 'the chosen one'?" John was full of dread, but he was determined to learn the truth.

"The master believes that you hold the spirit of the first horseman. Personally, I think you act more like a sniveling wussy than a warrior, but that's not my decision." Lori bared her teeth as her bones continued to crack and pop.

"I'm a cop for god's sake, not some horseman. This is just a bad dream. I'm going to wake up in a minute and all of this will go away."

"It can be a good dream, John—a great dream! All you have to do is renounce God and you'll be one of us. Money, power, sex, anything you want! Anything you can imagine can be yours, including me. I can take any form you want. I can be anyone you want me to be. But this is your last chance. Just say yes."

"No way I'll do that. You killed my daughter and you're going to pay." John's voice raged with determination.

"Pay? How am I going to pay? Are you going to arrest me, Detective Williams?" Her eyes, now serpent-like, remained transfixed, unblinking as though they had no lids. And her voice no longer sounded like Lori's sweet drawl. It was the raspy hiss of a predator. This thing, this ogress was not of this Earth.

"That's exactly what I'm going to do." Instinctively, John reached for his handcuffs. In his mind, he was still dealing with a member of the weaker sex and the cuffs should be enough to place her in custody. Unfortunately, the handcuffs were upstairs in his bedroom closet along with his Colt. Bad timing, really bad timing. His face appeared worried in the faint light. The creature recognized his dilemma and cocked her head upward and chortled.

"The only thing you're going to do, Johnny, is die!"

John stood without flinching a muscle. It was as though he was in a trance. He did move enough, however, to unwillingly bite his tongue as he watched her complete the mutation. Her svelte body thickened through the middle, growing leathery with grizzled black hair sprouting in all directions. He counted six sagging teats instead of the two upswept breasts he once cherished. Below were the cloven hoofs, flanks, and legs of a goat, and above was a horrid mixture of beast and human. Her eyebrows were heavy, curved upward toward her Medusa-like hair. Sunken temples and a square chin accented with a tuft of raven hair was the final touch. And a nightmarish finish it was. John tasted the blood welling in his mouth as he blinked at the beast now standing before him.

"Come give Lori a kiss, Johnny. One of those juicy French kisses you love so much. It'll be over in seconds." Her forked tongue flicked in and out, as she held out her misshapen arms and swayed from side to side in a taunting manner.

"Screw you!" It was the only thing he could think to say as he stepped back and turned sideways to assume a fighting position.

"It's too late for that, Johnny," She hissed.

John should have been off guard by her surprising speed, but he wasn't. Somehow, he sensed that he had to keep his wits about him. He knew that if he became unhinged, his mind would be scattered, and it would mean certain death. He anticipated her wild charge by sliding to his left and delivering a crushing forearm blow to her neck as she rushed by. The clothesline strike effectively knocked her off her hooves, sending her flying wildly across the room and onto an end table and lamp.

Glass shattered from her crushing weight and exploded in every direction. Meanwhile, John pivoted in preparation for another charge. He didn't have to wait very long. She quickly rose and grabbed her neck.

"You bastard!" She winced as the prickly hair bristled on her back. Angry and unable to breathe, the words had to be forced from her throat. "I'm going to smash your throat just like I did Sugar Bear's. I'll show you how it feels!"

John refused to show any fear. In disdain, he spat a mouthful of blood and saliva in her direction. It splattered on her teats and mixed with the blood that was oozing from her wound. Several large pieces of glass were embedded in her hairy black chest, causing her to wince in pain.

"Come ahead, you bitch!" He spat again.

Lori regained her poisoned breath and gnashed her exposed teeth in preparation for another assault. But this time, she was more deliberate, more calculating. This was a creature with vast intelligence. She slowly clopped forward and warily assessed his position until she was within four feet of him. After she stopped, she grinned as though she knew something that he did not. And she did.

As though hypnotized by some psychic energy, John blinked for a moment at her yellowish eyes and grinning teeth. It provided her the opportunity she needed. Before he realized it, he was falling backward, arms out, feet in the air, crashing to the floor. His failure to earlier see her posterior, especially the elongated tail that extended from her trunk was a mistake. She used the ugly appendage as a fifth limb by coiling it around his feet and yanking them out from under him. He never felt it.

However, he did feel the sharp pain in his lower back when he hit the floor. He also felt the heft of the beast when she landed on top of him, blowing her foul breath in his face. Her smelly shanks straddled his waist, keeping his upper body from twisting, while she pinned his arms with her skeletal hands. It was then that John realized how powerful she was. Unbelievably strong. *Weaker sex, my ass!* That was his first thought. His second was one of sheer terror.

"I'm going to send you straight to Hell so you can be with your foster mother again. I'm sure she'll be glad to see her Johnny boy." Poisoned spittle dripped from her teeth. John was so close now he could make out a set of curved horns and triangular ears in her tangled hair. Hell had surely arrived at the Williams' house.

"HELL NO!" He yelled. John's reply showcased a willingness to live, but for an instant he thought about giving up and dying. He thought about being with his family in the afterlife. But then the creature said something that transformed him into her worst nightmare.

"I'm really disappointed, Johnny. I'd thought you'd be more of an adversary than this. Hell, your little twit of a girl fought harder than you before she died. She scratched and clawed like a wild cat. Her mama was there when I did it. Did you know that? She even heard little Boo calling for you. 'Daddy, Daddy! Help me!'"

The beast cocked her head backward and cackled. She sensed that she had won the battle and was preparing to deliver a vicious bite. But she wanted to taunt him, to make him suffer before she finished him off. Her victory celebration was premature, for John had not given up and it was a mistake on her part to assume he had. He was filled with fight, preparing to deliver a vicious blow of his own. The tilt of her head was the opening he needed. He lifted his right leg upward and hooked his ankle across her neck, then thrusted her backward to the floor.

John escaped and sprang to his feet, prepared to unleash all of his pent-up frustration and anger. Lori's terrible words had triggered him. They had resurrected a man who had no reason to live by giving him inspiration to avenge his daughter. It was powerful motivation, but he also felt a higher power pushing him, a sacred intent that goodness should always prevail over evil. John felt that potent message in his heart and it gave him courage and inner strength. The silvery gleam in his eyes told the beast that the real fight was about to begin. And so it did.

For almost an hour, the fighting was intensely violent, savage, and incredibly fast. The furious blows were delivered and countered at short range. Lori was hell-bent on biting John with those snapping jaws and he was hell-bent on avoiding them at all costs. He had struck her with at least five or six hard blows that would have killed any mortal, but she seemed impervious to each strike. She chomped at him repeatedly. Neither opponent could gain an advantage so they fought in the dark from room to room until the den and kitchen were completely destroyed, until both had to pause to gain their breath. John's eyes never left Lori's repulsive face as he clutched his knees and gasped for air. He needed a new strategy, a good old fashioned 10mm Colt strategy. But he had a problem. The firearm was in his bedroom closet.

"Well, Johnny. It looks as though you're going down the hard way." Her chest heaved in and out as she attempted to regain her strength for another round.

"You're the only one going down!" John growled as though he was ready to resume the fight, but in reality, his arms and legs felt like dead weight. He reached up and wiped the dripping sweat from his brow, swallowed his breath and searched the den for an opening to get around her. The opportunity came unexpectedly. What he saw made him squint in disbelief. Boo had returned. The little girl who had once pledged to protect him was back. Those words had weight now. They were much more than the cute oath of a little girl.

He squinted again. He couldn't see Boo's apparition, but he knew she was there. A poker from the fireplace was floating mid-air behind the creature. It looked like a ghost movie from the sixties, that dangling poker bouncing up and down as though suspended on wires. And he could smell her flowery scent. Even though the room was thick with the goatish stink of the beast, John could still smell that sweet aroma. The creature smelled her as well, but it was too late when she took notice. With surprising force, the fire iron dropped on the back of the creature's skull as she turned to sniff the air. When it connected, it made a sharp crack that sounded like a small caliber rifle. Knees buckled, eyes rolled, and down she went. John wasted no time. He seized the opportunity by hightailing it up the stairs. It was good that he did, for when he arrived at his lightless closet, he couldn't find his holster and gun. Panic set in as he scoured the shelves. He needed more time.

"Good lord, what did I do with it," John whispered hysterically as he continued his search.

Meanwhile downstairs, Boo vanished about the same time the she-beast began to recover. The ogress lifted her heavy body from the carpet, eyes flaring like two lighthouse beacons on a pitch-dark night. Her face twisted from the cutting pain in her head and chest. To say she was livid would be a gross understatement. She cussed, hissed, and threatened to remove John's private part in the same manner as Rimmon and Pierce. That was her promise.

"You son of a bitch!" She howled. "Where are you?"

She had decided to begin her search upstairs and would have been there in seconds had a rustling sound at the front door not changed her plan.

"So, Johnny. You think you can sneak out the front and get away?"

She charged to the door and ripped it open, expecting to find John cowardly scampering from the house. She found nothing of the sort. What she did find, however, momentarily caught her off guard. The two deviant teenage boys had returned. Armed with two urine filled balloons, they were ready to have their revenge on the old fart who had made them appear foolish.

"What do you two pricks want?" She snarled as bursts of stinky steam exploded from that horrible mouth.

The two pricks stood frozen. Their skinny arms were cocked like two quarterbacks, but they were too terrified to deliver the balloons. This terrible thing in the shadows was anything but the old fart that filled their bags with rotten fruit.

"I asked you little fucks a question." She drew closer, allowing them a better inspection.

The shaking boy with the darker green hair lowered his arm and dropped the balloon. He also wet his low-rider jeans as he watched his true-blue buddy turn coward-yellow and run into the darkness. The amber urine splattered on the concrete stoop and then puddled under his high-top tennis shoes. The fact that the urine stained the mischievous boy instead of John would have been a wonderful case of poetic justice had the teenager's life not been in jeopardy. The beast seemed amused nonetheless, grinning, sniffing the air while her tongue lolled around her lips. Finally, she had a victim filled with fear instead of vengeance and she instinctively wanted to kill.

"Well, well, lookie here. Stud boy must be marking his territory." She reached out, grabbed the kid around the neck, lifted him into the air, and drew him within inches of her horrible face.

"Stud boy want a little kiss? Or maybe he wants to go all the way with Miss Lori. Is that what you want, stud boy?" Her nostrils flared and she licked the frightened boy's face with her raspy tongue. She was sampling his innocence, his virginity. The teenager could only turn his head side to side in disagreement.

"Please, let me go!" He cried.

"Let Lori have a little taste and then she'll let you go." Her mouth opened incredibly wide as though every jaw tendon had the elasticity of a rubber band. But before she could deliver the fatal bite, a voice from the darkness commanded her to stop.

"Let the kid go, you bitch!"

It was John. He had returned equipped with two pounds of steel. He waved a Bowie-like hunting knife in his right hand. It was a knife Papa Dan had given him on his thirteenth birthday, a knife designed for gutting and skinning wild animals. It was the only lethal thing his groping fingers could find on the closet shelf. But he was not concerned. In his skilled hands, a blade was as deadly as a bullet.

"Johnny! Where have you been?" The beast turned her grisly head toward John, and simultaneously flipped the teenage boy onto the front yard like a cigarette butt. John remained silent, poised for a charge. He knew he had to remain focused, as did the beast. So, in the darkness, the creature invented her own diversion.

"John, I've missed you so much. Boo and I wish you could be with us. We're so lonely without you."

The voice was soft, very recognizable to John. It was Rebecca's. John stared into the dark haze as puzzlement shaped his face. The shadowy silhouette before him belonged to Rebecca, not the deformed creature. For a moment, he wondered if she had returned much in the same manner as Boo. Perhaps she was there to warn him, he thought, for surely it was his sweet Becky who had earlier visited Boo and moved the Bible about the house. Earlier he doubted her presence and he didn't want to make that mistake again.

"Becky, is that you?" For a few beautiful seconds, he was held fast in a dream that his life would return to the way it was before the tragic deaths in his family. The sound of her voice had awakened that hope in him. Yes, it was that voice, that musical voice. The captivating voice of a siren. Lorelei the siren. The beast knew this was his weakness. His knife hand dropped to his side and he cautiously inched forward.

"I need to hold you, John. I'm so lonely...I need you to hold me right now," she pleaded.

The voice was plaintive, and it certainly sounded like Rebecca's, but the words seemed stitched together like a poorly sewn quilt. Yet, John wanted to believe so badly he dropped the heavy knife to the floor and reached out to welcome her embrace. It would have been a lethal embrace had the electrical power to the house not been restored. Never again would he berate the power company for being tardy.

FLASH!

At first, the light was blinding, but not so dazzling that he couldn't see those gleaming yellow eyes and predatory teeth coming at him. He had been deceived again, but there was no time for him to lament his blurry judgment. The fight resumed and the beast had gained a toxic advantage with a piercing bite to his shoulder. The pain was excruciating, much like the pain from a horrible burn. She drew back and was preparing to take another chomp when John retaliated by throwing a crushing uppercut with his right elbow. It was a defensive move, but it was effective.

The swinging blow landed squarely under her chin, causing her eyes to roll and grow cloudy. It was the opening John needed. He stepped back and pummeled her face with a series of hard blows that bloodied her nose and bruised her eyes, and as she staggered backward, he delivered what should have been the coup de grace. It was a long-range kick to her hairy chest. The blow struck with such speed and power that it drove several broken ribs inward toward her lungs and beating heart. Blood oozed from the corners of her mouth as she plopped on her backside to the floor.

"It's over you bitch!" John screamed as he watched her shoulders slump and eye lids slowly close. She was no longer hissing or thrashing, but to be sure, John stood in front of her motionless body for a long moment, long enough to convince himself that she was dead. Finally, he exhaled a sigh of relief and turned for the phone in the kitchen. After he made the 911 call, he sat in a dinette chair and tried to regain some margin of sanity.

A horseman? Good lord, how ridiculous is that? All sorts of thoughts churned through his head. He yearned for a rational explanation for this madness, but there was none to be had. Only the racking pain in his shoulder interrupted his crazy thoughts. It was unbearable.

"Damn that hurts!" He reached up and poked at the gaping wound. Blood poured freely from the gash, causing him to shiver and sweat even though the struggle was over. *Must be the poison that's doing it,* he thought. *Need to do something before I pass out.*

John grimaced as he struggled to rise from the chair. Every movement of his body made that inflamed shoulder hurt even more. He staggered to the stairs to get bandages and antiseptic from the upstairs bathroom. After grabbing the handrail to steady his body, he prepared to take the first step. But he stopped. Dead cold, he stopped. A nagging voice inside his head begged him to take another look at the creature, just to be sure. He wished he had ignored that little voice because when he stepped back to peer around the corner, a panic-stricken fear chilled him to the bone.

"Oh, my god!" John was breathless.

The beast was gone. But worse yet, so was the huge razor-sharp Bowie knife he had dropped to the floor. In the confusion, he had forgotten to pick it up. So, the beast must have found it. How could things get any worse?

John dismissed any thought of searching for the creature. He didn't have a choice. Blood had begun to ooze profusely from his lacerated shoulder, staining the carpet and marking his wobbly path up the stairs and down the hall. He lacked the strength to canvass the house for the monster, anyway. He could only hope that she had crawled off somewhere to lick her own wounds or, better yet, die.

Right now, he needed medical attention, so he hobbled down the hallway and into his bedroom. By the time he staggered into the bathroom, he was dizzy and had to fight to remain conscious. A cold splash of water from the faucet to his face helped awaken his senses, allowing him to maintain enough dexterity to find the first-aid kit and clumsily tend to his wound. It was a makeshift dressing, but it was effective. After a few minutes, the bleeding slowed, and the pain abated just enough for his head to clear. He located the aspirin bottle in a cabinet drawer to his left. After popping a few pills into his mouth, he braced his hands on the sink, slowly bent over and gulped the cold water directly from the faucet. It tasted great. His body craved the fluid due to the dehydration and loss of blood. He allowed the water to flow over his face for a moment before he rose and fumbled for the hand towel on the wall rack. John found the metal rack, but the towel was missing. He fingered the top of the sink cabinet, thinking it may have fallen, but he felt nothing.

"Shoot! Where's that towel?" John murmured as he continued to feel around for the cloth. He had all but given up when suddenly, he stopped and sniffed the air. "Oh, god!" He moaned.

The gamy smell hit him first. It warned that the horror had returned. Frantically, John hand-wiped the dripping water from his face and opened his eyes to an awful reflection in the mirror. Grinning and leering, the beast appeared pleased. It was standing behind him, holding the dangling towel in one hand and the shiny knife in the other.

"Looking for this, Johnny?" She mockingly shook the blue towel above his left shoulder. "Or could it be this?" She waived the blade above his right.

He fought to conceal his surprise as he studied her reflection in the mirror. She was still smiling that awful grin, but he could tell that she was still in pain. Her breathing was heavy, labored as though a lung had been pierced instead of her heart.

"Police are on their way. They'll be here in just a minute." He spoke calmly even though he knew she would attack again.

"I know that, Johnny. I heard you make the call. But we've got a little unfinished business, you and me." Her tongue flicked as she prepared to use the blade.

John expected the move. He also felt a renewed power in his body as though he was being infused with an unnatural strength from above. He sensed that the God he cursed so vehemently for being uncaring was really a God who does great things. How else could he explain the might and stamina that was restored in his physical being after every confrontation? That new strength helped John block the beast's descending arm with his right forearm. Instantly, he pivoted and delivered a left elbow to her damaged ribs. The sound that rose from her throat was one of shear agony, a guttural groan straight from Hell. He could still hear her crying as he stumbled out of the bathroom through the bedroom and toward the stairs.

As he moved down the hall, he could have sworn that he smelled his daughter's sweet scent. Even though he didn't see or hear her, he knew she was there. He was right. Boo's mission to protect him was not over. Patiently, she waited for the beast to charge from the bathroom, and charge she did—hissing, howling, and waving the knife while sprinting toward the bedroom doorway. When the creature drew close, Boo performed one of her haunted house maneuvers. With precise timing, she slammed closed the bedroom door in the creature's face.

"Ummph!" The sound was deep.

The beast smashed into the door with the force of a middle linebacker, but unlike a tackled running back, the solid oak door refused to go down. Instead, the beast was sent spinning backward across the room and to the floor. Blood spilled from her flattened nose as she bounced to her hoofs and charged again. But this time, she opened the door before charging past the doorway.

"You little bitch!" The monster spit venom in every direction as she burst into the hallway. "I'll kill you."

It was an absurd threat. It brought a giggle from Boo that echoed down the hall like a whimsical chime. Boo's amusement infuriated the beast even more since she could no longer be harmed. But John was a different story. He was of flesh and bone and her primary target anyway.

384

Boo's antics simply diverted her attention from her main objective to kill John. The beast plowed down the stairs, crazy mad and determined to sink that knife between John's shoulder blades. Had John not been so sluggish, he would have been safely out the front door by now. But the poison was coursing through his veins and damaging every organ and nerve in his body. By the time he reached the door, the room was spinning so wildly he struggled to find the knob. Fortunately, he opened the door with his last ounce of strength and looked up to find his guardian angel. No, it wasn't Boo. This was a burly, real-life version, a two hundred sixty-pound rendition. That was the last thing John remembered. Seeing his partner Victor....

55

It was a different smell that permeated his nose. Not the sweet smell of Boo nor the foul musk of the beast. This cutting scent was the antiseptic nip of medicinal alcohol. John knew where he was the moment he opened his eyes and sniffed the air. This was a hospital room. The setting was unmistakable. There were glaring lights, a rigid bed, and a television perched in the corner on the wall. The IV in his right arm and a petite nurse checking his pulse were the other dead giveaways. At first, he felt strangely disconnected, but slowly the sensations returned, and much like the nurse, he started to feel the thump, thump, thump of his beating heart. At least he thought it was his heart. The sensation he actually felt was coming from his throbbing shoulder, not from his chest. The awful pain from his wound had been roused from its sleep.

"Hey, partner. How are you feeling?"

John turned his head to his right and spied Victor sitting in an uncomfortable chair next to his bed.

"Hey, Victor. My shoulder hurts like hell but I'm still breathing. It could be worse." John attempted to ignore the pain and muster a smile.

"By the look of your house, I believe it. It looked like a tornado blew through there." Victor shook his head in disbelief.

"Yeah, I'm just glad you were there to see her, or should I say *it*! Did you get her?" John asked.

Victor answered with his own question, "Get who?"

"The beast! She was chasing me when you arrived. She was right behind me with my knife. She was trying to kill me. Don't tell me you didn't see her?" John's face twisted with pain as he sat up in bed.

"God, I didn't see anyone but you when I got to the house. I was about to knock on the front door when it swung open and you fell out. After that, the patrol cops and paramedics arrived, and the place was crawling with people." Victor seemed puzzled.

"What do you mean, you didn't see her? She was right behind me. I could almost feel her stinking breath on my shoulder." John was annoyed with Victor's answer.

"I'm telling you, John. There was nobody there but you." Victor was adamant.

"Well, who the hell do you think took this chunk out of my shoulder? Who do you think bit me?" John's annoyance was turning into resentment.

"I don't know how that happened. All I know is you had lost a lot of blood and were in shock when I got there. That's all."

"It was Lori. She's the one I was fighting. She's the one who bit me."

"Lori?" Victor's eyebrows flared with incredulity.

"Yeah, Lori! She's not who you think she is. She changed into some kind of monster right in front of me. Animal teeth, horns, black hair all over—really ugly! If it weren't for Boo, I'd be a goner right now." John looked as though he was possessed by a monster himself.

Shocked by the look on John's face, the attentive nurse became inattentive as she dropped a glass thermometer on the linoleum floor. She had the same look of skepticism as Victor, that perhaps John should be in the psychiatric ward with the other delusional patients. After all, talk of seeing monsters was common on that floor.

"Easy, partner. You've been through a lot and need some rest." Victor's words sounded reassuring, but his face was still brushed with doubt.

"Don't call me partner!" John snapped back. The image of Victor, the Minotaur, had just entered his mind and he was about to work himself into a frenzy. "I know what I saw!"

"When I talked to your doctor this morning, he said your blood had some kind of powerful toxin in it. Some kind of poison that attacked your central nervous system. Hell, he even said it could be something like rabies." Victor cracked a smile at the most inopportune time.

"Oh, so that's it. You think I'm nuts. That I'm a foaming-at-the-mouth mad dog that's making up all of this stuff!"

"No, no. I didn't say that. It's just that the doctor said the toxin could make you have hallucinations. That's all," Victor replied.

"Well, I'm not crazy and the animal that bit me was no hallucination. She was real—as real as you and me!" John's voice grew louder.

"What about Boo? You said Boo helped you. How?" Victor asked.

"Lori killed Boo. That's what Boo has been trying to tell me. That and Lori is this monster thing. Boo told me that last night right in front of Lori. That's why Lori changed."

"John. Boo is dead. How could she tell you anything?"

"I know she's dead! But her spirit came back to tell me!" John bellowed.

"John, take it easy. Everything is going to be all right."

"God, I can't believe this is happening." John collapsed back on the bed.

John realized how preposterous his story must sound. Victor's misgiving eyes made that very clear. The nurse confirmed the absurdity of the ghostly tale as well. She tripped on her own feet and almost fell down as she continued to back-peddle out the open doorway. Besides, had John not been there himself, he would certainly declare his tale a neurotic whopper. Yes, he was alone in his knowledge, yet somehow, he sensed that this was his destiny—to stand alone against the beast. All of this crazy horseman stuff aside, he wanted the chance to confront Lori again, to avenge the death of his daughter. No one would deny him that opportunity, especially Victor.

John still held no trust for Victor. That suspicious feeling had risen in him like a cold northeast wind. There was no way Victor could have missed seeing Lori, or the beast, or whatever the hell it was. And even if he did, how could he not have heard those maniacal screams and hisses emanating from the house? The little voice inside his head that kept raising those doubts also kept pleading for him to trust the same man.

John knew that the beast was capable of some incredible feats, some even superhuman. She could have slipped out the back door without Victor noticing. Who knows, maybe she even walked out the front door in the guise of another person. Maybe a cop or a paramedic. After all, she was a shapeshifter capable of assuming any identity. John was filled with so much confusion, he really did not know if Victor was telling the truth or not. However, he did know that he was completely exhausted and needed rest, so he asked Victor to leave. Victor quietly complied.

"Man, that hurts!" John groaned as he turned on his uninjured side, hoping to relieve the throbbing ache. It was a good maneuver. The discomfort in his shoulder had begun to ease a little, so he closed his eyes and hoped the pain meds would help his overwrought body relax. And for a minute or two, he dozed. But an uninvited whisper snapped him from his peace.

"Johnnnnny."

It sounded like mist.

56

The hospital staff were relentless in treating his injury and their dedication finally paid off with his dismissal on the fourth day. It was a rough stay for John. The poison from the creature's bite was a rare substance that caused him immense pain and violent trembling. And for a while, it baffled the doctors in their search for a cure. Yet, the venomous bite was not the sole cause of his suffering. Blood analysis by the hospital lab had revealed a significant level of alcohol poisoning in his body. Much of his convulsive shaking was delirium tremens due to his withdrawal from all the booze he had been drowning in after Boo's death. But the doctors had conjured up anti-venoms that cured both of his maladies and he had managed to force down enough tasteless food to regain his appetite and strength.

He had also regained his wits. He was focused now, no longer embroiled with jarring emotions that quarreled for his attention. He felt only one sensation. A deep and deadly rage had found his blue eyes and dilated them black with ferocity. His pupils had a feline look about them, as though he were on the prowl. That savage look warned that he could think of only one thing. The beast. She was on the loose and would certainly go on killing if he didn't stop her. He had purpose and was ready to leave, but there was one more interruption.

He had just finished dressing in his street clothes when he noticed her face peering around the half-opened door. It was hard not to notice that endearing smile. He half-expected to see her. Over the past two days, he had silently prayed for guidance, for someone of faith to tell him what to do. And here this gentle woman stood with a glint in her eyes and knowing look on her face. He wondered if she was God's sponsor, if the Almighty One had called and asked her to bestow words of divine direction on his behalf. Given her spiritual devotion, John was certain she had an unbroken line to his heavenly mansion.

"John, mind if I come in?" She asked.

"Dr. Brown! No, of course not. Please come in."

"Looks like you're getting ready to leave. You sure you don't mind?"

"No, no! Here, have a seat." John slid the bedside chair around for Dr. Brown and seated himself on the edge of the bed.

"Thanks." Dr. Brown sat down and placed her backpack and several books on the floor beside the chair. "I read about you in the paper."

"In the newspaper?" John appeared dumbfounded.

"Yes, there was an article in last night's paper," she answered.

"Why would anyone write an article about me?"

"Evidently a reporter has been following the murders and your investigations. It makes really good fodder, you know, satanism, bloodletting, dismembered body parts—all the weird stuff the public eats up. He even mentioned Boo's death." Dr. Brown's eyes held steady on John as she waited for his response.

"My god. Why would a reporter bring Boo into this mess?" John grimaced.

"Well, the story really wasn't about Boo. He just inferred that she had recently died under mysterious circumstances. The article was really about the police department, or more specifically, you. He tried to paint you as incompetent because the murders are still unsolved. He wrote that he was at your house the other night when you were injured. That he interviewed a paramedic who said you were delusional, that you kept mumbling something about a monster that was after you." Dr. Brown reached over and clutched John's hands. "John, talk to me. Something's up. I can feel it in these old bones. It's something bad, isn't it?"

Dr. Brown asked the question, but she already knew the answer. So did John. It had just taken a lot of pain and emotional suffering for him to accept it. His eyes softened as tears temporarily wiped away his rage.

"You were right, Dr. Brown. You were right the whole time; I just wouldn't listen to you. I just couldn't believe something like that monster could actually exist."

"You've seen the beast, haven't you?"

"Yes, I've seen her. She's the one who killed Boo. The one who tried to kill me when I wouldn't agree to renounce God."

"It's a she?" Dr. Brown's jaw dropped in surprise.

"It's the woman I was seeing...Lori. Can you believe that?"

"I would have never guessed it. Do you know why she is focused on you?"

"I'm not sure," John answered.

"There's got to be a reason, John. She wanted you to renounce God for a reason."

"Well, I know this sounds nutty, but she said her master thinks I'm a warrior, a horseman."

"Oh, dear!" Dr. Brown dug her fingernails deep into John's flesh, so deep, it almost drew blood from his palms. He was so stunned by the incredulous look on her face he never noticed the pain in his hands. Her grandmotherly features suddenly disappeared as her grainy skin was drawn as tight as the skin on a drum. Her thin lips formed a circle of dread and her eyes widened with awe as though she had just witnessed the toothy hiss of the she-beast herself. But her dread was rooted in something else, something more serious than the beast. Something prophetic.

"What is it? What's wrong?" John asked.

"I just had a horrible thought," Dr. Brown said.

"What?"

"A scripture," she answered. "'For He has set a day when He will judge the world.' That's part of the scripture from Acts 17:31."

"What are you talking about?" He asked.

"The Apocalypse!" She answered with an air of certainty.

"The end of the world?" John's face was shaped with doubt.

"Yes," she said.

"That's crazy!" John drew back in disbelief.

"Think about it, John. The book of Revelation refers to four living beings, Four Horsemen—the Four Horsemen of the Apocalypse. The first horseman has a bow, and he rides a white steed. He is a warrior—or better yet, he's the incarnation of war. That's why he carries a bow. It's a sign of military power."

"Oh, no!" John's stomach was tied in nervous knots.

"What is it?" Dr. Brown asked.

"Right after Boo died, I had a dream, a very vivid dream. In it, I was on a white horse. I was dressed in some kind of ancient body armor and I had a bow. Oh, and Boo was in the dream too."

"What did she do?"

"She placed this crown on my head and then she broke open a seal on an old book she was carrying."

"Then what happened?"

"Nothing, I woke up before I could find out."

"Consider this. The Apocalypse marks the end of Satan's reign on earth. It brings about his complete elimination because he is cast into the Lake of Fire forever! So, if by some chance you are the embodiment of the first horseman, if your spirit has been designated to fulfill that role, it makes sense that Satan would want to stop you. Aren't you an orphan, John?"

"Yes", he answered.

"Did you ever know your parents?"

"No, never."

"It all makes sense. If Satan thinks you're that person, that you have that spirit in you, he would want to convert you, to have you renounce God. Perhaps, he thinks if you come over to his side, he can stop the prophesied chain of events. Maybe he thinks he can prevent the Apocalypse, or at least delay it."

"And Lori was sent to convert me?" John asked.

"Yes! She could be his Jezebel, sent specifically for that reason. Boo's death and maybe even your wife's were parts of their scheme. Every terrible thing that has happened to you has happened for a reason." Dr. Brown picked up her backpack and books from the floor. "I need a cigarette. You mind if we get out of here?"

"No, after listening to all of this I need some fresh air."

John and Dr. Brown rejoined in the hospital parking lot next to her car. He leaned against the Honda's dented fender while she paced back and forth in front of him, puffing away between sentences.

"All of your visions, John. All of the visions you told me about could be flashbacks of some kind, glimpses of prior lives."

"I didn't think you believed in reincarnation."

"I don't. But in your case, I'm thinking there has to be some kind of connection between all the imagery you saw and what's happening now." Dr. Brown took a deep draw from the cigarette. "Don't you think it's too coincidental that in every one of your visions you were a soldier fighting an enemy? Do you think it's just a coincidence that Rebecca's

Bible kept showing up turned to the scriptures in Ephesians? Remember what those scriptures were telling you?"

"I remember some of it." John answered, still confused.

"They were telling you to put on God's armor, John. So, you can stand safe against the tricks of Satan, for you are not fighting against people of flesh and blood, but against the wicked spirits, against the evil rulers of the unseen world. That's the message! That's what Rebecca was trying to tell you."

"It all fits, doesn't it?" John was coming around to Dr. Brown's explanation.

"Yes, it does. John, you must never lose faith in God. And you must believe in yourself no matter what happens. Stay courageous and believe that you're capable of accomplishing anything. You must never doubt that," Dr. Brown said adamantly.

John and Dr. Brown continued to discuss her theory. They even talked about how the beast could possibly be destroyed. Finally, the conversation ended when she smoked her last cigarette and had to leave for her morning class. Dr. Brown left convinced that she was correct in her assumptions. John left still somewhat uncertain that he believed her literal interpretation of the Gospel. He was torn somewhere between accepting the verses as prophecy or as parable. After all, he remembered Mama Ruth saying God spoke to us in many ways.

Accepting the premise that he had some profound effect on man's existence was still a farfetched idea in his rational mind. Perhaps an angel appearing before him to explain his role would be sign enough to convince him. He really didn't know. What he did know was that he accepted the existence of the beast. He had seen, smelled, and touched that foul creature and knew it was real. He also knew that he wanted to avenge Boo. He was still tortured with a burning need to make that unsightly creature pay for what it did to his daughter. For now, that was motivation enough.

The rage returned.

57

Five days of home rest had allowed John's body to fully mend. It also permitted his hatred for Lori to simmer like a slow burning fire. Although he was still not convinced that his spirit was preordained to play some sort of apocalyptic role, he was certain his life had purpose. For now, that was the reason for his existence. Lori's death warrant had been issued and he would be the Grim Reaper who would serve it. The possibility that her demise might have biblical repercussions was secondary to his primary motive. He wanted to avenge his family...plain and simple. His only dilemma was locating the creature, although that quandary was resolved with a phone call.

At half past midnight, the shrill sound woke him from sleep. An anonymous caller had invited him to the morgue. The clouded voice had promised that he would find all the answers to his questions there, but he had to come alone—no other cops, no one else. Just him. It was a risky invitation, but he couldn't refuse. He quickly dressed and left the house with his heart filled with hate and his Colt filled with hollow points.

He was also eaten up with anxiety. He cranked the Chevy and drove while hunching over the steering wheel like a neurotic senior citizen. His thoughts were consumed with who, or what, would be waiting for him at the morgue—perhaps Lori, maybe Victor, possibly Connors. Each would be a worthy adversary.

Yet his mind kept screaming for him to consider the real reason for his disquietude. The demon of demons. The god of the underworld. Would the evil one be there waiting? How would he look? And of course, how should he address him? Satan? Lucifer? Mephistopheles? Asmodeus?

Beelzebub? Maybe Mr. Devil or the less formal ole' Scratch. There's a saying in the South that if you speak of the devil, he shall appear. In truth, John hoped he would never show up. He hoped he would never have to look into his hellish eyes or address him by any name.

His fight was with his female flunky and he reminded himself of that fact as he pulled into an empty parking space at the back of the county building. He sat there for a moment, allowing the car to idle until a twinge of pain in his shoulder sent him a second reminder. It was a timely cue, a notice that it would be foolish to think too much about anything other than who or what was waiting for him inside. He grimaced a little, took a deep breath, popped the gear shift lever into park and turned off the ignition.

He slipped past the unlocked back door and stopped long enough to withdraw his weapon from the holster. Then he quietly walked down the dark hallway with the Colt swinging slightly at his side. Along the way, John tested several switches on the wall, yet none triggered the much-needed light he sought. And since he had left the flashlight in the car, he was caught in a cop's worst nightmare—an in-the-dark search for a murderous felon. But luck was with him. He made it unscathed all the way down the dim corridor to the swinging metal doors that led into the morgue.

Silently, he bent over and peered through the narrow crack between the double doors for any sign of life. Nothing. Just the dim room that functioned as the receiving area. He positioned his back against the wall next to the door and listened for any activity inside. Silence. He pushed the door inward with his left hand. It made a faint creaking sound that surely announced his arrival. He quickly stepped inside and waved the Colt from side to side at eye-level, and slowly moved forward to the center of the open room while continuing to measure his surroundings with his eyes and gun. Luck was still with him, for the bright lights mounted above the two emergency exits on either side of the room aided his search. The light reflecting off the stainless-steel doors of the refrigerated cadaver compartments magnified its intensity even more. He quickly determined that the room was empty, or so he thought it was until he heard a familiar voice call his name.

"Hello, Johnny. How have you been?"

Something moved from behind the tall, refrigerated compartments, forcing John's eyes and the firearm to swing to his left. He expected to see the sickening visage of the she-beast, to again look upon that horrible face and smell that putrid odor. Instead, he saw his fantasy made real, the beautiful form that brought him to the brink of openly renouncing his faith. God help him, he was momentarily mesmerized by her beauty.

"What's wrong, Johnny? Azriel got your tongue?" Lori asked.

She had taken the shape of Lori, or more accurately, Lorelei the evil siren. Cascading black hair, sexy eyes, sensuous mouth and a round bosom that was swollen heavy with milk. And with all that glowing skin, she was gorgeous. Poor John was in a trance, still taken aback by her appearance. But all of that changed when she turned sideways to offer him a different view of her profile, a view he hadn't seen before. Her belly protruded outward like an over-ripe watermelon. She had the figure of a woman ready to deliver.

"What do you think we should call our little one, Johnny? It's time you know." She turned back to face John and began massaging her belly. "Maybe we can call it John, Jr. or how about Boo?"

"Kiss my ass, you bitch!" John shouted.

John's eyes took on a savage gleam and his lips curled upward in a snarling pose. The thought of emptying the 10 mm clip between those lactating breasts was burning his mind and ordinarily he would have squeezed off the rounds. But his eyes dropped to view that distended belly and his homicidal thought gave way to wide-eyed wonderment. How in the world could nine months of gestation occur in only nine days? His snarl turned into an open-mouth gape as he lowered the Colt to his side.

"Well, I see you're a little shocked by my condition, so I'll make the decision for us. I think it's a little ewe, so I'll name her after your little brat." She grinned wickedly as though she were enjoying herself. "I'll call her Boo!"

John lifted the gun when Lori opened one of the middle storage compartments that housed the dead bodies. With a whip of her wrist, she forcefully yanked the long metal drawer outward and stepped aside so it could roll freely on its tracks. The drawer made a loud clunking sound as it rolled and a noisy bang when it abruptly stopped at the end of the rails. The large body resting on the metal slab jerked upward and forward, landing a full ten inches off-center. Lori continued to smile malevolently while she bellied up next to the corpse. She grabbed the white sheet that covered the body and with a guileful look on her face, gazed across the room at John.

"Don't bother with the gun, Johnny. It's a useless piece of metal. Besides, I've got a little surprise for you."

Lori stood frozen, holding a corner of the sheet in her left hand while she continued smiling. John returned her gaze while thinking how odd she looked, like a pregnant magician ready to pull a rabbit from a hat. Lori was preparing to reveal an object, but it was anything but a little bunny.

"We've been keeping a friend of yours on ice," she said. "I think you'll be thrilled to see him. I know he'll be thrilled to see you."

Lori ripped the sheet from the body and, for good measure, accented the move with a loud "*tah-dum!*" All that was missing was a drum roll.

"What do you think, Johnny? It's your old friend Sugar Bear." She pointed at the naked body that was stiff from rigor mortis.

"You really are one screwed up bitch."

"Screwed up? If I'm screwed up, it's mostly your fault. I don't ever remember you kicking me out of bed!" She seemed pleased with herself.

"That's not what I meant, and you know it."

"Well now, Johnny. Don't you worry about ole Sugar Bear, here. He made his pact and now it's time for him to fulfill his end of the bargain." Lori began stroking Sugar Bear's furry chest as though attempting to wake him from a deep sleep. "Sugar wasn't very popular with the ladies. Hell, just look at him. It's no wonder. He was one ugly mortal. So, when I was nice to him, he said that he liked me, that he'd do anything if I would be his woman. He wanted me, Johnny. He wanted me so badly he was willing to give up his soul in exchange for some pussy. Can you believe that Johnny?" She snickered.

"Well, after Mr. Bear agreed to our bargain, he wanted to back out. We had just kissed a little bit, then I rubbed on him with my body and he lost it, just like you did our first time. He lost it before he could even get his underwear off. Well, Miss Lori could have no part of that, so I told him if he could get it up again, he could have me—but, he had to take me as I really looked, not like Miss Lori. So, when Mr. Bear saw me that way, he told me the deal was off. That's when I collected what Mr. Bear owed me. I own his soul now and can bring him back anytime I like. And I think now would be a good time. Don't you?"

John raised his weapon when Lori screamed an order.

"LAZARUS, COME FORTH!"

Lori looked across the room at John and giggled like a pubescent schoolgirl. "Oh, the irony. How silly of me. That line has already been used. I meant to say, SUGAR BEAR, COME FORTH!"

Sugar Bear's hairy body began to ripple as though an electric current was surging through his dead muscles. The trembling finally stopped after about ten seconds. When it did, the Bear sat up with a sudden jerk and opened his eyes. That's when John got a really good look at his bulky shape, a body that was still horribly deformed.

The severed nose was still hanging by a thread of skin, his face and torso were still battered and bruised, and the blood remained caked in his hair and beard. His eyes were like black marbles against his china white skin. Obviously, he had never received the skillful touch of an artisan mortician. He also had never been the subject of a thorough autopsy, nor he had never been buried. A closed casket funeral had everyone believing that Sugar Bear was six feet under the ground. Many loyal disciples had to participate in this charade, although John was thinking only of one… Connors.

Where was Connors? All of the hostility aside, John really wanted to question him, but presently, he had a more monstrous problem. Sugar Bear had swung his awkward legs to the floor and had clumsily lurched forward about three steps. With his arms outstretched, he had all the dexterity of Frankenstein and, with that ugly mug, all the bad looks as well. John had the Colt aimed at Sugar Bear's heart and was ready to fire when Lori interrupted his concentration.

"You'll have to excuse me for leaving, Johnny, but I'm sure Mr. Bear will entertain you. Besides, I've got a date with your housekeeper in about half an hour." Lori shaped her hand like a telephone receiver, held it to her ear and perfectly mimicked John's voice. "Tina! You've got to come over to my house right away. It's urgent!"

John was shocked. Not by how accurately she had imitated his voice, but by the horrible thought that Tina might be placed in jeopardy. Lori reveled in his anxiety. She cackled, opening her lips so John could see that the transformation to the horrible beast had begun. Those pearly white, orthodontically straight teeth were replaced by the yellowish teeth of the beast.

"You see, Johnny. I want all of your family dead, including your precious Tina. And as for you, well, Mr. Bear here is going to take care of you!"

John quickly moved to his right. He wanted to gain a clear angle for a shot at Lori, but Sugar Bear stumbled forward, blocking his line of fire and permitting her ample time to leave by the side exit. John was determined to pursue her, so he broke to his left like an all-conference running back sprinting for the end zone. He would have made it too, had it not been for a vicious clothesline tackle from Sugar. John never saw it coming.

He was instantly flattened, and worse, he fumbled the Colt. Sugar let out a savage growl and attempted to stomp John into the hard vinyl floor. Thank God for quick reflexes. Instinctively, John rolled out of danger and to his feet, but his problems were far from over. Sugar's tree trunk of an arm smashed him on his face. The forceful blow air-mailed him across the examination room and onto a gurney used for transporting stiffs.

It was an incredible sight. John was on his stomach, riding that gurney like a disoriented bobsledder until he finally crashed into an autopsy table that was used in an afternoon post-mortem. Glass containers, metal organ pans, and surgical instruments flew everywhere with John landing in the middle of the mess on the floor. Bruised and dizzy, he felt like someone hit him in the head with a brick. Still, he had his wits about him, and he knew Sugar Bear wouldn't stop with that love tap. And he was right. The big zombie was on his way. Fortunately, Sugar was as slow as molasses, still lurching forward as though his legs had no joints. His lack of speed gave John time to get up, square off and launch a hard fist at Sugar's cold black eyes. The heavy blow would have knocked any living being unconscious, but Sugar Bear was no living being. As though he had been tickled by a feather, he simply twitched what was left of his dangling nose and threw a another clumsy, side-armed blow that connected with John's skull once more.

This time John saw that hairy arm coming, but he was too mesmerized by Sugar Bear's indifference to his own punch to react. *A two-week headache,* that was the crazy thought that entered John's mind as he pinwheeled backward into that damn autopsy table again. Yet this time, he held his balance and quickly dismissed the thought. He decided to forego the blows to Sugar Bear's awful face, and instead, aim for the knees. It was a wise choice.

He was surprised at the brittleness of Sugar's bones against the rigid sole of his shoe; he went down so easily. Each leg snapped like an over-baked pretzel. Lori may have revived Sugar Bear's soul, but there was nothing she could do about restoring his decomposed body. The cold air of the refrigerated chamber combined with rigor mortis had taken its toll. But like a wounded animal, Sugar murmured a low grunt, stared straight ahead, and kept on coming. Several times, he attempted to lift his heavy torso from the floor in order to take a few steps. It was a useless effort. Those legs were worthless stumps, unable to support his heavy weight. Finally, he gave up and began to crawl on his hands and knees, his head cocked against his shoulders, still growling, still intent on getting to John. He looked like a big angry zombie crab.

"Unbelievable," John said. He almost cracked a smile as he watched the crazy sight.

"Well done, John. You've crippled our assassin. He's not worth a tinker's damn now, so I'll have to finish the job myself!"

John wasn't startled to hear Connors' voice. He had sensed that he was nearby. Although he was surprised to find Connors holding the gun Sugar Bear had knocked from his hand.

"Why, Charlie? How could you be involved in all of this?" John wanted to know the answer, but his question was more of a stall. He needed a plan.

"Power, John. It's all about power," Connors' voice was jittery, his eyes darted about, and his gun hand was shaky.

"Power? What kind of power can you get from these animals?" John was indignant.

"Power and control beyond your wildest imagination. Enough to shape the destiny of mankind," Connors answered.

"You are one sick bastard if you think that's what you're going to get from these lunatics." John glanced over his right shoulder at Sugar Bear. He was fifteen feet away and still crawling.

"That's exactly what I'm going to get. I've paid my price and I'll get it. I've made all the right sacrifices. Rimmon and Pierce were just the latest two I offered the master. He made me the shaman. I'm in charge now!"

A horrible thought hit John like a freight train, making him shudder with disgust. "The right sacrifices? The latest sacrifices? Don't tell me you had anything to do with the death of your daughter."

"She was sick—really sick. She would have died anyway. I just saved her from a lot of suffering," Connors' voice trembled.

John took a step toward Connors before the sound of the cocking gun hammer made him stop in his tracks.

"Don't move! I don't know how to handle this gun and I'm a terrible shot. If you move, I'm liable to hit you in a non-vital area. Just stay still and I'll make this as painless as possible."

"Yeah, just like your daughter."

"Shut up!" Connors screamed.

Connors had begun to inch forward to improve his accuracy when John noticed a featureless shadow moving behind him. The shadow moved closer and closer until he saw a reflection of light from an unmistakable bald head. It was Victor. John didn't know whether to breathe a sigh of relief or a sigh of trepidation. But he had to do something, and he had to do it quickly. Connors was close enough to pistol whip him, and at that distance, nobody's aim could be that bad.

"VICTOR!" John yelled in dire hope that he had misjudged his partner.

"That's a lame brain attempt, John," Connors said, refusing to turn around and look. He was certain John was trying to divert his attention.

"Go ahead, Victor. Shoot him!" John demanded.

"Give it up, John. I know what you can do with those hands and feet. I'm not taking my eyes off of you," Connors said.

"SHOOT HIM, VICTOR! NOW!" John yelled louder.

Connors grinned and chuckled, still thinking that John was bluffing.

"Drop the gun, Connors!" Victor barked the order like an army drill sergeant.

The sound of Victor's voice hit Connors hard. The surprise turned the medical examiner's face a ghastly white as his grin gave way to a panicky frown. He needed a clean look at the man behind him, so he reached upward and pushed his over-sized, black rimmed glasses back up on his nose. A slight tilt of his head gave him a clear line of sight. Sure enough, Victor was aiming his .38 Special at his back. His fear was con-firmed.

"No! You drop your gun, Victor. Drop it now or I'll shoot, John!" Connors shouted in a dither.

"No can do, Connors. You know a cop can't give up his weapon. Drop the gun and get on the floor face-down. NOW!" Victor yelled even louder as he moved from behind Connors, gaining a strategic position in front.

The standoff had Connors laboring. Sweat appeared on his brow as he nervously shuffled his feet. He knew that Vic-tor would squeeze the trigger if he didn't drop the gun and that scared him. But the thought of facing the she-beast and explaining how he failed to kill John scared him even more. He leveled the gun at John's heart and summoned the cour-age to fire. But, again, luck was on John's side. Everyone had forgotten about Sugar Bear. The possessed, grunting, angry Bear had continued to drag his carcass toward John's feet while the others were playing their game of chicken. The whip of Bear's powerful right arm swept John's feet out from under him at the same instant Connors fired the Colt. The bullet whizzed by John's toppling body and lodged harm-lessly in one of the middle-refrigerated compartments.

Connors was preparing to pull the trigger again when the slug from Victor's .38 exploded through his chest cavity, piercing his heart and left lung. He could only groan as he lay on his back, suffocating in his own blood. John instantly recognized the awful gurgling sound. It was the sound of blood percolating from the bullet hole through Connors' lung. Connors gasped for breath. John had been trained in the army to treat a sucking chest wound but, for Connors, he offered no assistance. He knew he would be dead within seconds anyway.

Just then, the irrepressible Sugar Bear pulled his dysfunctional body on top of John and hooked those terrible hands around his neck. For a second, John was spellbound by Sugar's disengaged eyes and his total lack of breathing. Since the Bear was dead, it wasn't as though he needed air. But those eyes, those horrible eyes were like a horrifying look into Hell. John felt as though things were in slow motion—that he was watching, but he really wasn't there—but when he began to feel the blood leaving his head, he snapped back to reality and responded with several solid punches to Sugar's awful face. Just like before, the blows were ineffective. The grip tightened and John's face grew numb.

John attempted to call his partner, but that strategy was no more effective than the punches. The chokehold had rendered him voiceless. Yet he couldn't help but wonder what Victor was doing and why his partner wasn't backing him up. Then out of the corner of his eye, John could see the Colt on the floor next to Connors' body. John didn't know for sure if it was within reach, but he had to try something. He strained with his right hand while he fought to remain conscious. He stretched every tendon until he felt the cold steel against his fingers, until he had slid the gun across a pool of blood and into his shaking hand.

The deafening sound of a 10mm at close range filled the room, as John fired every bullet in the magazine into Sugar Bear's face. When he finished, there was nothing left to recognize. Even Lori, with all of her black magic, couldn't resurrect this headless zombie.

John swallowed a mouthful of air and shoved Sugar's torso off his chest. "Damn!" His voice was a whisper. "Where have you been?" He hoarsely asked as he stared upward at Victor.

"I heard some noise in the receiving room and ran out there to check it out," Victor responded while reaching down to offer John his hand.

John reached up, grabbed it, and then struggled to his feet.

"Man, that freak almost killed me while you were out there. You shouldn't have left."

"Sorry! I wouldn't have left if I didn't think you could handle the situation." Victor's eyes scanned the messy remains of Sugar Bear on the floor. It confirmed that he was right.

"Well, did you see her?" John asked.

"See who?"

"Lori!" John replied

"Lori?" Victor asked.

"Yes, Lori!"

"No, there wasn't anyone out there." Victor shrugged.

John's old doubts about Victor's loyalty had returned. Victor had saved his partner's life, but he had also walked away leaving him in peril. But for now, those questions would remain unanswered. Tina was in danger.

58

The Williams' house was an appropriate setting for the final confrontation. It had been the scene of immeasurable joy and agonizing pain, of beautiful dreams and terrible nightmares. Perhaps for the monster, this emotional upheaval was an early victory in their battle—for to bring such chaos to the sanctity of one's home, the one place where a family should be able to share their love and feel safe, is a triumph of deceit, confusion, and wickedness of the worst kind—and that was Satan's abode. It was a fitting setting all right.

Few words were spoken. The distrust was like a thick fog that separated the two detectives. So, the car remained as quiet as a tomb until John hit the brakes and pulled the Chevy alongside the curb at the top of the driveway. He could sense that something was wrong, that something evil was pulling at him. The fact that Tina's clunker was parked in the driveway and the front door to the house was standing open confirmed his suspicion. It also meant he needed a quick plan of action. He was certain that the open door was an invitation from the she-beast, that the creature expected his arrival and wanted to draw him into some sort of deadly game of chess. He just didn't know if he was playing one opponent or two. Victor's loyalty was still in question.

"Victor, are you all right?" John asked as he withdrew the Colt from his holster.

"Yeah, I'm all right. But I've just got a bad feeling about this, John." Victor's face confirmed the worried twinge he felt in his gut.

"So do I, but Tina's in there. And I'll be damned if I'll let anything happen to her. Are you with me, Victor? Are you going to back me on this?"

"Yeah, I'm with you. Just tell me how you want to do this." Victor attempted to sound positive.

"Go around to the back of the house. There's a door to the basement. Here, take my keys. If it's locked, you can use them. Check out the basement and work your way upstairs. I'll go in the front and cover the main level and the upstairs bedrooms, and then I'll work my way toward you." Given the circumstances, John was surprised by the calmness of his own voice.

"All right. Give me a few minutes to get inside before you come in," Victor replied.

"Oh, and Victor?"

"Yeah?"

"Don't be surprised by what you see and hear. This thing, this creature, it can change its appearance and its voice."

"All right, I'll be careful." Victor promised.

John watched as Victor exited the car and slipped along the trees that bordered the east side of the house. After he disappeared into the darkness, John allowed him an extra minute before he departed the car himself. He made his way down the driveway, stopping momentarily to peer inside Tina's old Buick. It was empty, so he eased over to the open doorway to the house and stood outside long enough to listen for any movement inside. He didn't hear anything, so he poked his head in and out of the doorway several times in an attempt to get a visual of the den.

Two end-table lamps were on, so there was ample lighting for him to survey the entire room. It was empty. The beast was nowhere within sight, but she had left her mark. Strange words and symbols were scrawled all over the white den walls. Most of the hanging pictures had been ripped from the walls to make room for the red scribble. With one exception, none of the words or symbols made sense to John. He recognized an inverted red cross that had been smeared on one of the few pictures that remained on the wall, a picture of Rebecca and Boo. John was incensed.

He was tempted to bolt through the house in search of Lori, but that type of reckless behavior is exactly what she wanted. So, he resisted the temptation by focusing his attention on another matter. He squinted his eyes in an attempt to identify the strange red liquid on the picture. Was it red ink? Or possibly red paint? He swiped his left index finger across the fluid and held it about a foot from his face for a visual inspection. Suddenly, his eyes bulged, and his heart leaped. He had made the identification. It was unmistakable. It had been present at almost every murder scene he had investigated. It was blood. A horrible sense of dread hit him as he wiped his finger across his right thigh. The swipe left a short red smear that was quickly absorbed by his khaki trousers. He felt shaky, as though he had no bones to support his flesh. *Don't let it be Tina's. Please, don't let it be hers.* There was so much of it on the walls. *God help me, please.*

"Johnnnny? Are you down there, Johnny?" The raspy sound was coming from up the stairs in John's bedroom. John steadied himself, readjusted his grip on the Colt and turned toward the stairway. The sound of the beast was a good sign. It meant that the game was underway and, perhaps, Tina was still alive.

"Come on up, Johnny. I've got a little surprise for you, but you'd better hurry." She hissed.

John pivoted toward the stairs. Tina was up there and his need to protect her was much greater than any fear. He thought about Dr. Brown and her words of advice. *You must have faith, John. You must have faith.* He urged himself forward, up the steps and down the dark hall until he arrived at the doorway to his bedroom. The door was partially closed, yet the ceiling light was on inside. Lori, in the form of the beast, was sitting on the king-size bed, resting against the wooden headboard. In addition to seeing her, John could also smell her. That rotten stink had become very familiar to his nose and he hated the odor. He fought back the queasiness and continued to peer inside until his eyes found Tina sitting on the bed to the far side of the beast. The gap was too small to get a good visual of her condition, so John stood quietly outside the door for another half minute, straining to see anything else until he knew he had to make a move.

"Come on in, Johnny. I can see you sneaking around out there. Come in now or I'll rip Tina's heart out. I'm tired of waiting." She bared her teeth, signaling her indignation.

John reached out with his left hand and gently pushed the door. It made a low-pitch creak as it swung inward. He slowly eased into the bedroom while placing his left hand under the butt of the Colt. Once inside, his worst fear unraveled before his eyes. Lori's head lolled about as a stream of yellowish spittle oozed down her chin. How she could grin while gnashing those teeth was a true devilish dichotomy. She seemed to be enjoying herself as she watched him move warily forward. John watched her closely as well. Given her ability to strike without warning, he was reluctant to take his eyes off her. Yet he had to assess Tina's situation.

John centered the 10mm on the beast's hairy chest while his eyes darted back and forth in Tina's direction. He spied her directly to the right of the beast. Both had their lower extremities covered by the bed spread while the beast had her hideous arm draped around Tina's shoulder as though they were long lost buddies. But they were anything but friends. Tina's face told him that. She was terrified, trembling, and silent. John had seen fear on a person's face before, but never like the panic-stricken look in Tina's tearful eyes. Instinctively, he wanted to empty the clip into the beast and get Tina out of there. But that little voice in his head kept begging him to be patient. *Something's not right with this picture. I know it. Tina is trying to tell me something, but she's too frightened.*

"What's the matter, Johnny? You look puzzled." The beast continued to grin.

John ignored her question.

"I asked you a question, cop! Are you going to answer or should I bite a plug out of your dear little Tina?" The smirk was instantly replaced by an angry scowl as her bone-like fingers grabbed a handful of Tina's hair and yanked her head backward.

"Wait! Wait! Just wait a minute. I'll answer. I'm just surprised that you brought her into this, that's all. This fight is between you and me, not her! Let her go, and you and I can settle this." John pleaded.

"No can do, Johnny. Tina and I are just getting to know each other." The beast never took her eyes off John as she pulled Tina's face within inches of her own. She then licked her cheek with that reptilian tongue. Tina made a little squeal and tried to pull away. It was useless. The beast licked her again.

John took aim with the Colt and started to approach the bed. He had a clear shot and wanted to take it. But, again, that little voice asked him to resist the urge, to please engage the beast with words before he resorted to violence. Something was still wrong with this picture; he just couldn't figure out what it was. *What was the surprise that the beast had concealed?*

"I wouldn't do that if I were you, Johnny. Your bullets are useless against me and besides, you might hit my little friend here." The beast cackled.

The horrible grin returned as the beast withdrew her arm from around Tina. With that same arm, she reached down and threw the bedspread away, revealing the little surprise that had been neatly concealed under the cover between her misshaped legs. John looked on in shock. It was Tina's young

414

granddaughter, Carmen. *Tina must have brought her when she came to the house.* The beast wrapped her long fingers around Carmen's slender neck and lifted her above the bed as though she was a rag doll.

Carmen tried to scream, but the intense pressure on her vocal cords made it impossible. Tina screamed loud enough for them both as the little girl flailed her arms and legs wildly at the air. Like a woman possessed, Tina began to pepper the face of the beast with a wave of open-handed blows. But her slaps were nothing more than an annoyance to the monster and an absolute hindrance to John. In her zeal to protect her five-year-old grandchild, Tina had risen to her knees and gotten entangled with the beast. John's clear line of fire was no longer there and now he was in a state of panic. With no clean shot and Carmen's face turning as purple as a turnip, he had to do something quickly. He pointed the Colt's muzzle upward and fired three rounds into the ceiling. Maybe it wasn't the best decision, but it was the only thing he could think of given the trying circumstances.

POW!

POW!

POW!

The sound was deafening.

"Let her go, you bitch!" John yelled as he set the gun's sight back on the beast.

For a few seconds, all eyes shifted to him as the shrieks ended and the frantic activity stopped. The discharging of his weapon had at least accomplished that. It was as though everyone was suspended in time and unable to move. But with Carmen now unconscious, Tina quickly shrugged off the surprise and began her salvo again. The beast removed the bother with a vicious backhand swat that sent Tina tumbling from the bed and across the room. The sound of her thick body slamming against the wall was almost as loud as the exploding gun. Now there were two family members out cold. Yet for John, that was an advantage. With Tina out of the way, he had the opening he so desperately needed.

The double-tap blaze that exploded from the muzzle of the Colt was followed by a loud demonic groan. The bullets had found their mark. The beast instantly dropped Carmen to the soft bed, sprang to her hooves and slapped at the holes in her hairy chest, as though she were attempting to extinguish an excruciating fire.

"DAMN YOU!" She screamed.

All hell had broken out in the bedroom, absolute chaos. Fortunately for John, he didn't let the bedlam distract him. He was preparing to shoot again when the beast unexpectedly sprang from the bed and bolted out the bedroom door. It was so fast, John never got off another shot. His gut urged him to follow, but his good judgment insisted that he first tend to Tina and Carmen. Victor was surely in the house and had heard the shots. He would react, and hopefully, finish the job.

With all the melee in the bedroom, it was a miracle that Tina was still alive. Her faint moan signaled that someone from above was looking out for her well-being. John quickly knelt down and shook her hoping she would regain her senses. She responded with a second moan. The sound made it clear that even though her head was still spinning, she was going to make it. And so was Carmen. It took Tina only seconds to shed her disorientation and ask about her granddaughter.

"Where is my baby?" Tina pleaded.

Without hesitating, John stood up, turned and stepped to the edge of the mattress. He bent forward, slid his arms under Carmen, lifted her up and delivered her to Tina. And their emotions touched him, allowing him a brief moment to share in their special love. But his ardor was mixed with

416

anxiety. The beast was missing which meant the nightmare wasn't over. For John, it would never be over until that foul creature was dead. Yet, he knew he had to get Tina and Carmen out of the house now. Frantically, he hustled them to their feet and down the stairs. They scrambled, like an out-of-control fire drill until they arrived at the front door.

"Tina, get Carmen in the car and get the hell away from here." John issued the order as he firmly pushed the two of them out the front door.

Tina looked over her shoulder as she hurriedly helped Carmen onto the Buick's front seat. "What about you, Mister John? Aren't you going to leave?"

"Yeah! I'll be right behind you. Now get going!"

John words were without weight. He had no intention of leaving, yet he was more than willing to tell Tina a white lie in order to get her away from the house. After watching the old clunker sputter out of the driveway, he stepped back through the doorway and withdrew the Colt from his holster. He was prepared to begin his search for the beast when he was greeted by several bone-chilling sounds.

POW!

POW!

POW! POW!

The sound was unmistakable. Over the years, John had learned to recognize the calibrated sounds of all sorts of weapons, everything from a .22 automatic to an AK47 assault rifle. And this distinct bang came from a .38 caliber handgun, Victor's .38 Police Special. Like an echo from hell, the noise rose from the basement and reverberated throughout the house. John reacted by racing to the landing at the top of the basement stairwell. He wanted to rush down but good judgment prevailed, so he slowly moved forward, step by step, his back pressed against the inside wall. He would have continued his careful descent, but halfway down he heard an agonizing cry from Victor.

"John, help me," he cried.

Recklessly, John rushed down the remaining steps. Before reaching the bottom, a second cry drew his attention to a far corner of the open room. It was another troubled moan from Victor. At this point, John was so juiced with adrenaline, his feet never touched the last four steps on the stairway. Two more giant strides landed him in that same far corner where he found Victor sitting on the bare concrete floor, slumped against the corner walls among a stack of storage boxes. The barrel of the revolver he held in his right hand was still smoking from the discharge of the slugs. His weakened condition had left him unable to fire another round. His labored breathing and glassy eyes revealed the discord that was taking place in his body.

"Oh, no!" John knelt beside Victor and lifted the gun from his shaking hand.

"I never saw that damn thing coming, John," Victor gasped as he struggled to lift his chin from against his chest.

"Don't talk! Don't talk! Just sit still!" John frantically looked about for any sort of make-do bandage. There was nothing in sight but the usual junk and boxes one stores in an unfinished basement, nothing that would serve to stop the hemorrhaging. So, he did the next best thing. He applied pressure to Victor's open wound with the palm of his right hand. "I need to get this bleeding stopped and then I'll call the paramedics. They'll fix you right up."

"Don't bother, John." Victor gasped again. "I'm not going to make it."

"Yes you are!"

"No I'm not, John. It's bad, really bad."

"Don't say that! Yes you are!"

John's voice was filled with dread. He knew Victor was right. The wound was grotesque. Apparently, the beast had crept up behind Victor and viciously bitten his neck. A large chunk of flesh and a two-inch section of carotid artery had been ripped from his body. No amount of pressure was going to stop this bleeding.

"Forget it, John." Victor smiled as though he were unafraid of what he was about to face, as though a heavenly peace had begun to fill his injured body. "I got off four rounds. Can you believe it? Four rounds in its chest. And I swear I could see the first hole closing before...before I fired the last shot. What is that damn thing anyway?" Victor's gasps grew even more short and sporadic, as blood poured everywhere.

"Don't talk. Just be still. I've got to get to the phone. You need help!" John said.

"No! Don't leave me, John. Please don't leave me. I need to tell you something."

"It won't take but a minute." John answered. "I'll be right back and you can tell me then." John attempted to rise from his knees, but Victor pulled him back down.

"Please, John. Don't go! It can't wait. I need to tell you now."

Tears of guilt welled in John's eyes as he stared at Victor. His doubts and suspicions about his partner had been unfounded. Caught up in his own uncertainty, John had been unable to trust a man who was willing to help him fight his worst enemy, a fellow officer who was prepared to give his own life by protecting his partner. John knew exactly what that kind of sacrifice meant, and he was heartbroken to see Victor fading so quickly. He leaned closer and withdrew his hand from Victor's bleeding neck. He reached down, picked up his partner's left hand and clutched it between his palms. Victor looked up and smiled such a sweet smile, an innocent look that seemed so out of place on his rugged face. He knew the end was near.

"What is it, Victor? What do you want to tell me?" John asked.

"Tell my wife Mary that I love her, and I'll miss her. Will you promise to do that, John?" Victor's voice was soft, almost a whisper.

"Of course, I will, Victor. I'll tell her." John gave his word.

As John continued holding Victor's hand, his senses deepened with the knowledge that he was witnessing the death of a friend. Yes, Victor may have annoyed John at times with his brusque demeanor, but he was still his friend. Never once had he failed to cover John's back, and never once had he doubted John's loyalty. To a fellow police officer, that was the ultimate measure of friendship, and without question, Victor had more than measured up.

Although Victor's cloudy eyes remained open, John knew the exact moment he passed away. His broad hand fell limp as he slowly exhaled his last breath. Then quickly, his ruddy face turned chalky white, a certain sign that his heart had stopped pumping its life-giving blood.

"I'm sorry, Victor. How could I have been so stupid?" John whispered the apology as he gently closed Victor's eyes.

John remained at Victor's side for a moment. He just couldn't pull himself away, nor could he stop weeping. Victor's loss had rekindled the horrible grief that had scarred his psyche so many times before. The loss also made him question why he had not placed his doubts aside and gotten to know this man better. He couldn't explain why he had never met his wife nor even knew her name. Yet now, he would have to meet her to deliver his partner's dying words. Nothing on Earth could stop him from fulfilling that vow—not even the beast.

"Johnnnny!" The howling summons came from above.

John released Victor's hand and stood. There was no need to answer the invitation. He was certain the beast knew he would respond to her call. It was just a matter of how. He briefly considered charging up the stairs, opening fire like a wild man as he drew within range. He was filled with so much rage that he burned with the mad desire to finish the job, to put an end to the creature that had caused him so much misery. But the beast was too clever to leave itself open to a frontal attack, and an out-of-control wild man would give her a valuable mental edge. A second option would be to hide in the basement and wait, hoping to ambush her from the darkness. But he knew that she would never come to him. The rules to the deadly game had already been determined. And rule number one demanded that he go to her, to approach this thing on her own terms. The monster hungered for that pleasure and John was more than willing to feed her rabid appetite.

Moments later, John left his friend and began his search. Cautiously, he stalked though the house, room by room, upstairs and down. He opened every closet door at least twice, and when his search came up empty, he even resorted to looking under the beds. He was in the upstairs hallway, ready to give up when suddenly he was overcome by the feeling he was being watched. As he stood outside his bedroom, he was certain that a pair of friendly eyes were gazing at him, pressing at his backside like a subtly ocean breeze. Instinctively, he wanted to spin around and aim his weapon at this unseen force, but then his nose caught wind of a familiar scent, a scent that revealed the watcher's identity. Sweet roses. There was no mistaking the smell.

"Boo," John whispered as he slowly turned around. At first, he was shocked by what he saw. It was Boo all right, standing behind him. But her image had taken on a much higher degree of clarity. It was as though her ghost-like molecules had begun to take material form, giving her a life-like, solid appearance. Color had even found her face and arms, and her achromatic nightgown was now a faint shade of pink.

"Up there, Daddy." She confidently replied as she pointed upward at the ceiling.

Puzzlement appeared in John's transfixed eyes as he ignored her words and continued to stare at her face.

"No! Up there, Daddy!" Boo's voice grew in timber. She was obviously annoyed.

Once more, he refused to look up until his nostrils caught wind of another familiar odor. And this smell wasn't a bouquet of flowers. Instead, it had the mossy stink of evil. It was an omen, a horrible portent that John should have heeded Boo's warning, for what happened next caught him completely by surprise.

A malevolent shape crashed through the hallway ceiling halfway between Boo and John. Sheet rock, insulation and loose wiring exploded downward with the unwelcomed guest. KABOOM! John was so stunned by the unbelievable sight and loud sound he never reacted to the flailing arms and legs of the dive-bombing beast. A sharp kick from her right hoof firmly connected with his left thigh before he could clear himself from the action. The blow sent him reeling backward against the wall and down to his knees. It also sent a current of pain all the way down to his little toe. Yet the beast did not take advantage of his defenseless condition by continuing the assault. Instead, she turned, and in a fit of anger, screamed and charged at Boo.

"DAMMIT, JOHN. THIS STUPID BITCH OF YOURS DOESN'T KNOW THAT SHE'S DEAD!"

Obviously, the beast wasn't thinking clearly, for to threaten a specter with physical harm is certainly a waste of time and energy. Just the same, she charged. Swinging wildly, growling and cursing, she kept on coming. Her wild swings just

422

wisped through Boo's small spirit while she stood there and grinned. It would have been comical had the situation not been so dire. The beast grew more and more frustrated and cursed even louder while whipping her tail back and forth behind her. Meanwhile, Boo just kept on smiling that cute little smile. Finally, the beast grew tired of throwing the ineffective punches, so she momentarily stopped while attempting to regain her wind. The brief pause allowed her time to reassess her illogical strategy. It also allowed John enough time to reach his feet and aim his weapon. When she turned back to check his whereabouts, she found herself staring at the muzzle of the Colt. The look of surprise on her face was priceless.

BAM! BAM! BAM! BAM! BAM!

In quick succession, the five slugs pierced their intended target. The force of the bullets catapulted the beast backward and down the short flight of stairs to the house's main level. Head over hooves, she tumbled like an out-of-control gymnast until she landed hard on the den floor. She flopped on her back while ferociously clawing at the burning holes in her chest.

"You bastard!" She howled.

John heard all the commotion and had taken two steps in the direction of her fall. Victor's words were still fresh in his mind and he wanted to make certain the creature wasn't miraculously recovering from the wounds. Yet before he could take another step, he felt an emphatic tug on his hand. His eyes widened as he turned to find his ghostly daughter. She seemed frantic, almost desperate as she waived her small arm about. And the mischievous grin on her face had been replaced by a concerned grimace. He was confused about her intentions at first, but then he understood. She wanted him to follow her into his bedroom. That was why she was motioning with her arm. Any other time, John would have honored her wish, but he was still concerned about the beast.

"No, Boo," he said. "I need to check downstairs."

He turned away and was about to take a step when Boo demanded that he stop.

"No, Daddy! Don't go down there. Come with me," her voice was clear as she waived again.

Some innate feeling prodded John to forget about the beast and to follow his persistent daughter. That sixth sense told him that he might be vulnerable if he didn't. Moreover, the noise had stopped in the den which was a favorable sign. At least he hoped it was. So, his eyes held fast to Boo's petite spirit, and he followed her into the bedroom and to the door to his closet. Mysteriously, her ghostly image disappeared, and then the closet door swung open. It was as though she couldn't generate enough spectral energy to move objects and remain visible at the same time. John was surprised by the bizarre incident, but he was even more shocked by what he witnessed next.

Various items on the top shelf in the closet began to fall to the floor. The same items he had rummaged through several days ago when he had fought with the beast. Four baseball caps, two empty shoe boxes and several old police manuals tumbled downward in every direction. Boo was up there rustling around. But why? What was she looking for? Then the answer became obvious. Down from the shelf fell the old recurve bow Papa Dan had given him when he was a young boy. It landed squarely at his feet, with two arrows dropping closely behind. John had missed all of this archery gear in his earlier search.

"What the....?" John was perplexed. He stepped away from the closet opening, still unable to fully grasp Boo's intent. If the bow and arrows were meant for protection, he refused the offer. In his mind, the Colt automatic was still his

424

best option. It had served as effective protection for his years in the military and on the police force. Besides, it had been the demise of the beast by delivering five neat holes to her chest. Or at least, he thought she was dead. That panicky speculation prompted him to quickly discharge the magazine from the Colt. He wanted to replace the five missing rounds before settling that question. He snapped open his ammo pouch and dug for the extra shells. At the same time, he turned away from the closet, left the bedroom and headed for the den. *Please God, let her be dead. Please let this nightmare be over.*

John's prayer would not be answered. When he arrived in the den, the beast could not be found. An incredible chill rushed up his spine and encircled his brain. He felt powerless, as though he were standing naked on the frozen Arctic tundra. The unearthly thought that his Colt was useless sent his heart racing and his hands trembling. It also sent his brain into overdrive, searching for an answer to his dilemma.

You idiot! It's the bow. That's what Boo was telling you. Use the bow and arrows, not your gun. In a mad dash, John pirouetted and broke for the stairs. Just like before, he was so pumped up with adrenaline, his feet touched only two of the six steps before he reached the top. And for a brief moment, he sensed that he would arrive at his bedroom unhindered. He could see the narrow opening of the bedroom door at the end of the hall. Yet he was certain he could hear a thudding sound emanating from above as he raced up the stairs. The loud thud seemed to be moving just ahead of his own pace. A grip of fear made his feet move even faster. *Oh, dear god. It's the beast. She's back in the attic.*

THUD! THUD! THUD! THUD!

The beast was gaining more ground than John. It was a bad sign, but John was determined to continue his pursuit of the bow. He raced to the end of the hall, preparing to make

425

a sharp left turn through the open bedroom doorway. As he turned the corner, he was greeted by a familiar sight. Again, the sheet rock exploded from the ceiling. Landing only a few feet in front of John, the beast hit the floor with good balance and instantly began flailing her arms and legs. Wildly she swung in every direction until she connected with the handgun in his right hand. The force of the blow caused the automatic to fire a round as it sailed across the room. The sound of the exploding bullet was earsplitting. For a few seconds the action stopped as John and the beast stood frozen, each scanning their body to make certain they hadn't been struck by the misdirected slug. No harm had been done. The round had found the ceiling on the other side of the bedroom.

"The gun's useless, Johnny! It can't harm me!" Her eyes were wide with murderous hunger.

"I don't need the gun to kick your ass!" John raised his fists and turned his body sideways in a defensive posture.

The beast grinned that same horrible grin. "Oh, you're sooo bad. I'm really scared. Why don't you just close your eyes and I'll give you a little love bite like the one I gave your fat partner? It'll be over in seconds," she hissed.

"Fuck you!" John screamed.

"I believe we've covered that subject, Johnny. I've already slept in your bed. Hell, I've even slept in your attic, listening to you cry like a baby over your sweet little Boo. You could have had all the power in the world if you had come over to my master. But noooo, you refused. So now, you'll have to die, leaving your little one here an orphan." Lori rubbed her swollen belly with her misaligned hands.

"The only one who's gonna die is you and that creature growing in your stomach."

John's threat was not well received by the beast. His menacing words were enough to trigger a follow-up attack.

426

"You Bastard," she screamed and charged.

In their previous encounters, the fighting had been fierce, very fierce. Yet by comparison, their prior battles were minor skirmishes compared to this all-out war. It was the sound of Armageddon that rose from the house. The screaming voices and crashing furniture could be heard a block away. Again and again, the beast would mount an assault and John would parry, effectively blocking her frenzied blows. He would then counterattack, delivering what should have been crippling strikes to her head and neck, yet it was a waste of energy. The effort simply angered her while slowly depleting him of his own strength. Even with all of his hand-to-hand skills, he knew that he wasn't her equal. Nonetheless, for twenty more minutes, it was a whirling dervish of fists, elbows, knees and feet countered by hooves, teeth, claws and tail.

They continued fighting throughout the house, finally ending up in his bedroom where the battle began. It was there that John gathered enough strength to launch a final assault. With precision, his hands and feet violently struck every soft spot on that hairy body. His last blow, a savage front-kick to her chest knocked her from her hooves, sending her against the wall and down to the floor. The repercussion from delivering the strike sent John in the opposite direction, recoiling him to the floor on the other side of the room. There he sat, completely exhausted and completely disillusioned by his inability to kill this stinking creature. John confirmed that fact as he heaved for air, and watched the blood ooze from her mouth, nose, and ears.

"That's it, isn't it Johnny? You're completely spent. I can feel it." Her yellow eyes glowed as she licked the blood from the corners of her mouth.

"Hell no! I'm just getting started," John gasped. His words were meaningless.

"No, you're done. The dreaded horseman is finished. Your soul is screaming for me to take it. Can't you hear it, Johnny?" She cackled like a witch stirring a wicked brew as she prepared to rise from her haunches.

John remained motionless; she was right. He was twenty feet from the bedroom closet, just twenty feet from the bow and arrows he so desperately needed, but he didn't have the gristle to rise to his feet. His limbs felt like wet noodles. Even his thoughts had shifted from aggression to submission as he wondered if he would be reunited with his precious daughter after his death. Would he finally have peace? Yes, he had given up on himself and his ability to defeat this horrid thing, but fortunately, someone else had not accepted his unconditional surrender.

Hanging in the air, the bow and two arrows floated past the creature as she struggled to rise to her hooves. The beast saw it first, yet she was so surprised by the bizarre sight, she never made a move to intercept its passage. John was awestruck as well. He remained on his rump with his mouth agape and excitedly whispered her name.

"Boo."

Although she was invisible, there was no doubt that the spirit toting the weapon was her. How else could they be dangling two feet from the floor? It was Boo all right and she made it to her father without a hitch. John felt a renewed sense of power as the bow and arrows were dropped into his shaking hands.

"That won't help you, Johnny. Just give it up. That stuff won't help you." The beast stood in place, swaggering back and forth like a bombastic bully issuing a dare.

John quickly scrambled to his feet and seated an arrow on the bow string. He had a flashback of the powerful bow he held as the first horseman in his dream and sensed that the beast was worried. For the first time he could see a measure of anxiety in those awful eyes. The beast's trepidation grew worse as he drew back the string and attempted to align the arrow's shaft between the two top teats on her chest. Nevertheless, she continued to taunt him, to try to stare him down.

"Go ahead and shoot, you spineless piece of crap. You couldn't do anything to save your little Boo, so what makes you think you can save yourself. Better yet, drop the bow and I'll give you that little kiss I promised, just like the one I gave your whiny daughter." Her words were followed by a hellish laugh.

"Kiss on this, you bitch!" John held his breath and looked down the arrow's shaft with both eyes open. Like a good marksman, he exhaled a breath, let go with his fingers and listened as the arrow whizzed across the room. Confident that his aim was true, he was prepared to breathe a sigh of relief upon the beast being struck by the deadly broadhead. Instead, he found himself gasping in disbelief as his eyes followed the arrow to its final destination. His sniper-like accuracy with firearms clearly wasn't transferable to more primitive weapons. The arrow ended up stuck in the wall just to the left of the creature's head.

"Nice shot, Johnny! You couldn't hit the broad side of Virgil Rimmon's barn!" She cackled at her joke as she reached up and pinched the shaft between her bony fingers. She easily pulled it from the wall and snapped the fiberglass arrow in two as though it were a dry twig. "I've had enough of your feeble efforts," she hissed.

John could tell that she was enraged. Her grotesque face seemed to ripple, and her eyelids narrowed over her maniacal eyes. She was preparing to make a final lunge when he frantically bent down, grabbed his last arrow from the floor and reloaded the bow. Even though his hands were trembling, he found the strength to draw the fifty-five-pound string to its fullest length and aim the arrow at the swaggering beast. And then, the moment turned freaky.

"Don't hurt me, Johnny. Please don't hurt me." She begged.

"What the…." John thought his mind had snapped, that he had finally gone insane.

"It's me, Johnny. It's your Mama Ruth. I've missed you so much. Come give your mama a hug," she pleaded and held out her frail arms.

Sure enough, the person standing before John looked exactly like his foster mom. She was the same five feet three inches with the same sweet face and graying hair. She even sounded like her. John appeared puzzled at first as he gently eased the tension on the bow string. But then an awful stink began to fill the room, an unmistakable pungency that reminded him that this thing was anything but his loving Mama Ruth.

"YOU'RE NOT MY MAMA!" John shouted.

"Of course, I am, Johnny. Just look at me. Now drop that silly bow and come over and give me a hug. I've missed you so much." She eased two feet closer.

John paused for a moment as his gaze met the eyes of the lifelike clone. Perhaps his stare was one last assurance that this creature could not be Mama Ruth for he was certain he could recognize her soft brown eyes if he saw them again. The brief glimpse confirmed what he already knew. The only thing he discerned in her eyes was the hellish glow of fire and brimstone.

"NO, YOU'RE NOT!" He yelled.

John's emphatic reply was still echoing throughout the room when he pulled the bow string to its maximum draw. This time, in an effort to improve his erratic aim, he closed his left eye and peered down the shaft of the arrow with his right. Now he was aiming as though he was looking down the barrel of a rifle. The beast sensed that he had accurately marked her, and in anger, reassumed her satanic image. She lunged as a god-awful wail rose from her throat. It sounded like a thousand demonic voices.

John thought of only one thing as he released the string from his fingers. *You must have faith!* He had not forgotten Dr. Brown's sage advice.

The creature's final lunge abruptly ended five feet short of where John was standing. The thud of the arrow penetrating its leathery skin put an end to any additional attacks. It also stifled the demonic wail. The beast appeared confused as she reached upward to her chest and clamped her bony fingers around the arrow's shaft.

"You bastard! Do you know what you've done?" The beast labored as wisps of steam flowed from its gaping mouth.

"Yeah, I know," John retorted and stepped within inches of the beast's ugly face. "I've shot the piece of crap that killed my little girl. You're history, bitch!" John knew that it was a fatal blow, and he would be the last one standing.

Suddenly, the beast began to tremble. Small twitches at first but then it quickly grew to violent convulsions. Something awful was about to happen.

"There'll be others, Johnny." She bellowed and grinned, her mouth drawn back in a ghastly curl. "Others will come!"

That was the last thing John saw before the explosive flash of light blinded his vision. The supernatural force propelled him backward, smashing him against the wall and knocking him unconscious. It was over!

59

Was it Boo? Yes, it was. John could see her, dressed in a white nightgown, standing close enough for him to touch. Yet she seemed vague, ghostly as though she had no substance. And the surroundings had the same surreal quality. Misty white air, like a bank of thin clouds, swirled slowly around her. It was a peaceful scene, a heavenly vista. But was it real or an illusion? It seemed more like one of his visions than reality since he could only see himself in his mind's eye. *Perhaps it's a dream,* he thought. John really didn't know for sure. He did know, however, that Boo no longer held that restless sheen in her eyes, that she finally seemed at peace with the world. She was smiling and whispering something that he couldn't quite comprehend.

"Da—"

"What is it, Boo?" He asked.

"Daddy," she sighed.

"Yeah, sweetheart? What is it? What's wrong?" John strained to hear her response.

"Daddy." She sighed again and reached out with her right arm.

"I can hear you, Boo. What are you trying to tell me?"

"Daddy, wake up," she implored.

"What?"

"Wake up, Daddy."

"Huh?" He answered.

"WAKE UP!" She yelled.

The piercing sound of her high-pitched voice accomplished her mission. John's eyes snapped open like a mishandled window shade. He sat up in bed with the same breakneck speed. He was jolted, unable to believe the sight before him.

"What the devil?" he asked.

Frantically he rubbed his eyes and gasped for a breath of air. As his vision slowly cleared, he stared again and what he viewed chilled him to the bone.

"You wouldn't wake up, Daddy. You were snoring real loud and I couldn't get you to wake up."

"Boo? Is that you?"

"Yeah, Daddy. It's me!" She giggled, amused at his question.

Yes, it was Boo. She was standing beside the bed, dressed in a white nightgown. Yet she was of flesh and bone, not the ghostlike image he expected. And her stature had changed as well. She no longer held the size and look of a four-year-old preschooler. No, she appeared to be a smaller child, a two year old, perhaps. John was speechless and confused at how the hands of time had been spun backward, at how the two years he thought he had lived had been mysteriously lost. He was in shock, but his consternation was about to hit another high that would send him reeling beyond imagination.

"John, are you up?"

The sound of the voice made his body tremble and his heart race at an incredibly fast pace. He instantly recognized the tone and timbre. No, it wasn't Boo delivering the question, but Rebecca. He pulled himself up against the headboard and said nothing.

"John?" Again, the shout came from downstairs. "You need to get up. My mammogram appointment is at nine this morning and I need you to drop Boo off at the babysitter's."

He didn't answer. Instead, he sat motionless, staring blankly into space. He could only wonder if what he had experienced was real, or if it was just a bad dream...or god forbid, a vision.

And then, he thought about the terrifying warning.

"There'll be others, Johnny. Others will come."

...Coming soon...

...Turn the page for a sneak preview of R.G. Johansen's new novel...

Something
Sinister
Within

Read it at your own peril...

One

A PLACE FOR EVIL

It's not the way you want to start the weekend. The call came into the Gaston County Sheriff's Office late Friday afternoon around six o'clock. The caller sounded confused, his words garbled and disordered. The man kept saying something about finding two bodies on the bank of Ramsey Creek off Lake Norman. The location was just north of Mt. Holly, about a thirteen-mile drive for Deputy Sheriff Joe Griffin. With the deputy's shift ending in ten minutes, it was an untimely interference of a big weekend planned with his wife. He knew the trip and the preliminary investigation would likely last through the night and into the next day. But with a small department and two officers on vacation, the deputy had no choice in the matter. Reluctantly, he climbed into the black-and-white Ford cruiser and drove east on Highway 74. Twenty minutes later, he arrived at the Gulf filling station in Mt. Holly to meet the caller. Griffin immediately recognized the individual walking with a bowlegged stride toward his patrol car.

His name was Doug Dutton, but everyone called him Puck. No one knew how he got stuck with that moniker. The handle certainly had no connection to anything dreamed up by Shakespeare, although he looked very much like a hobgoblin...especially if you had consumed a jar of his high-octane moonshine. Puck was creepy, very creepy. He was a scrawny man in his forties although he looked every day of sixty.

And he was about 110 in weight, with a frame like the Hunchback of Notre Dame. His pockmarked face with the hook nose of a witch and the prick-ears of an elf were features best suited for a Halloween mask from Walmart. His only teeth were two lateral incisors on the bottom with an in-between gap just wide enough to wedge his hand-rolled cigarette. All his ugliness aside, it was comical to see him talk with an extra-long smoke bouncing in his mouth. The up and down and all-around motion looked like a music conductor waving his baton, only Puck never had to use his hand.

"Shuriff! I'd be the one that called. I found two dead peoples when I was fishin' up yonder on Ramsey. Looks like they'd been campin' out." Puck seemed agitated as his voice grew in pitch.

Deputy Joe knew this man, and his reputation. And it certainly wasn't for catching trophy largemouth up on Ramsey Creek. No, Gaston was a dry county, and he was famous for making illegal whiskey and stealing pigs. Puck figured when you have no education and you can't read nor write, you do what you must to make a living, even if it's against the law. The deputy's gut told him that Puck was most likely scouting out a new location for one of his stills when he stumbled upon the campers.

"Mr. Dutton, why don't you get in your truck, and I'll follow you to a point where we can park our vehicles and walk to where you found the bodies," he instructed.

It wasn't difficult to follow Puck's 1955 Ford F100 pickup. The beat-up truck was missing both bumpers, had a cracked back window, and sported multi-colored fenders that were discernible a half mile away, not to mention the trail of smoke belching from the exhaust. And if the deputy should by chance lose eye contact, he could still find his way to Puck by listening for the overloud noise from his absent muffler.

Fortunately, both men stayed together as they drove to the remote location past a local boat launch and down a chert road for almost a mile. Finally, they arrived, parked in the tall weeds along the roadway and got out of their vehicles. Puck wasted no time waving Griffin over to begin the journey—and a journey it was. The trip to the site would have been easier by boat as the deputy struggled to force his way through a labyrinth of briars, low trees, and thick bushes while Puck walked through the vegetation as though his skin were made of leather. Meanwhile, the deputy was getting angrier with each snag on his tan and brown uniform and prick on his exposed arms from the blackberry thorns. Beyond his ire, without the protection of thick leather boots, he was even more afraid a mean copperhead would add to his puncture wounds. He suspected Puck was leading him on a meandering path to make sure they weren't within eyesight of his whiskey stills and Deputy Joe was fighting mad about the deception.

"It's just up ahead, shuriff. We be almost there," he answered while waving his arm for the deputy to continue to follow.

And then without notice, the heavy foliage opened to a sandy area where two canoes were pulled up on the creek's bank. Deputy Griffin stepped into the opening beyond the narrow boats, whiffed the foul air, and scanned left to right at the camping site, wishing he could just wake up from this grotesque nightmare. The scene was surreal, and the fading sun and dark shadows added to the twisted visual. The wind moaned, calling from the tops of the towering oaks and thick pines which made the deputy even more jumpy and anxious. That bad feeling was confirmed when the shocking scenery revealed something sinister had, indeed, happened.

A young man with ash-gray skin was in first stage rigor mortis. He was on the ground in a defensive, fetal position near a small triangular tent some fifty feet from the water's edge. His clothes, along with the tent, were torn and ripped as though they had been shredded by the claws of a wild animal. Dried blood somewhat concealed numerous slashes on his face, torso, buttocks, and legs. That same caked blood helped cover the stab-like wounds deep in his throat around the jugular. There was no need to check for vitals. The deputy instantly knew that this horrific crime scene would need the professional expertise of a medical examiner and lab technicians.

"Don't get close to the corpse, Puck. I don't want anything disturbed. Where is the other body?"

"It's over yonder, next to that honeysuckle bush," Puck answered and pointed to an area some thirty feet away.

As the deputy cautiously walked closer, he noticed what appeared to be an animal track in an area of bare soil among the floor of pine needles and leaves. Or at least he thought it was the mark of an animal. The print also carried some unusual characteristics that appeared to be human. As he continued to move toward the tall honeysuckle, he gazed left and right at the camping supplies and unopened food items strewn about the site. He thought it odd that there were no sleeping bags or cots. He carried on with his search until his eyes found the blood splatters on the bush next to the body. It left a baleful warning that evil of the worst kind had been at this place, and Joe struggled to keep his emotions and visceral reactions under control. The early scent of decomposition mixed with the fragrance from the honeysuckle made him dizzy and twisted his stomach. But he knew he had to keep his composure, especially with Puck looking on, so he fought back the unwanted sensations.

After wiping the sweat from his face, his eyes widened to view a woman in her mid-twenties lying on her back among the leaves. Daylight had mostly disappeared, so Joe needed a double take and a flashlight to make sure this was not an illusion. The violence imposed on the woman seemed beyond human comprehension. Her limbs were grotesquely contorted as though every bone in her arms and legs were broken, her mouth agape from screams for help that no one heard. Her nude body made the deputy wonder if she had been sexually violated. And her lack of clothing exposed the postmortem lividity which was present across her entire body. Unlike the male victim, there were no slashes, just the massive bruising and a set of circular wounds on her neck. And worst of all, her pale green eyes were open, suggesting that she had a first-hand look at the killer before she died. Joe, a fifty-year-old father with a daughter about the same age as the deceased woman, couldn't help but think that this was someone's baby. He had seen death before, but nothing that wounded his soul like this.

"Do you think a black bar attacked these folks?" Puck's question sent the deputy's heart rate in overdrive. He knew Puck wanted this to be an animal attack so the investigation would be brief, so law enforcement wouldn't be traipsing through the woods looking for evidence and find his stills.

Red faced and livid, Griffin responded, "This was no damn bear attack. A black bear would never do anything like this! Now, let's go. It's getting too dark, and I need to get back to my car to use the radio. We can mark the trail on the way back if the techs want to walk instead of getting here by water."

"But I seed a bar the other day when I was fishin'," Puck retorted.

"Just shut up and let's go." The deputy had the look of a man in fear, a man who knew that evil had arrived in Gaston County. He could only wonder why.

CPSIA information can be obtained
at www.ICGtesting.com
Printed in the USA
BVHW062348210323
660854BV00011B/327

9 781087 975610